Bitter Almonds & Jasmine

Dominic Piper

Books by Dominic Piper

Kiss Me When I'm Dead

Death is the New Black

Femme Fatale

Bitter Almonds & Jasmine

1

WHATEVER HAPPENED TO YESTERDAY?

She hears it before I do.

'Daniel,' she hisses. 'Daniel! Is that your phone? Wake up. Hey.' She pushes my shoulder and then pushes it again, almost rocking me onto my side. This is Fenella. She's twenty-seven, Scottish, a personal shopping consultant at Harrods, divorced twice and presently naked. I met her and her friend Szonja last night somewhere. I'm sure the bar had a name, but at the moment it isn't forthcoming. The Dancing Skeleton? The Shabby Cadaver? No. It was Dirty Bones in Shoreditch. Fenella made me drink a cocktail with vanilla vodka and lavender in it and it was lust at first sight.

Szonja is an air hostess for Cargolux. She only drank Paganini Grappa, kept putting her hand on my leg and couldn't stop talking. There was a good DJ, from what I can remember. No. He was terrible. I could have done a better job.

'Mm?' My head is pounding from an embryonic hangover. I feel slightly nauseous. What time is it? I lean over and hit my alarm clock once, twice, three times until the display lights up. 3.56. What the hell?

'Quickly. It's coming from the kitchen. It could be something urgent.'

'OK. OK.' I roll out of bed and head towards the

kitchen. When I get there, I can see the blue light of my mobile flashing next to the oven hob. I scoop it up, take a quick look at the display – *unknown caller* – sit down at the kitchen table and compose myself so I don't sound rude or, worse still, surprised. Sometimes it pays to be cool, calm and collected. My head is spinning. This had better be good.

'Hello?'

'Is that Daniel Beckett?' Female voice. Thirties. Educated. Wide awake. Unapologetic. Calm, with a barely discernible tremor of anxiety.

'Yes, it is. How can I help you?' I put a hand in front of my mouth to stifle a yawn. Fenella appears and stands behind me, massaging my shoulders. I can smell her perfume; Bibliothèque by Byredo. I want coffee.

'And I understand you're a private investigator.'

'That's right. I…' Then I realise that she's modulating her voice. Skilfully done and it's certainly fooled me up to now, but at least I have Fenella, Szonja, disturbed sleep and alcohol as an excuse. The adrenalin starts pumping. I don't say anything. I have to be wary. I start to wake up. How did she get this number? What's she doing in the UK? What is this?

'It's so good to hear your voice again,' she says. 'I'll keep this short. We need to meet. I need to hire you. I've no idea what the protocol is. The money and so on. I'm sure we can sort that out later.'

'Where?'

'Do you remember D7?'

'I might.'

'Would this morning be too soon?'

'What time?'

'Whatever time you wish.'

'I'll be there. Once you see me, make your way on foot to D20. I'll make sure you're clean.'

'Will do.' She clicks off, leaving me staring at my mobile like an idiot.

'What on earth was all that about?' asks Fenella, before losing interest. 'As we're both up, shall I make coffee?' she says. 'I'm really dehydrated. I expect you are, as well. It might help things.'

'Sure. The stuff's over there. D'you want to make one for Szonja?' I run the back of my hand down the side of her hip as I watch her walk towards the Siemens coffee maker. She's a little over five foot, with a lithe, small-breasted, athletic figure and beautiful pale bronze skin.

Her straight, black hair reaches all the way down to her coccyx. I remember now that she said her mother was Indonesian, from Bandung. It was difficult to equate those exotic Javanese looks with her Edinburgh accent at first, but I quickly got used to it.

'No. Let her sleep,' she says. 'She was pretty hammered last night. She was a riot, though, wasn't she? I could tell you liked her. Have you got any painkillers?'

'You seemed quite keen on her yourself, Fenella. Too keen, some might say. I had to prise you apart on several occasions. I thought I might have to use a crowbar. Paracetamol in that drawer. Not that drawer.'

'Now, now. You'll make me blush. Hey! You've got Java Arabica. We always used to have this at home. My mum wouldn't drink anything else. Did you know that Java was once so popular that it became a slang term for coffee?'

'I do now.'

She tosses the caplets into her mouth and washes them down with water which she drinks straight out of the tap. 'Mm. Did you know that the market for oil is the largest in the world? Know what the second largest is?'

'No idea.'

'Coffee. Do you want to see me again? Without her, I mean?'

'Sure.'

'Good!'

While she makes the Java, I run over the telephone conversation in my mind.

It's so good to hear your voice again.

That wasn't a pleasantry. It was code. *Don't interrupt. Listen.*

'I'd love to go to Apsleys again,' says Fenella. 'I adore Italian food. Their foie gras terrine with cherries needs to have a shrine erected to it. And you should see what it looks like inside. The restaurant, I mean. Not the foie gras. You'd just die.'

'I'll see if I can book a table.'

'You're a sweetie, Daniel.'

D7.

Once you've painstakingly memorised the codenames for hundreds of clandestine meeting places all over Europe, they tend to stick in your mind forever. At the moment, D7 refers to the Crimean War Memorial in St James's, near Pall Mall, at the bottom end of Regent Street. The codename changes depending on what day and month it is. Tomorrow, it will be called K5.

There's a big Guards' Memorial and statues of Florence Nightingale and Sidney Herbert. It's the sort of place where you might see people with cameras around their necks holding tourist brochures and staring up at things. Good, clear line of sight in every direction. When she asked me if I remembered it, I said, 'I might'.

That meant yes.

While the bean-to-cup coffee maker does its stuff, Fenella finds a couple of coffee mugs and turns to face me. Despite the rude awakening, she looks both delectable and composed. 'If you had to choose between me and Szonja, who would you choose?' she says. She frowns. She's serious.

This makes me laugh. 'Oh, Szonja, every time. Isn't it obvious?'

'But seriously.'

'I can't make a comparison like *that*. You're different from her. Besides, I only met you both last night. I need time. Don't rush me. I have to do more research.'

Would this morning be too soon?

More coded talk. That means it's urgent. Very urgent. Whatever it is, it has to be today. I wonder what's wrong. I wonder what's *so* wrong that she managed to track me down after over three years and call me in the middle of the night.

All this covert doubletalk sounds like bullshit, but as someone once told me, 'bullshit saves lives'. Plus, it still defeats all technology.

I try to remember the background noises from that call. It sounded like she was out of doors. I could hear cars and street noise. A big lorry with a diesel engine and someone yelling in Russian.

Fenella places two mugs of coffee on the kitchen table and insinuates herself onto my lap. She puts her arms around my neck and kisses me. She takes my right hand and places it on one of her breasts. She licks her lips and tilts her head to one side. 'OK. So. If you had to choose between me and her as *lovers*, who would you choose?'

Whatever time you wish.

That means eleven a.m. and I agreed to it. I'm genuinely amazed that I can still remember all this stuff; though I suppose if you can still recall from school that the main industries of Sweden are telecommunications, pharmaceuticals and motor vehicles, anything's possible.

Fenella nuzzles my neck. I reach around her back and grab a coffee, taking three or four sizeable sips before placing it on the table again. That helps.

'You paid a lot of attention to me last night, I seem to recollect,' she purrs. 'I think *I've* got the advantage over Szonja. I could see it in your eyes.'

'I could have been faking it.'

She finds this very amusing. 'A man can *never* fake his lust for a woman. It is impossible. A woman always knows. *And* you said you would see me without her. *And* I know you meant it.' She bites my shoulder. I think she may have drawn blood. 'You *crave* me. I can feel it. You are craving me now. We are like the first man and woman. Naked. Passionate. Infatuated. Hungry.' She swivels around so she's straddling me, leaning back, both wrists resting on my shoulders. I hold the sides of her body, just below the armpits.

'Your Java's going to get cold, Fenella. What would your mother think?'

She kisses me again, her mouth open and warm. I grab a handful of her hair. She sighs. Her body reacts.

Once you see me, make your way to D20. I'll make sure you're clean.

D20 is the statue of Henry Irving, outside the National Portrait Gallery in Charing Cross Road. These surreptitious sites are generally statues or monuments of one kind or another; things which are likely to be there permanently, never supermarkets, restaurants, bars or theatres. Or charity shops.

Walking from D7 to D20 will take about fifteen minutes, and if she's smart, which I know she is, she'll get to D20 via Piccadilly Circus and Leicester Square, both areas being pedestrianised and packed out with tourists at all times of the year.

It's unlikely that anyone will be following her, but if they are, this will be a good route for me to take care of it; lots of long, wide roads, side streets and a distracted and/or disinterested populace. When I get to D7 at eleven, I won't even glance in her direction. My appearance will be her cue to get moving.

'I don't think I've ever been up at this time before,' says Fenella, rotating her belly at me. 'It's nice. It's exciting. It's like we're awake at some forbidden time. It's kind of like anything goes, you know? We could do anything right now and it would be OK. Anything *forbidden* you fancy trying, Daniel? Anything *taboo*?'

'I'll text you when I think of something.'

She shakes her head so that her hair covers her breasts. I place my hands on her hips to slow her down. She leans forwards and nips my earlobe. I don't have to turn around to know that Szonja's just arrived; soft footfalls, libidinous presence and the orangey scent of Poison Girl by Dior.

'Hey, what's going on? What are you two doing in here without me? Look at the two of you! Look at her face! Her eyes! God! It's like she's on heat! Have you been making coffee? Have you seen what time it is? Is there any coffee left? What's going on? Fuck. I feel like I've got an axe buried in my head. Have you got any aspirin or anything?'

Szonja is from Miskolc. Voluptuous, blonde, lots of

freckles. She has a husky voice and a cute Hungarian accent. She leans over me, puts her arms around my neck, leans forwards and kisses Fenella on the lips. I can feel her soft breasts pressing against my shoulder. '*Olyan puha vagy, bébi*,' she whispers to Fenella. All things considered, this is quite good for four in the morning; certainly an improvement on sleeping. 'So, what's happening? What's going on?' she asks.

'One of his girlfriends calling him up in the middle of the night,' says Fenella, grinning. 'I tried to get him to invite her round.'

'Oh Jesus,' says Szonja. 'That would be fun. What's her name?'

That's a good question. Her name is April Taylor aka Noemi Zetticci aka Alita Langlois aka Suzanna White aka Michèle Couet aka Engla Bergqvist and God knows how many others.

But her real name's Polly Greenburgh and we used to be colleagues. And whatever the trouble is, I'm obliged to help her. As it's her, and I know what she's capable of, I'm a little worried and wondering what can be wrong.

Fenella disengages herself from me. 'My bladder is *so* full. I've got to have a pee. Don't go anywhere. Don't do anything without me.'

Almost as soon as she leaves the room, Szonja takes her place on my lap. She's all-round bigger and heavier than Fenella and I'm wondering if my thighs can take the strain. I'm also wondering whether it's worth trying to go back to sleep. 'I'd like to see you without her. Without Fenella, you know?' she whispers. 'Interested?'

'When are you free?'

'For you? Anytime, *csillagom*.'

'I'll call you.'

'You better, huh?' She bares her teeth at me. 'You don't, I get angry. I am like a *fiend* when I am angry.'

'Maybe I'll anger you on purpose.'

'Yeah. Mm. That would be good.' She grinds her hips and bites her lower lip. 'I liked it that you were excited by my body. It is good. My body, I mean. I know it is. I saw that look in your eye. I could see you wanted to consume me. And I was ready to be consumed. To be desecrated. To be plundered. Submissive yet resisting. Yearning to be mastered. Aching for climax after climax. Longing for crisis after crisis.'

'Have we been introduced?'

'I have a friend, too. A good friend. Her name is Kamilla. You'd like her. She is *savage*. She's a Cool Hunter. Big girl. Like me. Very vocal. Like me. I know you are interested. I can feel it. I can feel it deep inside.'

She grins and bites my lower lip. I'm wondering what a Cool Hunter is. I place an arm around her back and another behind her knees, stand up, and carry her back into the bedroom, where Fenella is already waiting. Am I that predictable? Szonja laughs as I toss her onto the bed. I wish I could bottle the smell in this room; I'd make a fortune.

While I'm setting my alarm for nine o'clock, the women start without me. I quickly put Polly out of my mind. She's tomorrow's problem. Then I remember. It already is tomorrow. Whatever happened to yesterday?

'Daniel...'

2

PRETTY POLLY

I live in Exeter Street in Covent Garden, so decide to walk down to Pall Mall for my eleven o'clock meet. It'll take fifteen minutes, which means I'll get there at around half past ten. This will give me half an hour to check the area out, get a coffee and something to eat and have a think.

I stop at a branch of Boots the chemist and buy a pair of dark FCUK wrap sunglasses. I bin the bag and the case and slip them in my pocket. It's still pretty grim and chilly, but by the time I get to Trafalgar Square, the clouds suddenly clear and the sun is starting to dazzle, so it won't look too odd if I'm wearing them.

I pick up a tourist's map of London from a roadside seller. He tries to sell me a Buckingham Palace themed tea towel and a Beefeater bottle opener fridge magnet. I politely decline his suggestions.

After successfully negotiating the tricky choking traffic hell of the square with only two scary near misses, I set off down Pall Mall, looking for a café of some sort, but at the moment it's all embassies, bespoke tailors, art galleries, businesses and exclusive, overpriced restaurants and bars.

Just as I'm approaching the Crimean War Memorial, I cross over the road so I'm on the south side, almost getting run down by a black cab in the process. The driver spits out of the window. I take a quick glance at the memorial; no sign of Polly, but then I wouldn't expect there to be. Not yet.

There are half a dozen Japanese teenagers looking at Florence Nightingale and taking pictures with their mobiles. An overweight man in a turquoise suit is bending down, wobbling uncertainly and doing up a green shoelace on a pink suede shoe. A tall, well-dressed woman is shouting at her children in Italian.

There's a big Sofitel hotel on the corner of Waterloo Place and a fair amount of people going in and out. For an area with no traditionally famous tourist attractions, there are already a good number of sightseers crowding the streets, plus besuited businesspeople going wherever. This can be a good thing or a bad thing. It all depends on what happens in the next half an hour.

Two traffic wardens joke with each other as one of them prepares to slap a ticket on a striking, bright orange Saleen S7 Twin Turbo that's parked on a double yellow line. The owner, a heavily made up Arabic woman with great legs and a sexy, wicked mouth, appears and argues with them, pointing back at the Villandry St James's. I've spotted a dozen CCTV cameras, three of which are aimed directly at the monument.

I look for solitary males or females sitting in parked cars in restricted zones reading newspapers which are upside down but can't spot any. I look for innocent-looking family groups that have a weird vibe about them, London taxis that are parked with the engine running, people walking one way then changing their minds and walking in the opposite direction, backpackers who look too affluent to be backpacking, anyone who I spot twice in thirty seconds, anyone who makes eye contact with me, anything that looks inexplicably wrong, anything that *feels* inexplicably wrong. Nothing. So far, so good.

I find a small café, order scrambled eggs with smoked salmon and an Americano and sit outside at a small, circular table. There's a blue plaque on the house across the road; Nell Gwyn lived there, or at least she lived in a house that was on that site. Orange-girl, actress, mistress of Charles II and quite a wit, apparently. Died young, though. Thirty-something, if I remember correctly.

Three amazing-looking black girls approach the café and look in the window, trying to work out if it's worth getting any food here. They're speaking Czech. One of them asks her friend if I am her boyfriend and they all laugh. He is too good-looking for me, she says. Perhaps you should take him to your hotel room, says the third girl. Perhaps he will kiss you all over your body. They laugh again. I place a hand against my mouth. I'm trying hard not to smile. My food arrives and the girls turn to leave. '*Hezký den!*' I call after them. Just means 'have a nice day' but the shock effect causes them all to scream with embarrassed laughter and pirouette away at high speed. I think Nell Gwyn would have brazened that one out.

I have to admit, I'm intensely curious about what Polly wants. I didn't even know she was in the UK. It's a little under three and a half years since I last saw her. It was in Norway. I can remember giving her a jokey high-five in the foyer of The Thief hotel in Oslo before we parted company for what turned out to be the last time.

And, of course, she knew not to get in touch with me

and I knew not to get in touch with her. Yet she did get in touch. And that's another thing that I pondered briefly last night, or this morning, or whatever it could be called.

I've had my current mobile number for two years and four months. It was acquired when I was semi-commuting between here and Italy, just before I got my business cards made. I still can't work out how she got hold of it, though I have my suspicions. On the other hand, if she put her mind to it, I wouldn't put anything past her, no matter how difficult it might turn out to be.

I check my watch. Two minutes to eleven. I pay the bill and walk back over to the south side of the road, heading in the direction of the monument. I take another good look around. There's no one here who I clocked earlier and no suspicious silhouettes.

The orange Saleen S7 Twin Turbo is still in place and now it's got a parking ticket on its windshield. There's no one inside. I make a note of the registration and memorise it. The owner of that car was a pretty good-looking woman. When I've got the time, I'll track her down and engineer a meeting, maybe dinner, though if she's a regular at the Villandry St James's, she may be an expensive date, but expensive dates can sometimes turn out spectacularly well.

When I'm a hundred yards away from the monument, I see her. She's standing looking up at the Sidney Herbert statue, a map and some sort of guidebook under her left arm and a green and white tote bag slung over her shoulder. She's wearing big red-framed glasses and her long wavy blonde hair is in a ponytail which is tied loosely at the base of her neck and allows the rest of her hair to straggle over both shoulders. Very chic.

Her clothing look is well-dressed moneyed tourist; a

black cropped jacket, outsize orange t-shirt, black skinny jeans and white trainers with some sort of floral pattern on them. Two grinning, suntanned, camera-toting guys who are pretending to have a conversation about something can't take their eyes off her.

I can't blame them, though. Polly is what they used to call a 'looker': exceptionally pretty, great cheekbones, sexy mouth, exquisite blue eyes, ash-blonde hair, a slim figure with all the required curves and the cool poise of a ballet dancer on her day off. I just hope they don't try to hassle her. They won't believe what happens even while it's happening.

It looks like she's clean. I keep walking and check my watch. Five seconds before eleven. With my peripheral vision, I can see that she's made an abrupt one-eighty and is looking right at me. And off we go.

After maybe a hundred yards, I stop, look at my tourist map, and cross the road, heading back the way I came. I put my sunglasses on and stuff the map in my pocket. By the time I'm back at the memorial, I can see her in the near distance. She's on the right-hand side of Waterloo Place and is walking at a calm, touristy speed, taking everything in.

That orange t-shirt was a good idea; it'll make it marginally more difficult to lose her when the crowds get worse in five minutes or so. I cross over the road so I'm on the left, sauntering along, taking my sunglasses off as I stop and peer into various windows, always keeping her in my peripheral vision or in reflections where available.

I walk along and sink into a trance-like mode, staring straight ahead, looking at nothing in particular. There are small family groups, solitary women with shopping trolleys, roadworks guys, businessmen with briefcases and one large group of tourists following a guide holding a plastic Icelandic flag on a long, wobbly pole. It's a typical central London mix of workers, wanderers and foreign visitors. Polly stops for a couple of seconds and rummages in her tote bag before proceeding. Nothing stands out until I see a young black guy wearing a slate grey Nike hoodie crossing the road from Polly's side to mine. Not unusual on its own, but a plump, middle-aged woman wearing a burnt orange bobble hat walks over to Polly's side at almost the same time; rushing, like she's avoiding heavy traffic where there is none. Alarm bells ring.

I take a closer look at Polly. She has a grey-haired business guy in his fifties walking maybe a dozen yards behind her wearing a smart blue Oscar Jacobson suit and holding a tan briefcase in his left hand. He's limping slightly but matching her speed almost exactly. Bobble Hat is fifteen yards behind him and now, on my side, Nike Hoodie has sped up slightly, being almost adjacent to Polly but not quite, keeping a little to her rear.

She's in a surveillance 'box' and it's a professional one. I feel a sudden adrenalin rush. This is called the ABC technique. 'A' is Grey Hair, who is directly behind the target. 'B' is Bobble Hat who will be following A. 'C' is Nike Hoodie who stays across the road a little to the rear of the target.

What I saw earlier was 'B' swapping positions with 'C' when Bobble Hat and Nike Hoodie changed road sides. This is what they do: an ever-changing fluid and mobile stakeout that most people would find hard to spot and virtually impossible to shake off.

How do I know it's professional? Because it's *too* professional, almost clichéd, and doesn't take into account an observer like me, let alone the target being someone like Polly. The personnel that are being used prey on the preconceptions and prejudices that they'll assume (or hope) you'll have.

'They'd never get some cool young black dude to do this sort of thing.' 'Trained surveillance people aren't frumpy, overweight, middle-aged women wearing a bobble hat.' 'No way would a surveillance professional have a limp.'

But surveillance personnel are anything and everything. Any sex, any age, any number, any vehicle, any silhouette. That's the point.

Polly's aware, I have no doubt of that. That's the reason she stopped and looked in her bag; to give them a little shake so I'd spot them. As far as I can make out, none of them are wearing earpieces, and none of them have their hands in their pockets. This is a good sign. It probably means that they're not in anything but visual communication with each other, so I'll have to watch out for subtle hand signals or other gestures.

If they're using electronics, I'll find out soon enough. If at any time they're not all in each other's direct visual range, all it needs is an innocent little movement of the head to check their pals are still with them. This is going to have be fast and efficient, and I have to be invisible. No problem.

We're approaching Piccadilly Circus, so Nike Hoodie is shortly going to have to cross over the road and resume his 'C' position in the pedestrianised area by the Shaftesbury Memorial Fountain once we get there. I remember reading that the statue above the fountain isn't really of Eros but can't for the life of me remember who or what it's meant to be. I may ask Polly later. It's the sort of thing she'd know.

This little team will have no idea where Polly's headed, but once Nike Hoodie realises she's going to proceed down Coventry Street, he'll undoubtedly cross over and continue his 'C' position on the left-hand side of that road, unless one of the others replaces him. Unfortunately, he's not going to get that far.

I wonder what they have in mind. A snatch? A kill? Are they being shadowed by a third party in a vehicle of some kind? God knows what sort of trouble she's in. Nike Hoodie turns and looks in my direction for a second. I stare through him and past him. He hasn't spotted me.

As Polly walks past Lillywhites sports store, the crowds start to seriously thicken, and once we hit Piccadilly Circus, it becomes difficult for Grey Hair and Bobble Hat to keep their previous distance, particularly as we've just turned a sharp right, but I'm sure they're not worried, as the swarm of tourists will give them plenty of camouflage. Maybe it'll give them a chance to compare notes or high-five each other. Bobble Hat removes her bobble hat, stuffs it in her bag and pulls out a red scarf which she quickly winds around her neck.

Polly keeps to the right of the fountain with the two of them close behind. Doing the best he can under the circumstances, Nike Hoodie walks around the fountain on the left, keeping as far away from Polly as possible, hugging the kerb, perhaps getting ready to cross the road at the first opportunity. I asses his weight. Under those fashionable too-new hipster clothes, he's a fit two hundred pounds and he's switched on. OK.

There are so many people milling around, that for a moment, I can't get to him, then manage to catch up just before the traffic lights change and the impatient, revving traffic from our left starts its high-speed take-no-prisoners charge.

I flank him on his right, choose my vehicle, then turn sharply, and with all my weight and energy, thump him hard in the deltoids with the ball of my hand. He falls sideways, straight into the traffic and gets hit hard by a black cab. I don't stop. I keep moving and allow the resultant confusion, screeches, screams and rear-ending to take its course.

I cross over to the left-hand side of Coventry Street and take up the 'C' position that Nike Hoodie might have taken, had he not been indisposed. I take my tourist map out of my pocket, take my sunglasses off, and ask some guy dressed as a tiger how to get to Oxford Street.

As he's giving me directions, I keep an eye on the other side of the road. Polly continues in the direction she was heading with her surviving surveillance buddies in tow. Grey Hair and Bobble Hat are the only people ignoring the RTA that's got everyone else here rubbernecking and gasping in horror.

I can see that Bobble Hat has taken the 'A' position now and Grey Hair has dropped back into 'B' mode. Either they have zero colleague loyalty, or this is so important that the loss of one of their crew is secondary to the continuance of this job. Or maybe they didn't like him. Or maybe they don't give a toss about anything.

Polly stops to look at the menu in the window of a restaurant and this gives her two friends a chance to place themselves at reasonably correct distances once more. Grey Hair looks uncertain, and I know he's deciding whether to cross the road or stay where he is. He stays where he is, losing the limp and switching the tan briefcase to his right hand.

I remain on the opposite side of the road, but now I'm moving faster as I have to overtake them all. I can tell that Polly's aware as she slows down a little. They're all going to have to walk under a long tunnel of construction scaffolding in about thirty seconds and we're rapidly approaching Leicester Square, so I want to get this next stage out of the way as soon as possible.

I run across the road, turn on my heel and walk back the way I came. I can see Polly straight ahead of me and walk towards her. She's maybe thirty feet away and just entering the tunnel. I time it so that she and Bobble Hat are back on the open pavement just before I go in. Polly and I don't look at each other. I put my sunglasses back on.

Now I'm under the scaffolding and plastic sheeting. Grey Hair is on his own. There's no one behind him. He gives me a brief, friendly smile as we're both going to have to do a bit of a sideways walk to get past each other. I turn my body towards him, grab the back of his jacket collar and tug down hard while simultaneously chopping him in the throat with the side of my hand.

Before he has time to choke, I sweep his legs from under him with my right foot and jab my elbow into his solar plexus as he goes down. He lies on the floor, hyperventilating, gagging, coughing and moaning. I really don't see what all the fuss is about; compared to Nike Hoodie, he got off lightly. I turn around and catch up with Polly.

Bobble Hat still hasn't realised what's happened, but as soon as I walk past Polly and she notices me, she turns around to face her remaining pro-stalker. 'Keep away from me!' she shouts. People turn and look. 'Stop following me or I'll call the police!' Bobble Hat then gets a two-handed push in the chest which knocks her to the ground.

She doesn't get up. Too astonished, too frightened, too fucked. Even though it looked like Polly hardly put any effort into it, the ch'i invested in that blow would have felt like a strike from a sledgehammer wielded by a bodybuilder. Let's hope Bobble Hat doesn't have a heart attack from it. Let's hope she does.

I let Polly walk ahead of me into the claustrophobic chaos of Leicester Square and once the crowds hit a critical mass, I catch up with her, briefly place my hand on the small of her back and guide her into Leicester Place, a short thoroughfare leading to Lisle Street. Straight ahead is the New Plum Blossom restaurant. I've been here before. I look over my shoulder as we walk inside. No one about. That little bit of drama seems to be over.

Mr Ông, the proprietor, smiles as he sees me and makes the usual fuss. His son, Xueqin, a fractious, dangerous-looking individual, winks at me as if we're in on something crooked together. He holds up a waiter's pad and gets ready to scribble down my order with a red betting shop pen. I order a random selection of sweet and savoury dim sum and a couple of large coffees, then ask for a table in the upstairs dining area, which I know will be empty at this time of day.

Polly and I choose a table away from the window and sit down. We look at each other for a few seconds. She takes her glasses off and places them on the table. Plain glass. She's the first to break the silence.

'Well, *that* was exciting!'

'I really enjoyed myself. Who were they, Pol?'

'I've no idea. Well, *sort* of an idea.'

'What is it? What's going on? Nice you see you again, by the way.'

'You, too. I don't know where to start. I really don't.' She places her elbows on the table surface and covers her face with her hands. She takes a deep breath, perking up a little. 'Are you really a private detective now?'

'Top of the range. No job too small or sleazy.'

A frown, then some serious eye contact. 'Is everything OK with you?'

'So far.'

'I can pay you. I can't ask you to do this for nothing. It could take a long time and it could be dangerous; life-threatening, I mean. Is it safe here?'

'Safer than you could possibly imagine. We'll go somewhere else later. We just need to have a break, I think.'

'I'm sorry I called you at that time. I...'

'Forget it.'

Mr Ông pokes his head around the door and brings in the coffee and food on a black lacquer tray. He prides himself on his discretion and lack of inquisitiveness. He smiles at Polly and then raises his eyebrows at me.

'Is this lovely lady your fiancée, Mr Beckett? If – and I am not saying it *has* to be this way – *if* you should ever need a delightful Chinese buffet for your wedding celebration, I hope you will consider my establishment to supply it.'

'You'd be the first on my list, Mr Ông. But I'm afraid this lady is a work colleague, not a fiancée.'

'Ah! My mistake.' His expression darkens, and he shakes her hand. 'I am Keung Ông, madam. Pleased to meet you.'

'Andrea Cole,' says Polly, without missing a beat.

'I will leave you to your business talk. And remember, Miss Cole: all cats love fish, but fear to wet their paws. The coffee is Columbian San Agustin, Mr Beckett, brewed just as you like it! Enjoy, and an honour to meet you, Miss Cole.'

'You too, Mr Ông,' says Polly, flashing him a charming businesswoman's smile. She waits until he's gone and gives me a strange look. 'What's going on here? Are you his adopted son or something?'

'It's a long story. One day I'll tell you.' I watch her as she eats. I remember the delicate little movements of her fingers as she wipes away fragments of food from the sides of her mouth. I always had quite a crush on her. She sees me watching and pokes her tongue out. She seems to be ravenous and I wonder when she last had anything to eat.

'These are absolutely marvellous. What is this? Has it got taro in it?'

'Taro, mushrooms, shrimp and pork.'

'Totally delicious. This is the first thing I've had to eat today.'

I take a sip of coffee. 'So, what are you doing here? I didn't even know you were in the UK.'

'What were you expecting? A phone call and a night down the pub chatting about the old days?' She stops herself. 'I'm sorry. I shouldn't be crabby. I'm a bit frazzled. I've been back here for close on two years. I work for a specialist department in the Security Service. Overseas Fiscal Review Policies.'

I try not to seem taken aback. 'You are kidding, I hope.'

'Nope. It's called the OFRP for short.'

'Catchy. Sexy, even. So, who runs this OFRP?'

'Answerable to MI5, though we're about ninety per cent autonomous. We're not based in Thames House, though. They supply us with all the equipment we need, computers and the rest, and, of course, ultimately, the money comes from them, or from the taxpayer, I should say. Small unit, four personnel.' She smiles. 'Remind you of anything?'

'I don't understand. What do you do there? Overseas Fiscal Review Policies is one of those totally meaningless cover titles. I can't imagine you spend all day checking the tax returns of toothbrush factories in Monaco.'

She stops eating and looks at me. 'I'll be breaking the Official Secrets Act many times over telling you this, but I know I can trust you and at the moment I don't give a fuck. And official secrets, anyway. Pfft.' She makes a dismissive gesture with the fingers of her left hand.

'The function of the OFRP is the discreet eradication of potential or actual financial threats to the UK by whatever reasonable means necessary: blackmail, cyber damage, conversation intercepts, data analysis and I can see you looking at me and I know that look; we don't use violence and we don't kill people.

'A fair amount of this activity is aimed against so-called *friendly* countries, so it's all very *softly softly catchee monkey*; no kicking down doors or tying bombs under people's cars. Not your cup of tea at all. The OFRP has been in existence for close on nine years.'

I smile and nod my head. 'And who do they think you are?'

'They think I'm called Judith Hart.'

The absurdity, nerve and sheer outrageousness of this finally overwhelms me and I start laughing. 'Oh my God.

Well, that's some piece of work, Pol. You managed to wangle your way into a top-secret intelligence job, and you checked *out*? The *vetting*, I mean? No one realised who you were? What you'd been?'

She allows herself a little smirk. 'Not the slightest idea. I was note perfect the whole way. Took a while to create a convincing background. You know what it's like today. They'll send someone down to meet your old teacher's stepsister's goldfish. MI5, JIC, Interpol; they all had a hack at the coalface.

'It was pretty exciting, I have to say. A challenge. You can't imagine the buzz. You know how I get off on risk. After one of the earliest interviews, I had to go into the toilets to laugh.'

'I'll bet. Well, congratulations.'

'Thank you. I want to keep being part of it all in some way, you know? I liked it. The covert stuff. Secrets within secrets made it more exciting. Plus, I wanted to disappear. Had to disappear. We both did. I enjoy starting a new life. It's stimulating. And I'm like you; I didn't want to hang around in continental Europe indefinitely. But now...'

'Have you heard from the other two?'

A brief moue of concern across her lips. 'No. I've never pursued it, either. Not a good idea. Have you?'

'No. How did you get my mobile number?'

'Pure luck. It was quite a while ago now. I was in Milan. There was an article in *Il Giorno*. Some painting that had been stolen and recovered. By Pelliccioli, I seem to remember. Not my cup of tea at all. Too modern.

'There was a photograph taken with the gallery owner standing in front of the painting. And there in the background, there a very good-looking brunette standing next to what turned out to be you. It was only a side-on photograph, out of focus, too, but I recognised you immediately.'

'Was it my alluring and athletic body type?'

'It was that Sando leather jacket. The one you wouldn't throw away.'

'It had sentimental value. What did you do? I mean, how did you…?'

'I tracked down the woman. She was the manageress of that gallery, Volante Peccati. She seemed *very* fond of you. Can't imagine why. I told her that I'd seen the article about the Pelliccioli and asked for your name and telephone number.

'I told her that my grandfather had had a Brancaccio stolen almost a decade ago. He'd given up hope of ever seeing it again before he died. I fact-checked it in case *she* did. There were a few Brancaccios that had gone AWOL over the years. I was able to describe it to her.'

'And she fell for it.'

'I wasn't going to call you or anything. I just felt a bit better having your number somewhere. I never knew when it might come in handy.'

'And now it has.'

'Maybe.'

'So, what do you want to hire me for? Trouble with an Amazon refund?'

'Not quite. It's just that two men attempted to murder me last night, and I think my boss was behind it.'

Mr Ông pops his head around the door. 'Everything A-OK, Mr Beckett?'

I give him an eye-roll. 'Bit of trouble at work.'

'Ah!' He points a finger at me. 'Remember – defeat isn't bitter unless you *swallow* it!'

'Wise words, Mr Ông.'

'Not me. Fortune cookie.'
'OK.'

3

LAMASHTU & OLEANDER

I ask for some more coffee and some more food. I think it's late enough in the morning now for all of this to count as lunch. I leave the choice of food up to Mr Ông who, of course, is delighted to be given the responsibility.

I take a discreet look at Polly's face while we wait. She looks a little haggard, I have to say. She's about five months older than me, but at the moment it looks like five years. I don't tell her this. I don't think it would go down well.

We make small talk while we wait for the food to arrive; there's no point in starting on something like this and being interrupted halfway through.

If it's as serious as she thinks it is, I'll have to keep my wits about me and remember every single word she says. Apart from anything else, what she's just told me puts a whole new complexion on that surveillance team; who they were and what they hoped to achieve.

It concerns me that they knew she'd be at the monument at eleven precisely. Could have been luck, of course. I don't believe in luck. Thinking about it now, I didn't notice any of them hanging around when I did my initial recce and they weren't there just before the arranged rendezvous, either. They seemed to appear from nowhere. So, where did they come from?

I visualise the buildings around that area as Waterloo Place morphs into Regent Street. National Bank of Egypt on the left, then a disabled parking bay on Charles II Street on the right with a Prêt next to it.

A Japanese restaurant on the left, a gym on the right. Were they sitting in a parked car that was hidden from view? Were they in the Prêt having a coffee and waiting? Had they been eating *tonkotsu* or working out? It's both baffling and worrying.

'How much do you charge, by the way?' she asks. 'Money's no object. I'm just curious.'

'You don't have to pay me anything.'

'But I want to. I can't force you to take a financial holiday. I don't know how long all of this will take. I don't even know what this *is*. It could be weeks. Could be even longer than that.'

'A thousand a day plus non-negotiable expenses.'

'Is that all? That doesn't seem very much. To hire you, I mean. With all your, er, expertise.'

'It's to do with keeping a low profile more than anything else. That's a top of the range price for someone working on their own. Not part of a company, I mean. Any higher and it would attract the wrong sort of attention.'

'Have you got an office?'

'Sure. It's in a bad part of town. There's a big ceiling fan, scotch in the filing cabinet, dead flies on the windowsill, worn-out carpets, a stacked secretary who's in love with me and a chain-smoking dame wearing a fur coat and pearls in the waiting room.'

'Does she cross her legs so you can see her stocking tops and suspender clips?'

'Obviously.'

'No office, then.'

'No. The phone you called me on. How long have you had it?'

'It was a PAYG. I bought it about two this morning. I'd got rid of my other one. It was an everyday mobile. Nothing special on it. I took a journey in a black cab, turned all the tones off and left it stuffed down the side of the seat. If it was being used to track me, they'd have been following that cab around to wherever.'

'But my number...'

She rummages around in her tote bag and pulls out a small, worn, cheap-looking address book with a photograph of a squirrel on the front. She waves it at me. 'Sometimes the old ways are the best. I keep this in a secure location. Emergencies only. You're under O for Optician.'

'I see. Are there any implants of any sort in or on your person? Anything electronic that could be used to eavesdrop on nearby mobile conversations? Anything that could be used to track you?'

'Nothing. No one uses implants now, certainly not where I work. They're not deemed useful or secure anymore. The bugging/tracking arms race is too fast. It'd be a full-time job deciding when to upgrade and to what. You'd end up with lots of unsightly scars all over your body and I have enough as it is.'

She holds up a hand as if to stop me talking. 'Listen. Everything you would have done, I have done. There is nothing on my person – clothing, shoes, bags, girly accessories – that was there before the early hours of this morning. I'm clean.

'I know what you're thinking. You're thinking where

did that little tag team appear from at just the right place and time. Well, your guess is as good as mine. I was in a hurry. I'm a little out of practice, in the same way that you undoubtedly are. I accept that I might have been careless. Just wait until I tell you everything and you'll understand. Something may fall into place.'

'OK.'

Mr Ông appears with the food and a large cafetière of Columbian San Agustin. More dumplings, pork rice rolls, barbequed pork buns, steamed meatballs and a lot of things I can't identify. There's also a big bowl of orange and tangerine slices. Mr Ông points at the fruit.

'Oranges and tangerines both bring good luck and fortune. I shall tell you a brief story, if I may, Mr Beckett, Miss Cole,' He folds his arms. 'My brother, Chonglin, was married to a beautiful woman. Her name was Eu-fùnh. I was unmarried at the time. One night, I was eating a snack of tangerines and the telephone rang. It was Eu-fùnh. She was sorry to tell me that my brother had died. He had had a heart attack. Now I am married to Eu-fùnh. I will leave you to enjoy your lunch.'

Polly starts to eat one of the pork rice rolls and rolls her eyes at me. 'I think I'm going mad.'

After about ten minutes, she finally slows down her eating rate. I think this is a good time to get her talking. I pour her some more coffee.

'Where do you want to start?' I ask.

'It's difficult. Difficult to pinpoint where this slippery slope began. Does the name Dragan Vanchev mean anything to you?'

'Not anymore. I cut him out of my life. He was an energy drainer. He's dead to me now.'

She laughs. 'I'd forgotten about this. Are we going to

be able to get through all of this without a quip every five seconds?'

'Unlikely.'

'Anyway, he's a Bulgarian national. A diplomat. Fifty-three years old. Attached to the Bulgarian Embassy here in London. He's involved in the brokering of trade deals in the UK, but also travels to Croatia and Slovenia. He has a lot of contacts with industry in those countries.

'Without going into unnecessary detail, he was using confidential information he'd acquired here for personal gain when he travelled abroad.'

'Typical corrupt diplomat, then.'

'Precisely. He's well thought of in the UK and a trusted employee at the embassy economics division. Brings a lot of money into the country through his endeavours in Eastern Europe; some dodgy, some not. All the government finance nerds love him, and they don't seem to care where the business and/or money comes from.

'When he's here he's in Ass-lick City. An all-round good guy. They'll do anything to keep him sweet. He's just gone a little too far, that's all. That's why we stepped in.'

'So, you wanted him out of the country.'

She nods and takes a sip of coffee. 'We'd heard rumours that he led a dissolute life of sorts, so I was tasked with getting enough on him to either blackmail him or get him in deep shit with his boss. Either would do. We couldn't rock the boat too much, but he had to go. It had to be a delicate, low-key, ultra-discreet operation.

'The UK couldn't be seen to be upsetting the embassy and the country itself with an aggressive op against one of their staff. There was, for various tedious reasons, too much to lose. The Bulgarians are a little touchy and, relatively minor as our industrial dealings with Bulgaria are, there would be a multitude of financial knock-on effects from Vanchev's actions that could cost this country millions.

'On top of that, of course, is that he's viewed as a bit of a boy wonder here. Maybe he's being protected, maybe he's not.'

'OK. Blackmail first, and if that didn't work, really fuck him over by handing all you had to his boss at the embassy. None of this would be connected to your unit, presumably.'

'No. It would seem like anonymous and malicious criminal activity. By the time they got hold of it, it would barely matter where it all came from. I'm aware that people can get away with more and more in their personal lives nowadays, so I was looking for something pretty spectacular, if it was there.'

'He's married, yes?'

'To Lilyana. Two daughters who are both over here; Veronika, thirteen and Violeta, eleven. Adores them all, apparently. Both girls attend Queen's College in Harley Street. His wife has no idea what he gets up to and it would certainly be the end if she found out. She's a truculent woman – her father is a high-up in the National Assembly – and would take the kids with her if anything happened. She's much too young and attractive for him as well, which I suppose makes what I'm going to tell you that much worse.'

'So, your job was to build up a dossier of nastiness, beat him across the head with it and hope for the best.'

'That's about right.'

'Who knew about this operation?'

'Only me and my boss. As I said, we're mainly autonomous, so no one in Five was aware. They don't have a great deal of time for this sort of stuff, anyway; too busy with terrorism. They'd only be informed after the fact and even that would depend on whether the outcome had been useful. Or successful. Or stepped on the toes of something else. Or whatever. That's the way it has to be. That's part of our remit. There's often big money involved in what we do and where there's big money, you'll always find corruption of one sort or another. It's unavoidable.'

'Your boss's name?'

'Culpepper. Alistair Culpepper.'

'Where does he come from?'

'MI5. Liaison with NCIS. Support, advice, that sort of thing. This is his first boss job. Been at it for four and a bit years.'

'Was this a big thing for Culpepper? The Vanchev job, I mean? Notable in some way?'

'Not really. We've done worse. Or better, depending upon how you look at it.'

'So, what did you find?'

She sighs and drums her fingernails on the table surface. Something's wrong, I can tell. She's one of those people where everything starts to go into slow motion if they're uncomfortable. It's as if she's started a journey which she knows is going to turn bad. I can actually feel the frostiness in the air.

'OK. Just to give you a little one-phrase introduction to the man, he's an all-round sleaze and prize-winning hypocrite.'

'Par for the course for today's diplomats, I've heard.'

'I was hoping to get maybe half a dozen separate blackmail actions out of my surveillance on him. Less than that if I got one good major one. I'd know intuitively when I had what I needed.'

'And you are the sole operator on cases like this.'

'Yes. As I said, there are only four of us, Culpepper and three officers. The other two are not involved in field duties. One is a techie and the other is an analyst.'

'And those two wouldn't have known what you were up to.'

'No. Certainly not the analyst. They might see the result of jobs like this in the future, if necessary, but not while they're actually going on. Need-to-know. You know what it's like. I'd ask the techie for equipment and how to use it, but the why and wherefore would not be discussed at the time and in this case, she would not even be aware of Vanchev's name or what the operation was. It would always be set up so that I was the sole surveillance operator and was the only recipient of any information gleaned.'

'Presumably you draw a car from somewhere.'

'There's a central quartermaster's in Thames House. There's also another in Surrey; out near Ockham. OFRP use the one in Thames House. OFRP have a pool of five vehicles and I changed the one I used every day, usually.'

'And I take it that you don't tell them what you want the cars for.'

'Come *on*.'

'I have to check. How long had you been spending on this?'

'I'd been at it for just under five weeks. I stopped the day before yesterday. But that was an enforced stop, as you'll shortly discover, though my assessment was that I didn't have long to go before I had enough material for a satisfactory sting. Not a spectacular one, just a satisfactory one. Sometimes that's the best you can hope for. I can't believe you're a private investigator.'

'What was he up to?'

'In no particular order, he has a mistress in Stoke Newington, Beverly Sanderson. Twenty-eight. She's a secretary. Sees her twice a week, maybe less. That seems quite ordinary, except I've seen her walking around the place, and she is, or was, a guy. No doubt whatsoever.'

'Is he aware, do you think?'

'Hard to tell. Nothing wrong with that per se, but it wasn't really what I was looking for. I wanted something that was a shocking betrayal of his family and something good, or truly awful, tacked onto the side of it. A ghastly side order, if you like. The wife, for example, might be perturbed by Ms Sanderson, but his boss might not be.

'The current ambassador is Tihomir Katranjiev. He's a bit of a good-time guy – an alcoholic, actually – and is known to have liberal views. He'd probably just have a laugh about something like that and think Vanchev was either a wild and crazy guy or a hapless dumbass.'

'Keep going.'

'He's a regular visitor to a pair of dominatrices in Putney: Mistress Lamashtu and Mistress Oleander. They work as a team. Very attractive women. Classy, full-figured and elegant. I quite liked the names. Well thought out. Lamashtu is a Mesopotamian female demon associated with the bringing of disease and Oleander is a beautiful but poisonous plant. Sometimes his sessions with them would last two hours, and he was not averse to taking a long lunch break to be with them.'

'Have you got their number?'

'Ha ha. They specialised in prolonged torture and humiliation sessions, but whatever they did to him, he was still able to walk and function afterwards.'

'He should ask for his money back.'

'I also caught him attending what seemed to be a traditional wife-swapping party in Burnt Oak. His "wife" was a pretty convincing older call girl by the name of Yasmin Dupont, real name Hollie Bishop. She's from Kidderminster and admits to being thirty-nine. I would think she's in her mid-fifties, but what the hell. Bit of a cheat, really, not taking your real wife to these wife-swapping soirées. These people have no integrity.

'There were six other couples attending. Perhaps they were fake couples, too. I don't know who they were, and it didn't really matter. This party started at eight o'clock at night and finished, from what I could gather, at around three in the morning. That's when the guests started leaving, anyway. Is 'guests' the right word? Partakers? *Visitants*? Who knows?'

'Doesn't sound too spectacular so far.'

She shakes her head and takes a few sips of cold coffee. 'But then, two days ago, I got lucky; though in retrospect that may not be a good choice of word.

'I'd had Vanchev's telephone and internet conversations tapped from the moment I'd started all of this. Most of it was useless stuff; just little snippets like him arranging to take Yasmin Dupont to that party and lots of mawkish calls to his wife when he was in work. He calls her his little *выдра*. It means otter.'

'Because of her webbed feet.'

'Undoubtedly. And she eats raw fish. I was reviewing the morning's calls and there was a message left on his mobile that piqued my interest. It was a call lasting just over a second and all the caller said was 'nine o'clock'. It was a man's voice. I think it came from a mobile, but I couldn't trace the number. I got our techie girl onto it, but it was a poor signal and didn't last long enough. All she could say was South London or North Surrey.'

'Suspicious and creepy enough to be a lead.'

She nods her head. 'He had a two-hour meeting with MXC Capital, a merchant bank in the City, at four o'clock. I made the assumption that he wouldn't be going back to the office when it had finished, and I was right. But he didn't go home. He went to Brown's Hotel in Mayfair and booked a room for the night.

'I've no idea how he would have explained this to his wife. Maybe he doesn't have to explain things to his wife. I parked across the road and waited. He came out of the hotel at just after eight-twenty. He walked as far as Fleet Street. I tailed him on foot, wondering where the hell he was going. I'm sure there was a good reason for him not getting a cab or whatever, but I'd no idea what it could have been.

'I was about ten yards behind him when I saw a black Bentley Bentayga SUV a little further up the road outside St Bride's church. Parked on double yellow lines, engine running, empty apart from the driver who was looking in his rear-view mirror. I had a feeling, you know?

'I put a spurt on, overtook Vanchev, and just as I was passing the SUV, unclipped the shoulder strap on my bag and allowed the contents to fall all over the floor. A woman and a man stopped to help me pick everything up. While they were doing that, I put a tracker underneath the wheel hub.'

'This is really exciting.'

I get a counterfeit laugh. 'Shut up. Vanchev got in the

SUV and I got a black cab back to Brown's where I'd left the car. By the time I'd got the tracker display up, they were on their way to Richmond. This fitted with the techie girl's location assessment of that phone call.

'It took me around fifteen minutes to catch up with them. By the time I had a visual, they were going over Hammersmith Bridge. The chauffeur, or whatever he was, was a fast driver.'

'What were you in?'

'A black Lotus Elise.'

'Your department has too much money.'

'I followed them through Richmond town centre until we turned off towards Richmond Hill. Kept going until we got to a big detached house situated in some pretty expansive grounds, fairly well hidden by trees and large shrubs. I say house, but it was almost like a castle; turrets, arrow slits, the works. Big medieval doors; iron and wood. They looked heavy. You could imagine really having to put your back into it to open them.

'Not ancient, though. A folly, if anything. Probably early twentieth century. Five storeys, maybe more. It was hard to tell from the road. Hard to tell how big the whole property was, I mean. If it was a house, you'd be thinking of something with at least a dozen bedrooms, servants' quarters and long, spooky corridors.'

'An expensive place in your estimation? I mean, mega-expensive?'

'Well, taking into account that it was in Richmond, I would say five or six million plus. More if it was listed. Possibly more again if it was blue-plaqued. I had to drop back so I didn't get spotted. I parked behind a lorry and got my camera out. I was using a Canon DSLR with a Nikon AF-S lens, so I could see the entrance clearly from just over a hundred yards away.

'The SUV turned off the road and stopped at the entrance to the house. There was some sort of intercom to the driver's right. The window came down and he leaned out and said something.'

She stops and purses her lips.

'And then what?'

'Then?' She laughs, but the laugh doesn't reach her eyes. 'Then the fucking gates of Hell opened up.'

'Fancy a drink, Pol?'

'I thought you'd never ask.'

4

DOUBLE VODKA AND VODKA

We arrange to meet by the Young Dancer statue in Broad Court near the Royal Opera House and then on to my flat in Exeter Street. Whatever's going on has to be slowly teased out of her in a safe and relaxed environment if it's going to be useful and accurate, and we couldn't stay in Mr Ông's establishment indefinitely.

We leave the New Plum Blossom together, but separate when we get to Charing Cross Road, each taking our own route to the statue. She won't need me to shadow her.

We still have to be cautious after this morning's events, but whoever our friends were, their little unit is fucked now, and it'll seem like we disappeared into thin air, but it always pays to be a little paranoid.

On the way there, I pick up some Havana Club rum, Coke, limes and a load of various snacks. I remember Polly was a Cuba Libre fan. Also, Lychee Martinis, but only at the weekend.

She's sitting on the base of the statue next to various assorted tourists. She stands up and smiles when she sees me. She looks so tired and jittery. I want to lean forward to give her a hug or a cheek-to-cheek non-kiss but check myself just in time. No embracing – formal or informal – with Polly. No reason given. Past trauma? Who knows?

You just had to accept and respect. She falls in step beside me as we proceed along Bow Street. Out of habit, we both speak in an unobtrusive murmur, a little below the ambient street noise.

'Is it always free in that restaurant or is it only for you?'

'Always free. They're strongly anti-capitalist. It's a social experiment.'

She smiles. 'Huh. Where are we going? Where do you live?'

'Exeter Street. A third-floor flat.'

'You live in Covent Garden? That's really smart. Central but a pleasingly obscure road.'

'I thought you'd be impressed. Who's the statue of in Piccadilly Circus?'

'Anteros. God of unrequited love.'

'I knew that.'

'Sure you did.'

She looks puzzled as we take a right turn and walk through the tourist-heavy indoor market. 'Are we going shopping?'

'Yes. I want to pick up some hand-knitted children's clothing and artisan soaps.' I shrug my shoulders. 'I take a different random way back to my flat each time. I know all the reflecting surfaces in a big radius around it and I can feel it if things aren't right.'

'Stupid of me to ask.'

I can feel her grinning behind my back as I quickly deal with the two enhanced Yale cylinder locks attached to my front door. This is a pretty straightforward security measure and makes it difficult for anyone – burglar or otherwise – to access my flat when I'm not there.

You can't pick lock one and then proceed with lock

two. The first lock would click back to its original position after three seconds. It's a housebreaker's nightmare. Unless they've brought a battering ram with them.

'There's a nightingale floor up ahead,' I tell her, as I close the front door. 'There's a secret path through it to spare your ears. Follow me and watch where I put my feet.'

'I can see it. Just the right distance from the front door so you can't take a run-up and jump over it. That's if you recognise it for what it is in the first place. This is a big flat. Quiet, too, considering the location.'

'That would be the triple glazing.'

'Ballistic glass?'

'Level six.'

'You're paranoid.'

'Wouldn't you be?'

'I guess you're right.'

She follows me, making only one misstep that produces an ear-splitting squeak. She laughs. 'Shit, that's loud!'

She has a quick nose in the two bedrooms and the bathroom. 'Very nice. It looks as if someone cool lives here.'

'Yeah. I wonder who that could be.'

'This is just like that place you had in Echternach, but without the view. Are you sharing?'

'Very droll. This used to be a wood storage place up until the 1960s,' I say. 'They knocked the wall down between two of the original houses. I had it extensively refurbished when I moved in.'

'And whose money paid for that, I wonder?'

'Curiosity killed the cat.'

'Do you have a cleaner?'

'Are you offering your services?'

We go into the kitchen and she sits down at the table, looking around. I make myself a double vodka and soda and a stiff Cuba Libre for her.

'All the RSG200 metal bars on the windows. That's you, yes?'

'It's an impregnable fortress. I have to stop actresses and models from breaking in somehow.'

'That's understandable. Can you get onto the roof?'

'If you have to. I've checked it out. But you can't get in that way. More bars. In an emergency, rooftop travel can take you about five hundred yards in most directions. It's all pretty stable and safe up there.'

'So, who is she?'

'Who's who?'

She grins and sniffs the air. 'It was in one of the bedrooms, too. Leather, patchouli, violet, vanilla – the woman who wears Bibliothèque by Byredo.' She frowns with concentration. 'No. Wait. There's something else. Or should I say *someone* else. Orange. Rose. It's Poison Girl by Dior. You surely haven't had two different women with clashing perfumes in this flat at the same time, have you? It's regarded as being bad luck in some cultures.'

I place her drink on the table in front of her. 'Glad to see you haven't lost your nose for these things.'

She gulps down half of her cocktail and slaps the palms of her hands on the table surface. 'OK. Let's start. I want to get this out of my head as soon as I can and put it in your head.'

I take a sip of vodka and sit down opposite her. 'The fucking gates of Hell were opening up, I believe.'

'Pretty dramatic turn of phrase, hm? There was no way

I could get in through that front gate. There were cameras by the entrance and undoubtedly more elsewhere. But I had a feeling about this. It was different from the other stuff that Vanchev had been getting up to.

'I knew this would be good. The brief message, the pickup, the location; everything. It felt right. I just had to take the risk and get inside; in the grounds, at least. I parked my car in a small road about five hundred yards away, facing towards the town, so I could make a quick getaway if necessary.

'The camera, particularly with that lens, was a little cumbersome, but I managed to stuff it in my bag so that it was relatively unobtrusive. I walked down a road which took you to the far right of the grounds.

'I went maybe three hundred yards before I found a way in. A section of the wall which was only eight feet high or thereabouts. Looked left and right then took a running leap and vaulted over it.'

'Was the camera OK?'

'Fine. Thanks for asking. Once in the grounds, I just squatted down and waited for five minutes. Silence. No dogs, no nothing. No. Wait. I said no dogs, but I meant in the grounds. I thought I heard a single, muffled bark coming from inside the house, though I'm not sure if I imagined it. There was a lot of ambient noise where I was situated.'

'What sort of bark? What sort of dog?'

'A deep bark. Not a Chihuahua. When I heard it, I counted to a hundred, but it didn't recur. Anyway, I made my way towards the house. There didn't seem to be a security presence. At least not outside. No squadrons of humourless low-IQ bald heavies with earpieces, snarling Dobermans and Uzis.

'Whoever owned this place assumed that the big gate at the front and the perimeter walls would be enough, and I suppose they were right. But then this is Richmond, not Riga. That gate was the only way you could get a vehicle inside the grounds and if you were going to try and burglarise the place, I'm sure there was sufficient protection; alarms and so on.

'The first thing I noticed was several upmarket cars parked at the side of the house; I spotted a really nice-looking Lamborghini Aventodor. Yellow and black. Giallo Spica. Looked like a big wasp. There seemed to be something going on in a brightly lit room on the first floor. I saw shadows inside as if someone was walking around, but I couldn't see anyone.

'From my POV it looked like an old-fashioned ballroom. I could see part of an enormous crystal chandelier hanging from the ceiling. Now I know you're going to think this was unladylike, but I decided to climb a tree so I could see what was going on.'

'I always knew you were a tomboy at heart.'

'Once I'd found a comfy branch, I got the lens sorted out and managed to get a good look inside. As I suspected, it was a large ballroom or something similar. Empty. Rather unusual décor. The walls were covered in murals. Rather old-fashioned paintings of what might once have been exotic animals: camels, elephants, crocodiles, giraffes. Erotic scenes: once again, rather old-fashioned, but extremely explicit, perverse and kinky.'

'You had me at explicit.'

'Voluptuous women, multiple partners, lesbian, straight; definitely male orientated, I thought. It was like looking at some guy's secret, deranged, sexual fantasies that had somehow materialised in reality and got plastered all over the walls of his house.

'I'm no expert, but the quality seemed to be very good. I wouldn't have been surprised to discover they were copies of works by well-known artists, do you know what I mean? Very thick carpets. Two-inch pile, at a guess.'

'You were filming by this time?'

'Yes. Right in the centre of the room was something that looked like a low stage. Three feet above the ground. It was circular. Like a big circular bed. Diameter of roughly twelve feet. Some sort of red material covering it. Velvet; something like that. Looked soft. A scattering of colourful cushions: the shades and designs matched the murals.

'There were four-seater restaurant tables around the bed and a grand piano in the corner. You know those black-tie boxing dinners people go to? Reminded me of those, except it wasn't a boxing ring in the middle and they don't usually have grand pianos.

'There was food on the table. Snacks, really. Canapés and the like. Sushi. Stuffed dates. Things I didn't recognise. There were also half a dozen chaises longues sprinkled about the place and a load of stuffed animals. Mainly birds; swans, peacocks, quetzals, toucans, birds of paradise. There was money behind this, whatever it was.'

'But there was no one in the room at this point. No Vanchev.'

'Nobody. For a moment, I thought I was wasting my time, but I could tell it was a room waiting to be filled. I stopped filming and sat tight. After ten minutes, the big double doors opened and in trooped six men. I started filming again.

'All very well-dressed and mostly foreign; European, Arabic, one African-looking guy. Age range between forty and seventy at a guess. Vanchev was the third to enter the room. He seemed to know the others, but it was more like they were acquaintances and not friends. People who shared an interest, maybe. There was an atmosphere of reserved politeness, I thought.

'Very shortly after, a seventh man arrived. The others turned and clapped when they saw him.'

'They *clapped*? What – as if he'd made an acceptance speech or something?'

'I suppose so. They all looked happy to see him. He acknowledged their applause gracefully; bashfully, even. He waved it away with an elegant hand gesture. He was wearing a white tuxedo. Pretty tall. Grey hair. Black goatee beard.'

'Eye patch?'

This makes her smile. 'Calm down. But this is where it got a little strange. Right behind him were a couple of naked women – at least, I *thought* they were naked at first glance. One white, one black. Very tall. Same height. Stunningly, breathtakingly beautiful, like highly eroticised fashion models. They held big silver trays groaning with glasses of champagne. The full Bruce Wayne. Everyone started clapping again.

'The white one had long, red hair and wore nothing but silver body chain jewellery; like a necklace that had expanded to cover her shoulders and her breasts, you know? Though obviously her breasts and nipples were totally visible. They couldn't not be. She was excessively voluptuous. She wore silver heels and that was it. Nothing else.

'The black woman wore a dark green and bright yellow head wrap, maybe a traditional African one, I'm no expert. You couldn't see her hair. She also wore a triple strand white pearl necklace. She was very dark and the pearls looked striking against her skin. Nothing covering her breasts, but she wore a black leather waist cincher, perhaps eight inches wide. Big gold bangles on both wrists. Not voluptuous like the other one. Sleek, small breasted and athletic. But yet again, very tall. That was it for her apart from a pair of beautiful gold heels. Miu Miu, at a guess.'

I have to shake my head to get rid of the images that are currently scurrying around inside it. 'You could be describing my eighteenth birthday party.'

'Huh. You wish. So, Goatee Beard sat down at the grand piano and started playing. I didn't have sound, but I guessed it was classical.'

'This is pretty weird, isn't it?'

'A parallel universe office party. The two women mingled with the men and served them champagne. The black woman popped pills into their mouths from time to time, but I couldn't make out what they were; couldn't see the colour or shape.

'So, the men talked, the women served them with champagne and pills and Goatee Beard accompanied them on the piano.

'This went on for maybe half an hour, forty minutes. Occasionally, the men groped the women as they walked around: some half-heartedly, others a little more roughly. The women seemed nonplussed. At one point, the women embraced and kissed. I think this at the request of one of the men. Everyone was clapping and laughing. I couldn't get a handle on what this was, you know?'

She gets up, walks over to the kitchen surface and makes herself another Cuba Libre. 'What is it again?

Double vodka and vodka?'

'You got me. Whose house was this, d'you think? It's not that important at the moment, but…do you think it belonged to Goatee Beard?'

'I don't know. I never got a chance to check it out. It's something I was intending to do, but it had no urgency at the time. Then events overtook. The main thing was the stitching up of Vanchev. Any other stuff would come later.'

'Of course.'

She hands me my drink but doesn't sit down again. She leans up against the window. The light coming through means I can't see her face. She drinks a little of her cocktail.

'There was a sudden change of atmosphere. I could feel it. I noticed one of the men undoing his bow tie and stuffing it in his tux pocket. Another one of the men rubbed his hands together. The African-looking guy whispered something to Vanchev and laughed.

'Vanchev joked with the white woman, tried to grope her and kiss her, but she smiled and good-naturedly pushed him away. She kept looking over at Goatee Beard, as if she was looking for reassurance that this activity of Vanchev's wasn't her doing, that she wasn't encouraging it. Just my impression. It could be that she just wanted it to stop. Hard to tell. The black woman walked across the room, looked over her shoulder, smiled at everyone, then opened the double doors.'

'And?'

'And that's when the children came in.'

5

RICH MEN'S STUFF

It seems as if we've already gone so far down the road with this that I'm beginning to forget what Polly is doing here and what she wants. Two men tried to murder her, she said, but now that seems a long time ago.

Whether she realises it or not, her narrative is exhausting. This has an unpleasant, ominous, creepy feel about it, and I can't imagine where it's going. No wonder she seems a little agitated.

I'm intensely curious, but I still say, 'If you don't want to go on with this…'

She holds both hands up. 'It's – it's got to be said. All of it. This time tomorrow my telling you all of this will be in the past and you can get on with whatever you have to do. And I can get on with whatever I have to do. I just have to steel myself from moment to moment. Somewhere in this lot is the answer. Don't worry. It's OK. I'm OK.'

'I'll take you out to dinner tonight.'

She smiles, but it's a brittle smile. 'There. You see? I've got motivation to get through it now.'

'Just don't drink all of that rum. I'm having a cocktail party later on. Some very important people. Power couples, the works.'

'Any sports celebrities or fashion influencers?'

'More than you could imagine.'

'These children matched the décor and the furnishings. That was the first thing I noticed. They really blended in. Is that silly? They were all dressed in very fancy clothes: velvets, satins, silks, even fur. One of them wore a silver fox fur jacket. Lots of rich colours: crimson, turquoise, vermilion, gold, emerald green, tangerine; pretty amazing looking.

'Jewels, pearls; none of it looked fake to me, though from that distance it could have been. Under other circumstances you'd really appreciate it as a visual thing. No particular style, but clichéd ancient Egyptian and Moroccan came to mind. Almost fancy dress, but not quite. I got the impression these clothes had been custom made. Well, I mean, they'd *have* to have been.'

'What did everyone else do when they came in?'

'The women made a fuss of them, patting their heads, smiling at them and laughing. Their behaviour reminded me of infant schoolteachers or nursery attendants, you know? But these women were virtually naked, so it seemed bizarre and unhealthy. None of the children reacted to these women in any way that you might expect, naked or not. They just ignored them. I remember thinking that their indifference seemed rather impolite.'

'How many were there?'

'I counted twenty-eight of them. Boys, girls, some black, some white, some Asian. There was one cute little Chinese girl, or maybe Korean. Two of the boys were possibly Indian. A scattering of blonde, Nordic types.' She laughs. 'It was a real United Nations deal.'

There has been an almost imperceptible slowing of her speech since mentioning the arrival of the children. I'm nudging her along a little. Questions that she'll probably give me the answers to anyway, but if you create a collaborative atmosphere, she'll remember that there's someone listening, someone she has a link to, and won't dry up. That's the theory, anyway. Subtle interrogation techniques often turn out to be *too* subtle.

'Age range?'

'Between six and eleven, I'm guessing. Hard to tell with differing races. An eight-year-old French kid may look a different age from an eight-year-old Somali kid, you know? Anyway, they drank the champagne and ate the food.'

'Are you sure it was champagne and not some soft drink?'

'It was champagne. There were bottles of champagne apart from the glasses that the woman brought in. What the children drank was coming out of the same bottles that the men were drinking from. No doubt about it. The good stuff: Dom Pérignon, Armand de Brignac, Carbon. The black woman gave the children pills, just like she'd done with the men. I don't know if these were the same pills as the men got, though. Impossible to see properly.'

'What was the – what was the *demeanour* of these kids? Excited? Afraid? Indifferent?'

'They looked a little drugged; zombied out. But their, their *gait* wasn't abnormal. They were just quiet. Serious. Well-behaved, I suppose. They weren't staggering or shuffling or tripping up or anything. Or speaking. I mean, they didn't hold *conversations* with the adults there. They did speak sometimes, but usually in response to something one of the adults had said. At least that's the impression I got.

'Sometimes it seemed as if they were asking questions. Just an impression. My lip reading's still OK, but that wasn't important at the time. I thought I could deal with that later when I reviewed the film. But the main thing you noticed was that they were serious. A bit *Village of the Damned*. Like they weren't children anymore. Like their childhood had been surgically removed.

'Of course, it could have all been an act. I didn't have anything to compare it to. Oh, and everyone seemed to be *glowing*, you know? Sweating, I mean. As if the room was really warm. As if the heating was turned right up. Some of the men started loosening their collars after only a few minutes. Maybe it was so the two women didn't catch a cold!'

She sits down opposite me, Cuba Libre in one hand and my hand in the other. Her grip is uncomfortably tight.

'A lot of mingling, touching and stroking went on. It did occur to me that they were all a bit high, I suppose, but not out of control. Not yet, at least, though it did get that way later. I don't know what the black woman had been giving to all of them. What was in those pills, I mean. I wondered if it was MDMA or something like it. It can't have been too strong, or it would have presumably knocked the kids out. Plus, mixing whatever it was with the alcohol, you know?

'I don't think I saw either of the women take anything, though they were drinking champagne like everyone else. Neither of them seemed drunk, though. I think it was because they weren't guests; they were working. There was loads of champagne. I couldn't work out where it was all coming from. It just seemed to be magically replenished from time to time.

'Goatee Beard walked around among everyone, sometimes speaking to one of the men, sometimes crouching down and talking to one or two of the children, like a slightly sinister but friendly uncle. He was definitely the host, if you could use that word. One of the men started dancing with the white woman, a kind of inept waltz, but it didn't last for long.

'Vanchev was talking to two of the children, two girls, but they weren't talking back. They seemed disinterested. At that point, I realised that almost all of my right leg had gone numb from sitting in the same position in that damn tree for however long it was.

'Someone must have said something, because everyone started clapping again. The two women were virtually naked already, but they very slowly and carefully removed all their jewellery and their heels. The black woman undid her head wrap. She had very long hair underneath and shook her head from side to side. This got a round of applause. The hair covered her shoulders and breasts. She kept the waist cincher on.

'Both women got onto the circular bed and started to put on a show, I guess you'd call it. A sex show. Very artistic, very sensual. They were familiar with each other, I think it would be safe to say. After a slow start, it escalated pretty rapidly.'

'What are we talking about here, Polly? A real sex session?'

'Yes. No holds barred. I was initially surprised that the children were allowed to watch this. It was pretty vigorous, kinky stuff, you know? I was also – this is silly – I was also surprised that they were allowed to stay up so late. But like I said, it was as if they weren't really children anymore.' She shakes her head. 'I felt like a perve filming it.'

I take a sip of my drink. 'So, what was going on while

these women were on the bed or stage or whatever it was?'

'Some of the men sat on the edge of the bed watching, and some of the children as well. More champagne, more mingling, more touching, more stroking. I kept thinking "This is rich men's stuff. This is what men of the world get up to. This is the reward you get for being powerful and important and monied."'

'Goatee Beard wandering from person to person, seeing that their glasses were topped up. Keeping them sweet. Feeding them. Chatting. Laughing. Conspiring. Then it started. It was very, very gradual. I couldn't quite work out when it started going that way.'

'When what started?'

'The orgy. That's what it was. I feel uncomfortable using that word for some reason. It seems an indecent word to use under the circumstances. The children seemed to know what to do. They were *professional*. That's the word that kept occurring to me. Goatee Beard moved among them, helping people off with clothing, encouraging, assisting, smiling and finally joining in himself.

'He was doing things that got applause from the other men, almost as if he was demonstrating what could be done. I think you could say he was a well-liked figure. If the men there were sometimes not familiar with each other, they were all familiar with him.

'The women were not involved with the children; they were only involved with each other.' She laughs. 'They had plenty of stamina. Oh – and my impression was that this was a first time for a few of the guests. Just a feeling. I couldn't put it into words. Maybe not a first time with activities like this per se, but a first time doing it in this sort of company, a first time doing it with this sort of opulence and deference.

'I filmed for another ten minutes, but my stomach was heaving. Anything you can imagine was happening. It was ghastly. Ghastly and nightmarish. I started wishing I'd been holding a Barrett XM109 instead of a camera. I'd have taken out every adult in the room and enjoyed doing it. All sorts of things were going through my mind. "I'm quitting" being at the top of the list. I couldn't…'

She stops suddenly and places her fist against her mouth. Her eyes are filled with tears. 'I couldn't…'

She's going to throw up. For some reason, I manhandle her towards the bathroom and let her do it in there rather than the kitchen sink. Maybe I'm getting fussy in my old age. She doesn't quite make it to the bathroom in time. I stay with her for ten minutes, my arms folded, watching and waiting. Once I think she's over it, I make her stand up. We're going to have to get rid of her clothes.

'Listen, Polly. Get undressed. Have a bath. Wash your hair. Clean your teeth. There's some Thymes Goldleaf bubble bath, some Acqua di Parma shampoo and the yellow toothbrush is a spare. I'm going to go out and get you some new clothes. You're going to need a change of wardrobe anyway. There's a robe behind the door that'll fit you.'

She coughs. 'I'm sorry. How will you know what my sizes are in everything?'

'Hey.'

'Of course. Sorry to have doubted you.'

*

When I get back from the shops, she's sitting watching the television news. She's made herself a coffee. Her hair is wet. She smells of Thymes Goldleaf. I suddenly recall how I know about that product and the memory makes me smile. The robe is much too small for her and a little distracting because of those long legs. It belonged to a Malaysian Airlines stewardess called Regina-belle and it was too small for her, too, but I think that was intentional. I get a brief shiver down my spine thinking about her.

'Here we are.' I chuck a couple of shopping bags at her, one from H&M and the other from Bravissimo. 'Two pairs of skinny jeans, one black, one blue. Two t-shirts, one dark green, one red with an amusing melon print. One pair of trainers, black with rose pattern and no evidence of puke. One seven-pack of white trainer socks. Two Panache Clara bras, lilac and black, full cup, 38E, plus three pairs of matching knickers size twelve. Should keep you going for a while. Don't wear them all at once.'

'I feel like a kept woman.'

'You're lucky I got jeans otherwise it would be my taste in suspenders and stockings as well.'

'The mind boggles.'

'And seven-inch heels. How do you feel?'

'Better. Relieved I've told someone. Makes me feel less unbalanced.'

'Get changed and we'll go out. Get some fresh air and then maybe something to eat.'

Ten minutes later we're strolling down the south side of the Strand towards Trafalgar Square. Now it's late afternoon and pretty busy with tourists. It's still warm, but there's a pleasant cool breeze. Not quite summer, not quite autumn. Neither of us wears a jacket of any sort.

The chances of Polly being tailed again are virtually non-existent, so we can relax, as much as people like us can ever relax. We don't speak and we don't really look at each other. Polly looks in shop windows from time to time. She stops and buys a pair of gold mirror flash sunglasses from a branch of Topshop. I stand around like a boyfriend while she chooses them.

As we walk along, guys keep checking her out and she pretends not to notice. I don't really know where we're going, but this respite will give her a chance to get her thoughts in order. If I'm going to help her in some way, I need her to give me a narrative that isn't tinged with emotion.

Just before we reach the square, we veer left and walk down leafy Northumberland Avenue, eventually crossing the road by the Corinthia Hotel and finally ending up in Whitehall Gardens, where we sit down on a bench underneath some lime trees with a view of the Thames. I still don't speak. I just wait.

'I like looking at the river. It makes me feel sane,' she says.

I smile, turning my face towards her so that she sees it, but still keep quiet.

'I bet you think I'm losing it, don't you?'

'Yes.'

'Hm. How did I know you'd say that? It's just that…some of the things that were happening. Do you remember I mentioned there was a little Chinese or Korean girl? Some of the things with her in particular. They were…there were aspects that resonated with me, do you understand?'

'Sure.'

She glances at me to make sure I got the message.

Satisfied, she looks straight ahead at the river again.

'Once I'd got back in my car, I drove for hours. I had no idea where I was going. I ended up in Marlow in Buckinghamshire at one point. I drove past that famous pub, you know? The Compleat Angler? Weird to think that the Thames goes out that far. Then I made my way back into London. A really stupid route.

'I live in Devonshire Street. I came in through Windsor and headed up to Radlett. I didn't want to go home. I wanted to drive until I couldn't keep my eyes open anymore. I kept telling myself that I'd got enough on Vanchev to get rid of him permanently. Get him out of the country, I mean. I suppose the evening had been a success. But I didn't care. I didn't know what to think of him and I didn't know what to think of the others at that place. I felt numb.'

'What time did you get home?'

'Past three a.m. I'd been starting to make driving mistakes for about half an hour, so I got back, parked, and crashed out. I wanted to see Culpepper about all of this as soon as possible, so I slept until nine and went and saw him just before ten the next day.'

'This was yesterday.'

'Yes. I transferred the film to a memory stick to give to Culpepper. I also made another copy and put it in my safe. I have no idea why I did that. Made the copy, I mean. It's not something I'd normally do. I wiped the file off my computer once I'd done all that. Did a full purge. Crunched it. Compressed it. Shredded it. Eradicated it. Then I physically destroyed the memory card from the DSLR. Flushed the bits down the toilet.'

'So that film only now exists on the two memory sticks. Did you tell Culpepper you'd made a copy?'

'No. It's not that I didn't trust him at that point, but things like that memory stick have a tendency to disappear and I didn't want that to happen with this one. Do you remember that Alderney Street thing about five years ago?'

I remember it well. Nothing to do with me, but I was in Trikala at the time and heard the gossip about it from a local guy who was a former Interpol agent.

A long-term intelligence/police sting on a paedophile ring in Pimlico, South West London, produced damning indictments against so many senior politicians, churchmen, celebrities, police and members of the Royal Family that, as my contact put it: 'Your whole country would sink into the sea. Everyone you look up to is a bastard! All of them! All dogs!'

After instructions/warnings from somewhere on high, the investigation was killed overnight and, apparently, many innocent heads rolled, or at the very least were transferred into different jobs. People were bought off, blackmailed or threatened, and incriminating data was obliterated. Oh, and a mild rap on the knuckles for the perpetrators. Such is life.

'So, you just…'

'Just handed him the memory stick and returned the camera and lens to the quartermasters. I told him that there was enough on there to finish Vanchev and that we should now decide how to proceed with the sting. I told him to exercise caution when watching. Contents disturbing, all that sort of thing. He told me I looked a little peaky. Said I should take the rest of the day off and then tomorrow – that would be today – come in and we'd have a meeting about how to set everything in motion.'

'Then you went home.'

'Yes. Pottered around for a bit, then went to bed. I must have been more exhausted than I imagined. Got into bed to read for a while but went out like a light.

'The next thing I remember was my phone ringing. It was Culpepper. I didn't even know what day it was, let alone what time. I looked at my watch. It was four p.m. I couldn't believe that I'd slept for that long. He sounded anxious. Very unusual for him. Very dry, most of the time. Cool as a cucumber.

'He said that I was to get to a safe house ASAP. No questions. It was a direct order. He'd explain later. He said to go to 28. This was a large Edwardian place in Mornington Crescent. I hadn't been there before, but the protocols, key systems and pass codes were similar for all of them.

'I was not to contact anyone, including him. He'd get in touch with me. The fact that it had a two-digit designation meant it was unmanned, which I was rather relieved about. I didn't want to have to make small talk with anyone.'

'Had this ever happened before with your unit?'

'First time. At least for me. But I knew the score. I packed an overnight bag and got a cab to drop me in Camden High Street. I picked up some food and drink and walked down. It was a three-storey, solid Edwardian house. Well kept, as they all are. I think someone goes in to tidy up and see all is well two or three times a week. It's made up to look as if it's been converted into flats, so the neighbours are used to seeing strangers going in and out.'

'What did you think was going on?'

'I assumed it was to do with Vanchev, but I couldn't imagine how or why, and I was still too fatigued to postulate. I just thought I'd sit tight and wait until Culpepper deigned to explain things to me. I had something to eat and sat in the living room, reading. There were a lot of books. No television, though. I got bored reading and watched a film on my iPad while I finished off the food. And before you ask, no – my iPad wasn't linked to the Cloud or anything, no emails, no iTunes, nothing.

'Despite having slept most of the day, I was feeling pretty tired, so I turned in about ten o'clock. I went through all the locking up protocols and once I was in the bedroom, I locked the mortice and stuck a couple of wooden wedges in the doorframe: one top, one bottom. I can't help myself. Habit.'

'So, you just went to sleep.'

'Yes. But not for long. It was exactly midnight. A terrific crash at the bedroom door. I thought I was dreaming at first. I sat bolt upright. You know – what the *fuck*? My heart was thumping. I got up. I could see that the hallway light was on. I could hear mumbling. Male voices. Two people? Three?

'My first emotion was bafflement. How could *anyone* have got in here without setting all the alarms off? Who the *hell* would be doing this? Another loud crash. Whoever was doing it was ramming their shoulder into the door or was trying to kick it down.

'The noise was so loud that I wondered if they were using an Enforcer – you know those battering rams the police have? Whatever – the impacts told me they were strong. The third time they did it the lock splintered. Those wedges were the only things keeping the door from flying open.

'I thought "OK". I was only wearing knickers and a t-shirt. There was no doubt in my mind; whoever came through that door was not going out of it as a living being. There was nothing in the bedroom I could use as an effective weapon. I ran towards the door and flattened myself against the wall on the handle side. A second later, the door exploded off its hinges.

'Two guys. Big, stocky, serious. I turned into the first one before he could come in the room, pushed his jaw to the right then whipped his head to the left. Snap. Game over.'

'Fuck.'

'The second one tripped over the first and actually fell onto me, knocking me backwards. I managed to stagger to an upright position to discover he was wielding a fuckoff black combat knife.

'He got in a thrust to my abdomen, but I grabbed his wrist, broke his arm across my hips, then pushed him backwards, bringing my knee up as he was on his way down, breaking his back. I grabbed his knife in both hands and pinned him to the floor with it, straight through his heart. It was like a vampire movie.'

I turn to her and look concerned. 'I hope those clothes I bought you were alright. I can change them if they're not suitable. I wouldn't want to annoy you or anything.'

She laughs for the first time in a while. 'I put the light on and did a quick search of the bodies. No ID – goes without saying. No labels in any of their clothing including underwear. Both of them were hefty and muscular. Ex-military? For sure. Nationality? Who knows? European?

'Both Caucasian and a little swarthy. Over six foot, and two hundred and fifty pounds the pair of them. They both had Delta Evo Swiss Military watches on their wrists; popular with commandos the world over so that meant nothing. Great-looking watches, though. I should have taken one.

'The guy who got the neck break had had plastic surgery around the eyes, left cheek, mouth and neck. I got dressed and had a damn good look around the place. I expected to see signs of forced entry somewhere, but there were none. Everything was still locked up as I'd left it. None of my new friends had keys or burglar's tools. I suddenly had the horrible feeling that they'd been in the house all along and were waiting for me to fall asleep.'

'Did you have a good look around the place before you turned in?'

'I didn't take the floorboards up or look in the oven, if that's what you mean, but I did everything that you would have done. Stood still. Listened. Felt the vibes. No unusual smells, no sweat, no colognes, no perfumes, no gun oil, no freshness in the air. The place didn't feel like it had been used in a fair while. If someone had told me that I'd been the first person to open that front door in two months, I'd have believed them.'

'So, they'd have taken every imaginable precaution. Freshly showered, clean or unused clothing and, wherever they were secreted, they knew how to turn their presence off. They'd presumably have known the layout of the house pretty well. Either they knew it before they got there, or they allowed themselves half an hour or so to familiarise themselves with every nook and cranny.'

'Chilling, huh? Well, it seemed obvious to me. There could only possibly be one person behind this.'

'Culpepper. He was the only person who knew you were there. He intentionally sent you into a trap. Unfortunately – or fortunately – he didn't know what you were capable of.'

'That seems reasonably logical, but at the same time it doesn't really make sense. Why on earth would he want me killed? And even if he did, why do it in a safe house? Why make the whole thing so elaborate? If he ordered those guys to murder me, why not do it in the street? Why not run me down as I was crossing the road? Why not use a sniper? Poison?

'One of them was unarmed, the other had a knife. A bloody knife! Much too messy. Why not give them guns? Why two of them? Why ex-military? Why do it – or attempt to do it – in a registered government premise – albeit a secret one? It could only end in some sort of enquiry, the sort of enquiry that someone like Culpepper, if he was behind it, would do anything to avoid. If I was found dead there, it would cause trouble, and now it's going to cause trouble because those two thugs are going to be found dead there.' She laughs again. 'God bless them.'

'Did you photograph their faces?'

'No. Didn't think. Too much to do.'

I watch an incredibly pretty short-haired redhead wearing big-frame glasses wiggle by. A figure like Monroe's wrapped up in a sexy ruffled V-neck green dress. I wonder who she is? I wonder where she's going?

'I don't think anyone will find your two pals,' I say. 'If your boss is behind this, their corpses will have vanished by now. He'll have been expecting them to call it in and when they didn't…'

'Still. It's not the way I would have done it. "Don't do shit in your own backyard", you know?'

'Maybe the intention was that you'd be killed there, and your body would be taken somewhere else. It was just a good place to do it because it would be witness free. They sequestered you away somewhere so the act could be done in private; a place where the public would not be involved in any way. No witnesses, no worries.'

'Possible. It was a corner house. I've no idea who was next door, but it could have been nobody. That often happens. They'll purchase adjacent houses and make them look like businesses, so it isn't suspicious that the lights are off at night.

'The noise was what baffled me. It's a quiet area at night, a quiet street. Try getting a cab after eleven in that area. If they were professionals – and it's obvious that they were – why make all that noise trying to break down the door? At best, it's amateurish, at worst, incompetent.'

'Or they'd got too cocky.'

'It's conceivable. But from the street, I imagine it would have sounded like someone dropping a wardrobe onto the floor again and again. Maybe it sounded louder to me than it would to someone outside. Maybe the house had soundproofing that I was unaware of. Still pretty mind-boggling.'

'They were in a hurry. They didn't anticipate the wedges. It may not have occurred that you'd lock a bedroom door. Perhaps they panicked. Perhaps they weren't very bright. Perhaps this wasn't their usual thing. Lots of possible reasons.

'They weren't expecting the whole enterprise to be anything other than quick and straightforward. They also weren't expecting to encounter someone who could kill them, weapon or not, before they even realised they were in a fight.'

'But what the hell could have happened to set a shitstorm like this in motion?'

I stare at the statue of Henry Bartle Frere. I can't think straight. I close my eyes. Culpepper gets the memory stick. He looks at the contents at some point, then, possibly *hours* later, he calls Polly and tells her to get to a safe house.

Either before or after that, he gets in touch with two goons and tells them where the safe house is. They are to get there ASAP and then (if Polly's assumption was correct) hide until Polly goes to bed.

She would, in effect, be locking herself in with them. Then they are to go into the bedroom and murder her. And what was the next step? Leave her body there for whoever maintains that house to find? Take her body elsewhere and hope that no one spots them carrying it out of the building?

Getting into a house like that would set the alarms off, but so would getting out of it, unless you knew how to do it. This is insider intelligence stuff. Without a doubt, someone told them what to do and how to do it.

The combat knife I can understand, though. If the police ever got involved with this, evidence of firearm use would take the investigation into another league altogether.

'Do you think those guys were brought in from somewhere in Europe to *specifically* deal with you? Could it have been done that quickly?'

'I thought about that. As I said, Culpepper got the memory stick at ten a.m., he tells me to get to a safe house at four p.m. That's a maximum of six hours to get someone sorted and on their way over here. It's tight, but it could be done if those two were ready and waiting for the call, you know? Average flight time from, say, Berlin to London is two hours. Yeah. It could be done that quickly. Unless they were already here on holiday or something, loafing around waiting for work.'

'Were there any strange vehicles parked in the vicinity?'

'Not that I noticed. I'd have spotted anything unusual or noteworthy.'

'So, it was probably their intention to leave your body in the building, unless another team arrived later to remove it.'

'I suppose so. Hard to say. They weren't forthcoming.'

There's something not right here, but I have no idea what it can be. Not yet. Culpepper's department doesn't sound the sort of setup where you can just pick up the phone and order a foreign kill unit to go and snuff out one of your own operatives.

What did she say he'd done before? Liaison with NCIS? Sounds like a career pen-pusher to me. But you never can tell. Whatever this is, it has to be directly connected to what she filmed the other night and, at present at least, Culpepper is suspect number one.

It's also likely that her killing of those two goons is not going to be consequence free. Someone, somewhere, is going to be very upset and not a little stunned by that. It would have been useful to have one of them alive for a little light questioning, but under the circumstances, she couldn't have done much else. The big question here, of course, is *why*?

She stretches, folds her arms and crosses her legs. 'I packed up my stuff and got out. Walked all the way to Goodge Street tube before catching a black cab. Dumped the phone in the cab like I said. Got dropped off at Queensway. Booked a room in the Shaftesbury Hyde Park International. Paid cash. Started getting edgy as all the connotations started flooding in. Couldn't sleep. Took a walk around Queensway and Bayswater Road and then called you.'

'So, you've hired me to find your phone.'

'My God, Holmes; you never cease to astound me.'

6

UNDERGOING PROGRESSIVE MODERNISATION

We get a table at Boyds Grill & Wine Bar in Northumberland Avenue – a rather opulent and ostentatious eating place with huge chandeliers, copper topped bars and marble walls – and order a large sharing board of meats, cheeses, breads, olives and all the rest, plus a bottle of Veuve Clicquot 'La Grande Dame'.

I wouldn't ordinarily get a hugely expensive bottle of champagne like this, but it tells the staff that, as customers, we mean business. It gives us as long as we like to sit and talk, plus I give them subtle signals that we don't want to be hassled by the staff. Famous last words, as it turns out.

'Hello, Daniel.'

'Oh, hi, um, Priscilla.'

'Well, at least you remembered my name.' She flashes Polly a sub-arctic grimace. 'I'm the manageress. Just checking that everything's OK here. Is the table to your liking? We can move you if you wish. It's no problem.'

'The table's fine, thank you,' replies Polly, wondering, quite reasonably, what's going on. What's going on is I had an affair with Priscilla about a year ago and it didn't end well. I had no idea that she worked here. She used to be the manager of Texture in Portman Place, which is, as far as I know, the only restaurant in London which serves Icelandic cuisine. Their fermented shark is sensational, as is their chocolate porridge. The Reyka vodka's not too bad, either.

Her thick chestnut brown hair is tied back in a braided chignon and even the severe black work uniform can't disguise the alluring hourglass figure underneath. That fresh-faced, country-girl prettiness still makes my heart hammer in my chest, despite the disquieting chill in the air.

She speaks with what might once have been called a 'posh' accent. An affectation, I think, but that makes it rather charming; it sounds as if she's watched way too many Emily Blunt movies. I wonder if there's any way I can extract something pleasant from this situation. I doubt it very much. Priscilla turns her attention to me.

'My fiancé left me afterwards, if you're interested. Apparently, I was shouting your name in my sleep. I was saying some pretty explicit things, if you must know. Very explicit. Obscene and explicit. Obscene, explicit and cheap. My fiancé said that he'd never wanted to strangle a woman before, but he wanted to strangle me.' She turns to Polly. 'My apologies. Please don't think me rude. Is this business or pleasure?'

Polly smiles pleasantly at her. 'Purely business. Do go on.'

'Thank you. He was a wealthy man, Daniel. Went to one of the top public schools in the country. He was a senior analyst in corporate finance. A big man in many ways; not so big in others. We were going to be married in Ras al-Khaimah when he had the time. It's a very forward-looking country undergoing progressive modernisation.'

'So I've heard.'

'I fantasise about you every night. I'm sure you know what I'm saying. Or would you prefer me to be more direct, more earthy, more *smutty*? I know you liked it when I spoke like that. It's as if I'm addicted to heroin or crack cocaine. In fact, I wish I *was* addicted to heroin or crack cocaine. That would be easier to cope with. That would be like drinking a Slush Puppie compared to thinking about you.'

'Perhaps we could go out to dinner next week.'

'Yes.'

She turns on her heel and walks away. Polly raises her eyebrows, sighs with mild exasperation and laughs. 'Well, some things never change. She's very pretty, though. Do you remember Paris? That hotel – what was it called? The one where the birds never shut up outside.'

'Maison Souquet.'

'That's right. She looks like the girl whose ex-boyfriend tried to attack you in the bar.'

'I hadn't thought of that. You're right. What was her name again?'

'Melisande Boucher. She was former DGSI, remember?'

'She was sultry.'

'Good word.'

'Great breasts.'

'I'll take your word for it.'

'Very supple.'

'That's enough.'

We wait until the food and champagne arrive before we continue. I try to remember where we were. Oh yeah. 'Can I just go over something? For my benefit? You film Vanchev and his pals at this place in Richmond, you hand over the results to Culpepper. This is what the two of you have been working on for over a month. This, presumably, is a "result".'

'That's about it.'

'Then six hours later, Culpepper tells you – no – *orders* you to get to a safe house. Eight hours after that, those guys are battering your door down and wielding commando knives. Could it be that you just got a *bit too much* on Vanchev? What I mean is, could Culpepper have *not really wanted* Vanchev out of the country for some reason? Was he hoping that you wouldn't get enough material for blackmail, for example?

'I mean, you were the only witness to the goings-on at Richmond. If you were killed, then no one would know what Vanchev had been up to apart from Culpepper. That's assuming that Culpepper wanted to protect Vanchev in some way. Does that make sense? I'm clutching at straws. You did suggest that Vanchev might be protected. That he was viewed as being a bit of a boy wonder. Were you being punished for being too successful?'

She frowns as she spreads too much Echiré butter over a slice of grilled bread. 'But Culpepper could have just closed the whole thing down if he'd wanted to,' she says. 'He could have said that something else had come to light that would prevent Vanchev's dodgy dealings. That would have been it both for me and the other two officers. The operation would have stopped.'

'No. That's just too slapdash. You or someone else would eventually discover that that just wasn't true. That there was nothing else that actually *had* come to light.'

'It's possible. But Vanchev would just be off my radar then. I might not see anything on him ever again. I'm not going to open up his files a year from now when I feel like a bit of light reading. On top of that, I don't think that Culpepper would be so stupid as to try something like that. Especially with me.

'You never can tell, of course, but it would be a high-risk venture and that's putting it mildly. There would be too many people who might look into something like this, not just the OFRP staff. It might not happen now, but it could happen in the future. It would be like a ticking time-bomb.'

I take a sip of champagne and eat some olives. 'OK. I have to know. Could Vanchev's case be less black and white? Is he all that he seems: a greedy career diplomat and devoted family man with a thrilling sideline in deviant sexual activity? As far as you know, could there be something *else* going on with him? Is there anything at all that doesn't feel right to you about this? Anything you came across during this operation that rang alarm bells in any way whatsoever?'

'I've read everything there is to read on this man. I've had his computers hacked; work and home. I've read his emails, I've listened to his telephone calls, I've looked at his porn, I've burgled his house and I've followed his wife and daughters and had their computers hacked as well. I've accessed all three of his bank accounts and both of his wife's.

'If he was anything other than a cocky, greedy, corrupt, slimeball and pervert, I'd know about it. The kickbacks he gets from Croatia and Slovenia – and, more recently, Luxembourg – go into a single Swiss bank account under the name of Jürgen Drescher. It would have been relatively easy for him to set it up and I've been inside that, too. Dirty money, sure, but comparatively clean as a whistle.'

'Is it – and this is just a shot in the dark – is it possible that his nefarious activities could have left him open to blackmail from another source? That your unit was treading on somebody else's toes?'

She pouts and shakes her head. I admire her hair and look at her mouth. 'Well, if he's being blackmailed, he's not paying them anything regularly, unless it's in cash or kind, which is always possible. Perhaps it's New Age blackmail or something.

'Generally speaking, if you're being blackmailed – and in his case, it could really only be for the sex stuff – you stop the relevant activity with immediate effect. You don't continue going to wife-swapping parties with call girls in tow if someone's squeezing you for money.

'His outgoings are regular, predictable and minimal. He's mean as well as greedy. I'm guessing that the goings-on at Richmond would have cost him a pretty penny, though I'm perhaps erroneously assuming that he was a paying guest. Maybe he wasn't. Perhaps it was free. Perhaps it was a reward for something. And the sessions with the dominatrices in Putney would not be cheap. I have a feeling that there's a source of money that, for whatever reason, I haven't come across.

'It could be that he pays for his sex services in cash and there's an account somewhere that he uses solely for that purpose. It may not even be in this country. There may not even be a bank account. It could be that he brings cash in from abroad in the diplomatic bag.

'He wouldn't be the first diplomat or politician to smuggle currency using that method. All he has to do is to change it to GBP when he gets home. Remember, he's been to-ing and fro-ing from the UK to Europe for six years plus. It could have built up. He might have a suitcase full of money somewhere. Several suitcases.'

'OK. It was just an idea.' I pour out the rest of the champagne. 'Well, if you're hiring me, the first thing I'm going to do is to make you disappear until I can find out what's going on. We can't risk another attempt on your life. Next time they'll be prepared, and you've probably annoyed them a bit already. I'd like you to use one of your aliases for everything from now on. Who's free?'

'Jacinta Darke. All the stuff's in Coutts in the Strand.'

'Tomorrow, I'm going to stash you in a holiday cottage somewhere out of London. Probably Surrey. I'll take you there personally. We'll buy a couple of PAYG mobiles for our exclusive use. We'll do a shitload of shopping first, so you don't have to go out anywhere. You can start making a list when we get back to my place.'

She raises an eyebrow. 'Ooh, lovely. I adore food shopping.'

'I'll need the memory stick with everything you filmed on it. The copy you made, that is. You said you put it in your safe.'

'Why do you want it?'

'I don't know yet. Maybe I want to see what Culpepper saw. Maybe I can get inside his head. Something may jump out. If the contents of that stick are what this is all about, I don't think it should be left in your flat where someone could get at it. If the contents are valuable, we want to know why. Plus, if I'm going to get to the bottom of this for you, it could be used as bait.

'It may be that no one knows that you copied that file, but at some point, someone may guess or suspect that you have. I'm still assuming that the reason they tried to kill you was because of what you had filmed, what you had seen. Unless something else comes up, that's all I've got to go on.'

'Well, we'll have to go back to my flat and get it.'

'The stick? No. It's too dangerous for you to go back there. I'll go on my own. Just give me your address and the combination of the safe.'

'There isn't a combination; it uses an advanced fingerprint module. I have to be there.'

'You have to make things fuckin' difficult for me, don't you?'

'There's twenty thousand in cash in there, too. It's part of my emergency money. Look upon that as a deposit for your professional services.'

'You don't…'

'Yes, I do.'

'Right. Whatever's going on, we have to assume they're watching your flat after your killing spree at the safe house. They may *not* be, of course. They – whoever *they* are – may not know where you live, unless *they* are Culpepper or someone he's hired. But we'll assume that they do.

'We have to move fast on this, so the best course of action would be to go there when it's dark, quiet and when the streets will be deserted. That'll be tomorrow morning at four-thirty to four forty-five.

'Moonset will be about eleven tonight, so we won't have that to worry about. I'll go in first, ascertain everything's OK, then I'll come and get you. I'll need you to draw me a plan of your flat. Let me know which doors arc usually open and which are usually shut. Will you have left lights on inside?'

'No. And all the windows are locked.'

'Streetlamps?'

'One almost directly across the road from the front door, but my place will be dark when you go in; I keep the front curtains drawn when I'm out. The hall light switch is to your right at shoulder level by the living room door. The flat is on the corner of the north entrance to Devonshire Mews South. There are garages and mews flats which back onto it. There's an old lantern light hanging from one of the walls there. It's always on at night.'

'What about parking? Can anyone park outside your flat?'

'Only if they want a parking ticket or to be towed away. The whole road is permit parking, hospital vehicles, doctor parking, motorcycle bays and disabled spaces. The nearest parking meters are about two or three hundred yards away.'

'Where's the Lotus parked?'

'Didn't I say? That went back to the quartermaster's at Thames House at the same time I took the other gear back. Why?'

'Doesn't matter. It's just that if you parked it near your flat or in a private car park, I'd avoid going back to it. But as you didn't...'

'You're so meticulous.'

'Part of my charm. We'll book Dial-A-Cab to get us there. Do we have to approach your place from the front?'

'No. We can approach from the rear. If we get the cab to Weymouth Street, we can walk all the way up the mews, and the entrance to my flat will be on our immediate right.'

'How many floors? Which one do you live on and

who's in the others?'

'Three floors. I'm on the first. Ground floor is a retired theatre impresario and his former wife, Mr and Mrs Trengrouse. Second floor is a Tunisian widow and former cellist, Madame Scalesi.'

'How long have they been there?'

'Impresario and former wife thirty years, Scalesi forty plus.'

'Have you seen them recently?'

'All of them in the last week.'

'Any of them had visitors of late, familiar or unfamiliar?'

'Not to my knowledge.'

'How do you get in the main entrance?'

'Keypad. Eight digits. 18761973. 1876 and 1973. Madame Scalesi's idea, apparently. The birth and death years of Pablo Casals.'

'That old chestnut. *Everyone* uses that. What about your flat?'

'Banham M5000 mortice deadlock, a Yale PBS2 deadlocking night latch and a Schlage BE 375-V keypad, five digits, currently 99932. I change it every week. There's a fire escape door at the end of the entrance hall which leads out to the mews. It's an external security door with a full steel reinforced core. Banham and Yale like the front, but no keypad.

'Booby traps?'

'M18A1 anti-personnel mines and a spring-gun in the fridge.'

I laugh and then nod my head sagely. 'Pays to be careful.'

'But it's so hard to get replacement cleaning ladies.'

'Have you got one?'

'Mrs Klara Brutka. Gives the place a blast once a month. Last time was nine days ago. No keys. I let her in.'

'Let's get back to Exeter Street.'

On our way out, Priscilla materialises from nowhere and grabs my upper arm. 'I've bought some things. Just now. Online.' She leans forwards and whispers in my ear. 'No. Please. Please stop it. This is impossible. I hate myself.'

My eyes widen and I swallow hard. I can see Polly smirking as we head back to Covent Garden. I just knew this was going to be one of those days.

7

NICE BOY

I book a place called Honey Cottage in Godstone, Surrey, for two weeks, using Polly's aka of Jacinta Darke. She'll pay them in cash when she gets there. The woman's name is Mrs Coffin. Nothing like a good omen to start off the day.

'What time does Coutts open in the morning, Pol?'

'Eight a.m.'

'OK. Go in and fetch your ID stuff as soon as it opens, then we'll drive down to Godstone. I'll book a rental car from Boneville's, pick it up at seven a.m. and stash it Cavendish Square until you're ready. Be careful. Be switched on. After we've been to your flat, we'll come back here and have breakfast.'

'I'm sure I can rustle up something from the nothing that's in your fridge and cupboards. Or maybe you can get Priscilla to go shopping then come back and make us a full English. I'm sure she'd be more than delighted.'

'Bitch, bitch, bitch.'

She draws me a plan of her flat. Entrance hall, a living room on the right as you go in, first bedroom on the left, second bedroom on the right. Fire escape straight ahead. The hall takes a right turn, then there's a dining room and kitchen on your left and a bathroom and toilet on the right. Looks like a big place.

I sit at the kitchen table and call up Dial-A-Cab, arranging for a car to pick us up from outside the entrance of the Club Quarters Hotel at four-twenty a.m. When I've finished the call, Polly sits across from me and hands me a vodka. 'We walked past that hotel earlier on, didn't we? So that was just a random choice. I'd forgotten how…arbitrary you were.'

'I'm known for my arbitrariness. It's one of my strongest points. The chicks dig it.'

'This is some life we both have, isn't it? I sometimes feel like I'm in a parallel universe.'

'I know you secretly hanker after being a veterinary nurse.'

'True. And your psychological makeup makes you an ideal candidate for being a technical writer; washing machine instructions a speciality.'

'You better get to bed. I've made the spare bedroom up for you. We're both going to have to get up at about three-thirty.'

'I am a little tired. This has been quite a day.'

I fetch an old sweatshirt from my bedroom. 'Here. You can wear this. Forgot to get pyjamas when I was out shopping.'

'Thank you.' She takes the sweatshirt, heads towards the bathroom, then stops and turns around to face me, grinning. 'Daniel Beckett.'

'Hm?'

'I like it. It's a nice name. It suits you.'

'Go to bed.'

*

The cab drops us both off in front of The Harley Street

Clinic in Weymouth Street. It's 4.32 a.m. Two blonde girls stride past wearing identical grey trench coats and trilby hats with green goose feathers stuck in the bands. At first glance, they look like they might be identical twins, but they're not. I wonder where they've been.

'Hope everything will be alright,' the cab driver says to Polly.

'I'm sure it will be. Thank you.'

We wait until he's out of sight, cross the road and walk along Devonshire Mews South, which is all window boxes, hanging baskets, olive trees in terracotta pots and huge green rubbish bins. At this time of the morning, it's like the grave. I'm glad I wore a jacket, as it's pretty chilly.

Polly makes brief eye contact with me, but her expression is devoid of emotion or empathy. I'd forgotten that everything gets switched off when she's working. She's probably thinking the same thing about me.

She links her arm through mine, so we look like a slightly inebriated couple. I trip over once or twice. She giggles. I whisper nothing in her ear. We keep to the narrow, tarmacked areas next to the small apartments and garages and avoid the cobbled roadway.

I can see one parked car, but it's draped in a dirty red cover which looks as if it's been there for some time. Someone has written 'fuck' in the dirt with their finger and someone else, more recently, has written 'slut'.

There are one or two external lamps attached to walls, but the low wattage bulbs don't give off much light. Besides, we could live here and be coming home from some crazy party. There's a shivering pigeon dying by one of the bins. Polly stoops down and with a quick snap of her fingers helps it get where it was going.

About a hundred yards ahead, I can see the lantern light to the rear of Polly's flat and the barred ground-floor windows of the retired theatre impresario and his former wife. All is quiet. When we're ten feet away from Devonshire Street, Polly hands me her keys and I indicate that she should stand in the shadow cast by a large Butia palm which is guarding someone's pink front door. We agree that the next step should be executed as quickly as possible.

I walk up to the front door with a befuddled key-fiddling drunken stagger, in case anyone's watching, and type Señor Casals' dates into the keypad. There's a quiet click and I turn the handle and step inside.

I close the door behind me and acclimatise for a few moments. There are no sounds. The staircase that leads to the first floor is on my left. Ten cautious, silent steps later I'm outside Polly's flat. I type 99932, then use her keys to silently unlock the mortice and the Yale. I open the door an inch and wait, attempting to sense any presence. I stand there for maybe thirty seconds until I'm satisfied that it's empty. It's pitch black in here. I close the door behind me and wait for another thirty seconds before turning the hall light on, using the switch to my right.

Anyone outside would see that there was activity in here, but that's too bad. I just have to check out the place as fast and as thoroughly as I can, and that means putting the lights on in each room until I'm happy they're clean and have determined that all the windows are still locked. Using a torch would take too long and would be unreliable.

I deal with both bedrooms first, looking under the beds and in the wardrobes. Then the living room and dining room, even peering under the tables and behind the sofas. The robust fire escape door is secure, and the kitchen, bathroom and toilet seem fine, with security grilles and heavy-duty outdoor padlocks safeguarding the windows.

I take a final look around, turn all the lights off and relock the front door before exiting the flat. Then I go down to fetch Polly. She and the Butia palm are both still there. I snap my fingers quietly to attract her attention. She wrinkles her nose at me. I hand her the keys and we go back in through the front door and up to the first floor.

She goes inside and I close the door behind us. She turns the hall light on, and a dark shape says, '*Hey, bitch!*' There's the suppressed crack of two gunshots and Polly gets it in the head, the back of her skull blown away and her body crashing heavily into the wall before dropping to the floor.

No!

I don't even think about it. I flick the hall light off and make a headlong dive into the living room, roll over and get back on my feet as if this is some sort of training exercise. My brain is screaming 'What the *fuck?*', but I don't have time to listen to it right now. There are two of them and at least one is armed. Where could they possibly have come from?

'Hey, nice boy,' says a voice in an accent I don't recognise. 'Are you sad because your pretty bitch is dead? You going to cry, nice boy? Maybe you want to kiss her goodbye, no? Perhaps we will kiss her for you! Perhaps we will fool around with her, yes? You hear, nice boy? We make you watch.'

My eyes adjust to the gloom and I take a one-second

sweep of the place to look for something I can use as a weapon. Nothing. All I've got is the darkness. He speaks again. He's getting closer. Soon, he'll find the light switch.

'I'm coming for you, nice boy. Put your hands on the back of your head and walk out here. No problem. We're OK guys. We're cool. Piece of cake.'

I can hear the second man sniggering. He says something in what could be a Germanic language and the gun guy laughs. It's suddenly lighter. It seems as if the kitchen light has been switched on.

'My bro says we're going to party with you, nice boy. No problem. You ever been in prison, nice boy?'

He's about six feet away now. Despite being armed, he's cautious and moving slowly. Perhaps he heard about the incident at the safe house. I close my eyes and concentrate. In the second that I saw him, he was holding the gun in a two-handed combat grip, level with his collarbone. Both arms outstretched. Right forefinger on the trigger.

The little finger of his left hand will be exposed beneath his right wrist. I stand against the door jamb and wait. Five feet, four feet. I visualise what I'm going to do over and over again. Wait until he talks. Talking dulls reaction time.

'Hey, nice boy. I'm a cool guy. I…'

I quickly step out right in front of him, my hands clasped tightly together and in the same movement drive upwards against the base of both wrists, snapping that little finger at the knuckle, forcing the gun upwards. He squeezes off a round, and as I drive both sets of fingers down into the soft flesh above his collarbone, I feel a blinding pain somewhere around my right tricep. Have I been shot?

Just as he's dropping to his knees from the neck pain, I twist the gun out of his hands, grab a handful of his hair, send the suppressor crashing through his front teeth into his mouth and fire four rapid shots into his lower brain. But it's not over yet. His friend is armed, too, and has a similar-looking gun aimed at my head.

The pain in my upper arm is incredible. I risk a quick glance to my right. There's a five-inch diagonal rip in my leather jacket about four inches down from my shoulder and it's where all the pain is happening. A *ricochet*? A fuckin' *ricochet*? Well, that's a first.

'Gun. Gun.'

My new pal glares and points and I throw the gun over to him. I can't do anything else. He's angry and trembling, but just about keeping it together. This was unexpected and he doesn't quite know what to do next.

I take in his entire body; every miniscule twitch and flutter. He kicks the gun further away, walks up to me and aims his weapon, one-handed, at the centre of my forehead. Mistake. I duck out of the line of fire, grab the gun with both hands, twist it upwards and then wrench it down towards his gut, simultaneously kneeing him in the balls.

I push him to the floor. He groans and looks astonished. He throws up over my shoes, whether from pain or fear, I've no way of knowing. I unscrew the suppressor from his gun and pistol whip him into unconsciousness. I want this one alive. Polly's account of the attack in the safe house made me think it would have been useful if one of those goons had lived, but knowing her, that would never have happened. Now I've got one of them and I know exactly how to use him.

Under other circumstances, I'd have had two choices.

Either I'd disappear into the night and leave the surviving thug and whoever sent him wondering who the hell I was, or I'd keep on with the job. Of course, there's no choice at all. Polly and I once made a promise to each other and it's a promise I intend to keep.

I switch the hall light on and stoop down by her body, closing her eyes and running the back of my hand gently up and down her cheek. She's lying in a huge pool of her own blood and I wonder how long it'll be before it starts seeping down into the flat below. I squeeze her shoulder. *Sorry, babe.* She's wearing the red t-shirt with the amusing melon print that I bought for her.

First things first. I collect the two guns and take a quick look at them. They're the same: Grand Power K100 Whispers, made in Slovakia. They take 9mm rounds. Something clicks in my brain and I take a look at the faces of my two friends. *They're* the same, as well. I didn't really notice it in all the excitement, but they were obviously twins, right down to the same ugly gap in the middle of their protruding front teeth and their adorable monobrows.

The one that I've just pistol-whipped has a small one-inch scar beneath his lower lip. It looks old. But are these two Slovakian, like the guns? I don't think so. I don't know what language that was I half-heard, but it wasn't Slovak or Hungarian. But I can worry about that later. Right now, I have to act fast.

I take the guns and suppressors, memorising which was which, and place them on the kitchen surface while I attend to everything else. I head towards the bathroom, giving my new buddy a hard kick in the side of the head as I walk past. I put the bathroom light on, take my jacket and shirt off and inspect the damage in the mirror.

It's a superficial bullet wound, but it's pretty deep, hence all the blood that's pouring out of it and dripping off the ends of my fingers onto the floor. Four inches long and it's gaping. There's been a fair amount of cauterisation from the heat of the bullet, but not quite enough.

Looks pretty nasty and it'll need stitches. I guess that my heart rate went up dramatically during all the action, and that's made the bleeding worse. I must meditate more. Now my adrenalin is down a little, the pain is increasing, but I'll just have to ignore it as best I can.

I've got to find something I can use as a tourniquet. I can't make my dramatic escape with blood dripping everywhere and I don't want to faint from blood loss. There's nothing in here, so I press a toilet roll against the wound and start looking. Ouch.

I find what I need in what must be Polly's bedroom. There's a black satin kimono behind the door. I whip the belt off it and go back into the bathroom. I take the toilet roll away and the blood continues its worryingly copious trickle.

Applying a tourniquet to yourself can be a little tricky and this one is going to have to be pretty high up the arm, just below the armpit. At least I'll be able to see what I'm doing.

I wind it around a few times until I've got the two ends of the belt in my left hand. I wrap them around each other to tighten them until I can see the bleeding has stopped. I search the bathroom and finally find what I'm looking for in a small cabinet above the sink.

I take out three yellow hairbands and twist them over the ends of the belt again and again until they feel tight enough. This is pretty useless, but it'll have to do for the moment as I'm rather busy. My face has been sprayed on one side with Polly's blood and brain matter, so I soak a hand towel in hot water and give myself a quick decontamination.

Next up, a quick search of the terrible twins. Predictably, they have no ID and no identifying labels on their clothing. They're strikingly similar to the pair that Polly offed: hefty, muscular, six feet plus, well over two hundred pounds in weight, probably ex-military and certainly European.

Both also carry big black combat knives similar to the type that Polly described. The surviving twin has some sort of black pouch attached to his belt at the back. I push him over so I can get at it. It's full of superior glass-cutting tools. I take a quick look at the kitchen. So that's how they did it. Impressively quick work, I have to say. Quiet, too.

There's a kitchen window that overlooks the mews. It's four feet wide and less than two feet deep. Double glazed, but that didn't stop them, and the security grille and padlock, though effective burglar deterrents, didn't impede them either. They probably partially unscrewed the grille earlier and took it off completely when the opportunity arose. This tampering would have been undetectable from inside the flat.

Leaning out of the window, I can see the grille resting on top of an air con fan. There are two big suction pads by the sink and the panes of glass they cut out are neatly placed against the refrigerator.

They were too smart to wait in the flat. They must have been waiting somewhere in the street or somewhere in the mews; on a roof, maybe. As there were two of them, they could have covered both areas and been in communication with each other. Or they were somewhere close by with remote cameras: possibly in a vehicle.

They got to work the instant they knew I'd left the flat to fetch Polly. If they were speedy, professional, well-trained and well-rehearsed, they could have dealt with the window in well under a minute and Polly wouldn't have seen them (or heard them) from where she was standing. I lean out of the window again, and the Butia palm and pink front door are not visible from here.

A brilliant, unavoidable trap, and we walked straight into it. I wonder who they are? I wonder who they thought *I* was? The other thing that concerns me is how they knew that Polly would be returning to her flat and at what time. My hunch is that it was guesswork. Pure luck. It was all they had. She was hardly going to return to Mornington Crescent or the OFRP premises. They'd probably been buzzing around here since the safe house incident. If it was me, I'd have staked out this place for thirty-six hours before throwing in the towel.

Now I have to find Polly's safe. I check on the surviving twin's breathing and he's still dead to the world. I want to kill him so badly I can taste it. It'll happen, but not just now.

If I have to search each room for the safe, then so be it, but an accurate, educated guess would be quicker. Where would Polly have had it installed? Where is the last place in this flat that an intruder would look for a safe? Has to be the bathroom or the kitchen.

I try the kitchen first. There are three shelves of cookery books tucked underneath the kitchen surface. I clear each shelf as quickly as I can, but now even the slightest movement of my right arm makes the wound throb uncomfortably and I'm starting to feel nauseous. I give the back of each shelf a fingertip examination, but there's nothing.

Next stop is the fitted wooden dresser that takes up an entire wall. In the centre are four shelves. The top two are home to various pieces of arty crockery, but the third one down is covered in photograph frames, books, and various ceramic ornaments. Lots of stuff. Too much stuff.

Half of the pale pine at the back of this shelf is very slightly faded. No obvious reason. You'd barely notice it. I take everything down and tap along the back of the shelf with a knuckle. The right side sounds different from the left; more solid. This is it, but I can't work out how it opens.

There are cupboards to the right and left of this shelf. I try the right one first, but there's nothing out of the ordinary. It's full of tea towels and oven gloves. The left cupboard, however, has a strange-looking side panel covered with a different type of veneer from the other side.

Just on the off chance, I apply some gentle pressure with the ball of my hand. I hear five high-pitched bleeps and the panel behind the shelf slides to the side and there it is, a Burg Wachter Diplomat 35E with a SecuTronic Fingerscan lock.

Now the tough part. I go out into the hall, hook my hands under her armpits and drag Polly's body into the kitchen. This creates a wide trail of blood from the hall to the location of the safe. If the police ever get involved in this, they're going to wonder what the hell's been going on in here. The pain in my arm is getting rather worse.

Polly was right-handed like me. With a safe like this,

most right-handed people's instinct would be to use the index finger of their right hand, so I have to assume that Polly would use one of the digits on her left.

I hoist her up to a standing position, keeping her upright by hooking my right arm underneath her armpits. My chest is smeared with her blood. This would be difficult enough without a gunshot wound to contend with. I'll be glad when this day is over, and can almost taste the vodka on my tongue.

I press her already cooling digits against the fingerprint module and, of course, the last one I try – her little finger – is the one that opens the safe. Luckily, there was no discernible limit on the number of attempts.

I lower her to the floor and take a look inside. The first thing I see is her twenty thousand emergency money. My fee, in effect. Each thousand is made up of a neat pile of twenty pound notes with a wide paper band around them. They look like they just came out of the bank.

I take a look around the flat and find a large, smart-looking Jo Malone bag, filled with gift-wrapped scented candles, colognes and bath oils. I take them out, put the money at the bottom, and put the products back in. Not perfect, but better than nothing.

Right at the back of the safe is a passport under the name of Judith Hart, some other Judith Hart related documentation, plus a few items of jewellery. And there's the memory stick. I put it in my pocket and close up the safe, replacing the ornaments and photo frames.

Once everything's back as it was, I go into the bathroom and get my shirt and jacket on. Getting the jacket on is murder. I just hope the tourniquet holds.

I stoop down in front of my debilitated playmate and slap his face hard. He moans. I slap it again. He opens his eyes and looks at me, an unpleasant sneer spreading across his ugly face.

'Do you speak English?'

'Go fuck yourself.'

I still can't identify that accent. Dutch? No.

'Good. You're only alive for one reason.'

He laughs. He coughs. 'Ha. Because *she* wouldn't want you to kill me, nice boy? Your *whore*?' He laughs again. Speaking causes blood to pour out of his mouth. I hope he's got dental insurance.

'No. That's sentimental claptrap, girlfriend. *She* would want me to kill you over a six-month period using innovative and sadistic torture techniques. Then she'd make your mother eat your testicles. That might still happen if you're a lucky boy.'

I take the memory stick out of my pocket and hold it in front of his face. 'I want you to tell your boss I've got this. He'll know what's on it. He didn't know a copy had been made. Tell him he's just made a catastrophically stupid error of judgement. Use those words. Understand?'

He looks at me with loathing. '*Shun famin hool*,' he slurs, whatever that means.

I grab his jaw. 'I know you know what I'm talking about. Just tell him, whoever he is.'

'You and I will meet again, nice boy.'

'You can count on it.'

That jeering look appears on his face once more. I really can't stand it. I get up and kick him in the face so hard that his head bounces off the wall and he's out cold.

I go back into the kitchen and deal with the guns. I scrabble through a couple of drawers until I find a freezer bag and an unused pair of yellow Marigold gloves.

Medium size, but that'll do for now. My prints will be on both weapons, so I give each a thorough wipe down.

The first gun will have fired seven shots; two at Polly, the four I fired into that guy's head and the one that caused the ricochet. The gun belonging to my unconscious friend wasn't fired at all. I replace the suppressor of that one, apply some pertinent prints from the dead guy and put it back on the surface. It may be a waste of time, but I want to create as much confusion as I can while I'm here for the benefit of whoever comes to clean this mess up.

The surviving thug is still out cold. I close my eyes and visualise which hand he was using when he was aiming his gun at me. He's right-handed. I take his associate's gun and clasp his fingers around it, making sure his prints are everywhere they should be. He moans and drools.

For good measure, I put an extra thumb and index fingerprint on the suppressor and another couple of random prints on the side of the barrel. Then I stop with the prints; I don't want to go crazy.

Placing his right index finger on the trigger, I take aim and give it a slow squeeze, letting off a weirdly angled single shot that splinters one of the legs of a small pine table that's covered in junk mail. Then, just for good measure, I fire another shot about two feet wide of where the dead thug was standing.

This might be unnecessary, but I want gunshot residue from this weapon to be on his hands and clothing. It might also, in the future, suggest a scenario where the surviving thug shot Polly and then shot the other thug; after all, his are the only prints on this gun now.

I've decided that I'm going to keep this gun rather than leave it lying around. I don't want it to disappear, as it surely will if it remains here, and it'll be another time-wasting loose end for someone to worry over, as they'll find the bullets but not the gun that fired them.

It was used to kill not only Polly, but also her murderer. It's got this guy's prints all over it and now there'll be forensic proof that he's fired it. It may be useful; it may be not. But with possibly corrupt intelligence personnel involved, if anyone's going to be in possession of illegally tampered-with murder weapons, it's going to be me.

I go back into the kitchen, unscrew the suppressor and place it and the newly printed gun in the freezer bag. This is then stored in between the money and the scented candles and bath oils. The bag is now starting to feel heavy. I can't see all the bullet cases that must be on the floor but kick the ones I can see into random, illogical locations. I take the remaining, unfired gun and dump it on the sofa in the living room. More confusion for whoever.

I pick up my Jo Malone bag and head out into the dawn.

8

EARLY MORNING SOHO

It's a little after five a.m. now and starting to get light. I'm feeling a little fuzzy around the edges and can't quite decide which would be the best route back to Exeter Street.

I'm certainly not going to take a cab or use public transport. Much too early in the morning. Cab drivers or London Transport staff might remember someone like me if asked; sick-looking guy with strange posture wearing a ripped jacket and carrying a Jo Malone bag. Too memorable by half.

I just want to look like some normal working stiff on his way to a humdrum job with an early start, who just happens to be carrying a carrier full of scented candles, body crèmes, Pomegranate Noir cologne, twenty thousand in cash and a gun.

The strange posture is something I'm going to have to correct if I happen to walk past anyone. This is due to the tourniquet, which is now making my whole right arm ache like hell. On the plus side, this means the tourniquet is still doing its work properly, but the natural swing of the arms that walking causes is a source of considerable pain and discomfort; it makes you want to hold your arm at the wrist to stop it swinging or jam it in your pocket.

This would look very odd, particularly with the bag. I

walk along at a medium pace; any faster and I think it would look unusual and also make me feel slightly ill.

So, I'm going to have to take quieter roads to avoid seeing anyone, even though my natural instinct would be to take potentially busier thoroughfares so that I become invisible. I head back down Devonshire Mews South, cross over Weymouth Street and then continue along Wimpole Mews.

I can hear people having sex in Wimpole Mews. One of them is called Carlotta, and, apparently, she's a spiteful bitch. I'm feeling sweaty and nauseous. If I pass out and I'm taken to hospital, I wonder what they'll make of my tourniquet: a Victoria's Secret kimono belt and three yellow hair bands. Polly, I know, would laugh. I also wonder what they'll make of the contents of my Jo Malone bag. I'd forgotten Polly was a big Jo Malone fan. Wherever we were, she'd always find one of their stores. She had Jo Malone radar.

While I'm still in the land of the living, I attempt to run whatever's going on through my mind. I've just left a flat with two dead and one severely beaten. What's going to happen there next? I think these people will have organisation and they'll have backup.

I'm certain that those two thugs crawled from the same cesspit as the guys who attempted to murder Polly at the safe house, though at the moment, I've no idea who they might be, or what the motive of whoever hired them was. I wonder if they knew about the memory stick? I wonder if they knew about the safe? Were they just finishing the job their dead pals started?

If I was running this lot, I'd get some sort of vehicle to the flat in Devonshire Street ASAP, to remove the body of Thug One and get Thug Two some medical treatment.

Maybe give the place a thorough anti-forensics clean.

Interesting that they appeared to be twins. Is it a family business? Are they cloning them now? As for Polly, it's job done. I'd probably just leave her there and let the police sort it all out when someone discovered the body. Under certain circumstances, I might even call the police myself. Unless I had some reason for not wanting them involved.

It goes without saying that my blood and fingerprints are all over that flat. But then so are those of the other two, and at least my prints aren't on the guns. If the twins are spirited away and the police are called, it's going to look somewhat baffling.

My fingerprints and DNA aren't on any database and I'll bet anything that forensics, if they're requested, will come to a dead end with my thug homeboys. Of course, I should have foreseen this and worn a pair of latex gloves, but it just didn't occur. Sloppy.

The fact that Thug One and Thug Two were of foreign extraction probably means nothing. If Polly's boss, Culpepper, was behind this in some way, he may well have the contacts to buy people like this, unlikely as it may seem. Europe is crawling with kill-for-hire units, and if you have the money, they'll do whatever you want. There are many, many ex-armed forces people about, and they all have to earn a crust somehow.

If that's the case, though, it begs the question, where did Culpepper get that sort of money from? Is he independently wealthy? Did someone else give him the money? These people are not cheap, and whoever hired them/supplied them is going to be concerned about how three out of four of them died during two attempts to kill a single woman. Was it an official sanction? Did the

Security Service pay for it?

I was thinking about heading towards Oxford Street and maybe taking a more direct route down Tottenham Court Road, but by the time I get to Cavendish Square Gardens, I'm feeling a little more woozy and the sweat I just wiped from beneath my hairline almost covered the palm of my hand. More back roads, I think.

I keep moving east along Margaret Street and then work my way down through Soho. I dump the Marigold gloves in an overfull bin outside a branch of Burger King.

Wardour Street is a little more populated and many of the cafés are preparing to open. I walk normally, both arms swinging by my side despite the pain this produces in my right arm. I'm constantly listening out for cars. If I hear any type of vehicle, I accentuate my commonality; it could be police.

Homeless people shift in their sleeping bags in shop doorways. A one-eared dog belonging to one of them wakes up and silently snarls at me. Its owner is a girl in an old White Stripes t-shirt. Can't be more than fifteen. *Look after her, Fido.*

I'm starting to look a little less conspicuous. Guys are starting to set up road works before they start the serious head-split drilling a few hours from now. Why don't you ever see female roadworks people? Automated street cleaners hiss their water onto pavements and gutters. I can smell bread being baked and coffee being brewed.

A small Italian café has its doors open and the staff are busy inside. Even though it's not open to the public yet, I'll bet they'd let me buy a coffee and pastry if I sat outside. No time for that, of course, but it's something to think about. I feel hungry. I keep moving and walk straight into a sign on the floor saying *Diverted Traffic,* almost tripping over it. No one reacts to the clatter.

A pretty waitress from yet another café gives me a knowing grin, like she knows I've been out drinking all night and she's seen it all before. She has beautiful long black hair, gorgeous eyes and a sexy mouth. The sort of girl you'd ask out on a date while she was serving you, even if it meant making a total idiot of yourself when she turned you down in front of the other customers.

Outside her place is a black and gold lamppost with a brightly coloured hanging basket attached, which is surrounded by an immense amount of crap; cardboard boxes, paper cups, bin bags with their contents strewn everywhere, like an urban shrine to garbage. Or a twisted version of a roadside tribute to a traffic accident victim, but a victim that nobody cared for.

It's as if dumping it all around a lamppost made it OK. Someone's pissed over everything and someone else has vomited over it. The waitress sees what I'm looking at and raises her eyebrows in despair. I smile at her. I may come back here and ask her out.

My mind starts wandering. I start thinking about Priscilla and remember what she whispered to me as we left Boyds. She had a scurrilous line in sexual fantasy, and I wonder how her fiancé coped with her. Maybe he didn't. Maybe looking like that and talking like that meant she attracted the wrong sort of guy for her debauched purposes.

A scared-looking woman pushing a pram complete with loudly screaming baby almost walks into me. Where can she be going at this time of day? Is it her baby?

Another thing that's bothering me is the sort of professional surveillance that Polly must have been under yesterday morning before she met me at the Crimean War

Memorial, as well as earlier today.

She calls me on a brand new PAYG, arranges a meet in code at a defunct clandestine location, yet as soon as she walks up Waterloo Place, she's got a surveillance team on her case.

They didn't know about me, though, which is why it was easy to take them apart. They probably didn't know why *she* was there, either. This means that whoever's behind this isn't totally all-knowing, which is something of a relief.

At the moment, the only solution that I can come up with is that after she'd killed the guys at the safe house, someone, a third person, maybe a driver, saw her walk out of the house, thought 'OK' and discreetly tailed her until she got to the Memorial, calling it in, keeping a safe distance and organising one or more surveillance teams to keep an eye on her, while they sorted out the next attempt on her life.

But for what purpose? What were they doing? And how come someone as permanently switched on as Polly didn't spot them? Maybe she was a little distracted after her two surprise kills. She admitted that she was in a hurry and a little out of practice, but even so.

The two thugs in her flat weren't expecting me, either. Maybe they thought I was a boyfriend – Thug One's comments partially confirmed that – though God knows what their take was on me checking out Polly's flat before escorting her inside. And at half past four in the morning, too. Perhaps they thought I was being over-chivalrous and trying to impress her. Perhaps they didn't think anything.

Professional as they were, I got a feeling that they didn't quite know what to do about me. Maybe they didn't have any orders and couldn't improvise. Maybe they thought they'd get in trouble if they did something wrong.

It occurred to me before: did they have instructions to wait nearby until she turned up? What if she *didn't* turn up? Was there more than one team? Did they get relieved by another pair at ten o'clock or something?

I'm starting to feel a little panicky. This is beginning to sound as if there were a multitude of people with varying skill sets involved in this and it all started after she'd filmed Vanchev at the orgy and passed the film on to Culpepper; at least that's the way it seems.

Culpepper gets the film and less than forty-eight hours later there are four dead. Admittedly, Polly and I were responsible for three of those deaths, but let's not split hairs. What's going on? I'm having trouble concentrating, so I decide not to think about it anymore.

My arm is excruciatingly painful now. It's the combo of the tourniquet itself and the gunshot wound. I'd estimated that it would take me thirty to forty minutes to walk back to my flat. Am I there yet?

I cross Shaftesbury Avenue and traverse Chinatown. I look in the window of the Clouds and Rain Cocktail Bar and Dim Sum Diner. Haven't been there. Maybe I'll take Priscilla.

I feel like I'm walking through treacle. There's a bad taste in my mouth. I'm shivering. And sweating. I try not to stagger. I'm just about tolerating an overwhelming pain right in the centre of my head. I float through Covent Garden, not bothering with my usual convoluted routes home. It's so quiet that anyone trailing me would hopefully be given away by their footsteps.

I pick up a gigantic breakfast muffin and a large coffee

from a place called Kansas Fry-Up. I can hardly believe it when I finally turn into Exeter Street. I didn't think I'd make it.

*

As soon as I get into the kitchen, I take a huge bite out of the muffin and leave the rest on a plate in the oven. That's my reward for later. The pain caused by the tourniquet is killing me now, but I can't take it off until I've stitched this wound. I stagger into my bedroom and unlock my first aid kit, which is in a hidden compartment built into a wardrobe.

I take out two ibuprofen, two paracetamol, two aspirin, two dihydrocodeine, a single-use skin stapler and a curved suture needle with attached thread. I go into the kitchen, take the lid off my coffee and wash all eight pills down. I make a note of the time. Most of that lot will be in my system in ten to fifteen minutes. It won't help that much, but it's better than nothing.

In the bathroom, I get out of my clothes and dump them all in the bath. I'll have to get rid of the leather jacket, which is a real pain, but it's evidence, should evidence be needed. I check in the mirror that the tourniquet is still looking good. I get in the shower and let the hot water do its stuff.

I wash Polly's blood off my chest and allow the spray to clean out the bullet wound as much as is possible. It stings, but the pain throughout my entire arm is much worse. I dry myself off and use a separate towel to pat the wound. Despite the semi-cauterisation, there's a chance that this wound will be infected because of bacteria present in my shirt and jacket. I can deal with that later, if need be.

I get a bottle of vodka out of the fridge and pour myself a triple with ice. I take the bottle and the glass into the bathroom. I turn my back to the mirror, look at the wound and plan what I'm going to do.

This couldn't be any more inconvenient if it tried: a diagonal wound of varying depth, partially cauterised, back of the upper arm on the right-hand side and I'm right-handed. I suddenly get a flashback to trying to write with my left hand in school and being amused by the results. I gulp the vodka down in one, splash half of what's in the bottle over the wound, pick up the suture needle and start stitching.

With each stitch, I attempt to close the gap a little more. I don't want some damn huge scar there. Each time the needle penetrates my flesh, I have to purse my lips in an attempt to blot out the pain. But it isn't too bad.

I focus on what's going on in the mirror and just keep reminding myself that when I've finished, I can take the tourniquet off, pour myself another drink and finish off the rest of that breakfast muffin. It's a little unreal watching yourself do this in a reflection. It's almost as if you're doing it to someone else, apart from the fact that it's you who's feeling the pain.

By the time I get to the end of the wound, I've put in seven stitches and it took about five minutes. It looks pretty tight and it's no longer gaping. But it isn't perfect by any means. It's a little messy, in fact. I'm not sure whether they'd do something else in a hospital now. Maybe internal stitching.

The problem I have now is tying it off. I knew that would be next to impossible with one hand, so I use the skin stapler to fire a few staples into each end so that the suture doesn't somehow come undone. I look down. My hand is shaking.

Very slowly, I take the hairbands off the kimono belt/tourniquet and let it fall to the floor. I watch carefully for blood flow and there isn't any to speak of. I take another quick shower to clear up the blood from the stitching and splash some more vodka over my arm. I clean up the blood that's everywhere, soak Polly's kimono belt in some hot water, pour myself another triple vodka and sit at the kitchen table, finishing off my breakfast muffin, which has to be the tastiest I've ever eaten.

Now the tourniquet is off, my arm is getting back to normal and only the wound keeps throbbing away. I stretch my fingers and bunch them into a fist over and over again. I need to take another couple of dihydrocodeine, but I don't want to OD, so I'll have to save that treat for later. I go in the spare bedroom as if this was all a nightmare and Polly is still in there, asleep in one of my sweatshirts. She's not, of course.

I take a look at the stuff I bought her that she never got to wear. I paid with cash out of habit, and in retrospect that might have been quite a smart move.

I suppose, in a way, I let her down, but this was a situation where neither of us had the slightest idea what was going on, so we had no way of preparing for what happened or any way of properly defending ourselves against it. We did everything we could. Sometimes, that's just the way it rolls. Still, at least three of whoever they were didn't live to tell the tale, so that's something.

I drape two big towels over my bed to soak up any residual blood loss, lie down and pass out.

9

AN IMMORAL NIRVANA

I've been having quite a vivid but baffling dream, and when I wake up, it takes me a few moments to realise that it was probably the result of all the painkillers and alcohol. I was in a supermarket and there was a woman with a trolley walking down one of the aisles.

She wore a slim-fitting black cocktail dress with a cherry blossom pattern and black patent leather high heels. I wondered why she'd dressed like that for the supermarket and desperately wanted to see what her face looked like. I didn't want it to seem as if I was stalking her, so I hung back and pretended to examine items on the shelves.

After insinuating myself into the correct aisle and casually strolling in the right direction, I saw she was heading straight towards me. Even from twenty feet away it was obvious that she was extraordinarily beautiful. Now I could see that the dress was a cheongsam, and it was made from tussah silk.

She looked oriental but had the most remarkable blue eyes. She was smiling, as if she knew me. 'Do you not recognise me, Daniel?' she said. 'Has it been that long?'

I lie still and look at the ceiling, breathing deeply. I can feel tears pricking my eyes. I must be losing it. I hope I don't turn into one of those people who talk about their dreams.

I get up as slowly as possible but can feel my brain shifting in my skull. The wound resumes its steady throb of pain, so I head into the kitchen and down another couple of each painkiller. I look at the clock; eleven minutes past one. I slept for about seven hours.

I go into the bathroom and look at myself in the mirror. I can see bruising appearing around the wound and a little bit of redness that hints at the beginning of infection. At least it doesn't seem to have bled that much, so I must have done something right. I need to go to a chemist and get some sort of adhesive dressing I can put over this, preferably one impregnated with antiseptic. Maybe some iodine, too.

I shave, shower and wash my hair and feel a little better for it. I unload the Jo Malone bag; toiletries by the bath, freezer-bagged gun in my under-shower safe, money on the kitchen surface.

I load up the Siemens with Bourbon Espresso beans, then I order a delivery from Wagamama; teriyaki sirloin steak soba, four hirata steamed buns and a large slice of white chocolate ginger cheesecake. I intuitively feel I'll need the carbs and the protein.

But I'm still not thinking straight: that would be the dihydrocodeine and the vodka hangover. I drink a litre of mineral water. I need to be able to concentrate to work out what I'm going to do next.

Certainly, my first thought is that I need to lift Culpepper and get him in a soundproofed room somewhere, but that's more easily said than done. And although it seems plain that he's the bad guy here – and

Polly certainly thought so – it may not be as simple as that.

If he *is* behind this, I can't get my head around his motivation at all. He knew that Polly was observing Vanchev. It was he who set up the surveillance in the first place and he was running the operation. In a small unit like that, the who-does-what factor is pretty transparent.

I was tasked with getting enough on him to either blackmail him or get him in deep shit with his boss.

He would have worked out the whole thing in some detail. This involved damage to the economy, so it would have been regarded as important and serious work. One loose cannon diplomat burned, and the day of judgement postponed until the next Vanchev turned up. As far as Polly knew, this case had no special significance for Culpepper; it was just another job. Of course, that might not be true, but I'll assume for the moment that it was.

So, Polly set out to get what she could on the target. A mistress here, a dominatrix there; pretty average stuff. But then she comes across the big one. Vanchev is involved in stuff so bad that it turned Polly's stomach to even talk about it in the vaguest of terms.

Polly's revulsion may have been subjective – I always suspected that she may have been the victim of some sort of abuse as a child and a few of her comments confirmed it – but even so, what she was describing was pretty abhorrent and under normal circumstances would have put everyone in that Richmond house in jail, no matter what their wealth or status.

Unless, of course, they had diplomatic immunity, which would have certainly been the case with Vanchev and possibly some of the others.

Something happens when men of a certain type get wealth and status and it often ends up manifesting itself in activities like this. After all the striving, you finally reach an immoral nirvana where anything goes, and consequences are a thing of the past.

You are above everything and no one can touch you. Everything you ever wanted to do is handed to you on a plate. Your sociopathic entitlement gets free rein. It's as if the obvious, ultimate, logical conclusion/reward of success, wealth and achievement is perversion, corruption and debauchery. And you just *know* that they were nerds when they were teenagers.

But, often, intelligence services have to be as unethical as the people they're investigating. Despite the horror of Polly's discovery, the OFRP might have decided to keep it to themselves. They were, after all, not officially there, and so did not see anything untoward.

No intelligence unit worth its salt is going to go to the police and admit that while assembling a blackmail portfolio on a foreign diplomat, one of their agents, who was up a tree at the time, filmed an orgy that may be of interest to the authorities and, hey guys, here's a copy of the film for you and some popcorn – happy viewing.

They might keep the information on file, in case it becomes useful in the future. They may, at some point, decide to identify the other guilty parties, but only if it gave them some advantage in the Big Game. That's just the way it is. Often, the price that people have to pay for their country's security is that people like Vanchev and his fellow creeps don't go to prison, and it barely matters whose children they're raping.

Let's make an assumption. Polly said that she delivered the memory stick to Culpepper just before ten a.m. If I was doing a job like his, I wouldn't put the stick in a drawer and maybe take a quick look after I'd had an extended lunch and read the newspaper. I'd want to see what was on it without delay. After all, my chief operative had just told me that there was enough there to finish Vanchev and then some. This would obviously require my immediate attention.

Polly goes home, Culpepper takes a look at her work. Let's give him the benefit of the doubt, and say he finished looking at the whole thing and thinking about it by eleven a.m.

But it wasn't until four o'clock in the afternoon that he called Polly and told her to get to the safe house. What did he do during those theoretical five hours? Did he confer with someone? Is there another party involved in this that we don't know about? Did he get a rap on the knuckles from on high? Did he tell her to get to the safe house because he was genuinely concerned for her safety, or was he trying to sequester her for a discreet assassination attempt?

Is there a possibility that Vanchev was pulling the strings in some way? Was Culpepper in Vanchev's pocket? But then why start the investigation in the first place?

Was Culpepper under pressure to organise something where justice was being seen to be done? Did he not suspect that things would get this serious? Was what Polly discovered a bridge too far? Did Culpepper panic? Did it turn out not to be worth the gamble? To launch an investigation into Vanchev and hope — just hope — that nothing too bad turned up? And when it did, did he have no choice but to take drastic action?

It all seems a little mad, staking your entire career and

life on the possibility that one of your agents might not be very good at their job and sending them to target someone you didn't *really* want any harm to come to.

But, presumably, he would have known that Polly was good and, officially at least, he wanted serious harm to come to Vanchev. No matter how many times you go around in circles with this, Culpepper as the bad guy still doesn't make any sense, unless the whole thing is so smart and subtle that it's beyond my understanding. Despite all the painkillers, I'm getting a headache thinking about it.

My food delivery arrives. I take it all into the kitchen, open it up and start eating. I can't really taste anything, but that's no surprise. I decide to bite the bullet and take a look at Polly's film. Whether it's a good idea to watch this while eating I'll find out shortly.

I dump the computer on the kitchen table and make a large coffee with a slug of vodka in it. Something tells me I'm going to need it.

Once the memory stick icon appears on the screen, I click on it and wait for the images to start appearing. I just hope she hasn't put some sort of security shield on this or something that'll destroy my computer. There's ten seconds of red and grey signal interference and then there's the first-floor room with the chandelier.

The picture jerks around, disappears completely and goes in and out of focus for almost a minute, then I remember she was perched in a tree, so was probably attempting to get comfortable, and may not have realised she was filming.

It's as she described it to me: the chandelier, the stuffed birds, the thick carpeting, the red velvet stage, the dining tables, the classy buffet snacks, the chaises longues, the grand piano, the animal murals, the erotic paintings. Like Polly, I don't recognise most of the art on the walls but it's pretty good quality; the animals look like the work of Henri Rousseau or one of his biggest fans.

The erotic murals depict scenarios worthy of the Marquis de Sade: voluptuous and scantily clad nuns indulging in every imaginable sexual act with multiple partners of both sexes, naked Georgian or Louis XV ladies admiring themselves in full length mirrors while their maids lazily caress their bodies, drunken orgies with a never-ending parade of Rubenesque nudes, leering, naked men and priapic mythological creatures; all human and non-human life is there.

The only thing I recognise with any certainty is a skilled copy of one of Paul-Émile Bécat's illustrations for Verlaine's Fêtes Galantes. Surprisingly, it features a naked woman leaning against a mirror.

Then the doors open, and the guests start to file in. Polly said that Vanchev was the third. When he comes in, I freeze the image, expand it and take a good look at him. Not at all as I'd imagined. Medium height, sandy or ginger hair with a centre parting and a matching weedy moustache.

Spindly build, but with a sizeable gut and a double chin. There's something wrong with one of his eyes; either a divergent squint or a glass eye. A smart black Pal Zileri tuxedo, white shirt and a Turnbull & Asser polka dot bow tie in pink, blue and black. It all looks terrible on him. I want to write 'prick' across his forehead in black felt pen.

I've caught him smiling at another guest, a much taller, older, wide-chested, blond Nordic type wearing a similar tuxedo, but with a black open-necked shirt revealing a cluster of gold chains. He is not responding to Vanchev's friendly smile. Vanchev looks stupidly happy. Is this his first time at this elite gathering, I wonder? Has he finally *made it?*

Looks can be deceptive, but I try to match the Vanchev I'm seeing with someone who'd have the power and nous to manipulate an experienced intelligence executive like Culpepper. Impossible to tell, really, but I get a gut feeling that he's not the type.

I let the film roll on until all six men are in the room, then freeze it again. Some smile at others, some seem indifferent to everyone else there, as if they're too important to socialise with their fellow perves. I pick up an icy politeness, like people who are about to attend a business meeting full of unfamiliar faces, but who all have a mutual interest.

Then the man Polly referred to as Goatee Beard comes in. A palpable wave of relief ripples through the little crowd. This is something they all have in common; an appreciation of this man and his works. He's binding the room together.

They all turn towards him and applaud. He accepts their worship modestly. God knows what this is all about. It's hard to tell his age. He could be anywhere between forty-five and seventy. Nice white tux, blood red bow tie and matching cummerbund.

I freeze the film again so I can get a good look at the virtually naked women who are standing behind him with the champagne. Polly was right: stunningly and breathtakingly beautiful. Eroticised fashion models, I think she said, and that's a pretty accurate description, except the redhead is much too excessively busty for the catwalk but is not quite all-over big enough to get away with being a plus-size model. Her figure immediately reminds me of one of those provocative Bunny Yeager models, like Bella O'Dare or Diane Webber.

The black woman is like a work of art; a beautiful, captivating face, a well-toned, hard and ravishingly exciting body, and every piece of jewellery she wears draws attention to this fact, whether in shape, colour or location. This includes her green and yellow head wrap.

There's a concealed, simmering eroticism in this that I didn't appreciate when Polly described it. The anticipation of seeing it removed and seeing what she'd look like with long hair flowing over her shoulders and breasts is both thrilling and stimulating. There's a twinkle in her eye which makes you think she'd be a fun date, if she ever did something as ordinary as going on a date.

The white woman is her opposite, though just as tall; much curvier, more dissolute, with a scowling, sensual mouth. Her long, wavy hair is a startling amber shade. It doesn't look dyed to me, but there's nothing else on her body to compare it to. She has beautiful green eyes, but I think they're coloured lenses.

The body chain that covers her shoulders and breasts doesn't have the effect I'd imagined when Polly described it. It's far more lascivious, and the way it's draped over her breasts only serves to accentuate their shape, size and firmness, and emphasise her nakedness.

I could stare at these two all day, but I must get on. I take a bite out of one of the steamed buns and click 'play'. Goatee Beard says something to the black woman, and she laughs. It's a fake laugh. There is no sexual chemistry between him and either woman.

Then he walks over to the grand piano. The other guests watch him. He starts playing. Without sound, you can only guess, but as Polly surmised, I think it's probably classical. His body movements would undoubtedly be different if it was New Orleans jazz. A parallel universe office party, indeed. I take three or four sips of vodkacoffee. My arm continues to throb.

Everyone claps, laughs, pops pills and drinks champagne, and each woman is constantly being casually groped. The groping has an eerie asexuality to it. It's as if the men are entertaining themselves with these two women, playing with them as if they're dolls, asserting their power over them and, perhaps, their ownership of them. The women kiss, the men applaud.

The women occasionally exchange quick glances that the men don't see. Glances that contain expressions of boredom, contempt, ridicule, malice, revulsion, distaste. They must be being paid a fortune.

Then the black woman lets the children in. From then on, it's a sick-making blur that seems to go on for hour after hellish hour, rather than just over twenty minutes. Laughing, drinking, kissing, fondling, groping, distress, depravity, violence, horror and the two women eating each other alive on the little red velvet stage like none of it was happening.

Polly's assessment was that there were twenty-eight kids present. I would say it was more than that. Polly's focus was mainly on Vanchev and the other adults, but sometimes the odd child you noticed because of their exotic garb would disappear for a while and it looked to me as if new ones took their place from time to time.

This is guesswork on my part, though. It's all very confusing and, of course, I don't know how long all of this went on for after Polly stopped filming. It could have gone on for hours.

Whatever else it is, it's certainly a unique viewing experience and I can fully understand why it freaked Polly out so much. It would freak most people out, apart from the freaks who were presumably paying good money to be involved.

The expression on Goatee Beard's self-satisfied face throughout is paternal, knowing; it is as if all the guests, the children and the women were his offspring and he was gently guiding them through some charming and sophisticated erotic Elysium.

And then I wonder: is this what happens to abducted children? For abducted they must surely be. By no stretch of the imagination can this be voluntary. How do they keep them in line? Drugs? Threats? Behavioural programming? Some unimaginable neo-Pavlovian reward/punishment system? A combination of all of those things? Have they been trained (if that's the right word) from an early age?

And what happens to them when the party's over, so to speak? I can only assume that they have to be prisoners of some kind. You could never allow these kids to go back out into the world again after something like this. The risk would be much too high and, quite apart from that, they'd be damaged beyond belief. Where could they go? And – it's a chilling thought – what happens to them when they get too old for this, when they drift out of favour, when they become expendable?

And Polly's comment about them being professional; it's certainly true, but from time to time, blood-curdling distress peeks through and whatever was once under those experience-hardened shells raises its head in terror, despair and confusion.

When the film finishes and I'm left with a black

screen, I stare at it in a daze for almost ten minutes. Then the pain in my arm reappears as if to remind me where I am and what I'm doing. It's as if it decided to take a back seat out of sympathy while I sat through that bottomless pit of turpitude.

Fuck.

As I'm not going to be doing much of a practical nature today, I make another coffee, splash another slug of vodka into it and finish off the food. So, I wonder what would have been going through Culpepper's head when he was through watching this?

I download the file, find a spare memory stick and make a copy, stuffing the original in a big jar of Los Planes coffee beans and then thoroughly eradicating the file from my computer using überhacker Doug Teng's *Shangdi* program, which he was kind enough to give me. As Polly said, things like this have a tendency to disappear and, like her, I don't want that to happen in this case.

If Culpepper was on the straight and narrow, he'd be, in a relative sense, overjoyed when he saw the fruits of Polly's labour. He could lift Vanchev, get him in a room somewhere and project this onto the wall. Vanchev would be his; he could ask anything of him, manipulate him in any way he felt fit.

But this still doesn't explain what happened to Polly Greenburgh. Then a possible answer pushes its way through the dense vodka and painkiller fug. It's so obvious that I'm astonished I haven't thought of it before now. I slowly sit up in my seat.

What if Polly's death, the surveillance teams, the hit squads and all the rest had nothing to do with Vanchev at all? What if she had inadvertently filmed something far more important than a bent diplomat with a taste for off-colour sexual activities?

What if there was *someone else* at the orgy who was, in some way, of far greater significance? What if she'd accidentally stumbled onto something so sensitive that she had to be wiped off the face of the planet, and quickly.

I'm going to have to get hold of Culpepper. He has to be the first contact and he's still my best bet as main suspect. But without Polly around I have no idea how to reach him. I don't have a location for the OFRP, and I can hardly walk into MI5 or the JIC and politely request an address and telephone number.

It would be very unlikely that Culpepper is in the directory, so giving him a call or popping round to his house would not be an easy option. Polly's mobile might have been useful, but that's probably still silently touring London in a black cab somewhere.

In fact, I don't have any way of getting hold of the most basic information about him. It could take days or even weeks to track him down and I don't have that kind of time and I certainly don't have access to those kinds of resources.

But I know someone who does.

10

THE WALK OF SHAME

I get up early the next morning, stuff ten thousand of Polly's money in my battered leather messenger bag and dump my bloody, bullet-damaged clothing in a bin outside a seafood restaurant in Dean Street, just before the refuse collectors arrive.

I get a cab to Cromwell Road and walk the length of Stanhope Gardens, passing the house I'm going to visit and taking a cursory glance at all five floors. There are plenty of brightly coloured hanging baskets outside: yellow begonias, fuchsias, lantanas, lotus vines, portulacas, so I know the place is inhabited and I also know who's still inhabiting it.

These houses are probably among the most expensive in South Kensington, and I'm guessing that this one would be worth over three million by now.

It's sturdy Victorian, with a freshly painted white exterior, black cast iron fencing that stops you getting down to the basement, fat Doric columns around the fuckoff front door and a pleasant view of the well-kept gardens themselves, which are just across the road.

Permit-only parking, archaic street lighting, spotless pavements and a wealthy silence that belies the proximity to one of London's busiest thoroughfares. I turn back and cross the road.

There's a big ground-floor room either side of the front door and the blinds are down on each one. I walk up the three steps and press the buzzer. I can hear movement inside, and after about a minute, the door opens. A man who looks to be in his seventies, but by now must be well into his eighties, gives me a blank stare lasting exactly half a second before realisation dawns and his eyes widen.

'Oh, Jesus Christ.'

He's fast and strong, but I'm used to having doors slammed in my face and, without thinking, smack my right palm flat against the wood. The shockwave that this sends up my arm makes the bullet wound give me a sharp reminder of how much it's still hurting. I don't allow the pain to show on my face. It wouldn't do.

This is Lothar Koch, broker of dark and sensitive information to the highest bidder. At the last count, he had nine contracts out on him and it's only through being a bigger bastard than the perpetrators and their henchmen that he's still alive. Not bad going in his business.

He's also been condemned to death in his absence in both Russia and Romania. His very existence brings a new meaning to the words 'slippery', 'unscrupulous', 'unethical', 'venal' and 'untrustworthy'.

He's a fit guy, and, despite the fey personality he chooses to affect, possesses an underlying physical menace that most people would find extremely intimidating. He's a little taller than me, maybe six four or six five, with piercing gunmetal grey eyes that match his thick, rather foppishly styled hair.

He still has an athletic bearing; he was, apparently, a gold medallist in the 1955 World Fencing

Championships, the year it was held in Rome. Foil or épée, I can't remember which. This story may be apocryphal.

Though you'd never guess it from the way he speaks, he was born in Salzburg and, as a young man, attended the Medical University of Vienna, qualifying as a doctor sometime in the 1950s, getting struck off shortly thereafter (rumours abound) and ending up as psychological torturer in residence for whichever intelligence service had the lack of scruples to employ him. I've no doubt that there are countless people around even today who have had their brains turned to warm Camembert thanks to this man.

Somewhere along the line, thanks to information extracted from his gibbering, straitjacketed victims when they were dosed to the gills with LSD, Haldol, Mefloquine and the rest, he started trading in secrets, and through a system of exchange, barter, threat, blackmail and violence, truly became a man who knew too much. I've no doubt that that's just the tip of the iceberg. It could also be total bullshit, as could the rumour that he fathered a child by a world-famous Hollywood actress at the age of thirteen.

I push my way into the entrance hall. He's wearing a dressing gown with Beardsleyesque peacocks all over it and I'm suddenly reminded of the murals in the house at Richmond. He reaches for a large stainless-steel Georg Jensen candle holder sitting on a hall table, but I slap his hand down before he can get a grip on it.

'Don't.'

'Are you here to kill me?'

'No.'

'You *would* say that, wouldn't you?'

'If I was going to kill you, I'd have done it already.'

'Not necessarily. You might want to get inside first so you can do it inconspicuously. You might want to rub my nose in the indignity of it. You might have some self-righteous monologuing planned. I don't think I could stand that. I'd rather have a bullet in the brain.'

'Lothar. Shut up. I'm not going to kill you. I want to give you money.'

'Ah. Well why didn't you say so, old chap? Let me close the door.'

'And you can put that gun somewhere where you can't touch it.'

'And I thought I was being so subtle. *Quel dommage!*'

He takes a Beretta 950 out of his robe pocket and places it on the hall table, covering it with a blue and white Corneliani silk handkerchief. The gun is an antique. I wonder where he gets the bullets. I am ready to drop him if he pulls it, eighties or no; I've had enough of guns for a while.

I can smell a strong perfume. It's Maison Francis Kurkdjian. Also, tobacco smoke. Rothmans. And cannabis. Smells like Zero Zero or Katama. He's got visitors and they'll have to go.

'Who's here, Lothar?'

'Ah, yes. No problem. Yes. No. Come in. I'll introduce you. It's a bit of a bear garden in here, I'm afraid. Am I the only person who uses that expression nowadays? Could it be so? Bear garden. Goes back to the days of bearbaiting, of course. And I can tell *you* of a couple of places in this fair country where that barbaric sport is still practised. No names. No royal titles. Keep it under your hat. You don't want to be sent to the tower. Ghastly décor, apparently. Par for the course with royals, of course. No taste in anything.'

I follow him into a large sitting room. This is man whom, to a degree, you have to humour and be patient with if you want something. There's a bed in the centre with two people lying on it. One is a naked woman in, I would guess, her mid-fifties. She's lying on her side with one hand propping up her head, like a super-curvy life model.

Her breasts are enormous. Her dark red lipstick is smeared. Her eyes are half-closed, and her cheeks are flushed. Sweat is making her black hair cling to her forehead. She's smoking a huge joint and tipping the ash into a saucer with a medieval-looking nude on it.

She looks like she's just had sex and the prime suspect is lying next to her; a young guy in his early twenties with a shaved head, a big ladybird tattoo on his chest and the sort of body you'd have if you spent twelve punishing hours down the gym every single day. He's also sweating and smoking a fag. They don't look at each other. Perhaps they haven't been formally introduced.

There's a comfortable looking blue armchair right next to the bed, presumably so that Lothar can get a good look at the hot action. Next to the armchair is a small black Chinoiserie coffee table with a half-finished bottle of Château Lafite on it.

The room is decorated with a series of paintings, all featuring naked women of one sort or another, and I'd guess they're all originals: Tissot, Falero, Richir, Poynter and Gallhof. Overall value incalculable. If you robbed this room alone, you'd be worth millions.

If it isn't art, it's big tinted mirrors and William Morris wallpaper. The woman on the bed smiles at me. It's a lazy, post-coital, semi-stoned smile. I smile back. Lothar rubs his hands together like he's about to chair a meeting.

'Um, I'm afraid we're going to have to curtail today's activities, boys and girls. Some urgent business has come up. I'm sure you understand. And have no fear – you'll both be paid in full and the cabs home will be my treat.'

He leans forwards to speak directly into the woman's ear. 'And a little bonus for you, my dear. I always appreciate a woman who goes the extra mile.' He nods at me. 'This is Mr Cambridge, an old, er, *colleague* of mine. Mr Cambridge, this is Mrs Kay Gardiner and her associate Mr Raymond Henry Ambrose.'

Mr Raymond Henry Ambrose blows smoke, smirks indifferently and nods at me. Mrs Gardiner sits up and offers me a hand which I shake. She has soft skin. I can't stop looking at her breasts and she knows it.

'Pleased to meet you, Mr Cambridge,' she says, smiling. She has a charming, soft voice with the remnants of a southern Irish accent.

'And you,' I say. I look at my watch. It's eight-forty. There are certain milieus where the time of day stops being relevant or important.

Lothar shoos them out to wherever they go to get changed, and opens the curtains and a couple of windows. He rolls his eyes at me as if all of this is an everyday hassle that everyone can relate to. Mrs Gardiner is quite short; exactly five feet, I would say. I watch her as she wiggles her way out of the room; it's an exaggerated wiggle for my benefit, I think. She glances over her shoulder and smiles at me. Once again, I return her smile.

Once he's paid them off and they've gone, he returns and hands me a piece of paper. 'Mrs Gardiner's telephone number. She was most insistent.'

'Thank you.'

'She's a class act and she goes the extra mile.'

'I'll keep it in mind.'

'Nothing quite like a big, languorous woman of mature years, eh?' he says, giving me a friendly slap right on the bullet wound. I spit out an expletive.

'Everything alright, old chap? You look a little pale.'

'It's nothing. Just a bit of bad luck. A ricochet.'

'Ooh. Chance in a million, I understand. That *is* bad luck. You stitched up yourself, yes?'

I nod my head.

'Come on. Upstairs. You're right-handed and I'll bet anything you made a pig's ear of it. Right at the back of the arm, eh? Always a bastard.'

I'm too spaced on painkillers to argue. I follow him up the stairs to a room that smells of antiseptics.

'So difficult to find a woman who is actually a *lady* nowadays, don't you find? A lady in the old sense of the word, I mean. Every lady is a woman, but not every woman is a lady. Mm? Take Mrs Gardiner there. Now she's what I would call a *lady*. She was a very good actress when she was younger. Rep, mainly: Shaw, Wilde, O'Neill. Her Electra was electrifying, I'm told. Have you ever read *In Praise of Older Women* by Vizinczey? Ambrosial. One of my favourites.'

This room is what you imagine a doctor's surgery would have looked like in the 1950s. Big wooden desk, leather-backed chairs, oppressive green wallpaper, thick pile carpet, eye chart on the wall and bookshelves groaning with ancient leather-bound medical texts in several languages.

It's homely and comforting, apart from the glass cases full of scary-looking surgical instruments, large gas cylinders and a semi-electric hospital bed with gynaecological stirrups attached to the base. Did I mention the antique rosewood cocktail cabinet and small refrigerator?

There's a cheery painting of daffodils in a vase on the wall next to Lothar's doctor's certificate from the Medical University of Vienna. He catches me looking at it.

'Ah, Vienna! The streets of Vienna are paved with culture, the streets of other cities with asphalt, is that not right, Mr Cambridge? It's been so long since I've been there. It's probably stuffed to the gills with mediocre buskers, foul-smelling fast food joints and rundown branches of La Senza, Hotel Chocolat and Sports Direct by now. Take your jacket and shirt off and sit up on the bed, there's a good chap.'

'Are you sure you don't want me to put my feet in those stirrups?'

'Ah-hah. Yes. Yes indeed. The wit of the damned. Hard not to notice them, isn't it? Antique now, of course. I've had several offers from connoisseurs, but I would never sell. Place your right hand on your left shoulder so I can get a good look. Don't move. Just going to remove this cheap and vulgar dressing you've covered the wound with. On the count of three…'

Predictably, he rips it off on two. He puts on a pair of gold-rimmed half-moon glasses, and without touching the wound, takes a long look at it.

'The stirrups. Yes. Yes indeed. This *particular* house was actually purchased from the proceeds of my MRPs. That's menstrual regulation procedures to you, Mr Cambridge.'

'What are those?'

He sighs impatiently. 'Under-the-counter abortions, ducky. I don't mean that I actually do them under a counter. God forbid. That would be insane. But quite amusing. Perhaps I should start. Depends which shop.

'Some folk out there still like the sort of discretion that they can buy from someone like me. More fool them. I despise them all. Many of my patients are the hapless mistresses of Conservative Members of Parliament. I have no idea why that should be. Perhaps there's an academic paper in it! Should I publish, do you think? I could be famous!

'And of course, the blackmail material I've accumulated is incalculable. I've squeezed about fifty thousand out of some of this country's top politicians just in the last fortnight. They're all vermin, of course. I'd like to bleed them dry until they were empty husks. By the way, if you ever chance upon anything I could use as blackmail fodder, I'd pay extremely well for it. Extremely well. You'd get a cut, of course.'

I think of my copy of Polly's memory stick which is in a concealed pocket in my jacket. 'I'll keep it in mind. So, what do you think?'

'This is, I have to say, not a bad field dressing, but I'm afraid it needs better. It isn't a total catastrophe, all things considered, if that means anything to you. You're right-handed, it was in a virtually impossible position to stitch with any semblance of accuracy, so well done you, relatively speaking. The bullet presumably went through some clothing?'

'A leather jacket and a cotton shirt.'

'Mm. That's where the Lilliputian infection here would have come from. It hasn't got a grip yet, so that'll be no problem, but I'm going to have to take this stitching out and start all over again. Unless you want an unsightly scar accompanied by several gallons of the finest pus, of course. Maybe that *is* what you want. Who can tell nowadays?' He drapes a white towel over my lap, presumably to catch the blood. 'Now. What have you been taking and when did you start taking it?'

I give him all the painkiller and booze details and receive an exasperated roll of the eyes in reply. 'Well, um, I'm fresh out of local anaesthetic, I'm afraid. I'll give you a pinch of pain relief later on. The later the better, I think, from what you've just told me. For the moment, you're just going to have to put up with how much this will hurt as it's not healed properly, but I suppose a teensy-weensy little cocktail can't do much harm now, can it? Is it really too early? I think not. Am I bad?'

He goes over to the cocktail cabinet and starts decanting and shaking. After about a minute, he hands me a cold, pink concoction filled with bubbles. He flutters his eyelids as he gulps down half of his.

'*Magnifico*! I call this The Walk of Shame. Four parts Filliers Dry Gin 28 – pink edition, of course – three parts Veuve Clicquot, one part Campari and one part Absolut Raspberri. Shaken with crushed ice and served in an extra-large martini glass. No lime slices available, I'm afraid, but you'll thank me in five minutes. Keep that arm where it is and try not to move. This won't take long.'

I sip at the drink as he uses a stainless-steel stitch cutter on my handiwork. The Walk of Shame is a killer despite its innocent appearance: it's destroying my teeth and clawing at my brain. I must ask him for the recipe, which I've already forgotten. I feel very slightly ill once more.

'What, er, what happened to the, er, *perpetrator* of this wound, if I may ask such a question of you?'

'He'll have had a bit of a headache the following morning.'

'Hm. Right. I see. Well. That's all your stitching removed. Nice touch using a skin stapler to tie up the ends. Have you ever entertained thoughts of being a heart surgeon? Keep still.'

He dabs the wound with alcohol and then with something else. This stings quite a bit. I take another couple of sips of my cocktail and watch as he unwraps a suture kit.

'Sir Harold Aitchison. Odense. Four years ago. Was that you? Had all your hallmarks. That is to say, no hallmarks whatsoever. Sometimes a conspicuous absence can indicate an inconspicuous presence, if you get my drift.'

'I'm not here to give you compromising information which you can flog so you can afford live sex shows.'

'*Touché!*'

He uses a middle finger and thumb to narrow the gape of the wound and starts stitching. It's incredibly painful and I realise I'm clenching my teeth.

'So, what is it I can do for you? You mentioned something about money.'

'I need some information and I need it quickly. Speed is absolutely of the essence. This would be intelligence you could undoubtedly pluck out of the fire expeditiously, but something that would take me a lot longer to acquire.'

'Alright. Tell me what it is, and I'll give you a price and a timescale.'

He ties the knot at the end of the suture. He applies a collagen dressing to the wound, ties a bandage around my arm and tapes it in place, tunelessly humming "Für Elise" to himself all the while.

'Not too tight?'

'Fine.'

'Try to avoid showering or bathing. You mustn't get this wet for around two days. Or you can wrap a supermarket carrier bag around it, if you must. I know this will be a waste of time, but if you were a normal patient, or a normal *person* for that matter, I would advise a few days' rest. What's the information?'

'I need an address or addresses for an individual called Alistair Culpepper.' I spell both names for him. He nods. 'Plus, anything you can get on him at short notice: CV, where he buys his ties, anything. He's in charge of a specialist department in the Security Service called the OFRP. This stands for Overseas Fiscal Review Policies. Four personnel. Been going for nine years.'

Lothar laughs. It's a chilling sound. 'Overseas Fiscal Review Policies! Now if that isn't a vapid and meaningless appellation, I don't know what is! Where does he come from, this *Alistair*?'

'His background is with MI5. Liaison with NCIS among other things. This is his first big appointment and he's been in the job a little over four years.'

'Predecessor? Just out of interest?'

'No idea.'

'Would you mind terribly holding on for a moment, old chap?'

He goes to the refrigerator and opens the door. For a moment, I think he's going to make another cocktail, but he takes out three glass ampoules, each one a different size and each containing a clear fluid. Then, kicking the fridge door closed, he noisily rummages about in a drawer and produces a bunch of sterile packets containing disposable plastic syringes, needles and pre-injection swabs.

'What's in those ampoules? SP-117?'

'Ha! Now *that* would be a good morning's entertainment. God almighty – I'd simply *love* to get someone like you babbling away into a recording device of some sort. The mind boggles, it really does. Are you allergic to anything?'

'Normal life.'

'No surprise there!' He fills up a syringe and squirts some of the content into the air. 'Just a shot of penicillin. Kill that infection that's starting and give any lingering syphilis spirochaetes a kick in the balls! Left arm permissible?'

He jabs the needle in my left shoulder and has a quick chortle to himself. 'I'll be honest with you, Mr Cambridge: I quite like sticking a needle in people. Always have. I should have been an anaesthetist. They used to get all the nurses. Have you ever slept with a nurse? I'm sure you have. Swiss are the best. Followed by French. French nurses. They almost make one want to believe in God. Is this OFRP in Thames House?'

'It would seem not. I've been told that Thames House supplies the OFRP with equipment and, ultimately, the money comes from MI5's budget.'

'So, they're pretty autonomous.'

'About ninety per cent.'

'But answerable to MI5 at the end of the day.'

'Yes. What's that?'

He's got another syringe ready and, swabbing my arm again, gets ready to stick the needle in. 'One of my own inventions, designed for occasions just like these. Seven B vitamins, vitamin C, magnesium chloride and just a tiny soupçon of amphetamine. Don't worry – not enough to keep you awake all night grinding your teeth and talking bollocks. Just enough to give you an edge in case you need it. Can you give me a minuscular idea of what the OFRP do? Scottish nurses. They're very agreeable, too. Perky and blunt.'

'Eradication of financial threats. Blackmail. Cyber damage.'

'No extrajudicial executions?'

'No. Is that enough? I just need to see this guy face to face.'

'How soon?'

'Yesterday.'

'Five thousand. Cash.'

Not as much as I'd thought. 'Done.'

'Excellent! I wish everyone was like you, Mr Cambridge. Not literally, of course.' A little snort of laughter. 'That would be horrific. It truly doesn't bear thinking about. Just one more jab. Tramadol. I know you're pretending that your arm doesn't hurt, but you can't fool your Uncle Lothar.'

'When I leave here, do you think I should get a cab or just float back?'

'Ha ha. As I said before; the wit of the damned. Another cocktail?'

'Just the one, then I must get back to the wife. We've got people coming.'

This gets a big laugh. 'The old *trouble and strife*. They are such a millstone around one's neck, aren't they! Cor blimey!'

11

YOUR SON IS A DOG

After one more Walk of Shame, we retire to Lothar's kitchen. He insists on my hanging around for thirty minutes so he can make sure I'm not going to OD or throw up. I think he just wants the company. I sit down at his sturdy red oak table while he makes coffee. He drinks Hacienda La Esmeralda, Geisha Jaramillo variety. He has a Jura Giga X3 Pro C bean to cup coffee machine. I'm jealous.

There's a large television screen behind me which is switched on but with the sound off and, across from me, a Ruark Audio music system sitting right next to the oven hob. It's playing some sort of baroque harpsichord music which I don't recognise. Lothar keeps glancing at the television screen. I look at my watch. I can hardly believe it's only nine-thirty a.m.

'The amount we spoke of. You have it with you?'

I take the five thousand out of my messenger bag and push it across the table. As he's counting it, he takes several sly looks at where it came from. I know what he's thinking, but I also know he wouldn't dare risk it.

'Mm. Very good. Very good. I don't think I could *quite* manage this by yesterday as you requested, but, um, if the gods are with me, I may have something for you by the end of today. After all, it's still only early.'

'OK. That'd be great.'

'Things have changed since the old days, sadly. It's not an easy matter to scrabble around in Security Service files and pull out confidential information. This isn't the 1960s. Biscuit?'

'No thanks.'

I drink some coffee and stretch back in my seat. I feel weird, but that's no surprise. The harpsichord music is echoing around my head. Lothar is eating a Marie biscuit and tapping the crumbs away from the side of his mouth with his little finger. I try to concentrate. It's not easy. So much has happened in the last twenty-four hours that I'm not really fit to give it a good comprehensive analysis. I can only hope that everything will fall into place once the alcohol and pharmaceuticals are totally out of my system.

My sinuses hurt. Assuming that the film of the Richmond orgy is what this is all about – and I think it is – then someone, hopefully, is going to be tracking me down right at this minute.

I start thinking about Thug One and Thug Two at Polly's place. Showing Thug Two that I had the memory stick *has* to bring me to the attention of whoever is behind all of this. Who on earth was I? How did I even know the stick was in the safe? How did I know the significance of it? How was I able to neutralise two of their men, one of them permanently?

They'll have a lot of questions that will need to be answered. They'll be worried. If I'm lucky, they may even panic. And they're going to be wondering why on earth I would do something like that. I could have just disappeared, but I chose to get them on my tail. They'll be puzzled as well as perturbed. And so they should be.

By now, if they're smart, they'll also have linked me to

the disassembling of the surveillance box around Polly in Waterloo Place. They'll need to identify me, and they'll also require a fairly urgent tête-à-tête, probably with a view to my elimination. This is what I want.

But if they're not that smart or lucky, it may be quite a while before I run into them and discover who they are. I have no doubt that Lothar will get me a lead to Culpepper, but in case something goes wrong with that, or it turns out to be a blind alley, or if Thug One and Thug Two are not connected to Culpepper in any way, I have another cunning plan that involves taking advantage of Lothar's bad nature; playing him to my advantage in more ways than one.

You can always rely on Lothar to sell you out to the highest bidder, even if you're on good terms with him. But that has its uses. This is a high-risk strategy. It's one hell of a gamble. It might work. I'm going to do it.

'Another five thousand.'

This perks him up. He finishes chewing his biscuit. 'What's that, old chap?'

'This would be a concurrent job. Same urgency. I came across two expert hitmen in the early hours of yesterday morning. Central London. Probably European, probably ex-military. Ultra-pro. Big, powerful guys. Over six feet. Two hundred pounds plus. Both used Grand Power K100 Whispers with suppressors, and both had matching combat knives; I think they were Mac Coltellerie Z08s.'

That little altercation already seems like it took place a month ago.

'Italian knives, Slovakian guns. It would be like looking for a needle in a haystack. Anything else?'

'No ID. Black combat clothing, but discreet. No labels on the clothing…'

'Goodness me! Matching clothes, matching guns, matching knives – it sounds like they were twins! *C'est délicieux!*'

Of course. 'That's it. They *were* twins. At least I think they were. Ninety per cent sure. I didn't notice it at first. Both had the same gap in between the upper central incisors, both had the same dark monobrows. Similar face shape. Similar eyes. At the very least they were closely related. One of them had a small white scar beneath his lower lip. A little over an inch long. Probably a few years old.'

Lothar makes an unrecognisable hand gesture, flicking his three middle fingers rapidly upwards several times. 'Twins. Hm. Well, that's a teensy-weensy little bit better. Did they speak to you at all? Any polite exchanges? Recipe suggestions? Reading lists? Pickup lines?'

'They both spoke English, but there were a few phrases in a language I didn't recognise. Germanic, I think, but I can't be more specific than that.'

'Mr Cambridge, I am shocked. Shocked! You mean to say that there is a European language that you're not fluent in? Can you remember anything? Anything at all? I do understand that you're doped up to the gills. I don't expect miracles. But just a little scrap of something might be enough.'

I remember Thug Two sitting on the floor with blood pouring out of his mouth. The contempt and loathing in his eyes. What was it he said? It was certainly an insult of some sort and not in English. I close my eyes and try to bring it back.

'One of them said something like "Sun or shun fan. Shun famin hool." He was slurring a bit, so it wasn't too clear. Haemorrhaging from the mouth, too. Probably concussed. And I had a spot of tinnitus. Does that ring any bells?'

'*Soan fan in hûn?*'

'Yes. Yes, that's it. What language is it? What did it mean?'

'It's Frisian. West Frisian, at a pinch. Well that *is* interesting. And most helpful. I'm not quite sure how that would translate into English. Was he angry when he said it?'

'Livid.'

'He said "Your son is a dog".'

'What?'

He scratches his head. 'No! Wait! It must have been "You son of a bitch." Does that seem reasonable?'

'He was pretty pissed with me.'

'So, we're looking for a couple of identical twins, we think…'

'One deceased.'

'Ah. Alright. Hm. We're looking for one of a *former* couple of twins; an only twin, ha ha – but the twin *thing* will help with the identification, do you see? Hefty ex-military chaps, gap in front teeth, monobrows, same taste in sinister clothing and weapons and probably working for someone's kill-for-hire unit, *or* it's a little business they run themselves. Additional information: both use Grand Power K100 Whispers and possibly Mac Coltellerie Z08 combat knives. How sure were you of the knife make?'

'Seventy-five per cent.'

I try to recall something else from that nightmare in Polly's flat. Something Thug One said. I close my eyes and put myself back in that hallway.

My bro says we're going to party with you, nice boy. No problem. You ever been in prison, nice boy?

'Wait. One of them referred to the other as his bro. That could have been just the way he spoke, but if it wasn't, it kind of confirms that they were real brothers. Also, one of them asked me if I'd ever been in prison. That they were going to party with me. He called me nice boy. The other one used that phrase, too.'

'Mmm. That was a threat. They were toying with you. Almost certainly ex-cons; civilian or military.' He glances at the television screen and picks his teeth. 'Too many little slip-ups here. Far too confident and cocky. They were one hundred per cent assured of success!'

'That's it. I can't think of anything else. The whole event didn't last long and there wasn't much chit-chat.'

'Frisian speakers are relatively low in number. I would hazard a guess and say that there are about half a million people who speak it and they're scattered around quite a bit. The Netherlands, Germany and, of course, the Frisian islands themselves. There're also little enclaves like Heligoland, of course. These chaps are probably of the Netherlands variety.

'There's also the question of whether your Frisian friends entered this country legally or not. But speaking that language, even a single phrase, in front of someone like you was a mistake. It was slapdash and amateurish. They should have stuck to English or kept their mouths shut. Anything else? Anything else at all? It all helps.'

What the hell. 'Yes. A little over twenty-four hours before the encounter with our Frisians, a similar pair of professionals were encountered by an acquaintance of mine. Much the same appearance and build. Absence of ID and clothing labels once more. This time, there was no speaking. Neither had guns. One carried a black combat knife, but with no confirmed make. This was an aggressive attack with a view to assassination.'

'Hm! Why no guns, I wonder?'

'It's conceivable they were not expecting resistance.'

'And the outcome?'

'Fatal for both.'

'And you think they were connected to your two?'

'Eighty per cent sure. I'd be very surprised to discover they weren't. One of them had a distinctive feature: signs of plastic surgery around the eyes, left cheek, mouth and neck. Nothing more specific than that.'

'Now I'm intrigued, Mr Cambridge, I truly am. Could it be there's a link between your OFRP gentleman and these Thuggees? Well, no matter. I'll find him and them, you may have no doubt about that. Friesland, eh? Or is it *Fryslân* they like to call it now? I can't remember. Never mind.'

He makes us another couple of coffees. I hand him another five thousand. He counts it. He takes the other five thousand, goes away somewhere, probably to a safe, and then returns, having worked himself up into an indignant frenzy in the interim.

'Saints preserve us! All these ex-armed forces types wandering around looking tough and threatening people so that their boss or whoever will give them a pat on their freshly shaved heads. It's so vulgar.

'They should sterilise them or lobotomise them once they leave the army or whichever military rock it is they've crawled from under. Or just push them off a cliff. Coffee top-up?'

'Not for me.'

'I should be very careful regarding any contact you may have with people like this, Mr Cambridge. Call me superstitious, but I've always thought that we are all allocated a certain modicum of luck in our lives. Particularly people like us.

'You don't want to find yourself in some sort of embroilment with our Frisian friend when you're not in tip-top condition. I don't have to give you a full medical to know that, quite apart from all the alcohol and medication, you're not one hundred and ten per cent fit.

'There's a sense of *dégringolade* about you. The vitamin jab I gave you will help. My advice: take a holiday when all this is over. Might I suggest Cambodia? One of those private islands like Song Saa. Take a woman. Take a Tunisian nurse. In fact, anywhere that was a relatively recent war zone is a good holiday destination in my opinion. Bosnia-Herzegovina is very nice this time of year, I'm told.'

'I'll certainly think about it. How are things with the hits on you nowadays?'

'Only four that I know of. It was five until last year. One of the contractors died of old age! Can you believe it? Makes me feel like Methuselah. Used to be over fifty at one point. "My salad days, when I was green in judgment, cold in blood…"'

'You're getting nostalgic for a time when more people wanted you dead?'

'Ha ha! People have no idea, do they, Mr Cambridge. The alternative world of which we are the denizens. All the murders, the manipulations, the schemes, the plottings, the duplicities.'

He waves a hand at the television screen which is behind my head. 'I mean – look at that! Some Bulgarian diplomat dies of a heart attack on his way to work. Heart attack my *arse*. Outlived his usefulness in one way or another, I'll wager. Caught with his hand in the till. Blew the whistle on all the corruption. Shagged the wrong married woman. Or is *rogered* the correct term amongst the hoi polloi nowadays? I always quite liked *putting the devil into hell*. So, anyway; someone decided their life would be a little better without him in the world. Sofia! There's another pleasant holiday destination for you, if you're a fan of contemporary dance and performance.'

I get a cold feeling in my stomach as I slowly turn to look at the screen and read the text.

Dragan Vanchev, aged fifty-three, a commercial policy officer with the Bulgarian Embassy collapsed of a suspected heart attack close to the Embassy of the Republic of Bulgaria in Queen's Gate, South Kensington, London, yesterday morning. He was taken to the Chelsea and Westminster Hospital where he was declared dead on arrival. The ambassador, His Excellency Tihomir Katranjiev, expressed his sadness at Mr Vanchev's untimely passing and said his thoughts were with Mr Vanchev's wife and two daughters.

For a moment, my mind stops functioning. Completely. It's as if I've entered some zen-like state, where my thoughts arrive and pass away without meaning or context or comment.

Vanchev dead. What can this mean? Did he fall or was he pushed? Lothar's first instinct was that he was pushed, but then he's a cynical old bastard. If he fell, well, tough shit. But, after all that's happened in the last thirty-six hours, it's more than likely he was pushed. But by whom? And why? Everything has just got a little more complex.

I write my mobile number on the back of a yellow post-it note and push it over to Lothar. 'That's my mobile. Give me a call the moment you find anything. I've got to go now. I'll find my own way out.'

'ASAP, dear fellow. ASAP. You'll hear from me tomorrow, or even today if Fortuna is with me. And don't forget to rest, and don't get that dressing wet for at least two days.'

'I'll try not to. And thanks for your help.'

'My pleasure. And cut down on the alcohol, it'll only reduce the effectiveness of all those injections. Oh, and those stitches will dissolve in just over a week.'

His voice fades away as I head down the hallway towards the front door.

Then someone turns the volume up.

'Mr Cambridge! Mr Cambridge! Quickly! Come here!'

I sigh and walk back the way I came. 'What is it, Lothar?'

'Look. The television.'

He's frozen the screen. It's a police facial composite that looks like it was produced by PortraitPad software. I don't like the look of this guy at all: surly, sinister, thuggish, but not bad looking for all of that and rather cool, if truth be told.

It's me, and I'm the chief suspect in the murder of a thirty-four-year-old female civil servant at a flat in Devonshire Street in Central London.

'Fame at last!' cries Lothar, grinning all over his face. 'It's been a long time coming. Another Walk of Shame or something a tad stronger?'

12

HELP REQUIRED

From Stanhope Gardens, I take a long, erratic, switched-on walk to the DoubleTree hotel in Queen's Gate, changing direction twice and checking any and every reflective surface to make sure I don't have any company. Paranoid? Me?

Once I'm at the hotel, I rudely push through the tourist queue, hop in a black cab and get it to take me to the Victoria Embankment, so I can work my way inconspicuously across the Strand and up to Exeter Street, keeping the counter-surveillance dial on eleven the whole way. I have no doubt whatsoever that I'm clean, but an overly suspicious little voice keeps telling me I have to make absolutely sure.

When I get back to my flat, I put the coffee on, remove my jacket and shirt and take a look at Lothar's handiwork in the bathroom mirror. Nice dressing. No blood seeping through, which is always a plus. I fire up the computer, find an A4 cartridge pad and a V5 and sit at the kitchen table. I take a look at my watch. It's still only 10.41.

I notice a single black stocking on the floor. I think it belonged to Szonja. What was her savage friend's name again? Kamilla? Kamilla the Cool Hunter. I'll certainly look into that when all of this is over.

The first thing I do is review the television news. Tempting as it is to look at stuff about myself, I search for information about Vanchev on three different news channels first. He's the fifth or sixth item on each station and each one says much the same thing as the BBC report I saw at Lothar's place. All they've got is the official embassy statement and there's nothing much there to embellish.

This isn't really very big news; they just haven't got anything better at the moment. If it was the ambassador it would be more prominent and if the ambassador was a famous public figure it would be even bigger than that, but it's only poor old Dragan and he's a nobody. Correction: he was a nobody. If he hadn't died in the street, it probably wouldn't have made the news at all.

Polly said that his wife's name was Lilyana and that she was much too young and attractive for him. Truculent, too. Interesting. A cynical part of me wonders if our paths will cross now that she's recently widowed. I wonder what she looks like. I wonder what their sex life was like, if they had one. I wonder if she knew about Dragan's indiscretions.

I fill a French coffee bowl with enough Yirgacheffe to kill a herd of antelope and start Googling his name to look for more information. There's a little more detail, but not much.

He was found lying face down on the pavement in Prince Consort Road outside the Royal College of Music and across the road from the Albert Hall. A passer-by thought he'd tripped over some traffic cones which were cordoning off road works.

This happened yesterday morning and one site gives more detail: the ambulance appeared at nine-forty a.m.

Was he on his way to work? One assumes so, unless he had other business there. Prince Consort Road is just around the corner from the Bulgarian Embassy, so he was a few minutes away from his workplace.

If this was a hit, and if he was a creature of habit, the perpetrator or perpetrators would know the route he took to get to work. They would have known the side of the road he walked on and they would have roughly known the time he'd be there. They would also have had the professional chops to do this in broad daylight.

I have no idea how busy Prince Consort Road is at nine-forty, but I can't imagine that it was deserted, not with a big college nearby and an even bigger university just up the road. Lots of posh flats in that area, too.

The other possibility is that they followed him from his home. I don't know his home address and I don't know how he got to work. It may have been in an official car or even a cab. Maybe he asked them to drop him a little way from the embassy so he could have a healthy walk. If he took the tube, which is unlikely, he may have walked from Knightsbridge or Gloucester Road underground stations.

It would be nice to know for sure how he died. If he really died of a heart attack, then that's that. I have to assume that was not the case. If he was in some way poisoned with a drug that made it *look* like he'd had a heart attack, then there are maybe a dozen drugs that will do it effectively.

For about half of those, all it needs is a quick, shallow jab through clothing or directly into the flesh and death would be virtually instantaneous. Maybe two or three of those drugs would not show up in a post-mortem examination. The others would, but only if you were assaying for them. I press a number on my mobile.

'Hey, Mr Beckett. How're things? Tell you what, man: the most amazing thing. There was a police e-fit on the news last night that looked just like you! It could have been a frikkin' photograph! They're getting pretty good software now, huh?'

This is Doug Teng from Marton Confidential or Marton Computer Solutions, the name depending on whether you're looking at his website or speaking to him personally. There are good, complex reasons for this, which he's never fully explained to me. Whatever he's calling himself, he's an expert hacker/counter surveillance expert and is also trustworthy.

'Hi, Doug. Listen. I need something pretty fast. Are you busy?'

'Up to my eyes in it until the end of the month.'

'Two thousand.'

'Go on.'

'It's a DOA at the Chelsea & Westminster.' I spell out both names. 'Got there around ten yesterday morning. I need the full records and any pathology that may be lurking. Check again in four hours for the pathology if there's nothing now. Text me as soon as you've got *anything*. As swiftly as possible, please.'

'Sure thing. Guess what?'

'What?'

'I've got a full-time girlfriend! First one in nine months.'

'Oh, really? Well, congratulations. What's her name?'

'Haizea Ybarra. Pretty exotic, eh? Basque.'

'What – she wears one?'

'No. What? Her name is Basque. Like in Spain. Her folks are from Bilbao.'

147

'Well that's great. You'll have to introduce me to her.'

'No fucking way. That wasn't you on the TV, was it?'

'See you, Doug.'

I click him off and stare at the computer screen. I half-heartedly Google Vanchev's name a few more times, but as I expected, nothing of interest turns up. Out of curiosity, I have a look for photographs of Lilyana, but no luck there, either. I scribble a few possibilities on my cartridge pad, just to get things clear in my head.

1. Vanchev died of natural causes. This is nothing to do with the OFRP investigation or Polly Greenburgh's death. It is, as they say, just one of those things.

2. Vanchev was murdered by hot-stuff professionals who were able to make his death look like a heart attack. This murder took place five to six hours after Polly was killed. This makes it extremely likely that the two murders were connected. It is unlikely, however, that the perpetrator was Thug Two, the only survivor of the attacks on Polly. Firstly, he'd been seriously assaulted by me and would have been in no fit state to take on a job like that. Secondly, you wouldn't use the same sort of personnel for a high-risk, broad-daylight, subtle assassination of that type. That is not to say that the order for both killings did not come from the same source.

3. It's already a strong possibility that Culpepper, Polly's erstwhile boss, was responsible for her death. Could he have ordered Vanchev's death as well? If he did, his motivation is a mystery. He ordered the investigation into Vanchev with a view to booting him out of the country using blackmail. Polly gives him what he needs, so he makes a couple of calls which result in the murders of both Polly and Vanchev. Firstly, that defeats the object of the whole investigation and secondly, the OFRP don't

do extrajudicial killings and would undoubtedly be in a whole heap of shit if they started. Thirdly, it's insane. Once again, Culpepper as the bad guy just doesn't pan out.

4. Finally, I speculated that there might have been some illicit connection between Vanchev and Culpepper. That Culpepper was in Vanchev's pocket in some way. Maybe Culpepper's way out of a situation like that would be to kill Vanchev. But the risk would be too high on a number of levels and he has to be too bright to get himself into a mess like that. His CV, what I know of it, points to an intelligent, careful, loyal guy. I've got to get to Culpepper. It's the only way to sort this out. I just hope Lothar does his stuff as quickly as possible.

I make another coffee and look out of the kitchen window while the machine fizzes away. It's that damn memory stick. Everything that's happened is connected to it. Culpepper, and maybe persons unknown, saw what was on there and then the deaths started happening.

Then something else occurs to me. With Vanchev deceased, whether by accident or design, the OFRP investigation would be immediately shut down. If you were running a department like that and your target died suddenly, you'd just stop and move on to the next job. Any further investigations would be for the police, the Bulgarian Embassy, or some other government department, if they were interested.

But if the investigation was suddenly shut down, whose interest would that be in? It's speculative, but if I was the bad guy behind this, having the target die would be all well and good, but I'd also have to get rid of anyone who knew about the operation.

That brings me back to the idea that Polly had

accidentally stumbled onto something unconnected to Vanchev. Something sensitive. Something important. Something that got her killed. But Vanchev's unexpected death may still make him relevant. I just don't know how. Not yet.

There's also something nagging me about the hit on Polly at her flat. Just before he shot her, Thug One said, 'Hey, bitch!' Now it may be that all women were bitches to him and that was his normal MO when killing a woman. But it might also be something else. I close my eyes and try to recall his words in as much detail as I can. Only two words, but the nuance was very slightly angry and hate-filled, as if he was trying to be coldly professional but couldn't keep a lid on some rage or other.

This could be nothing, but it kind of confirms that the Frisian goons were related to the two that Polly killed and that Thug One had taken it personally in some way. I'll keep that on the back burner.

I turn on the BBC news and wait for my facial composite to reappear. I don't have to wait too long; it's still the main item on the news and the sordid details are ticker-taping across the bottom of the screen. Now there's a photograph of the murdered civil servant, Judith Hart, placed alongside my composite.

Those two faces together on national television; that's something I never thought I'd see in a million years. My heart is beating rapidly, and I deep-breathe to try to calm myself down, then I remember it's Lothar's amphetamines doing their work.

Judith Hart was apparently attacked while she slept. The whole thing is being presented as aggravated burglary. She was beaten to death by a blunt instrument, possibly a baseball bat or similar, but the police found no evidence of the murder weapon at the scene.

A neighbour heard a suspicious noise of some sort, called the police and was able to give them a detailed description of a man, probably in his early thirties, who was seen leaving Ms Hart's Devonshire Street apartment yesterday at around four-thirty a.m.

There's a hotline number to ring if you have any information and I'm not to be approached. Well, at least that's something; I hate talking to strangers. There's a brief shot of a police cordon outside the Devonshire Street flat, the entrance to Devonshire Mews South is closed off and a couple of uniformed officers stand around next to a squad car, then another news item appears about some shooting in America, followed by the reporting of a severe national threat level in the UK. That means a terrorist attack is highly likely, so maybe it'll push me further down the news ladder.

If the police had really been called by that enigmatic and sharp-eared neighbour, they would have gone into the flat and found two people dead of gunshot wounds to the head. One of the dead, a woman, had been puzzlingly dragged into the kitchen. Another man is sitting on the floor, having been expertly beaten unconscious by person or persons unknown.

The dead man and the unconscious man have no identification, are dressed similarly and even *look* similar. Both carry black combat knives and one carries glass-cutting tools. An unfired gun of foreign manufacture is on the sofa. The double-glazed kitchen window and its exterior metal security grille have been carefully and professionally removed. The hall, living room and bathroom are covered in blood.

The flat would have been cordoned off and a police forensics team would have been called in immediately. It would be a major crime scene. They would have discovered the blood and fingerprints of a fourth person. Those fingerprints would not be on file anywhere, and the blood samples would not link to any known DNA profile. That would be highly suspicious. The unconscious man would have been taken into police custody.

After all of that, the police would probably *not* conclude that Ms Hart was the victim of some solitary, baseball bat wielding burglar. So, someone's been playing games and, whoever it was, they had very quick and fancy footwork.

My guess is, that as soon as Thug Two regained consciousness, he made a call. At the moment, who he made that call to is a mystery, but it certainly wouldn't have been the police. 'People' arrive at Polly's flat and assess the damage. Discreetly, they get a team in and clean up the place to their specifications. They spirit Thug Two away to wherever he came from and he tells them what happened and gives them a good description of me.

He'd have had to sit down with a PortraitPad artist. For a number of reasons, it wouldn't have been an easy, quick process. Police? Probably not as he wasn't officially there, and his appearance would have raised questions. So, who would have produced my image to give to the media? He also tells them, whoever they are, that I waved a memory stick in his face and gave him a little message for his boss.

They concoct a story to give to the police. If this was the Security Service, they'd have got hold of a sympathetic police department/officer and probably delegated the handling of the local police to them. Someone – it could be anyone – writes an official police statement and then this whole septic tank of bullshit is force-fed to the media who swallow it whole.

It would be important that no one saw Polly. If they did, the entire story would collapse. It's possible that her body could have been disposed of and replaced by one with more credible and relevant injuries. Maybe they had a spare female corpse hanging around with a crushed skull and that informed the statement. It has been known to happen.

So why not cover the whole thing up entirely? Why go to all that trouble and have the police buzzing around? That would be down to me. Once Thug Two said his thing, they'd realise that – whoever I was – I had to be hunted down with extreme prejudice.

It's quite reasonable to assume that the police statement was geared to getting both the cops and the public on my tail. It's what I would do under similar circumstances and it's pretty smart.

Once I was apprehended, I could be spirited away to whoever's running all of this. If they didn't have that wide and legal reach, looking for me would be like searching for a needle in a haystack. This is useful. This tells me that whatever this is, it's serious and important.

They would have good cause to believe that, for some reason, I *wanted* to be found, but my motive would be unknowable and rather baffling. They'll be putting a picture together, and if I was them, I'd be spending a great deal of time and energy on apprehending me.

Quite apart from the police, I'm sure that Thug Two will be making his own investigations into my identity, with a view to tracking me down, unless that's being done for him by someone else. After all, I killed his twin brother, if that's who it was. He won't realise, of course, that through Lothar, I'll be investigating *his* identity at the same time. Maybe we'll meet somewhere in the middle. I'm hoping that we will.

I send out for some lunch and while I'm waiting for it to arrive, I fish the copy I made of Polly's memory stick out of my jacket, stick it into the back of the computer and run the film. A meeting with Culpepper aside, I'm still interested in the idea that someone else at the Richmond orgy may be the cause of all of this, so have decided to give that thread a tug.

I create a file called 'Richmond'. I take five screen captures of each adult at the orgy; four face shots from contrasting angles and one full body shot. I create a sub-file unique to each individual and give them an identifier, using the letters of the Greek alphabet.

The last two, THETA and IOTA, are the women. Polly said that Vanchev was the third to enter the room, and I've taken that as being correct, but I'll still call him GAMMA for the purposes of this file. Once I've finished, I place everything on a new memory stick. This all takes me about ten minutes.

The guy from Smack Lobster Roll turns up with my lobster & shrimp brioche and chilled can of Coke and I sit and eat while staring at my Richmond file. Despite the amphetamines, I still seem to have a good appetite. My arm starts throbbing again as the painkiller jab starts to wear off.

Not a bad day so far, all things considered. Got Lothar Koch working on Alastair Culpepper and the Frisian goons, got the bad guys using the police to hunt me down, got my facial composite on the national news, got

Doug Teng checking out Vanchev's death and just got a text from Priscilla Nichols saying 'I ache for you. I am in pain. Use me.' And it's still only nearing lunchtime of Day One.

Despite all of that, I have a gut feeling that I'm not moving fast enough, and that the trail will soon be getting cold. Under normal circumstances, someone like Thug Two would be out of the country by now. This would be par for the course if you were a foreign assassin doing a job here.

Once the job was complete, you'd be on your way to Heathrow. I can only hope that his desire for revenge against me will keep him here a little longer. Another possibility is that his employers will be extending his contract due to recent events.

Vanchev's death has muddied the waters a little, but I'm sticking with my possibly erroneous theory about his presence at the orgy being a side issue and, apart from a face-to-face with Culpepper, I'm sure that the answer lies with the identification of the other guests at that house in Richmond. But that identification could take a long, long time and it's time I don't think I have.

There's only one thing for it.

I'm going to have to hire a private detective.

13

FRANCIE

I do a rapid computer search, using the phrase 'private investigators London'. As I expected, a ton of stuff comes up, most of it preying on the paranoia and/or insecurities of prospective clients. Are you suspicious of your partner? Is he/she cheating? Is someone hiding something from you? Is your husband/wife a major dick? Are your children seeing other parents? Is someone else walking your dog?

If it isn't infidelity surveillance, it's debtor tracing, proof of cohabitation, process serving, background checks, litigation support, employee theft, false sick leave, illegal subletting, child custody, GPS tracking and a host of other tedious and slightly depressing items. I keep seeing the same buzzwords over and over again: discreet, motivated, ethical, dedicated, integrity, honesty – what an awful business to be in.

Most of these companies brag about their ex-military and ex-police personnel, but for me, particularly at the moment, these are negative qualities, not positive ones. I'm already dealing with people like that and I don't want fear, law abidingness, loyalty or prejudice colouring any potential investigation. Apart from that, these companies are all too slick, too professional and the 'besuited big business built on people's misery and fear' quotient is off-putting.

I don't really know what I'm looking for, but I'll know it when I see it. That's always been my philosophy even though it's rarely worked. Then, twenty dreary minutes later, it jumps out at me. Dakota Private Investigations, 14 Bedford Row, London WC1 3HE. Executive director and owner Ms Frances Martinelli BSc (Hons) Criminal Justice, MSc Computer Science. An unusual combo of qualifications for a PI, but my subconscious has been searching for unusual.

"I have been a private investigator for many years, both in the US and UK, specialising in financial cold cases, corporate fraud, cybercrime and missing persons tracing. At DPI, the client comes first. Each case is given my full and exclusive attention. Initial consultation is free. All cases are taken on in the strictest of confidence. An extensive list of testimonials and references are available on request. Dakota Private Investigations – where results matter and you matter."

And there's a photograph. A head and shoulders shot of a strikingly attractive woman in her late thirties/early forties. A strong, Italian face with great cheekbones. Beautiful, amazing brown eyes, long, expensively styled, thick jet-black hair swept back to reveal a widow's peak, a wide, sensual mouth and a cute, dimpled chin. There's humour and mischief in those eyes and a rather smug smile on her lips.

She's wearing a charcoal grey business jacket with a dark green blouse underneath. There's a gold chain around her neck. It looks like a publicity shot for a glamorous American newsreader and it occurs to me that it might put people off, maybe not in the US, but certainly here.

I just know she's the one.

I'll bet anything it's a one-woman business, and the address is a little north of Chancery Lane, so it's well within London's legal zone, which means that most of the work she'll get will be boring barrister bullshit.

The website is a little over two years old and I'm guessing this is a fairly new enterprise. I turn off the computer, carefully ease a jacket on to avoid damaging Lothar's handiwork and go outside to find a cab.

*

Bedford Row is filled with well-kept Georgian terraced houses and lots of trees. It's an expensive area, so she undoubtedly rents, which would be usual around here.

I find number 14. She's on the third floor, above a health insurance company, a solicitor's office and what looks like an advertising agency. I'm about to ring DPI's bell, when a young Indian woman comes out and holds the door open for me, so I flash her a fascinating and charming smile and go in.

No lift, but I need the exercise. When I get to the third floor, there's a reception area with a small desk, but no sign of a receptionist. This is separated from the large main office by a glass partition and I can see Ms Martinelli sitting at her desk with her feet up, shoes off, reading a battered paperback copy of *Delta of Venus* by Anaïs Nin and swigging coffee from a Starbucks cup. She's obviously having a frantic day. I poke my head around the door and tap twice on the partition window.

She looks so surprised that for a second I think she's going rock back on her chair onto the floor, but she composes herself, and in one fluid and fast movement places the coffee on her desk, puts her shoes back on, stands up and walks towards me, hand outstretched.

She's tall, maybe five feet ten in her heels, has a compact, hourglass figure and a noticeably slim waist. She's wearing a knee-length dark green dress with three-quarter-length sleeves.

Around her neck, there's an oversized plastic orange bead necklace and a matching bangle on her right wrist. Her watch is a Clé de Cartier; white gold case, face set with real diamonds and a pink strap made from alligator skin. Probably worth around thirty-five thousand. I'm in the wrong business. Hold on. I'm in the *same* business. Ah well. She looks like she's on her way to a fashionable cocktail bar or a meeting at a top US legal megacorp.

I breathe in slowly and get a whiff of aniseed, bergamot and neroli. It's L'Heure Bleue by Guerlain. Her presence is warm, welcoming and compassionate. In her photograph she was attractive; in person she's rather gorgeous and not a little overwhelming. I take her hand and give it a brief shake. My mouth is dry, though that may well be the amphetamines. I lick my lips. I receive a slick, megawatt smile.

'Hi! I'm Francie Martinelli. Welcome to Dakota Private Investigations. How may I help you?'

A seductive, soothing, husky, alto voice. Not Bourbon-soaked but getting there. We're both looking at each other as if some matchmaker has introduced us at a dinner party. She straightens her dress at the hips. I imagine kissing her neck. I force myself to snap out of the desire haze I'm in.

'Hello. My name's Daniel Beckett. I'd like to hire you. If you're not too busy, that is.' I put humour into my eyes, so she knows I'm kidding her about the busy part.

She looks slightly stunned. 'OK. Great. Come in the office. Would you like a coffee?'

'Please. Black with a dash of milk. No sugar.'

'Surely. Please take a seat, Mr Beckett. I'll be with you in just a moment.'

The office is classy and modern. It smells new. Everything is mainly cream, black, pine and chrome. I sit down on one of two black leather sofas and take a quick look around. Lots of books, mostly legal, many on computing and a couple on wildflowers.

On a bottom shelf, a smattering of well-thumbed paperbacks: Jacqueline Susann, Anne-Marie Villefranche, Georgette Heyer, Pauline Réage, Colette and Vanessa Duriès.

There's a large monochrome print of Lee Miller in profile by Man Ray on the wall behind her desk and a larger print of *Knight Errant* by Millais next to the window. In the corner, next to the coffee stuff, a big, old-fashioned one arm bandit fruit machine. I look at her bottom while she makes the coffee. Either she's put on weight since she bought that dress, or she bought it a size too small on purpose. Both options are sexy.

'You like it?' she says, and for a moment I think she's caught me out. I look for reflections where she could have seen me staring at her ass. There are none.

'Sorry?'

'The one arm bandit. I saw you looking. It's a classic 1941 O.D. Jennings Bronze Chief. It's a kind of hobby of mine. Well, not a hobby, really. I just get a kick out of winning, even though it's me that feeds it with the five cent pieces. Crazy, huh? I used to spend a lot of time in amusement arcades when I was a teenager and it became an addiction. Still haven't hit the jackpot, though. One day, yeah?'

'Sure.'

She sits down on the sofa across from me, places the coffees on the glass coffee table and leans forwards confidentially, giving off reassuring and comforting vibes. Her dark red fingernails match her lipstick. The perfume and the ample cleavage are making it hard for me to concentrate. Her hair is incredible; it's so *big*, and I wonder how long it takes her to dry it in the morning. Perhaps I'll find out.

'Now, Mr Beckett. How can be of assistance to you? I have to say that anything we discuss here will be in absolute confidence, so you can speak freely.'

She gives me a concentrated burst of prolonged eye contact to build intimacy and trust. I'd considered bullshitting her when I was on my way here, but now I've met her I can tell that there's no way she won't see through it. But I'm going to overdramatise to get her undivided attention and to get her on my side. Also, understandably, I won't be giving her the whole story. Not yet, anyway.

'I'm a private investigator. I'm working on a high-risk case where speed is of the essence and because of that there are aspects I need to delegate. I need assistance in identifying nine individuals from screen captures I made earlier from a clandestinely shot film which is technically the property of the Security Service here. The moment you start work on this, you'll be breaking the law and you'll be in breach of the Official Secrets Act of 1989.'

All of this is actually true; it only *sounds* demented when you say it out loud. She looks at me as if I've just announced that I'm a time traveller from the future with an important message for dolphins.

Bafflement, doubt, incredulity, suspicion, wariness; they're all taking it in turns to flit across her face. She runs a hand through her hair. Her eyes dart around the room. She has a small but noticeable diagonal scar that bisects her left eyebrow. This was removed from the photograph on her site. She recovers, her eyes quizzical and humorous.

'Get *out* of here.'

I try not to laugh. 'I'm not kidding.'

'The Security Service.'

'That's right.'

She pins me to my seat with a piercing stare. 'You're shitting me, yeah? Because I don't have time to waste on delusional crap. You have to be straight with me. I don't take cases where I'm not two hundred per cent sure of what the fuck's going on.'

This makes me laugh. I like her already. 'No. This is a difficult and complex case. I can't see any way of not taking you into my confidence because of what you may discover, but you have to understand that working for me could put your life in danger. I'm not being dramatic. Two people – well – *five* people involved in this have already lost their lives in the last thirty-six hours. I don't fully comprehend what's going on and I'll completely understand if you don't want to be involved.'

'Five people.'

'Yes. Not four, not six.'

'Dead.'

'As doornails.'

She frowns. 'Are you saying that it might be too dangerous for me? Too difficult? Is that what you're implying?'

'Not at all. How much do you charge?'

She shakes her head from side to side in an attempt to bring herself back into the room. 'Er, six hundred pounds per day plus expenses.'

'OK. I'll pay you eight hundred per day, plus a payment of two and a half thousand now and another two and a half thousand when the job is finished, however long it takes.'

I'm ripping through Polly's money, but it's what she would have wanted.

Francie Martinelli looks at me. I can tell from her expression that she now knows I'm serious. She sits back. Her eyes widen. She digs her fingernails into her thighs. I hope she doesn't ladder her stockings. I'm trying to get a feel for her trustworthiness and her character. Eager to please but prickly. Superficially confident but mildly defensive. The way she sits is unusual. Straight backed, knees together, hands on thighs. Bit of a closed posture. Interesting.

She composes herself and gives me a warm smile. 'OK. Why did you choose me? I hope you don't mind my asking that of you.'

'Intuition. You just seemed right. I needed someone smart and I needed someone right away. I took a gamble. You're in a highly competitive business, particularly in a city like this. I think you'd be at a slight disadvantage because you're a woman and because you're American.

'Being from the US makes you conspicuous and an outsider. My guess is that you do a fair amount of pretty dull work for lawyers in this area that's been making you bored shitless and you'll have come across your fair share of sexism and xenophobia. Because of all of this, I reckon you'd have to be at least five times as good as the men in your field to break even.'

She snorts. 'Make that ten times.'

'I had a hunch that something more exciting and unusual would appeal to you. Also, you wouldn't be intimidated by me or suspicious of me in the way that the big, slick, cop-heavy investigation companies might be.

'The outsider part is important. You're not part of the establishment. I don't think you'll go running to the police after what I tell you. I think you'll be able to keep your mouth shut. I think you're tough and you're going to need to be.'

She sits up in her seat, arching her back and pursing her lips. It's as if she's preening herself. She liked that, which was my intention.

'Can I ask you something?' she says, narrowing her eyes. 'Are you on drugs? You seem hyped up, you're talking nine to the dozen, you keep licking your lips and your pupils are so dilated I can't see what your eye colour is. I'm not being judgemental. I'm just curious.'

Honesty is the best policy. It'll also have the advantage of making the whole thing more intriguing for her. I give her a blast of the prolonged eye contact she was trying with me. She quickly looks down at her knees.

'I acquired an injury early yesterday morning,' I say. 'It was a ricochet wound from a 9mm round. I couldn't go to a hospital, so got an acquaintance to sew it up properly after I'd made a bit of a botch of it. Among other things, he gave me a multivitamin jab laced with amphetamines. You're seeing the side effects.'

'What happened to the guy that fired the shot?'

'I have blue-grey eyes, by the way.'

'I see.'

She gives me a long, hard stare. She crosses her legs. She drums her fingers on her thighs. I keep eye contact.

She licks her lips. Her breathing is rapid. I try not to look at the rise and fall of her breasts. I can almost hear her thought processes. She doesn't like people who try to put one over on her and she hates being underestimated.

'Are you on the level?'

'No. I'm a crook.'

She raises her eyebrows and looks mildly amused. 'Hm. I've got two other jobs on at the moment.'

'Cancel them.'

'Why should I do that?'

'Because your painfully acute perception is telling you that this is hot as balls.'

She laughs once. Then again. Then she can't stop.

'Oh, Jesus. Jesus Christ. Yeah. Sure. OK. You got me. You got me. Fuck. I admit it. This sounds like awesome sauce. What did you say your name was again?'

'Daniel Beckett.'

'Have you got a business card, Daniel Beckett?'

I hand her my card. She inspects it carefully, bending the thin, silvery metal and, as everyone does when they see it, pinging it with her finger to see if it makes an interesting noise. It doesn't.

'So, what do you want to do first, Mr Beckett?'

'Let's sit down at your desk and I'll show you what I've got.'

'Wait. Let me make a couple of calls.'

Her desk is big, and it has to be. There are two Dell U2917Ws with twenty-nine-inch screens, plus an Apple MacBook Pro which is almost falling off the edge due to lack of space. There are two big black CPUs on the floor, one of which has a Matt Murdock bobble head resting on top.

I grab a chair and place it in front of the screens, while

listening to her fob off two different clients with some excuse involving women's trouble. She's clever; no one ever argues with that.

She walks over and sits down next to me. Interestingly, she gives off quite a bit of heat, as if she's been sitting by a fire. Her perfume expands into the air around us. I've decided that I won't volunteer the whole picture, but I'll answer any questions she has, within reason. I don't want to make her an accessory, though an accessory to *what* I have no idea.

'A couple of minor corporate fraud cases,' she says, waving a hand dismissively through the air. 'Low priority for them and for me, so fuck 'em. Let's have it.'

I hand her the memory stick with the screen captures and she pushes it into one of the CPUs. My Richmond file instantly appears on the screen to my left. It looks better on her computer; sharper, almost borderline professional.

'Like I said, there are nine people I want identified, seven males, two females,' I say. 'I've tagged them with letters of the Greek alphabet for the moment, as I know being pretentious fascinates women.'

'Ha!'

'You can replace those with their names if and when you find out what they are. Once you've made the identifications, I'll want absolutely anything and everything you can get on them. There is a time limit on this, but don't worry if you fail on a few of them. At this stage, anything will be a bonus for me.'

'Can I open one and take a look?'

'Sure.'

She clicks on ALPHA. This is a saturnine individual with male pattern baldness, long black sideburns, bushy eyebrows and dark skin. Nationality unguessable: he could be Arabic, but I can't be sure. This is probably the worst example as I couldn't quite get a decent full-face shot, but the body shot is clear and shows a hunching of the left shoulder.

'So, this is what you've got for each of the nine, yes? Four facial, one full-length?'

'Not enough?'

'It's fine. OK. I'm just going expand one of the face shots. Hold on.'

She clicks the mouse and the image fills the screen. Simultaneously, a small software box appears on the right. Lots of numbers start scrolling by at high speed, then a chunk of ever-changing monochrome computer code appears in the centre of the box.

Small purple dots start appearing all over the face and soon each dot is given an identifier: left orbital upper, right lip lower bend, nose tip, right eyelid lower – until every dot has a name, the whole face shape is covered in dozens of identifiers and each dot is connected to the others by a thin lavender line. It looks mind-bogglingly amazing and I'm aware that my mouth is hanging open. I've never seen anything like it.

She clicks the mouse again and the other three facial images get the same treatment. Then a fifth facial image appears, looking like a composite of the other four and the dots and lines start moving around. Francie clicks once more, and everything stops.

'Where did these images come from? I mean, how were they taken?'

'They're all stills from an HD film taken using a Canon DSLR with a Nikon AF-S lens. Distance approximately one hundred yards, through glass that may have been double or triple glazed.'

'OK. They're not perfect by any means, but I think I can work with them. I'll be using Web XAA, which has all the best qualities of BioID, Betaface, ScanEx390 and NEUROtechnologija.'

'I didn't understand any of that.'

She smiles. 'Me neither. I'm just trying to impress you. I don't know what I'm talking about. Only kidding. I can only do one ID at a time. It'd be fantastic if we could do them all simultaneously, but the software isn't up to that yet and would probably crash the computer.

'It would be nice to get the source material so I could do my own captures using TechFine which is compatible with XAA.' She drinks some coffee. 'The end visual result would probably be roughly the same, but it would maybe cut the digital identifier time in half. You said speed was of the essence, I recall.'

'It is.'

'You don't happen to have...'

I lean back and look at her. 'Yes, I do happen to have. But what you'll see on that source material is not pleasant. In fact, it may brand itself on your brain forever. Despite the time it'll save, I'm not sure that I want to inflict it on you.'

She turns to face me and crosses her legs. She has big, firm thighs. I imagine dragging my fingernails down them and the goosepimpling effect that would have.

Once again, I get pinned to my seat, this time with a blasé smirk. 'Look. I've seen some pretty bad shit in my time. I'm forty years old. OK. I'm forty-two years old. I'm not some wet-behind-the-ears kid who's going to run screaming into the street just because of some shock-fest on a memory stick. What is it? What are you not telling me? Give it to me.'

'It's a kind of orgy.'

She sighs quickly and wriggles in her seat. 'Well, look. You know. I'll be straight with you, Mr Beckett. I'm a woman of the world. I'm a pretty big fan of porn. It's like my hobby, if you like.' Despite her forthrightness, she's blushing. 'Has been for years. Well, maybe hobby is the wrong word. It's like Pandora's box once you get started. I've had therapy for it. A lot of therapy. It hasn't worked. I could have bought a car with the money. Is that TMI? I'm not ashamed of it, so don't get all sympathetic and understanding. I can do without that, thank you very much. Anyway, there's not much I haven't seen. If you think…'

'This is kids. Both sexes. Possibly drugged or the victims of some sort of behavioural programming. Or both. Or something else. I don't really know. The seven men are participants, but the two women are not directly involved. They're more like part of the entertainment. The whole thing makes pretty grim viewing. It's certainly the worst thing *I've* ever seen.'

Her face changes. 'Kids?'

'Possibly aged between six and eleven. Around thirty of them, but that's just a guess. It's hard to work out what's going on. They come and go.'

'Oh, fuck. Oh fuck, that *really* shits. OK. I'll do it. I'll still do it, I mean. Don't worry about me. Is this the case? The kids, I mean? Are you tracking them down or something?'

'No. This is just unpleasant collateral. I'll be honest with you; I don't even know if this will turn out to be a useful lead. It's just a hunch, I suppose.' I shrug my shoulders. 'It's the only thing I've got, and it seems like the next natural stage. I suspect that the majority of these people will be visitors from other countries, though I could be mistaken,' I give her my copy of the stick with Polly's full-length feature on it. 'It's on here. Don't lose this. Have you got a safe?'

'Yes. Don't worry. It's a Barska Biometric wall safe. This stick will go inside it whenever I'm not using it.'

The Barska is virtually impossible to break into (unless you're me). Should do the job. I suddenly get a flashback to using Polly's fingers to open her Burg Wachter safe. I put the image out of my mind.

I take a quick glance at the office door; looks like a Bluetooth smart lock and a Yale. Windows look secure, with both Wedgit Twist Security Bars and Canzak Restrictor Cables. The ground-floor entrance had a Schlage Camelot Keypad Entry, a Kwikset 660 Deadbolt and a bump-resistant Kwikset 991 Juno. Probably the solicitors on the ground floor being paranoid.

She takes the stick and places it next to Matt Murdock. 'Right. Well, this is how it will go. Once I've duplicated your work from the source material, the software will digitise the images of each individual. What you saw on the screen just then was the software booting up, basically. It wasn't really doing anything even though it looked pretty cool.

'The composite image will be compressed and fed into various file sources. I'll start with social security, DVLA, police files, hospital files, social media, then widen the search to UK passport control. It sounds like a lot, but by the time the software has sorted out the compressed image, it's just pressing a button and letting the programmes get on with it.

'This is a new thing. Sometimes they'll crash,

sometimes they won't. If they do, you just have to start over, which can be a pain in the ass. But you get there eventually. Once I've exhausted the UK possibilities, I'll start work on Europe, the Middle East and the rest, though I doubt if it'll come to that. If they've been to this country, this should find them. It's cool beans.'

I like listening to her voice. 'Hold on – so you'll be hacking into all of those sources?'

'I know what you're thinking. You're thinking that this is activity that may cause alarm bells to ring somewhere, which I assume you won't want. Have no fear. It doesn't work like that, it's not detectable and this is definitely not hacking as you may know it. We're not going after the same information as a hacker might and similarly, we're not aiming at specific targets. It isn't as...*bulky*, I guess you might say. Does that make sense? And I don't have the skills for hacking, anyway. I hate math.

'I use DataScope B66. It's legal in this country at present, admittedly because no one knows it exists or what it can do. Developed and manufactured in Moscow about two years ago. One day soon they'll find out about it and I'll have to use something else.

'It automatically senses when internet traffic is at its busiest and then it goes to work. Try to imagine the Empire State Building as UK passport control. Then try to imagine a moth flying past on the eighty-ninth floor. No one would notice. The moth is DataScope B66. It's incredibly fast.'

'So, you'll be using software that's like a fast moth.'

She pauses for a few seconds. 'OK. The Empire State Building and the moth sucks as an analogy, but it's the best I could come up with at short notice.

'It's not perfect. These things never are. I can't get you

their addresses and telephone numbers or school reports or favourite colours, for example. This is purely image ID and it's potluck what gets dredged up with it.

'But we can usually – seventy to eighty percent of the time – link an image to a name and that'll be something, don't you think? And with the other shit that comes down, we can usually get some vital textual info. Don't worry. I'll identify these fuckers.'

'I have no doubt that you will. Here's the first two and a half thousand.'

I take the money out of my jacket pocket and hand it to her. Her eyes widen.

'You always carry this much cash around with you?'

'It impresses waiters.'

'I'll bet. Nice to do business with you, Mr Beckett.' She looks at the wad of notes, points to it and grins. 'I feel I should stick this down my cleavage.'

'Don't let me stop you.'

She laughs. 'Maybe I'll let you do it!'

'I've done it in my head a dozen times in the last ten seconds. Can I take you out to dinner tonight?'

'Oh, Jesus! You're the real fuckin' deal, aren't you?'

'You don't know the half of it. Wear something hot.'

'Just you wait, honey.'

I like her.

14

GOING GREY

We arrange to meet in the Clouds and Rain Cocktail Bar & Dim Sum Diner at eight, so I book a table for two in their Camelia Room. I have a vague memory of walking past this place yesterday morning on my way back to Exeter Street after the altercation at Polly's flat. The rest of that journey was a painful blur, apart from the pretty waitress in Wardour Street.

Taking Francie out isn't exactly work, but there's not much more I can do today until I get the info from Lothar. Besides, she's a sort of colleague now, so it counts as a business meeting. That's my excuse, anyway, and I have to eat sometime.

I'm still not sure how much to tell her about all of this; I'm just going to have to play it by ear. In one way, the less she knows the better, but she's not dumb, and eventually there are going to be questions she'll want answered. I don't want to spoil her commitment or focus. Maybe this *is* a business meeting.

I walk down to Holborn and then head towards Kingsway. I was going to walk back to my flat to help clear my head, but after a few minutes I start to feel a little fatigued and decide to get a cab. Just as I'm about to flag one down, my mobile starts ringing. It's Doug. I can hardly hear him because of all the traffic noise. My sudden stop causes a smartly dressed businessman of about twelve to walk into me. He tuts loudly and gives me a tough look.

'Hey, Mr Beckett. I know what you're thinking. How could he be that fast! Anyway, Dragan Todor Vanchev, aged fifty-three years. Cause of death, myocardial infarction. Post-mortem didn't throw up anything they liked, so they're doing a toxicology assay. No results on that yet. Thought you'd like to know.'

'That's great, Doug. Check again in a few hours to see if there's anything else.'

'Okey doke. Later, man.'

Interesting. That means that they've found no obvious physical reasons for him to have dropped dead of a heart attack. Now they're looking for other causes. I don't think I have to wait for Doug to get back to me to reach a conclusion, but it'll still be interesting if they find anything unusual – or nothing at all.

I forego the cab and find a small café opposite the Rosewood Hotel. I've never been inside the Rosewood, but it's rumoured to have a superb restaurant. Does great desserts, apparently; their mango and coconut pavlova is reputed to be almost holy. Perhaps Priscilla will be appreciative.

There's too much traffic to sit outside, so I order an Americano and a slice of carrot cake and sit at a table near the window. The owner is a fat, unshaven, surly bastard and barely looks up as I order; too busy reading his newspaper. The teenage girl he employs seems to do most of the work. He bosses her around like she's nothing. I bet he pays her shit, too.

I start thinking about Vanchev again. I'm sure it'll all make sense eventually, but I'd love to know who had him killed and why they did it. Has to be related to Polly's death. It's all a bit perplexing. As the girl places my coffee and cake on the table, I can feel her boss looking at me. I turn and meet his gaze and he quickly looks away. No doubt watching out for flirtatious customers. For all I know, he may secretly fancy her.

God knows what it must be like working all day long with someone like that. I'll leave her a big tip. I'm sure she deserves it. He disappears into the back and she starts cleaning the other tables, even though they all look pretty clean to me.

Just as I'm finishing my coffee and cake, the owner reappears and starts giving the girl more orders. He can't stop himself finding things for her to do. Getting his money's worth, no doubt. He looks at me again, but there's a slightly different expression on his face. Hard to read. Then it hits me. The newspaper. The temporary disappearance. My heart rate increases but it's too late. A dark green Ford Mondeo pulls up outside the café. Two plainclothes police officers are inside almost immediately. Both big guys, one in his fifties and the other in his twenties. Fifties Guy flashes me his warrant card. Looks genuine. I think these are real police. Shit.

'Good afternoon, sir. We are police officers. My name is Detective Inspector Christopher Hooper, and this is Detective Sergeant George Taylor. I'm arresting you on suspicion of the murder of a young woman at a residence in Devonshire Street, London W1, in the early hours of yesterday morning. You do not have to say anything, but it may harm your defence if you do not mention when questioned something which you later rely on in court. Anything you do say may be given in evidence. Would you stand up please, sir?'

There's something not right here. I could be an innocent citizen who happens to resemble that PortraitPad likeness. Suspicion of murder? Too much, too soon.

Hooper is Scottish. DS George Taylor speaks to the owner. Probably thanking him. The owner laughs and attempts to high-five Taylor who just glares at him in response. I very much doubt that I'll patronise this establishment in the future. The girl looks upset rather than frightened. I stand up.

'Now,' says Hooper in a firm but friendly voice with only a modicum of underlying threat. 'Are you going to be a good boy or are we going to have to handcuff you?'

I don't say anything. I wonder if they're going to search me now or when we get to the police station. Going to the police station is out of the question, of course. I'd never get out of there and my investigation would grind to a halt. I can't have that happening. I can feel my heart thumping.

There's a fifty-fifty chance that they'll search me at the station. If they search me here, they'll have my wallet and mobile and they'll know who I am. In a manner of speaking, anyway. Whoever's behind this, I'd prefer it if they didn't have a name.

Hooper gives me a suspicious look and nods at Taylor. Taylor gets the cuffs out. 'Hands behind your back, please, sir.'

Damn. They're a pair of nickel plated rigid folding cuffs. Not impossible to get out of, but bloody difficult when they're locked behind your back. Hooper places a hand on my shoulder while Taylor attaches them. They're on too tight and they hurt my wrists.

We go out to the car. A few passers-by stare. I get in

the back seat with Hooper. Taylor is doing the driving. I try to lean back, but cuffs are making it uncomfortable and now my shoulders ache. I wonder if I can get one of them to give me a Swedish massage.

As we drive off, Taylor calls it in. I try to work out where we're going. I hope it's not Seymour Street station. I have a contact there, DI Olivia Bream, and I don't really want to get her mixed up in whatever this is, and I'm positive the feeling would be mutual.

It's a certainty that these two have the official story as reported on the news. They do the footwork, and when I'm safely in custody, whoever performed the cover-up at Devonshire Street comes in for a quiet chat with a cricket bat while their pals dig a shallow grave somewhere.

I can't wait to discover who the puppet-master is. It's a funny thing. Sitting here with these two, I immediately feel like an eleven-year-old who's been caught shoplifting. It's my guilty conscience acting up.

I can see the reflection of this car in the shop doorways as we zoom along Holborn. No siren, but the blue flashing lights are on. In two minutes, we're bearing right into New Oxford Street and then Taylor hits the horn a few times as we cautiously jump a red light and turn into Tottenham Court Road.

I'm trying to work out which police station we're going to. Charing Cross? If so, we're going the wrong way. There's a lot of traffic here, but they're not using the siren to get past it. Does that mean I'm not an emergency? I'm insulted.

In five minutes, we'll be hitting Euston Road. I don't want to be too hard on these guys; they are the police, after all, but they're being played as much as everyone else. So here we go.

'Which police station are we going to?'

This gets a laugh out of Taylor. 'It speaks!'

'It's just that I've got a date tonight. DI Hooper's mother. I don't want to stand her up. She's really frisky at the moment. I think it's the heat.'

Taylor glances in the rear-view mirror to check his boss's reaction. Hooper's playing it cool. I turn to face him.

'You know what she's like, Chris. Demanding. She insisted I start going to the gym. I'll be quite honest with you: I can't keep up with her. What with the gym membership, sex toys, lingerie and the Viagra, it's killing me financially. You should see my overdraft. In fact, I was going to ask if you could help me out. I'll pay you back.'

'Just keep it up, sonny. Just keep it up.' says Hooper. He's attempting a grin for, I think, Taylor's benefit. He's clenching his teeth. I can suddenly smell his body odour. It's acrid. And he had a curry last night.

Taylor isn't laughing. Too respectful. He's also looking a tad perplexed. Do murderers usually talk this way? I've got to drag him into this to make it a little worse.

'Of course, I'd never have met her if it hadn't been for your sergeant there. He recommended her to me. She was one of his cast-offs. He said all the lads at the station were laughing at you. He did warn me about her, to be fair, as did your Chief Superintendent and two of the cleaners. Do you remember what you told me everyone called her, George? Hooper the Trooper.'

I don't really know what that means, but it has the desired effect. I can see Goodge Street tube station flash by on my left. Until now, I'd thought we were going to Paddington Green station, but then remember that it's closed. Hooper leans forwards and touches Taylor's shoulder.

'Take a right into Capper Street, George.'

Taylor swiftly changes lanes and turns right into a road I'd never really noticed before. It's narrow with lots of roadworks. At the end, it's right turn only, but Hooper points to a mews that's almost straight ahead but not quite, so Taylor has to take a brief but illegal left turn to drive down it.

I thought it was a dead end, but it continues for about a hundred yards. Then Hooper taps Taylor's shoulder once more and we turn into what looks like a deserted builder's yard. A couple of tons of rusty scaffolding, two big piles of bricks, four wheelbarrows and a stack of rotting planks. It looks like someone planned to do something here but gave up five years ago.

Taylor stops the car. Hooper gives me a weapons-grade smirk, gets out, walks around to my side and opens the door.

'Come on, mister comedian. Out you get. Don't fret; we won't leave any marks.'

Taylor turns the engine off and joins his boss. He's smiling. This is really not on. Ordinary folk pay their taxes to employ these people and look what they get up to.

I stand up and stretch my shoulders and spine. 'I insist that you let me keep the handcuffs on. I want to give you two pussies a chance.'

Hooper looks at Taylor and shakes his head. He has big hands. I'll bet his fists are enormous.

'We're not animals,' says Hooper.

'I wish I could say the same for your mum, Chris.'

His face goes a kind of reddish purple. Dark plum, it might be called, though perhaps closer to carmine or madder. 'Take the cuffs off him, George,' he says. I'm not that keen on his tone of voice.

I visualise Taylor's position and posture. I hear the key click in the lock. Two seconds for the first single strand to come off the wrist. The moment my right hand is free, I step back and sweep my arm across Taylor's throat, taking his balance and looping my forearm under the back of his neck, bending his whole body backwards and upwards. A button pops off his shirt.

He looks up at the sky, makes a gargling sound and waves his hands, hopelessly attempting to correct his posture and stand up straight again. It won't work. I could break his neck with hardly any effort now, but as I'm in a good mood, I just give him a hard hammer fist in his balls and let him drop to the floor.

Hooper looks astonished, but the astonishment promptly turns to anger. He actually roars as he charges at me and attempts a roundhouse punch to the side of my head. As I'd guessed, his fists are huge and must not make contact. I also have to limit the use of my right arm.

I block his fist with the side of my left forearm and stuff the fingers of my right hand into his open mouth and straight down to his tonsils. The gag reflex he's experiencing will stop him biting me. I can feel his wet tongue wriggling wildly against the palm of my hand.

He makes a noise like a death rattle. I walk straight into him and he has no choice but to walk backwards to avoid choking. His eyes are bloodshot, and tears run down his cheeks. I can feel him retching and attempting to cough. He tries to grab my wrist, but I just push my fingers deeper down his throat. This is a scary technique to be on the receiving end of and it's difficult to work out what to do to make it stop.

As I'm a nice guy, I make it stop for him. I remove my saliva-covered digits from his mouth and before he can work out what to do next, I hook my left hand under his right arm, place my right hand on his shoulder and press hard against his elbow joint, bringing him to his knees. Once he's down there, I bring my knee up hard against his chin and he's instantly out cold.

Taylor, meanwhile, has managed to stand up and makes a brave rush at me. He looks pissed off. I move out of the way at the very last second, grab the back of his collar and bring him down with a forearm chop across his throat. He lies on the floor and moans.

I wipe Hooper's saliva off on Taylor's jacket, find the key for the cuffs and undo the part that's on my left wrist. Just before I go, I take the car keys out of the Mondeo and slip them in my pocket. When these two recover, I have no idea whether they're going to pursue me or not, but at least it'll take their car out of the equation for a while, unless they can hotwire it, which is always a possibility.

But one thing's for sure, I'm in a lot more shit now than I was five minutes ago. I'll have the words 'dangerous' and 'violent' added to my profile and a large chunk of the Metropolitan Police on my tail. Though in fairness to me, I acted in pre-emptive self-defence.

Now I have to disappear.

I decide to head back the way we came. It's tempting to sprint, but that would only make me conspicuous, so while I'm in a fairly deserted road, I jog ten steps, then walk ten, watching all the while for witnesses.

Once I'm back in Capper Street, which is a little crowded, I settle for a brisk walk and avoid making eye contact with anyone. I run across Tottenham Court Road, walk importantly down Howland Street, then traverse Fitzrovia until I'm in Oxford Street. Now for some power shopping.

I know exactly the look I'll be going for. I pick up a pair of black Oakley Crosshairs in Sunglass Hut, then cross the road to Clark's to buy a pair of desert boots in blue/grey. That's two carrier bags so far. Now I'm starting to look like a shopper, as opposed to a murder suspect who attacks police officers in deserted builder's yards and puts his hand in their mouths.

Two squad cars with sirens blaring pass by. Is that for me? I look in a shop window in case it is, but I don't think there's any need; I've already vanished into the teeming chaos of the West End and now I'm just another anonymous consumer.

I feel vaguely annoyed. If I didn't have enough to do already, I've now got to somehow convince the authorities that I didn't murder Polly and be exonerated for beating a couple of cops up. Should I sue them for false arrest? At least they don't know who I am. Not yet. But that facial composite has to be taken down from the media. How I'm going to manage that, I have no idea. Maybe I should get in touch with DI Bream after all.

I buy a beige cotton summer suit in Selfridges plus a tan belt and rather rakish lavender pocket square to go with it. Across the road to Marks & Spencer for a couple of powder blue linen shirts and then a final stop at a large branch of Boots for three cans of L'Oréal Colorista hair colouring spray in graphite grey, a tube of lubricating eye drops, three plastic bath ducks, several unnecessary toiletry items, a packet of multivitamins and a tuna and horseradish sandwich.

Heading back to the busiest part of Oxford Street I

can find, I dump the cop car keys in a bin, hail a black cab and get him to take me to Piccadilly Circus.

'Been shopping have you, mate?'

'Wife's birthday coming up.'

'If yours is anything like mine…'

And so on until the end of the journey. I hate pretending to be ordinary; it gives me such a headache.

I walk back to Exeter Street via Trafalgar Square and the Strand, get inside and dump all my bags on the kitchen table. I was afraid I'd see blood seeping through the dressing on my arm after the police scuffle, but it looks OK.

Wrapping a Selfridges carrier bag around my right bicep, I take a shower and wash my hair. While the coffee machine is doing its thing, I get out everything I've bought and hang it up. I carefully place the plastic ducks by the side of the bath. Each is a different colour.

After I've eaten the sandwich and had three coffees, I read the instructions on the hair colouring spray and head for the bathroom. Dying my hair grey would look more convincing and last longer, but I don't have the time or inclination to faff around with all the preparations and bleaching that that would involve, so this will have to do for the moment. Depending on how things go, I might have to visit a salon and get it done by someone who knows what they're doing.

I wrap a towel around my shoulders, shake the first can and start spraying. Having dark brown hair, this takes a little longer than I'd imagined, and I use up the first tin pretty quickly. I have to keep stepping out of the bathroom to take a few deep breaths because of the smell. I also feel slightly dizzy. It's only when I re-read the instructions that I see the solvent abuse warning.

The result is better than I'd imagined and in ten minutes I'm a convincing grey-hair, as long as you don't get too close and as long as you don't run your fingers through my hair in a moment of uncontrolled passion. I notice a silvery sheen over my face and wash it off. And I've still got one and a half tins left.

Next, it's back to my Burton Claymore Underfloor safe hidden away under a removable stone tile on the shower floor. I remove the tile, type in the five-digit code and take out a pair of rimless plain glass spectacles and a small case containing a dozen coloured non-prescription contact lenses. While the safe is open, I retrieve Polly's original memory stick from the coffee jar and place it inside.

Looking at myself in the mirror I select brown lenses, which mysteriously seem to match my new hair colour the best. I haven't had to wear lenses for a while, so put a few eye drops in each eye before inserting them. It still stings when I put them in, and I have to blink a lot for five minutes. They look OK. More importantly, they don't look like coloured lenses, but then these are the best you can buy.

Next, I try on the plain glasses and look at my reflection once more. It works. I no longer look like the facial composite on the news. The mysterious neighbour who gave the police that detailed description had my age down as early thirties.

I haven't been able to change the way my skin looks, or my eyebrows, or my height and build, but the grey hair alone would fool a casual and/or semi-distant observer into thinking I was mid-forties or thereabouts, and certainly not the guy on the news. That's what I'm hoping for, anyway, and the clothes I purchased will help.

I've got a while before I have to go out and meet Francie, so I turn on the computer to see if there's any further news about Vanchev or my impending capture. Just as I'm reading an anodyne newspaper report on Vanchev's death, my mobile rings. Unknown number. When I answer it, I almost say 'Daniel Beckett', but stop myself just in time.

'Mr Cambridge? I am the bearer of glad tidings. The Frisian matter is *opus in profectus,* and I have been able to resolve the first matter of which we spoke and that was my first priority, as I'm sure you will understand.

'I thought I'd better give you a tinkle as soon as I had anything. Do you have a pen or is it all computers, networking and designer touchscreen gloves where you are?'

'I've got a pen. Let's have it.'

'The address of the gentleman you were interested in is number 72 Foxmore Street, London SW11 9DH.'

'Battersea.'

'Precisely. Quite a lovely road, if memory serves. Houses are not cheap, but not ostentatious, which is a vulgarity that I simply cannot abide. Modest back gardens. A much sought-after residence with many amenities close by and quite close to Battersea Park. Excellent public transport routes, both train and omnibus.'

'You should be an estate agent, Lothar. Did you manage to get a telephone number?'

'Alas, no. There is simply no landline associated with that property. I assume, like so many people nowadays, the gentleman relies purely on his mobile telephone, and what will happen when *that* fad kicks the bucket, I ask myself?

'Also, with that *particular* gentleman, there might be security issues in play. I am, however, still seeking a mobile number for our friend. Sometimes that can be a relatively easy task, sometimes not. In this case, it is not. Have no fear. I shall persevere.'

'Anything else on him at all?'

'Yes indeed. Mr Culpepper is fifty-four years old. He was married to Lucy-Ann Culpepper, née Jernigan, a photogrammetrist. She passed on six years ago. No issue and he has not remarried. Attended Aylesbury Grammar School in Buckinghamshire, then studied law at the University of Aberdeen. Excelled at hockey and track sports. Likes playing squash. Fluent in Spanish and German.'

'Security Service?'

'Worked as a legal researcher in the Home Office for three years, then on to MI5. *They* approached *him*, not the other way around. It's *so* nice to be wanted.'

'In a nutshell?'

'Clean as a whistle, dear chap. This isn't an in-depth study, as I'm sure you'll appreciate, but I've taken a look at his finances and his personal life insofar as they might leave him open to blackmail or coercion of any sort and there's nothing there at all. He's a bit boring, if truth be told. A likely philatelist, at a guess. Oh, and he buys his ties in Hawes & Curtis of Jermyn Street. Well, you did ask, ducky.

'I'm not saying, however, that some spectacular piece of intelligence might not leap up and change this assessment. It can happen from time to time, but if my gut feeling is anything to go on, I don't think it'll happen in this case.'

'What about the OFRP?'

'39 Mecklenburg Square, London WC1 9DG. Bloomsbury, don't you know. Charming, leafy area and just around the corner from the Charles Dickens Museum. I used to know a young lady who lived not far from there. Mrs Harriet Åkesson, if memory serves. Swedish. Originally a native of Eskilstuna. A keen flagellant. Mortification was her middle name. I suggested she join Opus Dei; they're always looking for suitable candidates.' He has a quick snicker at his own comment. 'The OFRP are on the third and fourth floor of the building. There are four personnel: Alistair Brodie Culpepper, of whom we have spoken, Jameela Rabia Rafique and what a charming, feminine name that is, Alex Wictor Carlsson and Judith Elizabeth Hart. I don't have addresses for the other three, but I can look into it, if you wish.'

'Don't worry.' It seems odd hearing one of Polly's aliases reported as fact. 'That's great, Lothar. Thank you. We can dump this now. You can focus on the Frisians.'

'Homing in on the little brutes as we speak, Mr Cambridge. I'm using personal contacts and chit-chat in the main, but a little computer finessing can add a soupçon of supplemental sheen. Modern computing is marvellous, don't you think? I can remember the days when computers were the size of a bungalow and you had to feed them with live cattle and trainee teachers.

'Computering aside, I have a few discreet telephone calls to make and one or two diplomatic tête-à-têtes, but I may have something for you sooner than I thought. Fortuna's wheel is spinning like a bugger today. And I must thank you for these little assignments. It's nice to have something one can really sink one's gnashers into. Gets me out and about, don't you know.'

'Don't mention it.'

'Oh, and two other tiny details that popped up. First of all, the OFRP is also designated the appellation Section 567. This would be for administrative purposes; pay and so on. It is partially financed by two other government departments, who are probably unaware of their contribution to such a shady consortium.'

'Which ones?'

'UK Export Finance and the Department for International Trade. No further details. Questionable significance. Probably nothing. Inter-governmental finances are always a tad incestuous and tricky to evaluate, particularly when it comes to intelligence funding. It's what they're like. If they don't think they're getting enough money from their official sources, they'll grab it from somewhere else. Clandestinely, of course.'

'OK. When you get something on the Frisians, call me immediately. Any time of the day or night.'

'*Bien sûr!*'

I don't waste any time. I get into my new identity, walk down to the Strand and get a cab to Battersea. Good old Lothar. Well worth the money.

15

DEAD END

Foxmore Street is full of early twentieth-century terraced dwellings which are modest but expensive looking. The road is quiet, tree-lined, uncommonly leafy and very well-kept. Nearly all the houses have venetian blinds on the ground floor. Permit holder parking on both sides of the road. Middle-range cars with a smattering of Range Rovers and sports models.

There's no one about. I walk along confidently, as if I'm visiting a friend. When I get to number 72, I take my Oakleys off, stride up to the front door and press the buzzer. Nothing. Smiling to myself, I take a step back and look up at the first-floor windows, as if I'm expecting Culpepper to poke his head out and wave. About three feet above the front door there's a yellow Yale outdoor siren box, so he's got a home alarm system.

I try the buzzer again. The house feels like it's empty. I should have got Lothar to find out the hours that the OFRP folk worked, but as it's almost two-thirty, it's probable that Culpepper's still at the office. Could be wrong. I push the buzzer a third time. Still nothing. I look over my shoulder to check for pedestrians or curtain twitchers, slip on a pair of latex gloves, get out my burglar's tools and start on the locks.

The mortice lock is open, so it's just the Yale. It takes

three seconds. Why was the mortice lock open? I close the door behind me and wait for the alarm system to start bleeping. I'll have a short time to disable it before it starts making a racket and the police or private security staff start arriving.

No bleeping. I take a look at the control panel which is a couple of feet away from the front door. It's been disabled. Either he doesn't use it or he's already home. Maybe he's asleep somewhere. Maybe he's sitting in his modest back garden.

I stand still and see if I can sense any presence. Nothing. My intuition about the house being empty is correct. I do a rapid scan of the walls and ceiling. I'm looking for motion sensors or cameras. Nothing in the hall, so I start on the other rooms. The last room I check is the kitchen. The kitchen looks out onto the garden. There's no one in the garden.

I cautiously make my way upstairs. Once I'm on the landing I take a look at what's there. Two bedrooms, a bathroom and a separate toilet. There's a print of *The Mulberry Tree* by Van Gogh on the wall and a faint smell of Bay Rum cologne. I reckon he moved here after his wife died. This is too small and poky for an affluent couple, but just right for a single guy.

The front bedroom door is closed. I turn the handle and push gently. Nothing happens. Perhaps I'm not turning the handle properly. I try again and the door opens a little, but it's fighting back. It feels as if someone has leaned a sofa up against it.

I keep the handle turned down and manage to push the door open an inch. I slip the fingers of my right hand through and run them up and down the edge. This is useless. Very carefully, I put firm pressure on the door with my left shoulder and manage to push it open another five or six inches.

This time I can get my whole hand in and most of my forearm. Then I touch something. A rough fabric like tweed. It's the shoulder of a jacket. And there's someone still wearing the jacket. I don't think they're alive.

I know immediately what this is and roughly what I'm going to find. I push a little harder and the door reluctantly swings open. I walk into the bedroom. Culpepper – I'm assuming it's him – is hanging from a sturdy metal door hook, a leather belt around his neck, his head drooping to the side.

His neck is stretched. His face is dark and bloated, almost black. His tongue protrudes from his mouth. It's swollen and blue, and it looks like he's bitten the tip off it. One of his eyes is open, the other closed. I have no idea why that should be, but it's pretty eerie.

I don't believe for a moment that this is a case of autoerotic asphyxiation gone bad. It's just meant to look that way. Everything's been arranged to make it obvious to any professionals who find him that it couldn't possibly be a traditional suicide. This was well researched. Suicides don't wrap a hand towel under the ligature – in this case the belt – to avoid discomfort. Suicides like to die fully dressed. Culpepper is not fully dressed.

He's wearing a pale green striped shirt with the top three buttons open. No tie. On top of that, a dark brown tweed jacket. No trousers or underpants, but he is wearing a woman's suspender belt and fishnet stockings. The belt is lavender and lime and the stockings are some sort of beige colour. No shoes.

I stoop down in front of him to take a look at his feet. His toenails have been painted dark red. I have no intention of touching him but take a good look at his corpse. I can't imagine how you would set this up. I can't imagine how you would fool whoever was going to do the post-mortem examination. No one is going to voluntarily collude in their own death by hanging without putting up a fight.

I press my fingers into my eyeballs. No. You'd have to disable him first. There's no other way you could do it. Disable but not kill. You can't asphyxiate yourself if you're already dead. But you couldn't leave any marks if you were the perpetrator. It hardly matters now, but I suspect that Culpepper opened the door to his murderer and let them inside. Someone he knew? Maybe.

I think about the possible cause of Vanchev's heart attack. A quick tap on the back of the neck with a poison-tipped needle might have done it. At worst, it would feel like a wasp sting. That could be what happened here, but with a non-lethal, possibly untraceable drug. Something to knock him out. Would the police and medics be searching for a tiny puncture mark after they'd found this lot?

I step away from him and take a look around the room. The first odd thing I notice is that the curtains are open. That's unusual and maybe a bit of a slip-up. Most people who practise AEA want privacy and seclusion; they don't want the people across the road having a quick look and taking photographs with their mobiles. This is an activity that is usually very secret; loved ones are frequently shocked when they find out about it. I can see a red bra on the floor by the window.

There's a small bookshelf next to the bed. Alarm clock, a couple of paperbacks and a wedding photograph of a laughing couple in their thirties. The man in the photograph is the man hanging from the door, though he looks in slightly better shape than he does now, and the wedding rings are the same. So, this is definitely Culpepper.

We have three deaths in a little over thirty-six hours (Frisian punks excepted), or at least discovered over that time. Varying techniques, executed by experts in making one type of death look like another (but not *that* expert). All three tricky and/or daring. High-end cover-up skills. Manipulation of the police and probably the Security Service. I'll probably get the blame for this one, too, if I'm lucky. I'm intrigued.

Did this occur before or after Polly was killed? Hard to say. The house is cool but not cold and the cause of death and its physical effects, particularly on the head, make it difficult for me to assess just when this could have happened. Culpepper was alive almost exactly three days ago when he told Polly to get to the safe house, but a precise time for this episode is anybody's guess.

A dressing table with a large mirror has been dragged across the room so that Culpepper could presumably watch himself in the purported act. Scattered on the bed are a few copies of a thick paperback called *Mein heimliches Auge*, which I've never encountered before. It's more like a book-shaped magazine than an actual book. Full of erotic photography, art and what look like stills from pornographic films. Avant-garde, retro, deviant – it's all there. All of the text is in German. Didn't Lothar say Culpepper spoke fluent German? Somebody has done their homework.

Scattered across the floor are a series of glossy black and white photographs of the same woman; a shockingly pneumatic pin-up with severe but sexy features. She's usually naked but will sometimes deign to wear stockings or négligées. I don't know who she is, but her hair, eye makeup and the picture quality place these somewhere in the late fifties or early sixties.

I get a shock when I get to the end of the pile. There are three photographs of Polly, all the same. They look like blow-ups of the sort of photo you'd find on an ID card and are probably from her official file.

I can't get my head around what the perpetrators were trying to do here, and I think that was the intention. Any police investigating this might think that Culpepper had a weird sexual infatuation with his co-worker.

But they'd have to make an effort to discover that that's who she was. It would be time-consuming and that may be the point.

Is this meant to link him with her death is some way? He hears about it and treats himself to a grief-stricken bout of AEA with formal-looking photographs of her face mixed in with his retro porn? If the police are lucky, if the police are even *involved*, eventually they'll make the connection. Or perhaps they'll get an anonymous call telling them about it. But from whom?

One thing's for sure, whoever did this was behind Polly's death and quite probably Vanchev's. If they're attempting to obfuscate, they're doing a good job; a great job. I find another bra under the bed; a purple one this time.

At least this makes it fairly clear that Culpepper wasn't the bad guy. He's the dead guy. Of course, he could be the dead guy *and* the bad guy, but intuition tells me he's just the dead guy.

This is all very weird, and much as I'd love to hang around here all evening and chill out with a bottle of wine, I have to get moving. I can think about the implications of this new death later. I go to the window, take a quick look at the street, go downstairs and let myself out.

I get back to Exeter Street and sleep for two hours. What a fuckin' day.

*

What was it I said? Wear something hot? Famous last words. She looks wonderful. I've only just inhaled the pert bouquet of my first double vodka and soda when she appears in the doorway of the Clouds and Rain Cocktail Bar. It's a black velvet Cavalli mini dress with a deep V-neck. The wrap front style accentuates her bust without it being too tacky and I'd somehow missed it this afternoon due to her sitting down most of the time, but she has quite amazing toned legs. No stockings.

I'd noticed the big, firm thighs but hadn't seen the whole picture. The black five-inch Saint Laurent heel sandals do amazing things to her calf muscles. I try to stop it, but my mind wants to speculate about her underwear; what she'd look like in it, how she'd take it off. Slowly, I think.

Her makeup is minimal but effective: a dusting of dark bronze eye shadow and raspberry red lipstick on those full lips. Both colours complement her light olive skin.

Around her neck there's a slim silver necklace with a white gold pendant hanging off it. Matching silver earrings. There's a pattern on the pendant. It's a triskelion inside a circle. I'm sure that has some significance, but I can't remember what it is. All these designer clothes and the Cartier watch: where's the money coming from? I'm sure I'll find out.

She looks around for a moment as if she can't see me, then I remember my new bespectacled, grey-haired appearance.

'Hi, Francie.'

She frowns as she walks over to me. 'What? Have you had some sort of terrible fright since this afternoon? I'd heard a sudden shock can turn your hair grey, but I didn't know it could change your eye colour as well.'

'It's a long story. I'll tell you later. Take a look at the cocktail menu.'

'Like the glasses, by the way. They make you look intellectual.'

'There's a first time for everything.'

She sits on one of the bar stools. I must stop looking at her legs. I can't stop looking at her legs. She peers at me through half-lidded eyes and licks her lips.

She's wearing L'Heure Bleue again. She orders a Kumquat Mojito and I have a Tom Yam. After the first couple of sips, the maître d' appears and lets us know that our table is ready, so we follow him into the Camelia Room, holding our drinks. This is simultaneously interesting and weird; I've never been out with a private detective before.

The Clouds and Rain is more like a *Chinese themed* restaurant, rather than an actual Chinese restaurant. It's part of a chain: there are maybe a dozen of them dotted around the country. But they have a great reputation and a fantastic drinks menu.

The Camelia Room is small and intimate, the walls covered in colourful retro Chinoiserie advertisements for Prosperity cigarettes, Dolly's Brandy, Ewo Beer, alongside communist propaganda art and Tang dynasty calligraphy.

Without thinking, I order a bottle of Veuve Clicquot and suddenly get a flashback to drinking the same champagne with Polly in Boyds. When was that? A little over forty-eight hours ago. It already seems like a lifetime.

The menu is so big, complex and varied that we order a dim sum platter and a sea food platter so that neither of us have to think too much. I smile at her and she smiles back. I think I need this break from all the drama of the last couple of days, but I still find I'm letting the mystery of Culpepper float around my consciousness.

'So, what do you think?' she says, smirking, arching her back and tracing a line from her shoulders to her hips with the tips of her fingers. 'Hot enough for you?'

'You look fantastic, Ms Martinelli.' The champagne arrives and a waiter fills our glasses. She drinks half a glass and rolls her eyes. She puts the glass down, places her hands on her thighs, lowers her head then looks up, briefly making eye contact with me before breaking it off.

This behaviour and the unusual way she was sitting earlier today; that straight-backed, closed posture. I get it now. Very subtle and very smart. She notices the slight smile of recognition on my face and blushes, her eyes darting everywhere.

'I've prepared everything I need for your project,' she says. 'All the software, I mean. I'll start work on it first thing tomorrow morning.'

'Good. Call me when you've got enough stuff for a presentation.'

'Will do. Could be lunchtime, could be before. Bring some coffee and a sandwich.'

'So, how did you get into this business, Francie? Being a private investigator, I mean. It's…'

'Unusual for a woman?'

'It's unusual for an American woman to be doing it in London.'

'I guess you're right. My dad was one. We're from Raleigh in North Carolina. He was a lawyer originally. We never had heart-to-hearts about it, but I think he felt he could help people more directly or something; felt the legal world was a little constricting, maybe.

'He didn't have any training. He just went out and did it. He was successful. Had his own company. Employed eleven people eventually. Called it Dakota International. Pretty grand name. He was from Sioux Falls in South Dakota.'

'So that's why…'

'Yeah. Following the family tradition.'

'Well, it caught my eye.'

'My mom was a famous stripper. No one believes me. He met her on a case. Corny as hell, huh?'

'What was her name? Professional, I mean.'

She smiles. 'Lina Lopez. Her real name was Brianna Hernandez before she got married. Not very glamorous, so she changed it. She was very popular. Had a super-hot body. She was a cage dancer for a while at the Whisky a Go Go. Met The Doors. I sometimes fantasise that I'm really Jim Morrison's love child, except the dates don't pan out even slightly.

'Can you imagine how cool that would be, though? I'd be the Lizard Queen! She quit quite a few years back and now she helps distressed horses or something. It's usually one animal or other.'

'Hernandez. So, you're an Italian/Spanish mix.'

'Yeah. I guess that makes me pretty fiery.'

'Hard to handle.'

She laughs and leans forwards, her eyes wide. 'I need

to be *tamed*.'

'Enslaved.'

'You better believe it, honey.'

'You were saying?'

She looks flustered. 'Sorry. About what?'

'How you became a PI.'

'Oh, yeah. Hold on.' She finishes her champagne and I refill her glass. 'So, Dad taught me a few tricks. I worked for him while I was in college, then worked for him full time for a couple years, then I went back to college, then I worked for him full time again.

'Also, my uncle, my dad's brother, was a lieutenant commander in Raleigh PD. He showed me lots of useful cop stuff. Then somewhere around three years ago I got married. A lawyer. Pretty rich, as it happens. It didn't work out. We weren't compatible.

'I won't go into detail, but it was a physical thing. Or maybe a mental thing. Stuff he couldn't or wouldn't do. Don't ask. And he freaked when he found out I'd been bi in college and still had the itch. So, I left him. We were married for a little over three weeks. End of. Never marry a wealthy man, Daniel; they're always fucks.'

'Too late. We're already halfway through the wedding list.'

'To be quite honest, I wondered if I'd become temporarily insane marrying that guy or marrying at all. I don't even remember meeting him. I can barely remember the ceremony. I think I'd been spiked with hallucinogenics. Now and again I even wonder if it was a bad dream and it really didn't happen at all. Have you ever slept with a nicotine patch on? It was like one of the dreams you get with those. I don't even remember what he looked like. Sometimes, I have to concentrate to remember his fuckin' name.'

'So, you still love him.'

'Oh yeah. *À corps perdu.*'

The food arrives. She's doing all the talking, which I'm quite pleased about, as I'm still feeling pretty wiped out. I just roll with it, nodding and smiling occasionally to show that I'm listening and interested.

'My dad had been working on corporate fraud cases for a few years and I'd helped him out on many of them. Some of them involved companies in the UK and it suddenly occurred to me that I needed a change after the separation, so he made a few calls and explored the possibilities of using his contacts here to set me up in my own business. He loaned me ten thousand dollars to get going and it picked up and here I am. I paid him back the money in full a year ago.'

'So, you're still legally married to this guy without a name?'

'No. Yes. This food looks delicious. Am I talking too much?'

I laugh. 'It's fine. You're taking my mind off things. I've had a busy day.'

She uses her chopsticks to dip a crab and samphire dumpling into a small bowl of ginger sauce. 'So, what about you? How did you become a PI?'

'It was my grandmother's dying wish.'

'She leave you a bunch of Chandler paperbacks in her will?'

'And a Colt Detective Special.'

'Nice gun. Anyway, I have two sisters and one of them, Rosa, is a kindergarten teacher.'

'What about the other one?'

She doesn't answer immediately. She stops chewing,

narrows her eyes and gives me a hard stare that I can't make sense of. 'Are you liberal?'

'I like to think so.'

'I mean, are you easily shocked or outraged by stuff? Conservative?'

'I don't think so. I...'

'OK.' She takes a sip of champagne. 'Well. Her name's Angie Martinelli, but she's better known as Shelley Saint. She's a kind of porn actress. Well, not a "kind of" porn actress, she actually *is* a porn actress. She's quite a big deal; in the US, at least. I can give you one of her DVDs if you like.'

'Sure. So, I mean, she's pretty famous? Like, people know her name?'

'Yeah. I would say so. She's big business. DVDs, Blu-rays, signed photographs, used underwear; you name it. I told you earlier that I was into porn. It was only when she gave me a load of freebies a few years back that I started getting into it. God – what must you think of our family? Angie performs in it, I watch it and our mom was a cage dancer. Jeez!'

I have to laugh. 'You're all going to hell!'

'As long as you can order Domino's down there, I won't give two shits. Hey. Did I tell you what my middle name was? Guess.'

'Herbie.'

'Ha ha. It's Luigiana. Can you frikkin' believe it? *So* embarrassing. I'm only telling you because I've been drinking. It was my father's idea. It was his grandmother's first name. She was from Palermo. Am I boring you?'

As we eat and make small talk I think about Culpepper. His death means that the three principals in the Vanchev case are now deceased. What will happen now? The OFRP is as good as finished and that case will almost certainly be consigned to the dustbin after a cursory glance by whoever. Can of worms. Too much trouble. Are the others in danger? Unlikely. Offing those two would be pushing it, even for whoever is behind this. But I wouldn't put it past them.

Polly referred to the techie as 'she' on one occasion, so that would be Jameela Rabia Rafique. Alex Wictor Carlsson would be the analyst. They'll probably be transferred. They were need-to-know guys, after all, and apart from supplying technical help in Rafique's case, neither of them would have known precisely what was going on with Vanchev. I wonder if it's worth getting in touch with either of them, if not now, then sometime in the near future. If they're still alive, of course.

No doubt, someone in MI5 will get them in a room and ask them about Culpepper. It'll just be a formality. His cause of death will be an open and shut case, unless they've got someone extremely smart who's got the time and inclination to look into it in detail. But how will Polly's death look alongside that? And what will they make of Vanchev's death?

If I worked for MI5 and was even *casually* looking at all of this, I'd think it stank to high heaven, no matter how plausible and convincing the deaths were. Three dead in two days? All of them connected to each other in an important intelligence matter? Has to be suspicious. *Has* to be major investigation material. Someone is manipulating this. They're manipulating the police and God knows who else. And they think nothing of murdering people.

'Are you thinking about the case?'

'Sorry. Is it that obvious?'

'Anything you want to share?'

I take a sip of champagne. 'I told you this afternoon that five people involved in this had lost their lives. Now it's six. But, er, three of those are the really bad guys, so it's not as horrifying as it sounds.'

'Fuck all the way off. What happened?'

She waves a waitress over and orders another bottle of champagne.

'I said before that this involved the Security Service and that as soon as you started work on those images, you'd be in breach of the Official Secrets Act. Well: in for a penny, in for a pound. I can't – *won't* tell you everything, but I'll tell you what I can, and I promise I won't bullshit you. Keep in mind I don't fully know what's going on myself. And don't forget the client confidentiality.'

'I'm having a lady boner already. Go on.'

'OK. Forget the really bad guys for the moment. We'll call the three deceased A, B and C. A is the bad guy. B and C are the good guys. B tells C to get something on A that can maybe be used for blackmail purposes.

'C films A at the orgy and gives the result to B. Less than forty-eight hours later, C is dead. About twenty-four hours after that, A is dead. I can only guess at the timescale, but something like twelve hours after that, B is dead.'

Francie nods her head and drums her fingers on the table. 'And that's why you want the people at the orgy identified. You think C filmed someone important apart from A and they're attempting a cover-up.'

She's quick. 'It's a possibility. It's all I can think of. At first, I thought B was behind it, but then I had my doubts. Now, I don't think he had anything to do with it; not directly, anyway.'

'So, who is your client? Wait. It has to be C.'

She's right, of course. But: 'What makes you say that?'

'It's obvious. OK. Here's *my* thesis, if you will. A is the bad guy, B and C must be spooks, operatives, agents, whatever you call them here.' She nibbles at a fingernail. 'Our bad guy wouldn't have approached you as he probably wouldn't have known he was under surveillance, and even if he *did*, it's unlikely he'd have gone to a PI for help.' She pauses as a new bottle of champagne is placed next to us. 'You said you thought B was behind it at one point. Why would you think that if B was your client? B told C to do the job. If C gets bumped off, B is not going to hire a damn PI. It has to be C.

'Shit. So, this is like a *posthumous* case. So, where's the money coming from? Were you paid in advance or something? Nope. Can't be that. Neither of you could know how long this would take. But you're paying me well over the odds. Shit. I'm out of breath after all of that and I'm starting to get a migraine from the mental strain.'

She gulps down some champagne and waves both of her hands in the air. She points at me, speaking slowly. 'So, why are you continuing with this, Mr Beckett? Someone is in trouble. They hire you. They get killed. That's the end of the case. Unless – *unless* – you have some sort of obligation to finish this. An obligation to C, whoever the fuck that is. And why would a spook come to *you* for help? Oh, Jesus Christ. What the actual fuck is going on here? You're not going to tell me, are you? I love this. I could get a damn book out of this. And you've suddenly changed your appearance. Someone's after *you* now. Is it the police? Are they trying to pin C's murder on you? This is Badass City.'

I have to laugh. 'You're very good, Francie.'

She raises an eyebrow. 'You don't know the half of it.'

'I think I can guess.'

'I think you can. Say; were you good in school? My biological clock is ticking away and I'm looking for a handsome high IQ guy to knock me up. Interested?'

'I...'

She laughs. 'Gotcha! You should see your *face!*'

She slams both hands on the table. I wave at a passing waiter. 'Could we have another couple of cocktails, please?'

*

Half an hour later, we're heading to Charing Cross Road via Lisle Street. Despite it being a weekday, it's very busy here and it's not even ten. So many people are pouring out of Leicester Square tube station that I wonder if there's been some sort of terrorist alert. Francie links her arm around mine and we walk towards Trafalgar Square without saying anything.

'I enjoyed that,' she says, smiling. 'That's the first time I've been out with a guy since I was married.'

'What did you think of it?'

'Interesting. And a little bit scary.'

'Is it *me* that's scary?'

'Not you. The whole thing that you're describing. It's got a kind of take-your-breath-away conspiracy vibe to it. And your vagueness – all the ABC stuff – makes it a little worse. Or better. Or what-the-*fuck?*'

'Where you do live, Francie?'

'Craven Terrace. Lancaster Gate.'

I flag down a black cab and give the driver her address.

'Give me a call when you're ready. I'll see you tomorrow. And I probably don't have to tell you this, but be careful, be observant.'

'Sure. And I'll give you a little bit of feminine advice. I don't know why you've dyed your hair and I'm not going to ask, but what you've obviously used is a spray-on. Do it properly as soon as you get a chance. I recommend Colorista Permanent Gel. The colour you want is called smokeygrey. One word. It'll be fiddly. Good luck!'

We air kiss. She gets in the cab. She's gone.

I find a branch of Boots that's open and pick up a carton of the hair dye before I forget what it was called. I don't feel like going back to the flat yet. I have to think. I turn into the Strand and walk all the way to Ludgate Hill before turning back and taking my regular irregular route home. I have to admit, I found Culpepper's death a little disturbing. Not the actual method used, but the almost simplistic, childlike logic behind it all. 'We get rid of her, we get rid of him, and then we get rid of *him*. And then everything will be alright.'

The arrogance behind it, the smugness behind it, the *entitlement to success* behind it.

Well, everything's not going to be alright. I'll make sure of it. I *have* to make sure of it.

16

LA DESTINÉE

Just as I'm walking past St Clement Danes church and looking forward to sinking into a hot bath, my mobile starts ringing. It's Lothar.

'Not too late for you, is it, Mr Cambridge?' He laughs to himself. 'Not tucked up in bed with some legal secretary, artisan ceramicist or social media coordinator? Not facetiming with a recently widowed dental hygienist from Helsinki?'

'You know me so well. What's up?'

'We need to meet. This is not really telephone call material. Too much of it and I'll need to display certain facial expressions, concerned gesticulations and melodramatic moues.'

I check my watch. Dead on eleven. 'I'll get a cab. I'll see you in ten to fifteen minutes.'

'Ah – ah. No no no no no no. Nothing personal, Mr Cambridge, but I'd prefer not to meet you at my home. You're a little too *hot*, shall we say. Identikits on the telly, wanted for murder and all that palaver. I'm calling from La Destinée. Do you know it?'

'No.'

'Oh, you'll love it. A charming little drinking club. Past its best now, I fear. Do you know the Nellie Dean of Soho pub?'

'Corner of Carlisle Street and Dean Street.'

'That's the chap. You want the Dean Street side. Past the newsagent, past the dilapidated sandwich place and just before you get to St Anne's Court, there's an alley with a cast iron gate. Push the gate – it won't be locked – walk about twenty feet and then you turn left into a small yard. It's rather dark and dank. I hope you won't be *scared*. Then up the fire escape to the first floor. There's a bell push on your right. Push it twice. Ask for Crazy Bob. Only kidding. Don't worry. I've told them I'm expecting a friend.'

'I'll be there in five minutes.'

I flag down a black cab and get it to drop me off in Soho Square. I walk up Carlisle Street and can see the Nellie Dean ahead of me. I stop, take a look at the menu in the Pizza Express window, make sure I'm clean and then cross over the road into Dean Street.

Once there, I find the gate that Lothar mentioned and walk down a narrow alley into a grimy area filled with graffiti-strewn green wheelie bins, steel beer kegs, cardboard boxes, broken shop display shelving units and three used condoms on the floor to my left.

It smells of fried food, rotting vegetables and stale urine. There's a dim orange light at the back of what must be the sandwich bar. If it wasn't for this bulb, I'd never have seen the guy staring at me.

For a brief moment, I get a surge of fear. He doesn't move. He doesn't speak. He's a monstrous individual: short, stocky, hunched, bald, wrestler's shoulders, thick, muscular arms, low forehead and a severely prognathous jaw. His eyes are like black marbles, sunk back in his skull, staring at me and staring right through me.

There's something not right with him, poor guy. As

my eyes adjust to the light, I can see he's carrying two big crates of Carlsberg. So that's it. He must work at La Destinée. I can see the fire escape to his left and he's blocking the entrance. I'll have to say something.

'Hi. I'm looking for La Destinée. I'm meeting someone there.'

He keeps staring at me. Five seconds pass. Then he nods towards the fire escape stairs and says 'Uh' and moves out of my way, not taking his eyes off me for a second. I take the stairs two at a time and press the bell push. I don't look over my shoulder in case he's right behind me.

For a moment, I don't recognise the woman who opens the door to me, but it's probably because she's dressed. It's Mrs Kay Gardiner, Lothar's friend from this morning. Apart from the clothes, she looks different and quite amazing.

Her black hair is tied back off her face, accentuating a charming, soft prettiness that I hadn't noticed earlier and she's dressed in a saucy French maid's outfit: a low-cut short black dress, lace-tied at the front, black fishnet stockings with matching garters, four-inch heels, lace cuffs, white apron and a white, frilly mob cap perched on top of her head.

To complete the look, she's holding a black feather duster under her arm. Her voluptuousness makes her décolletage outrageously indecent. I want to kiss it. I think I'll probably call her when all this is over. For a millisecond, I forget what I'm doing here.

'*Ah! Bonjour, Monsieur Cambridge. Ça va? On se revoit.*'

A convincing French accent, then I remember she was an actress. '*Ça va bien, Madame Gardiner,*' I reply. '*Vous êtes ravissante, ce soir.*'

She smiles, takes one of my hands in hers, stands on tiptoe and kisses me lightly on the mouth. Her breasts briefly brush against my chest. *'Vous êtes trop gentil, monsieur. Allons. Suivez-moi.'*

I follow her into the depths of La Destinée, looking at her bottom. It's like stepping back into the 1950s. Maybe it still *is* the 1950s here. Nothing would surprise me about Lothar's hangouts.

French café music ("La Mer" is playing as I walk in), retro Perrier posters and faded autographed photographs of celebrities I don't recognise scattered all over the nicotine-brown walls. Take one of those down and you'd be snow-blind from the original white emulsion that's undoubtedly underneath.

My eyes start watering from the reeky, honey-sweet stale alcohol smell of a joint that's open twenty-four-seven and probably has been since the forties without a single break. There's a creaking sticky wooden floor, but no sawdust. A well-stocked bar with a giant Howard Chandler Christie nude reclining behind the optics and a thickset barman in a bow tie who looks like he'd cosh you if you ordered an unfashionable cocktail or requested a pork pie.

It seems to be all preoccupied couples here and no one looks up as we walk through. Thankfully, none of them are wearing berets or stripey Breton shirts. Apart from the front door, I can see an exit you can access by walking behind the bar. Where that might come out, I have no idea; the geography of this place is a little confusing.

Mrs Gardiner looks quickly over her shoulder at me. *'On devrait se rencontrer, Monsieur Cambridge. Vous serez épaté, j'en suis sure. Avez-vous toujours mes coordonnées?'*

'*Oui. Je vais le garder pour toujours, madame.*'
'*Vous m'excitez, monsieur.*'

There's a window to my left with bars and another straight ahead without. To the right of that window is a pair of swing doors decorated with what looks like fanged demons climbing up honeysuckle with a naked woman lying underneath, smiling and caressing herself. That's where we're heading.

It's a small room with more faded celeb photographs on the wall and a large, unused Edwardian fireplace adorned with flowery ceramic tiles. Above the fireplace is a large print of *Nude with Red Dress* by Van Offel. It smells of expensive male cologne in here: notes of Jamaican Lime, gin, Scots pine, cedar and eucalyptus. It's Royal Mayfair by the House of Creed.

Lothar is sitting at a table on his own. There's a glass of red wine to his right and a couple of pink document wallets to his left. He's eating some unidentifiable meal from a bowl with paintings of sailing ships on the side. It's almost ten past eleven, but with Lothar's lifestyle, it's hard to tell what meal this could be. Breakfast? Lunch? He looks up when he hears us come in.

'Ah! Right on time as usual. No blue flashing lights or sirens on your tail? Like the grey hair and specs, by the way. Makes you look like a university lecturer who's just slaughtered his entire family.'

'That's exactly the look I was going for.'

'So, Mr Cambridge. Be honest. What do you think of Mrs Gardiner as a French maid? Pretend you didn't witness her denuded post-coital splendour this morning. Be objective.'

'Very alluring.'

'Would you like a drink? We have vodka here, don't

we, dear?' he says to the hovering Mrs Gardiner.

Mrs Gardiner smiles at me. 'We have Beluga Gold Line, Diva Premium, Crystal Head and Snow Queen.'

'What would you recommend, Mrs Gardiner?' I ask.

'Diva Premium's very nice.'

'OK. I'll have a double with soda.'

'Anything to eat, Mr Cambridge? Anything at all?' she asks, smiling and raising an eyebrow.

'Not for me.'

'Shame.'

Mrs Gardiner leaves. I place my hair dye pack on the table. Lothar glances at it and smirks. He pats the pink document wallets with the flat of his hand. 'Your money was well spent, Mr Cambridge, even though I do say so myself. A difficult job, but very stimulating. Rather like a difficult crossword puzzle. You have half a dozen clues that simply *will not* surrender their secrets. Then suddenly – bang! How could you not have remembered that Hine-nui-te-pō was the Maori goddess of death and the underworld?

'Having said that – and isn't that an *awful* phrase? – I'm not saying I've got all the answers, but I think you'll be pleased with what I've managed to trawl from the quagmire of iniquity where these swinish vulgarians dwell. Particularly taking into account the short notice.'

He drinks some wine and wipes his mouth with the back of his hand. 'A few favours were called in, I can tell you that for nothing. What I was hoping for was to find the actual location of the surviving Frisian, if he is still in this country, but that has proved to be a little too difficult in the limited time that I had. But – I shall keep digging. I want you to get your money's worth. Oh! Forgot to ask. How did you get on with the OFRP chappie? Culpepper, wasn't it?'

'Dead end.'

'Hm. I won't ask.'

We wait until Mrs Gardiner returns with the drinks before we get stuck in. She places my vodka in front of me. 'Just let me know if there's anything else you want, Mr Cambridge. Anything at all.'

'I'll be sure to, Mrs Gardiner.'

'Did a little bit of minor surgery on Mr Cambridge this morning, my dear,' says Lothar to Mrs Gardiner, grinning more to himself than anyone else. 'Keeping the old hand in. Very good musculature, in case you're interested. And could you ask Niculaiu to turn the music up slightly in the bar and turn it down in here, please, *ma petite tigresse*? There's no room in this marriage for the two of us *and* Edith Piaf. Oh, and ask him to keep an eye on the doors here. We'd like a little privacy.'

Mrs Gardiner gives me what could only be described as a 'look' and wiggles her way back into the main bar.

'That woman,' says Lothar, smiling. 'Her thirst cannot be quenched. I've no doubt you saw Niculaiu behind the bar there. Niculaiu Flamini. Ring any bells? No? Corsican. On the run for almost a decade now for murdering two policemen with his bare hands in Porto Vecchio. Quite an artist. Watercolours. Reminds me a little of the work of Peter de Wint. Are you alright for porky scratchings, scampi fries or honey roasted cashews? How's the arm? Holding up?'

I'm suddenly feeling fatigued. 'It's OK. What have you got?'

He slides four photographs, undoubtedly police or military mugshots, out of one of the document wallets and spreads them across the table in a row. My heart rate increases slightly as I recognise the brainless faces of Thug One and Thug Two. But there's something not right here. It looks like there are three photographs of the same person. The fourth photograph is of a different person altogether.

'What is this? What's going on?'

'All will be revealed!' He takes a sip of wine. 'You have certainly kicked the hornet's nest, Mr Cambridge. In fact, you've set fire to it and then poured petrol over it. The conflagration can be seen from space!'

'You better explain, Lothar.' I can hear the impatience in my voice. I'll have to try to disguise it.

'You have had a close encounter with possibly *the* most frightening and feared kill-for-hire unit in Europe, if not the world. These illustrious gentlemen are responsible for an *extraordinary* amount of hits. It's a very odd story; what I have been able to piece together of it, anyway.'

He sits up straight in his seat and rubs his hands together. 'Three brothers. *Triplets*, would you believe. Surname is Salo. Forenames are Wolfert, Redolf and Eemil. Thirty-seven years old. They work with their cousin, age unknown at present, who goes by the name of Jitser Vonk. I *love* it. My personal favourite, that one. Jitser Vonk.

'Salo, I believe, is more commonly a Finnish surname, but that's neither here nor there. Vonk is a fairly common Frisian surname, should you ever involve yourself in a pub quiz about such matters. Now. I'll just give you some essential background. I'll keep it brief as I can feel there is an undeniable urgency in this matter for you.

'All three are from Leeuwarden, capital of the States of Friesland, as I'm sure you're aware, which means that my guess at the language you heard being West Frisian was correct. You're welcome. Mata Hari was from Leeuwarden, did you know? Charming woman, apparently. Self-conscious about her small breasts. A *grande horizontale* who made a lot of errors of judgment. A *victim* of men, really, not a victimiser. Poor M'greet.

'Did you ever meet her?'

'Ha ha. I'm not *that* ancient, old boy, particularly as she was executed in 1917. Blew a kiss to the firing squad, apparently. Anyway. Back to the story. All three brothers and their cousin – that's *Jitser Vonk*, in case you had forgotten – served in the Netherlands Marine Corps.

'This unit is nicknamed The Black Devils or The Men of Steel. Terrifically arduous training, lots of hardship, scary reputation. I could not discover what the Salo specialities were, but take it as read that it was the usual special forces rigmarole: mountain warfare, heavy weapons, underwater sabotage, jumping out of aeroplanes tied up, blindfolded, carrying a sheep while urinating and all the rest.

'All three triplets served in Afghanistan, but no detail of rank or time or unit, except in the case of my very good friend Jitser Vonk, who served in the 24th Combat Support Squadron during that little squabble. Now. There is a little information lacuna after this. The next time that I pick them up was twelve years ago and they were already rumoured to be working as mercenaries, but the details are sketchy. Then I came up trumps! Both Wolfert and Eemil were arrested and charged with robbing a bank in Minsk, of all places. Not a very professional job, by all accounts.

'One of them – I don't know which one – went a little crazy with the customers as the police arrived and put two women and three men in hospital. One of the women almost died and it was lucky she didn't; Belarus still has capital punishment.'

'OK. So, what about the other two at this time. Were they bank robbers as well?'

He shakes his head. 'No idea, I'm afraid. I didn't really have access to any official files for this time of their lives. All of this was mainly through word of mouth, if you get my drift. Then we skip forward three years and the fun really begins.

'It's hard to know who did what, or which combination of personnel was used, but my sources have them down as definite culprits for a series of major hits in a career that has continued to this day. They're daring and highly skilled. They're the cat's pyjamas for deniable assassinations and charge top rates. They've worked for government departments in the UK, Hungary, Turkey, Sweden, Syria, Macedonia, France, Ukraine, Israel, Uzbekistan and Chad and I'm sure those are just the tip of the iceberg.

'Now. Hold on. I've got it here somewhere.' He pats his jacket pockets and finally fishes out a black and silver Fancii LED magnifying glass and pushes it across to me. 'I need this bloody thing to read the newspapers nowadays. Not that I ever *read* the newspapers, of course,' He pokes the Salo triplet photograph on the far right. 'Take a look at the mouth.'

The photograph is grainy, but I see it straight away. There's a small scar beneath the lower lip. It's a little darker than I remember, but there's no doubt it's the same scar. 'So, which one is this?'

'That one is Eemil. The sole survivor as he shall now forever be known. That means that the other Salo you encountered must have been either Redolf or Wolfert.

Jitser Vonk – *exquis!* – was involved in some sort of accident ten years ago. My source believes it was an automobile mishap. Quite serious petrol burns to the face.

'Now you mentioned that twenty-four hours before *your* Frisian encounter, an acquaintance of yours – God *alone* knows what sort of creature that must have been – came across two similar professionals and one of them showed signs of plastic surgery around the eyes, mouth, face and neck. I don't think it's *too* much of a leap of faith to assume that those two were *mon très bon ami* Jitser Vonk and one of the other Salo triplets, once again, either Redolf or Wolfert.

'That vagueness is irritating, but there it is. Par for the course with triplets. Freakish, I call it. Nature playing tricks. Oh, and Redolf had a weakness for high-class prostitutes, to the extent that the word *weakness* could easily be exchanged for the words *addiction* and *obsession*. There may be a little corespun thread to be tugged there.

'What else? Oh, yes. Eemil has a strong dislike of both dogs and curry, so no taking him out for a paneer tikka masala at Crufts, or serving him spaniel korma. He is also said to be short-tempered, pathologically impatient and a narcissistic psychopath. The girls must be queuing round the block!'

'OK. I think we can assume that under normal circumstances, people like this would leave the country after completing a job of this sort.'

'I would *certainly* say so, Mr Cambridge.'

'But in this case, I don't think he'll be going home just yet.'

'Revenge on his mind, I'll wager. What a lucky boy you are to have such a distinguished and maniacal executioner hunting you down! He's going to be a tad miffed with you, isn't he? What will his family Christmas celebrations be like this year? A little quiet and sombre, I suspect. Let's hope there's something good on the telly. I hope he hasn't already started buying presents. What a waste of money.'

He leans forwards. 'On the other hand, if I was him, I might think twice about coming after *you*. I don't know who your acquaintance was, but between the two of you, you've bowled out three quarters of one of the most lethal assassination teams in Europe. Possibly in the world. Well done you! Someone's going to want your head on a stick, I suspect. Oh! I forgot something. Just to put the Sato Nishiki cherry on top of the cake, when Eemil was doing *stir,* as the lower orders say, his prison nickname was the Raper. Wolfert was known as the Fuck Troll, if you please!'

This is a little too much for both of us and we start laughing. Lothar wipes tears out of his eyes. 'Well, holy mother of balls. I might also add that the Salo triplets and their cousin had a reputation for *never* failing. Under *any* circumstances. From what I can gather, this would be the first time they had taken on an assignment or assignments and had cocked it up in some way or other. They *certainly* do not suffer casualties.

'I assume Eemil will have to audition replacements if he is to continue his savage calling. Perhaps *you* might volunteer, Mr Cambridge. You may end up the best of chums. Go out to sleazy nightclubs and pick up hotel receptionists together!'

'I'll put that to him when we meet.'

'Ah, yes. As I said earlier, I'll keep filing away at the prison bars. There is, as we have discussed, a chance that he may not be returning home, wherever home might be. Some grim concrete abomination in Maastricht with IKEA furniture and drab orange nylon curtains, I wouldn't wonder.

'I'll be in touch the moment I find the seedy stone he's cringing under. I won't keep you any longer. You look terrible. Get some sleep. And watch your back. Oh, and if you need any muscle, I can tip Niculaiu the wink. Whatever it is, he'll do it for nothing. He is without a soul.'

We shake hands. 'Thanks, Lothar. Good work.'

'You're welcome, old horse.'

"Les Feuilles Mortes" is playing as Mrs Gardiner escorts me to the odorous outside world. I inhale her scent. Appropriately, she's wearing Chanel N°5. '*N'oubliez pas,*' she says, as she returns to the club interior.

I decide to walk back to Exeter Street. I need the exercise and I need to clear my head. A fine rain has just started, but it's not too savage yet and it feels good against my face. Heeding Lothar's words, I take every precaution to make sure I don't have company. I'm trying to be calm, but my heart leaps every time I hear a police siren.

It's a little past eleven-thirty now and the streets are still busy. I cross over into Soho Square, then turn down Greek Street and take a left into Old Compton Street to get to Charing Cross Road, keeping my mind blank and checking out every reflective surface that I can without making it too obvious what I'm doing.

I'm almost at Cambridge Circus when I get a little tingle of suspicion, so I cross over the road and lose myself in the crowds coming out of the Palace Theatre, doubling back down Romilly Street which is deserted from beginning to end. Then back up Shaftesbury Avenue, crossing the road and turn into Charing Cross Road once more.

I never find this sort of thing boring. It's quite enjoyable; relaxing, even, and I realise I'm smiling. A tall blonde girl in a lime green fake fur coat and a very short tangerine miniskirt smiles back at me as she passes. I wonder where she's going. Two policewomen walk by. I avoid looking at them.

The news about the Salo guys hasn't fully sunk in yet, though that may be because I'm a little wiped out from everything that's been going on. I think I need to sleep on it. It's pretty obvious, though, that that noxious little team, when they were still firing on all cylinders, seemed to be well out of the pay scale of a small setup like the OFRP.

Plus, quite apart from the financial aspect, it just wouldn't happen. This is big-time international stuff. So, who could have hired Eemil Salo and his compadres and why? With a reputation like theirs, whoever it was would expect no margin of error. Whoever it was had to use pricey, deniable European freelancers. Whoever it was had money and could access it quickly. Whoever it was wanted the very best.

You'd want to aim them at the target or targets and be damn sure your prey was exterminated quickly with the minimum of fuss. All three assassinations were completed in a very short space of time and, it would seem, at very short notice, though I can't quite see how that little group would have been responsible for Vanchev and Culpepper after their unexpected encounters with Polly and me.

Perhaps Eemil is a fit, versatile and motivated guy with a rapid recovery time. Maybe there are more people involved with this than is immediately apparent.

What are OFRP staffers Jameela Rabia Rafique and Alex Wictor Carlsson going to make of it? Will someone let them know how Culpepper died or will it be kept from them? Will they be discreetly inserted into some other department and everything will be swept under the carpet?

God, those two goons must not have known what had hit them when they walked into that bedroom and found themselves on the receiving end of Polly's skills. But they didn't lose heart and give up. They just regrouped and sent the next lot in. I keep forgetting Polly's dead. Mustn't forget. The rain is a little worse now and the ricochet wound is throbbing again.

I approach Exeter Street from the east side, turning into Catherine Street from the Strand. I walk on the right-hand side of the road, across the way from a busy Italian restaurant and trip over a green bin bag that's on the pavement. I can get a good view of the whole road from here.

There's someone standing outside the entrance to my flat, looking pretty soaked through. It's a woman. I cross over Wellington Street and pass the Lyceum Theatre. My heart sinks as I realise who it is. She's looking the wrong way, waiting, a dark blue Mulberry shoulder bag in her hands. I tap her on the shoulder. It makes her jump.

'Priscilla, what are you *doing*? This is dangerous. You shouldn't hang around here at this time of night on your own. Why didn't you call me? Look. You're soaked through.'

She's wearing a rather nice dark red feather print dress and black ankle boots. The dress is so wet you can see her bra through it and that's looking pretty much soaked, too.

Her hair is still tied back like it was the other day, but the water is dripping down her face from it. She needs to come inside.

'Come on. Come upstairs.'

'No. I mustn't, I mustn't. I don't feel anything for you. You must stop looking at me. Turn me away. Oh. Oh, I feel…I don't know what I feel. Can we go to bed? Immediately? I feel like I'm being driven insane by lust. I should be in an asylum. I should be in a straitjacket. They should throw away the key. I should become a nun. I should be locked up in a monastery.'

'Priscilla…'

'I just want to talk. Maybe for an hour. Maybe longer.'

'What sort of talk?'

'Crude. Explicit. I've prepared myself the way you like. You know what I'm talking about. My fiancé didn't care for it. He thought I was perverted. Perhaps I am. I know I am. *You* know I am. You can get me a cab afterwards. I won't mind. Send me back to my flat. Send me packing. I didn't know you wore glasses. Why is your hair grey?'

'You mean a nunnery, not a monastery.' I take her hand. 'Come on, let's get you out of those wet things.'

'Oh, God yes.'

17

ALPHA & CO

When I wake up, Priscilla is virtually lying on top of me. I can't wake her, so roll her onto her side and check my alarm for the time. It's 6.21. I inhale her perfume from the side of her neck. She's wearing Yves Saint Laurent Libre Eau de Parfum. I like Priscilla. She's nice, if a little mad. And a great lover.

She rolls back and lies across my chest, smiling to herself. I push her away again. She moans softly in her sleep. I shift her onto her back and in the same movement, get up off the bed and head for the bathroom.

I can see that the pillow, the sheets and a good part of Priscilla's face, hands, breasts and the inside of her thighs are stained with the 1-Day grey hair spray that's been on my hair, which is still a little damp from the rain last night. This stuff is going to have to come off.

Once in the bathroom, I check Lothar's handiwork on my arm. It's still looking OK, but then it was less than twenty-four hours ago that he put it on. What did he say? I mustn't get this wet for two days? I'll take the dressing off sometime tomorrow and see how it looks. I peer at myself in the mirror. A little pale, but then the hair dye plays tricks on your eyes.

I'm still not feeling fully up to scratch. Arm still

painful, but not nearly as bad as yesterday. I ponder whether to take more painkillers and decide not to bother. I'll take a couple of paracetamol after breakfast to eradicate the slight hangover I've got from last night. I think Mrs Gardiner put a quadruple vodka in my drink.

The more I think about it, the more confident I feel that Eemil Salo will not have fled the country. Now the information that Lothar gave me has had more time to sink in, I can't see him wanting to do anything else apart from hanging around in the UK until he gets a chance to off me.

He'll be waiting to see what happens with the police, which he must know about as my facial composite was certainly his work and he's probably seen it on the media by now.

But if he's still working for whoever, they're going to want him to capture me alive because of the memory stick. I'm assuming he's got a modicum of professionalism left after his recent sudden bereavements.

I take a shower, wash all the grey out and turn the Siemens on. While that's cooking, I wrap a towel around my waist and look for some paracetamol, but the pack's empty. Fenella must have taken the last of them the other morning or night or whatever it was.

I open the hair dye pack and take a look at the contents. There's an instruction sheet, a bottle of developer cream, a tube of post bold colour mask (whatever that is), a small bottle of colouring gel and a small plastic bag with something black in it. I open it up. It's a pair of black plastic gloves. It says on the pack that it's high intensity shimmering colour. Looking at all of this stuff is giving me mild anxiety, so I leave it on the kitchen surface and take two coffees into the bedroom.

Priscilla wakes up, stretches and smiles at me. She has a knockout figure and it's difficult not to want to start over. I lean forward and kiss her on the mouth. 'Coffee. Don't knock it over.'

'D'you know what time we finally went to sleep last night?' she purrs.

'No idea.'

'2.22. I'm sorry I was so…you know.'

'Don't worry about it.'

'But I was saying terrible things. I'm a monster, I know I am.'

Oh, God. 'You're not a monster, Priscilla.'

'But the self-disgust I'm feeling is…hm. So many wicked thoughts in my head. I imagined my ex-fiancé was watching us. And I could see him watching. I held his gaze while you consumed me; while you ravaged me. Do you want me to leave my job and move in with you?'

'Um. I can't really think about that while I'm working.'

'I was like a dam waiting to burst. All those things I said. I couldn't believe that filth was coming out of my mouth. I've never said things like that to anyone. I feel ashamed of myself now. But the shame is making me stimulated as I think of it. What happened to your arm?'

'Nothing. Just a scratch. Didn't want to get blood on my shirt.'

'Your hair's dark again.'

'Yeah. Look. I'm on a job and I have to have a different hair colour from my own. But that dye was only temporary. I bought this permanent gel in the chemist yesterday. I've never used it before. Could you take a look at the packet?'

I fetch the pack from the kitchen. I've had my hair dyed many times before, but it's always been a professional job, never this way. When I get back in the bedroom, she's sitting up and drinking her coffee. I can't take my eyes off her breasts. It's their indecent shape. She reminds me of one of those delightfully vulgar black and white 1950s pin-ups. *Delightfully vulgar.* I'm starting to sound like Lothar.

I hand her the pack and she glances at it. 'Yes. I've used this stuff. Not grey, though. Bright red. It was for a party. Your eyes are a different colour, too. I love your eyes. Would you like me to apply this for you?'

'Really? That would be very kind, Priscilla.'

She arches her back and wriggles her bottom on the sheet. 'But there's a price. And it'll have to be paid in advance. Like right now. And don't be gentle.'

*

Forty-five minutes later after a final rinse under the shower and an application of post bold colour mask, I take a look at myself in the mirror. Yes. Francie was right. This looks much more convincing and my complexion isn't as vampiric.

Priscilla is panting again. I wish she'd get dressed. My mobile starts ringing. For a moment, I think it must be Francie, giving me a time for her presentation, but it's Doug Teng. And so day two of the investigation begins.

'Hi, Mr Beckett. Not too early for you, I hope! I've been checking the info on this Dragan Vanchev guy every hour or so, but nothing came up until just now. Well, I say *now* – it was actually ten minutes ago. Anyway, they're just so *slow* there, y'know? I mean, it's the twenty-first century. Dragan! That's such a cool name. I wish I was called that. Dragan Teng – Computer Violator.'

'What did you find?'

'Usual mystifying medical terminology. They tried cardiac resuscitation in the ambulance, but no joy. The word 'unsurvivable' is in the notes. They also did something called VBG which I had to look up. It means venous blood gas. No results there. Also, the word 'acidotic'. I think that's to do with poisoning and that's why they do the VBG. Toxicology assay negative. The report is complete.

'Looks like your guy had a straightforward heart attack. It can happen, apparently, even in *your* world. My feeling is that they wouldn't have bothered with half of this stuff if he'd hadn't been so relatively young, but what the fuck do I know? Oh, and time from his reported collapse to the ambulance arriving was fourteen minutes, if that's any use.'

'OK, Doug. Great. Thanks. Cheque's in the post.'

'Ha ha. Not PayPal? I do PayPal now. I'm modern.'

All pretty predictable, then. Could be completely innocent, but under the circumstances, I'm thinking 'undetectable poison'. Then I get a text. It's from Francie. It says 'Your presentation awaits, Sir.' She's a hoot. My eyes feel heavy from keeping those damn lenses in all night.

*

I look at my watch as I'm buzzed into Francie's building. It's 9.09. She must have been up early. Either that, or she didn't go to bed last night.

'Hey, Mr PI. Come in. Everything's ready for you. Well, almost everything. Would you like a coffee?'

'Yes, please. Have you got any painkillers? Paracetamol

or something?'

'Sure thing.'

She looks very professional. She's wearing a figure-hugging black blazer dress that stops six inches above the knee and makes her jet-black hair look even blacker. Same orange bead necklace, same matching bangle and the same Clé de Cartier wristwatch. Silver stiletto court shoes with pointed toes that do great things to her calf muscles. Different perfume today, though. Not L'Heure Bleue. Sambac, jasmine, tuberose, maybe a hint of chocolate; I don't recognise it. Sexy, though. I believe they call jasmine 'the perfume of love'.

'I see you took my advice,' she says, handing me a coffee and a couple of Panadol capsules. 'It looks much better. The hair, I mean.'

'Took a while, but I think it was worth it.'

'Thank you for last night, by the way. I really enjoyed myself. Made me feel, I don't know, a bit more *feminine* than I've been feeling lately.' She gives me an arch, pursed-lipped grin as if it was her that I'd slept with last night and not Priscilla.

'It was my pleasure, Francie. You're great company.'

She smiles at me for several seconds. Strong eye contact. Then she turns on her heel and taps something on her laptop. A small black and silver cube on her desk that I hadn't noticed projects a large white rectangle onto her office wall. So, this is going to be a real presentation rather than a casual chat. OK. It means I can just sit back and enjoy it.

'I came here and set this going after I left you last night. Got that cab to make a detour and got another home after I'd finished. The program had to do one of these people at a time or the software would crash the system, so an overnight job was the obvious option. Once you kick the software's ass, it does it all on its own, though I was a little afraid I'd come in this morning and the computer would have melted. Took five and a half hours to come up with the goods, which is not bad, I guess.

'Oh, by the way. I had a few moments free this morning, you know? Just having a coffee break. Did a little research on you. Just out of curiosity. Want to see the results? Did a printout.'

'Sure.'

She swipes a sheet of paper off her desk and hands it to me. It's totally blank. I have to laugh.

'Not bad going in this day and age. Who the fuck are you?'

'I'm the Scarlet Pimpernel.'

'"They seek him here, they seek him there".'

'It's why I never go to Paris.'

She's looking edgy. 'Do you mind if I just do something before we start? Won't take long.'

'Sure.'

She walks over to the Bronze Chief in the corner of the room, puts a coin in the slot and pulls the lever. I can feel the tension as the reels spin. They stop on three lemons and a load of coins chug out into the tray.

'Yes! Yes! Fuck! Yes!' She turns to me. 'Pretty good, but it's the three bells I'm after. They're just old cents, but you know. Like I said. It's the buzz. Is this unusual? It just kind of gives me a release, you know? From stress? D'you know anyone else who does this?'

'Perfectly normal, Francie. All us PIs do it.'

'OK. Um. I took a look at the full film on that memory stick last night, too. Just to get better images of some of the subjects like I said yesterday. For the software, I mean. Just so you know. I can't think of anything to say. The words simply won't come. I had one fuck of a stiff drink when I got home. Just those kids. I mean, who the hell are they? Where – where did they get them from? What sort of sick fucks are running this whole thing? Are these the kids that you hear about going missing? I'm just at a loss. It's…fuck.'

'I don't know, Francie. I don't know what's going on. All I can tell you is that there's someone at the top of the pyramid who organises this and I'm going to find them.'

'You've got to let me in on this. You've got to let me help you in a more practical way than all this stuff,' She points at her laptop. 'If there's any kind of real-time help you need, it's imperative you let me know. I'm not a kid.'

'I'll keep it in mind.'

'OK.' She squints at the computer screen and touches it a few times. 'I'm not going to bore you with lots of text and I'm going to be brief, as I think that's what you want. I'm working from my own notes here, which you may look at afterwards if you wish. Pithy first impressions are always the best and generalisations are the only truth. That's what my dad used to say, anyway. If you have any questions, just ask.

'Like I told you yesterday, we can usually link an image to a name and as a side effect we get some decent info coming down the line. Just don't expect an authorised biography.

'I'll tell you who they are and what they are and why they may be relevant. I'll keep it short and sweet. You're not doing a frikkin' degree on these people. Like I said; potluck. Some of it's a tad sketchy and there are a couple of omissions. Can't be helped. Let's go.'

I sit down on one of the black leather sofas. At the top of the white rectangle on the wall the word 'ALPHA' appears. Then there's the dark, saturnine face, the bushy eyebrows, the male pattern baldness, the long, black sideburns. The way this software manipulates the image, it's as if he's in the room and is slowly looking from side to side. It's creepy. A full-body image appears to the left of the screen, the left shoulder hunched.

'This is Reda Desplechin. Age forty-nine. He's from Mauritania. Keeps slaves as it's legal there. Nice place. I may go there on holiday. French father, Mauritanian mother. Since the discovery of offshore oil at the beginning of this century, there have been ongoing and largely unsuccessful attempts to enter into trade agreements to purchase said oil.

'There are oil reserves elsewhere in this country, but details are perfunctory. Desplechin is the go-to guy. He's been schmoozed by the UK for some years now. If the UK are buying, then no one knows about it. He's not in the UK at this time.'

Mauritania. That's a long way to come for an evening's entertainment, whatever your interests may be. The screen goes white and the word 'BETA' appears. A rather handsome chap in his fifties. A full head of greying hair. Distinguished appearance. Confident smile. Good teeth. Nose job. Distinctive bright green eyes.

'Here we have Keld Mouritsen. Born in Denmark, currently domiciled in Saudi Arabia. Official nationality unknown. Aged sixty-seven. Father was Flemming Mouritsen, a successful arms dealer who made a fortune supplying arms to terrorist organisations of any stripe for over five decades. That is not to say that Keld Mouritsen supplies arms to terrorists. At least, there's no proof. But he is a kind of weapons broker.

'He is a frequent purchaser of arms from the US, the UK, China and the Czech Republic. From what I can gather, the UK is his biggest supplier by far. Second is the US, but that's way behind. What happens to these arms once he's bought them is not clear. Seems he also advises the Saudis how to look good to the rest of the world. Not in the UK at this time.'

So far, so big-time. Francie smiles at me, as if seeking my reassurance that it's all good enough. I nod my head. She blushes. The screen goes white and then the word 'GAMMA' appears. I know who GAMMA is, of course, but I didn't tell Francie. There's a chance she may have dug up something I didn't know about.

'This is Dragan Vanchev. Aged fifty-three. He has a wife, Lilyana, and two school-age daughters, Violeta and Veronika. Head of the economics division at the Bulgarian Embassy here in the UK. Travels abroad a lot. Thought to be a bit of a dodgy dealer. Probably only mildly corrupt as far as his own people are concerned as the Bulgarians aren't keen on that sort of thing and would boot him out if he got clumsy or went too far.

'Seems to have a knack for bringing a lot of trade to the UK from countries such as Slovenia, Albania, Montenegro and Croatia. It's not obvious how this is done or precisely what that trade is, but I reckon it's big bucks. He seems to be highly valued by the UK who may turn a blind eye to whatever it is he gets up to in his spare time or his professional time. Died yesterday morning in London. Heart attack.'

She flashes me a suspicious look. 'Did you *know* about this?'

I look innocent. It's not easy. 'News to me.'

She narrows her eyes. 'Hm.'

Next up is DELTA. This is an extremely overweight, totally bald guy who looks to be in his eighties. Bit of a mad stare on this shot. He reminds me of Aleister Crowley in his later years. Slightly Mediterranean look to his features. Not the sort of face you'd want to see peering through your bedroom window at midnight with a torch under his chin. I remember him from Polly's film and feel rather nauseated. I think I'd like to kill him.

'OK,' says Francie. 'This is my first fail. The software could not find anything, anywhere about this guy. There could be a number of reasons for this, but it's unimportant what they are. If someone was trying to eradicate his image from everywhere, that may be a cause. He could have gained a lot of weight, or had plastic surgery immediately after this, this *debauch*, or it could be an unknown complication with the software. But anyway. Sorry. I'll press on with him after you've gone.'

'That's OK. It adds to his mystique. You're doing a good job so far. Let's have EPSILON.'

I remember EPSILON. I can remember Vanchev trying to be mates with him right at the beginning and not getting any response. In this photograph, he looks a little bored. In fact, he looked a little bored all the way through the orgy, as if this was something he'd been doing a few times every day for several decades and was now experiencing a certain *ennui* about the whole thing. A blond, Nordic type. Wide chest. A fit-looking fifty or thereabouts. Gold jewellery.

'This is Grischa Rasputin, would you believe. No relation, as far as I can tell, though wouldn't that be great? Sixty years old. Originally from Kaliningrad. Hard to work out where he's domiciled now. Could be either

Norway or Iceland, but neither are certain. Another source said, ah, Republic of Ireland.

'This guy has been an important international money launderer since the 1980s at least, particularly in Poland. He also acts, from what I can tell, as a kind of private bank to the high and mighty. There are unfounded links to about a dozen senior British politicians to whom he's loaned large amounts of money at good rates of interest and also to at least four high-up members of the British Royal Family. Not in the UK at this time.' She looks over at me. 'These really are the crème de la crème of assholes, aren't they?'

'Elite vermin.'

'You said it, buddy. OK. Let's get ol' ZETA up there.'

I remember this one, too. Being a big uncle type to all of the kids there. Even in context, his behaviour was creepy. He's a very handsome, slim black guy and I'm putting his age as somewhere between thirty and fifty. Polly described him as the African-looking guy.

'This gentleman, and I use that word inaccurately, is from Eritrea. I say that before giving his name as I, or rather the software, had a few problems with this. The naming conventions in Eritrea are unusual and don't have what we would know as family names. Confuses the software.

'It looks to me that a child will take the first name of the parent as what *we* would call its surname. So, taking that into account, it seems as if his name is Mebratu Sesuna.

'Now Sesuna is a girl's name, which may be his mother's forename, but this guy also turns up as Mebratu Udinesi, which is an Italian name, so God knows what's going on. Might be he had Italian forebears as Italy used to own this country. Thought I'd better mention it in case it comes in useful.

'So! He's aged fifty. This guy is a notorious peddler of cheap generic pharmaceuticals. They're not *bad* pharmaceuticals, it's just that somehow, he manages to undercut legitimate sources. It's pretty unethical but complicated. The British buy a lot of these to save money but keep it to themselves and don't pass the savings on to whoever the customer is; the taxpayer, I guess. So, he saves the UK a major shitload of money, but I don't understand how he's rewarded for this. Basically, I've got more on this guy's name origin than I have on what he does, but there you go. Now for ETA.'

I remember this one alright. The master of ceremonies. The piano player. The one Polly called Goatee Beard. The one everyone applauded. The one who schmoozed his way around the evening's festivities. The one who the women kept looking at when things started going weird with the other creeps. Is he a guest with benefits or is he somehow in charge? I thought I caught an amused look on Francie's face just then, but whatever it was, it passed. In this photograph, the goatee beard is absent.

'This is Simon Randwijck van Cutsem. He's either fifty-seven years old or sixty-one years old. He's on record as getting his money from being a consultant in financial engineering, though who he did this for or when he last did it is unknown. It's not clear whether his skills are used to the advantage of the UK or not, and we don't know if that's the reason he's at the orgy.

'Financial engineering involves using math to help with monetary problems and drifts into the fields of statistics, computing and applied mathematics. That's in case you were wondering what it was. Now you know.

'He is a UK citizen. His mother was the semi-famous concert pianist Lieke van Cutsem and Simon himself was a bit of a prodigy on the piano, giving frequent concerts in this country from the age of fourteen. His father, Wigbert van Cutsem, was a mergers and acquisitions lawyer until his death, but I couldn't find out when that was.

'All this was gleaned from a solitary newspaper article that the software turned up. Simon van Cutsem is currently residing in the UK.' Another amused look flits across her face. 'A little more on him later. Now let's move on and take a look at THETA.'

The rather startling image of the black woman at the orgy fills the screen. I can imagine this being a print. In the composite 3D still that Francie has chosen and projected, she's wearing the green and yellow head wrap that Polly thought might be traditional African garb of some sort. I'm not so sure. Looks to me like contemporary high fashion. What a face. She's absolutely mesmerising.

Francie laughs. 'Are you ready? Have you recovered? Well, it's bad news, I'm afraid. This is the other fail. Or at least it is so far. Nothing came up for her at all,' She coughs to clear her throat. 'Zero. Zilch. Zip. By the way, I'll keep the software working on her and DELTA. Might be a software problem. There may be some reason that it failed to ID them that isn't obvious at the moment. I'm quite surprised, though. She's quite a beauty. I thought she might be a model or something, but you never can tell,' Once again, she smiles to herself, as if she's keeping something back. 'But I had much better luck with IOTA.'

The equally striking face of the redhead at the orgy is

projected onto the wall. Very pale skin against the luxuriant amber hair, the silver body chain over her shoulders and breasts and the loveliest green eyes. Once again, I suspect she's wearing coloured lenses, but then so am I. Maybe it'll be a talking point if we ever meet.

Her beauty has a greater erotic charge than the other girl. It's the expression on her face and it reminds me a little of Mrs Gardiner. A full mouth, but with a slightly cruel downturn that matches those knowing, mocking eyes. I can't get the image of her and THETA at the orgy out of my mind. Perhaps I never will.

'We are now looking at Ms Liva Mette Søndergaard aka Heidi Savage. Age is twenty-eight or thirty-three or thirty-six. There are a variety of sources for that detail, none of them are official, or, I would guess, reliable.

'She's a Danish national. From what I can glean from the fragmented information on her, she's been living and working in the UK for almost five years and seems to have liberated herself from the need to have work permits, visas and so on and so forth. Either she's been very lucky and has somehow slipped under the radar or someone influential is pulling strings for her.'

'Interesting. I wonder who might be able to pull strings like that, if that's what's happened?'

'No idea. It might be worth looking into if all else fails. But what a scoop, huh? This is a supershit deal. Heidi fuckin' Savage! I recognised her straight away but still ran the programme just to be one hundred per cent sure!'

'I don't understand.'

'Heidi Savage! Don't you watch porn?'

This makes me laugh. 'Obviously not as much as I should.'

'She's huge. I mean, she's the *bomb* in porn DVDs.

She's probably been around for maybe a decade now. At least. *Space Bitches? Latex She-Demons? Alien Lesbian Housewives? While Her Husband Watches? Secretary School?* No? Jesus Christ, that's some gap in your education there, honey. You should see her in action. You'd faint. I'll lend you some Blu-rays.'

'Thank you.'

She walks over to the coffee area and starts to make two more coffees. 'OK. Let's forget about Heidi for the moment and see what hits us about all those...did I tell you about my sister? I did, didn't I. Just wait until I tell her about this, which I would never do as it would be totally unethical and impinge upon Heidi's privacy.

'You know — I think she was in a film with Heidi a couple years back. In fact, I'm sure she was. What are you getting from the guys I've managed to profile so far? What jumps out? Hold on.'

She touches something on her computer and a new image appears on the wall, the six identified males in two neat rows, staring out at us like some sinister, unhinged and malignant Warhol screen print.

She sits next to me on the sofa, turning to face me and placing her coffee on the table in front of us. I look at her legs. Once again, I'm aware of the heat of her body and the bouquet of that perfume. She says, 'Now if that ain't a frikkin' rogues' gallery, I don't know what is.'

'Well, first of all, they're all roughly in the same age range, approximately fifty to sixty-five,' I say. 'That may have no significance whatsoever, but there it is. Maybe that's when you start getting into this sort of stuff. Maybe that's when you start getting powerful and rich and get *given* this sort of stuff.

'Secondly, they're all involved in big money

occupations: oil supplies, arms, international trade, money laundering, private banking, pharmaceuticals and finance. Thirdly, in one way or another they all seem like crooks.'

'That's exactly my impression, Daniel, but crooks that this country has to suck up to in some way. People that they can't afford to get on the bad side of, maybe. People they *need*. In one way or another, they've all got something that the UK wants, and it seems to be almost always connected to big money. They all have *semi-legal* stamped all over their faces.

'So, when these guys – and they might not be the only ones, remember; we may be only looking through a narrow window – when *these* guys come over here, they have to lay on a little entertainment for them. They have to cater to their tastes. It doesn't matter how twisted and perverse those tastes are, your government will bend over backwards to get it for them. Is it distasteful for them? The government, I mean? Who knows? Maybe they simply have no choice.'

'You always have a choice.' I finish my coffee before it gets cold. 'The whole thing would require elaborate secrecy and sophisticated planning. There would be a lot of money involved.

'Just for a start, wherever those children are coming from, someone would have to organise that, someone would have to organise the transportation, someone would have to be in touch, perhaps regularly, with human trafficking personnel. That's only a guess, but I can't imagine it's far from the truth.

'Also, those kids looked zombied out. How is that done and who does it? Do they employ medical staff? Doctors? Nurses? Scientists? If so, who are they and where do they come from? Who maintains these kids, dresses them, feeds them? Perhaps a little more worryingly, what happens to these children after the orgies? I can't imagine they'd be allowed to return to their former lives, or even their former countries.'

'Shit. I feel a bit sick.'

'There's also the question, which may not be relevant, of why these little get-togethers are in groups of this size. How specialist is this? Is it at the request of the participants? Do they like other men who share their tastes being there? Do they like being watched? Do they like watching? Is it some sexual kink that we're not aware of?'

'Would ten of them be too many? Would four of them not be enough? Do they get bonded in some way that's relevant to all of this? Do they retire to some room with brandy and cigars and discuss important business afterwards? Is the van Cutsem guy a participant or is he working?'

'Plus, of course, the women,' Francie replies. 'I mean, what's that all about? Considering what these guys are getting up to, those two seem a little out of place. And – fuck – how can they *do* that? How can they allow themselves to be a part of it? And the guy playing the piano. I'm holding a big bag of WTF here.'

'Yeah. It's confusing. The women could be just a form of decadent eye candy. You could argue that they fit in with the champagne, the stuffed birds, the salacious murals, the caviar, the piano playing; they certainly enhance the erotic ambience. Maybe the guests like to pretend they're in ancient Rome.

'And once again, that brings us back to the money being spent here. You say that Liva Mette Søndergaard aka Heidi Savage is a big star in her field. They'd *have* to be paying her. I can't imagine that she and the other woman would be doing this for nothing. And they'd have to find a way of guaranteeing that neither would blab.

'Either they'd have total and absolute trust in both of them, or they'd pay them off in some way; some sort of immense financial benefit. Maybe the women are ashamed and would never talk about doing something like this.

'Maybe the women are frightened. Maybe they've been threatened, though threats would be no basis for hiring professionals of this sort. Maybe, at some time in the future, they get "disappeared". Who knows?'

Then, of course, there's the slightest whiff of a security leak and they can afford to get the big Frisian guns out and swiftly eradicate Polly, and possibly Culpepper and Vanchev. Polly's film of that evening's events set such alarm bells ringing, that someone thought nothing of ordering the murders of those three. Yes. There's a lot of money about.

'I tell you what, Daniel,' says Francie, now looking a bit pale. 'I know you're a hot-shot, hot-shit PI and all the rest of it, but can I give you some advice on how you should proceed from here?'

'Of course you can, Francie.'

She leans forwards, taps her computer and isolates the image of Simon van Cutsem, whose image obliterates all the others on the wall. That amused look I caught on her face earlier is back.

'Call it a hunch, call it female intuition, but if I were you, I'd make *this* guy your prime target, your next lead or whatever you want to call it.'

'Because he's the only one in the UK at the moment? Because the others seemed to look up to him? Because he was more of a master of ceremonies than a regular guest?'

She turns to face me. 'No. Because he died three years ago.'

18

RAISING THE DEAD

It takes me and Francie two and a quarter hours on her computer before we come up with a satisfactory, if sometimes vague, picture of Simon van Cutsem and what happened to him.

It looks suspiciously like a load of whitewashing has gone on, some of it fairly recent, but whoever's responsible didn't have their heart in it as there's quite a bit of information hanging around that's easy to access.

Maybe someone didn't think it was worth the trouble as he's officially no longer in the land of the living. We look at everything. You never can tell when something apparently irrelevant will become useful. I guess we could visit libraries and look at old newspaper cuttings, but we simply don't have the time.

He was born sixty-one years ago in Wonersh, Surrey. We already had a few details of his parents, but he also had an older sister, Suze Hannah van Cutsem, an architect, who died thirteen years ago from PNP, which turns out to be something called Paraneoplastic pemphigus, a rare autoimmune disease.

We already knew that his mother, Lieke van Cutsem, was a concert pianist, but we didn't know that she committed suicide when Simon was fifty-eight. We found several photographs of her, mostly three to four decades old, and these were usually promotional shots for her concerts, which seemed to be mainly in the UK, but also in France, Switzerland and Poland. She was quite beautiful; dark, and always with a rather melancholy expression on her face. Sad eyes. Nice hair. Good figure.

Following in his mother's footsteps, perhaps, Simon started piano lessons when he was four years old and was taught locally by Professor László Geöcze, a Hungarian who had moved to the UK after the uprising. By the time Simon was seven, he had progressed to giving concerts in local town halls etc and it was thought that he might take his mother's career path. He continued to take lessons and give occasional concerts, but it never became a full-time thing.

His father, as we already knew, was a mergers and acquisitions lawyer and it seemed that he commuted to London every day to work in a company called Archambeau & Sons. He was a member of the Wonersh Bowling Club, which was founded in 1925. He was an Old Carthusian and sent the thirteen-year-old Simon to Charterhouse School in nearby Godalming, where he spent the next five years. His father died from polycystic kidney disease just after Simon took his A-Levels.

We then have Simon studying Mathematical Sciences for three years at Oxford University, graduating, then going into financial engineering, working for a company called Quinn de Carteret Consulting in the City of London, a job he acquired through friends of his father, and which, apparently, he was quite good at.

This job, and in fact this *career*, came screeching to an abrupt halt when Simon, at the age of twenty-five, was charged with causing a person to engage in sexual activity without consent. Other than that titbit there are no details of this case anywhere on the net. I assume they've either been wiped or are tucked away in inaccessible police files somewhere.

It doesn't look like the case made the papers. I had considered giving Doug Teng another call, but at the moment, just knowing about it may be enough. I'm also trying to keep my 'researchers', Lothar, Francie and Doug, in the dark about each other's existence and what I'm asking each of them to do.

Whatever, it doesn't look like van Cutsem went to prison for this. If I have to, I'll consult a lawyer and find out what could have happened; sentencing chops and changes as the years go by. There was also an article that Francie turned up about him being suspected of holding a child to ransom concurrent with all the other stuff. Nothing further on that. Perhaps he was just expanding his business interests.

Then we lose him for about thirteen years. By now he'd be in his late thirties and he's being charged with administering a substance with intent. We find one newspaper report about it. The victim was a woman called Patrice Bridgewater, aged twenty-six, who reported him to the police for putting some sort of benzodiazepine in her drink in a pub called The Admiral Codrington in Chelsea. But we could find nothing else on that case, and once again he seems to disappear into the ether.

But in the same article, it mentions that he was once suspected of kidnapping and false imprisonment of a minor. Whatever was going on there, he either got away with it or the report got something wrong.

It doesn't turn up again, but links in a roundabout way to that other report of holding a child to ransom. Or perhaps it doesn't. Whatever, none of these things say much for his character and I won't be taking him on as an apprentice.

Then, a little over three years ago, he comes back with a bang. He was arrested for procuring or pandering (the same thing, I think) and for multiple counts of sex with a minor, arranging or facilitating the commission of a child sex offence and, yet again, administering a substance with intent.

I don't think he suddenly went mad at this point. I think this type of activity had been going on for quite a long time, and the law had finally caught up with him. Maybe he got too cocky and slipped up. Maybe it was karma or a tough break. As there was something like a two-decade gap between the sexual offences that we found on here, I think he was just careful, lucky, or was paying people off. We may never know.

It went to trial and he was given eleven years. This was a big story, but not one I can recall reading about at the time, which is not too surprising as I was out of the country.

The press managed to dredge up who his mother was and that's when she committed suicide. She was almost eighty at the time and botched her suicide quite badly. She used paraquat, a highly toxic weed killer that's not only effective, but quite cheap. Not easy to get hold of here nowadays, though. From all accounts, it's a ghastly, painful way to go. Death can take anything from one day to three weeks.

We find an article about his arrest. There's a grainy photograph of him; the first one we've found. He doesn't have the goatee beard yet. I smile when I see that one of the arresting officers was a Detective Constable Olivia Bream. Well how about that.

'What're you grinning about?' asks Francie.

'I'm acquainted with one of the arresting officers.' I tap the screen with my finger. 'That one. Olivia Bream. She's an inspector now.'

'Looks like she won't take shit.'

'That's a pretty accurate assessment.'

Anyway, Simon van Cutsem didn't hang around in prison for too long. Eleven years must have seemed like such a fag to a man of his sensibilities; such a bore. So, nine days into his sentence, he hanged himself in his cell.

We had a damn good search but couldn't find out how he did it or whether there was an enquiry. Prison warders are not prone to allowing you rope, leather belts or other ligatures when they lock you up for the night, so it's a bit of a puzzle.

And now, three years later, as if by magic, he's hosting sex parties for wealthy and influential scumbags in a big house in Richmond. Hanging yourself ain't what it used to be.

Francie clasps her fingers behind her neck, closes her eyes and arches her back, which is probably stiff from all the sitting. I try to stop myself, but I'm forced to look at the effect this has on the jut of her breasts.

'I may have my eyes closed, but I know where you're looking, Mr PI,' she says, smiling to herself.

'I have no idea what you're talking about.'

'Yes, you do.'

'No, I don't.'

'I'm going to open my eyes now and catch you red-handed.'

I lower my gaze so I'm looking at her legs. 'See? Just admiring your firm thighs.'

'Hm. Flattery will get you everywhere.'

'That's what all the girls say.'

She smirks. 'But they *are* firm. Wanna squeeze?'

'One at a time or both together?'

'Oh, Jeez.'

She gets up and makes another couple of coffees. We sit on opposite sofas so we can look at each other while we speculate.

'OK,' she says. 'He's not dead. First of all, how did he get that done?'

'It would have been tricky but not impossible. Because of the nature of his offences, he would have been a Category A prisoner. But I can't see how you'd do it without the collusion of the prison governor and one or more prison officers. Maybe even a medical officer or a coroner. It would all depend on where he was being kept.

'We don't have that information, but it's unlikely he was in a cell where he had immediate neighbours. If you were organising something like this, you would not want witnesses hearing or seeing things they shouldn't.

'Maybe they found a way of getting him in solitary confinement; some jumped up charge or other. Maybe he feigned illness and was taken to some sort of medical enclave. Whatever, the avowed hanging could not be observed by anyone, as it hadn't really happened.'

'Sure,' she says, nodding her head. 'So, once it had happened, or *not* happened as is obviously the case here, other prisoners and people in the outside world would just have the word of the prison authorities that such an event had taken place. I mean, my first thought was that you'd have to get a lookalike fresh corpse from somewhere and string it up in the cell, pretending it was him, but you wouldn't even have to do *that*.'

'No. I mean, if you were a fellow prisoner, you'd

probably hear about it the next day from other inmates or maybe from a warder. The news would get around fast. It could just be planted with one person and in an enclosed society like a prison, it would become general knowledge very quickly.'

'Would you like a cookie?'

'Yes, please.'

She returns with a large plate of chocolate and hazelnut cookies and places them on the coffee table. I take one.

'So, Mr Beckett. I'm not that familiar with the way UK prisons work, but if there was collusion going on, my guess is that once he'd been isolated, he could, in effect, just walk out the front door, undoubtedly wearing a big hat and a false moustache.'

'You're probably right. Though I think your point about getting hold of a fresh corpse has some relevance. It's not that difficult to get hold of a dead body if you know where to look and *someone* had to be buried or cremated, just for appearances' sake. There was no report of a funeral, but I assume there was one. Normally, there would be a coroner's inquest, but they obviously avoided that little problem, as well.'

'Yeah, but why bother with a funeral at all? They could have got away with a fake one or just not bothered. I mean, his parents and sister were all dead. He didn't seem like the sort of guy who'd have a shitload of buddies, and who was going to give him a send-off after what *he'd* been doing? Other perverts? Maybe he belonged to a club. Perhaps they looked under a stone and there were all his debauched amigos.'

'Yes, well, whatever happened, it went to the press and was done and dusted.'

'Until now. So, second of all. Who would do this and why? Who sprang this dude?' She stands up and starts pacing, running a hand through her hair every now and then. I watch the sway of her hips as she walks. She has a great ass.

I usually like complicated cases, but this is both complicated *and* tiring. My being less than one hundred per cent fit isn't helping things and I feel a little drained after last night's session with Priscilla followed by four hours' sleep. I stifle a yawn.

'This is just speculation,' I say. 'But we have to start somewhere. Let's look at what he was being charged with. We may not know the whole story but let's work with what we've got. Take the procuring first. What sort of individual was he procuring and who was he procuring them for?'

'Could it have been kids?'

'It could have been. Look at Richmond.'

She narrows her eyes. 'So, who was he doing it *for*? The rich and influential like our little bunch of creepy pals here?' She taps her finger on the computer screen.

'Maybe not directly. Maybe a third party was, for want of a better word, *employing* him to procure for people like that.'

'And they didn't want him languishing in prison *because…*'

'Because he knew too much. Perhaps he'd threatened them with blackmail, perhaps he'd threatened them with going to the media, perhaps he'd threatened them with writing his memoirs.

'One way of doing it would be to hire someone to whom you give a copy of, for example, a memory stick. You call them every day. If you don't call them by a certain time, they send the memory stick to the newspaper or newspapers or media outlet of your choice.'

'So why not bump him off? Why not pick him up, taser him and stuff him in an industrial meat grinder?'

'I don't know. There must be some reason for that, but we just haven't got to it yet. That other thing – *arranging or facilitating the commission of a child sex offence.* That kind of fits in with our theory, too.

'I'd imagine that at the time of his arrest, even the police didn't quite know the extent of what was going on, what he'd been up to, what he was doing, why he was doing it.'

'So, someone from Spook City has him spirited out of prison,' she says. 'We know not why.'

'And they must have given him a new identity. It would have been the only course of action if they wanted him out on the streets again, so to speak, and continuing where he left off, which is plainly what he's been doing.'

'And we have no idea what that identity is.'

'But there's one thing for certain. The reason that my client is dead, was because she'd filmed van Cutsem. Suddenly this big secret was in danger of being exposed.'

'It was a *she*?'

Sod it. I think I can be straight with her now. Relatively straight, anyway. 'Yes, it was. Her name was Judith Hart (more lies) and her boss was called Alistair Culpepper. They both worked for a small unit within the Security Service. They were trying to get material to blackmail the late Dragan Vanchev; he was GAMMA on our list.

'She filmed that orgy and that's when all the trouble started. She thought her boss had sold her out and it was in some way connected to Vanchev. She was killed, then

Vanchev, then Culpepper, though maybe not in that exact order. It was as if someone was attempting to tie off the whole operation complete with its subject and personnel and hope it would go away.'

'But they didn't bank on you.'

'No.'

'She was a friend of yours, wasn't she?'

'Yes.'

'OK. Here's my plan. Let's take it as read that van Cutsem organised the entertainment for that little shindig. He was also acting as the maître d', if you like. Forget the piano playing for the moment. From what we know of him so far, I think the delightful musical accompaniment was him just amusing himself or showing off.

'It may not have been his house, he may not have picked the guests, he may even have had nothing to do with supplying the kids. But I'll bet you anything he organised the entertainment and hired those two girls, otherwise, what the fuck would he be doing there? We've only ID'd one of them, but if we can get hold of *her*, we can maybe find out what he's calling himself now and that'll be a start.'

I decide not to give her any detailed info about the Salo aspect of the case I think that would be a little too much. I don't want her to come unglued at this stage of the game. Maybe later.

I think of contacting Doug Teng once more, but this wouldn't be his area of expertise. He can hack, but he has to have a hackable target, like a company or organisation. This is different; and as Francie discovered, Heidi Savage aka Liva Mette Søndergaard seems to have been living an untraceable, off-the-books existence for five years or more.

'That seems logical,' I say. 'But we don't have addresses or telephone numbers for any of the people on that list. We have about as much chance of locating her as we do of locating van Cutsem. Someone like that; she'd *have* to be difficult to find. Mad, obsessed fans and all the rest. It'd be like looking for a needle in a haystack.'

She gives me a smug little smile. 'Not necessarily.'

19

TASTE OF GIRL

I eat another cookie. The pain in my arm is back. Francie paces around the room once more, mobile in her hand. 'Come on. Pick up. I know it's early. You damn lazy bitch.'

'Who are you…?'

She holds out a hand to shut me up. 'Hey, fucko! How you doin'? Is it early there? Really? Shit. I'm sorry. Were you asleep? It's not quite lunchtime here yet. Just wanted to know how things were going with you. It's been about a month. No, I can't call later, I've, er, I've, er, got a big job on. Yeah. Then I've got a hot date with this guy I picked up in a bar yesterday. His name? Nigel. Yeah. Yeah. All English guys are called Nigel. Ha ha. Yeah, they're mostly fags. Yeah.'

She's funny. I'm getting into this conversation now, whatever it's about.

She sits down and puts her feet up on the desk. 'How's Mom? Really? You're kidding me? Black-footed ferrets? I've never even heard of them. I thought it was still northern spotted owls. OK. OK. OK. Yeah. Yeah. Yeah. No. No. No.

'Did Dad get that dental implant afterwards? How much? You're *kidding*. They need to round all dentists up and stick them in prison. And they call themselves doctors now; can you believe it? They're doing it over here now, too. They're not frikkin' doctors, they're dentists. In fact, they're not even dentists, they're crooks. If they had the brains to be doctors, they'd be doctors. If they want to be a crook that badly why don't they rob banks? I'll tell you why – no guts.

'Yeah. Yeah. Yeah. Mm-hm? Listen, can I ask you something? No, it's not about *that*. It's *not*. Jesus, can you shut up for a moment? Let me speak. I said let me *speak*. Listen – d'you remember that film you did with Heidi Savage? Heidi Savage. *Savage*. Danish chick. Big red hair. About seven foot tall. Tits. Could have been two or three years ago now. Can't for the life of me remember what it was called. Really? Was that it? Are you sure? *Taste of Girl?* Yeah. Yeah. Actually, now that does ring a bell. You do? Did you? Wow. How many of you? Jesus. What was that like? Oh, fuck. Did she? Yeah? Send me a copy. I want.'

This sounds like it's going to take some time. I make some more coffee. Francie rolls her eyes at me in exasperation as she listens to the voice on the other end for about a minute.

'Aw. I hope you dumped her, baby. Yeah. You're too good for girls like that. Listen. No. It's just that I was thinking about Heidi Savage the other day and I was talking to a friend of mine about her movies and you can't get them over here. Tell you, I was just wondering if you could go right to the source, you know?

'Yeah. Yeah. She lives in the UK somewhere now. Nope. I have no idea. Yeah. No. I tried Amazon, but they don't stock them. Too hardcore, I guess. Yeah. That's her. Liva. Liva Mette Søndergaard. Yeah. Yeah, it is a nice name. Is that what it means? Really? South farm? Wow. Didn't know that. That website I use here – *they* didn't have them, either.

'Say, you wouldn't happen to have a number or an email address or anything for her, would you? Just a shot in the dark, really. Worth a try. I really talked her up to this friend of mine and it's really damn frustrating that you can't… OK. I'll hold on.'

She gives me a slightly insane grin that could indicate anything. But I realise what she's doing now. She's pretty slick. Maybe we should go into business together. Get an office with a secretary like in the movies. She opens a drawer in her desk and pulls out a pizza takeaway menu and a black Surcotto rollerball pen. She scribbles away.

'Yeah. Yeah. OK. Got it. And this is a recent number, yeah? OK. Well let's hope I strike it rich! Is she? Is she? Aw. Sure, I'll say hello from you. I won't forget. OK. Have to go now, hun. Don't forget what I told you about Lindy. No. No. OK. Love you, babe.'

She hands me the pizza menu. 'Heidi Savage's mobile number. My sis thinks it's recent. Want to give her a call?'

This is something that Doug *can* do. 'No. There's a guy I work with who's a bit of a wizard with stuff. I'll get him to find the address that this phone is registered to. Once he discovers the network, he can find the customer details. It's never a good idea to tell someone you're going to visit if it's a job like this. They can just say no or go out. Surprise is always the best option.'

Ten minutes later Doug Teng rings back. The account associated with that mobile is registered to a Miss L. Søndergaard, 139 Fife Road, East Sheen, London SW14.

'That was amazing, Francie. I can't thank you enough.'

'You're welcome. And hey – be nice – my sister said she's really sweet.'

'I promise I'll be on my best behaviour.'

'That's what I'm afraid of. There was no point in trying to contact her any other way. Just ask my sis. Like you said, these girls get hit on/hunted down by rabid, mouth-frothing, knuckle-draggers all of the frikkin' time.'

'Is that how you see me?'

'Of course.'

I get my jacket on and head out of the door. It's not even mid-day yet. That was a good morning's work.

*

I pick up a black cab outside a branch of LA Fitness in Theobald's Lane and get it to take me to East Sheen. The driver doesn't look too pleased. This is a fair way out of Central London and it's unlikely he'll pick up any fares on the way back. On the plus side, his surliness means I don't have to bat off any tedious chat, which is good, as I'm not in the mood.

East Sheen is right next door to Richmond, and I wonder if this is just a coincidence. Maybe Liva only agreed to the orgy as it was just around the corner from where she lived.

Fife Lane is affluent and remarkably leafy with Richmond Park right across the road from all the houses. I imagine that this is an expensive area to live in. There are lots of big metal security gates, conspicuous CCTV cameras, digital keypads and proximity readers. If you can spot any cars in the well-hidden driveways, they're almost always BMW 320s, Lexus IS-250s or Chrysler 300s, with one Jaguar F-Type in burnt orange.

The numbering of the houses doesn't seem to make any sense. It stops at number 41, then there's a gap with a bit of woodland, then there's a large, stone-built nineteenth-century church, with lots of pink roses and lavender bushes in the grounds. Right next to that is number 139, which I walk past while giving it a quick indifferent glance.

It's a detached, well-kept five-bedroom house, maybe built in the 1930s. Probably worth a few million, considering its size and location. A large, brick conservatory to the right with pink honeysuckle up the walls. No security gate, but an ADT bell box above the front door. It all seems very welcoming and open compared to some of the houses further up the road.

There's a blue Alpine A110 sports car parked on the gravel drive. It looks brand new. I keep walking and try to think of what I'm going to say to her when she opens the door. I can't just leap in and start interrogating her about van Cutsem. I have no idea what she's like (apart from being really sweet according to Francie's sister) and I don't want to upset her and make her dry up. I'll just have to play it by ear and see what pops into my head. This never works.

I turn back, walk up the drive, press the bell push and wait. Nothing happens. Is she out? There are blinds covering the ground-floor windows so I can't see inside. The front door is solid wood so I can't look in the hall.

Then I hear a mortice being unlocked and the door opens. It's her. It looks like she's just got up. She's makeup free, her hair is tousled and she's wearing a short blue silk robe with lace trimming. God almighty; she's gorgeous.

Her eyes are hazel, so I was right about the lenses. Long, long legs, beautiful face, noticeably busty, sensuous, stunning and striking. She could almost be my height. I'm in love with her. She looks suspicious.

'Yes?'

I turn on the full Hugh Grant. 'Hi. Miss Søndergaard? I'm *terribly* sorry if I've woken you up. I can come back later if it's not convenient. I only want a quick word.'

She frowns. 'What is it? What do you want?' Only a hint of a Danish accent. If I didn't know where she was from, I wouldn't have caught it.

I give her what I hope is a charming smile and hand her one of my business cards. She has a lovely mouth, not so cruel in real life; full, kissable. I must concentrate. 'My name is Daniel Beckett. I'm a private investigator. I would be *so* grateful if I could just have five minutes of your time to ask you a few questions.' I laugh. 'Nothing personal; you have my word as a gentleman of honour.'

Was that self-deprecating enough? It certainly fooled me. She looks at my card. She looks at me. She looks at my card again. A Bengal cat rubs against her legs then attempts to escape. She picks it up in one hand and tosses it into the house. She smiles and then the smile disappears.

'It does not say you are a detective on this card.' She pings it idly with a middle finger to see if it makes an interesting noise. It doesn't.

'I was trying to be subtle when I had them made. No one likes a show-off. Besides, the cool quotient of my job can be overwhelming for some.'

She smiles. She laughs. Then she's serious. 'You are quite charming.'

'Thank you. No one's ever said that to me before.'

She looks very slightly alarmed. 'Am I in trouble?'

'In trouble? No. Not at *all*. I'm not the police. This is just...this is just...'

'Come in.'

She walks into the house. I close the door behind us and follow, looking at her legs. I don't know if she's entirely responsible for the decor, but this place looks marvellous. It's like an Art Deco museum. The wallpaper in the hallway is an eye-catching black and gold peacock feather-inspired design, covered in framed 1930s posters for various Monaco Grand Prix events, Old Gold cigarettes, Onyx bicycles and Bonal aperitif, plus a silver-framed print of Marie Laurencin's portrait of Coco Chanel.

To my left is an enormous clock which looks as if it was designed by Sonia Delaunay and underneath that, a beautiful sepia-tinted photograph of Liva herself, naked, up a ladder, in what looks like an artist's studio. She has her back to the viewer and is looking over her shoulder. It looks like she's got hair extensions in. Sexy bottom.

Her sitting room is even more astounding: huge bevelled mirrors in wrought iron frames, a sizeable brass display cabinet filled with Lalique vases and small glass sculptures, a three-panelled lacquer screen featuring a naked woman holding a cat and a three-piece suite in dark walnut and white leather.

Next to a flowery stained-glass window, there's what looks like a 1930s drinks trolley covered with crystal obelisks of calcite, obsidian, lemon quartz, carnelian, red jasper and amethyst. There's so much stuff that it's overpowering. I quickly scan the room. I'm looking for something to hang on to; something to talk to her about. She senses my amazement.

'Do you like my house?'

'*Det er magisk!*'

Her eyes widen. 'You speak Danish?'

I smile at her. 'Enough to flatter your taste with, Miss

Søndergaard.' I'm such a slimeball. Then I spot what I'm looking for. Three large etchings on the wall to the right of the fireplace that *have* to be by Louis Icart. I walk up to them, take a quick look and then turn to face her.

'Louis Icart. Are these originals?'

She smiles and her whole face lights up, any uncertainty suddenly vanishing. She looks delighted. 'Yes, they are! I bought them at auction. Sotheby's. Do you know it?'

'I know *of* it. I've never been inside. Were they expensive?'

'Oh, but you should *go*. The one in the middle was only 3,500 pounds and the other two were 4,800 each. I was so happy. Look.'

She points to the one in the centre. Three virtually naked girls lie on the grass. It looks as if three men have left them and are heading towards a church. One of the girls has her legs spread. The church has the sun behind it and casts a long, phallic shadow.

'He is making fun of the church, I think. Those men are meant to be priests, leaving the women behind to go and pray to their god. But the shadow of the church. It is like a giant penis, yes? I love it. It is so erotic. Those girls are so ready. And this one.' She points to another etching of an elegant young blonde woman in eighteenth-century clothing who is baring her breasts. 'This is one of Icart's illustrations for *Félicia ou Mes Fredaines* by Andrea de Nerciat. Is it not delightful? I would like to have met her. She is so pretty. Of course,' she frowns a little, 'he may not have used a model. Have you read the book?'

'No. I'm afraid not.' This is all slowly slipping out of my control and I'm beginning to forget why I'm here. But I'm going to run with it. She goes to a bookcase, removes a hefty hardback and hands it to me.

'You may borrow it. You read French, I assume?'

'Yes, I do. And thank you, Miss Søndergaard.'

'My pleasure. What was it? Daniel? You must call me Liva. Oh, and this.' She fetches another book from the same bookcase. '*The Romance of Perfume* by Richard Le Gallienne. Drawings by Barbier. I have just finished it. It is a history of perfume and its uses. You must read it. Would you like some tea?'

'That would be very nice of you. Thank you.'

'Le Gallienne once had an affair with Oscar Wilde, did you know? His wife's maiden name was Nørregaard and I am Søndergaard. She was Danish, too. It is a strange coincidence, is it not? Please sit down. I'll be back in a moment.'

I sink down into one of her sumptuous Art Deco armchairs and look down at the books in my hands. I have to laugh. This is so weird. She's dazzlingly beautiful. Maybe a little lonely. I can't really work her out, but I think I've gained her trust a little, at least. Maybe she'll come back in here with a gun instead of tea. I just have to keep it cool. Sometimes you have to be patient in situations like this. Her cat reappears, sits down and stares at me. Amazing markings. Looks like a miniature leopard.

In a few minutes she returns with a sterling silver tea tray. She points at the tea set, a strangely shaped, flat-sided teapot with matching cups, saucers and milk jug. Orange and white with a curious tree pattern on each piece. The leaves on the trees are yellow, blue and green.

'Designed by Clarice Cliff in 1932,' she says. 'From the *Fantastique Bizarre* range. This set is called *Autumn*. I love it. Once again, I was lucky at Sotheby's. Only 2,400 pounds for the entire set.'

She'd love my IKEA crockery. She must be worth a fortune. A burglar with the right knowledge and contacts could retire after robbing this place. I watch her as she pours the tea into the cups. As she leans forwards, I can see more of her breasts. I can feel my blood pressure rising.

'You like them?' she asks.

'They're very nice. Enchanting.'

She looks up quickly, a shrewd smile on her face. 'And what about the Clarice Cliff crockery?'

This makes me laugh. 'Almost equally enchanting.'

'That was a good answer.'

'Thank you.'

She smiles at me, the smile swiftly turning into a laugh. She flicks her hair away from her face. This action makes her breasts wobble. She sits down opposite me. My mouth is dry. I have no idea what I'm going to say next. At least she's not wearing any perfume.

'So, what is it you'd like to talk to me about, Mr Daniel Beckett?'

I recover and take my glasses off to demonstrate openness and trustworthiness. 'As I said, I'm a private investigator. I'm working on a missing persons case. I'm looking for a gentleman called Simon van Cutsem.' I watch her face. No recognition. 'He may not be using that name now and it may not be a name that you know him by. Nevertheless, I think that you may be familiar with him.' And here we go. 'He was one of the people who attended the private party that you performed at about five days ago. In fact, I suspect he may have been the person who hired you for that party. Do you know who I'm talking about?'

She places her teacup in the saucer. She doesn't say

anything. She looks anxious. 'I don't know which, which *party* you are referring to. I think perhaps you are wasting your time with me. I do not perform at parties.'

'Shall I tell you how I got your address?'

She nods briefly. She looks as if she's right on the verge of crying. I feel terrible. I wish she'd tighten up that robe. The cat leaves the situation.

'I am working with another private detective. She is an American. Her name is Frances Martinelli. She has a sister whose name is Angie. Angie Martinelli. Does that ring any bells?'

She shakes her head. She has a pale complexion, but it's getting paler.

'You may know Angie Martinelli by her professional name. It's Shelley Saint. Do you know who I'm talking about?'

Her eyes widen. 'Shelley. Shelley! Black hair. Beguiling eyes. Yes. Yes, I know her. I love her. We did a film together!'

'*Taste of Girl.*'

'Yes! Yes! That is it. It was, ah, it was quite a long film. Something like over eighty minutes. Eighty-two minutes, I think. It was exhausting to make. But fun.'

'Then you'll understand that I know what you do for a living. I have no objection to it, and the reason I am talking to you is not connected to it. Not directly, anyway. Shelley knew that I would be seeing you and she said to say hello.' I smile at her. 'She also said that you were very sweet.'

Liva blushes and looks down to her left.

'She said that you would be willing to help me. She knows how important this job is to me and she knows how important this job is to her sister. All I need is a few small details, then I'll be on my way. You have my word that I will not tell anyone that I have spoken to you.'

'I don't know. I don't know that I can help. You must understand that the party was a confidential occasion. I could be in trouble if I talked about it to anyone. I could be in trouble if I talked about any of the people who were there.'

I don't say anything. I don't move. I keep staring at her with the same expression of sincere, heartfelt understanding on my face. Somewhere in the house, I can hear a clock ticking. Some dogs bark over in the park. About two minutes pass before she speaks again.

She takes a sip of tea. 'They paid me a lot of money. They paid me and Jael an extra bonus for never mentioning the party to anyone.'

'Jael was the other girl?'

Shit. How would I know about that? I'm getting careless. But I think I got away with it that time.

'Yes. Jael. Jael Caspari.' She suddenly becomes animated. 'She is from Switzerland. Her mother is a famous microbiologist. I am going to stay with her in Neuchâtel next year. At least I think I am. She said she'd email me when she had a chance. I haven't heard from her yet, though. She is so fit. Do you know, she runs three miles every single day!'

I smile at her. 'Neuchâtel is a very nice place. You'll have a great time there. So. Who was it who approached you to perform at this party?' I'm vaguely worried about using the word 'perform' all the time, in case she takes offence or something, but she seems OK with it so far.

I also have to keep back the fact that I've seen what's on that memory stick. That would leave me with much too much explaining to do. I'd like to say something like

'Who was the piano-playing creep with the goatee beard at the orgy?' but I know that that simply wouldn't work. I'm getting impatient now, but I have to persevere.

'It was this guy,' she says. 'He was very polite. Very funny. Very well-spoken. Quite tall.' She touches her chin twice with a pinching action. 'Funny little beard. Grey hair like you. He said he knew this girl who I had worked with about six or seven years ago. I think she recommended me. I know she did. I think she did.

'She had quit the business and was settled down somewhere. In Scotland, maybe? Her name is Venus Temple. She is funny. But her real name is Paloma Medina. She is Spanish. She is from Cadaqués. I stayed there with her two years ago. It was fun. Dalí's house is there! But I haven't seen her for a while. Some people just disappear out of your life, you know?'

This is it. 'So, what was this guy's name, Liva? The guy with the funny little beard?'

I can hear a car pull up outside. Two car doors being slammed, one after another. Quick footsteps up the gravel drive. Someone knocking on the door, not bothering to use the bell. Liva stands up. I gently take her wrist in my hand.

'Are you expecting anyone, Liva?'

There's fear in her eyes and incipient tears once more. 'No. No one comes here.'

Blinds covering the downstairs windows. Solid wood front door. 'Is there a room upstairs where I can look out and see who that is? Without them seeing me, I mean?'

'Sure. My bedroom. But…'

'Show me.'

We both take the stairs two at a time. I'm distracted for a second by the sight of her bedroom: an enormous brick fireplace, distressed black oak floors, big circular bed, black silk sheets, massive Art Deco crystal chandelier, tarot cards on the floor and a boggling amount of erotic prints covering every inch of every wall: Erich von Götha, Amandine Doré and Jean Cocteau to name but a few.

I stand a few feet back from the window and take a look outside. I can feel Liva's warmth behind me and I can sense her distress and anxiety. There's a dark blue Audi A6 parked outside. Two guys in suits standing outside the front door. The car is the giveaway. This is the police. They bang on the door again.

'Listen, Liva. There are a couple of policemen outside. I have no idea why they're here. They may want to come inside the house. They'll need a warrant for that. If they don't have one, you don't have to let them in. Once you open the door to them, I will be behind you. Just go along with anything I say or do. OK?'

She nods her head. She looks frightened. After what Francie said about her lack of work permits, visas and so on, I can quite understand why.

But I don't think this visit is about that. She's been working and living here illegally for quite a while and only *now* do they decide to check up on her? I don't think so. We go downstairs. I put my glasses back on and keep out of sight as she opens the door.

'Miss Liva Mette Søndergaard?' He pronounces it 'Soundgar'. Surly voice. Discourteous. Slightly derisive. South London.

'Yes.'

'Good afternoon, *miss*. My name is Detective Sergeant Peter Moss, and this is Detective Constable Roland Driscoll. I wonder if we could come in and have a quick word with you? It won't take long.'

'What about? Why?'

He puts a laugh into his voice. 'Well, if we could come in, we can tell you. Here's our ID.'

'Do you have a warrant to come in here?'

Laughter again. 'Well, you could just give us your permission to come in, *miss*, then we wouldn't need to get a warrant. We don't want to make a fuss on your doorstep. Neighbours. I'm sure you know what I mean. Don't want to get tongues wagging, do we?'

Now it's my turn. I walk up to Liva and stand just behind her, looking over her shoulder.

'What is this? Who are you? What do you want?' As I hadn't had time to practise, that was a pretty good Danish accent, even if I say so myself. I'm hoping that my grey hair and glasses will give me a suitable air of outraged authority. Add a slice of icy superiority and we're ready to go.

Moss raises an eyebrow and smirks at me. 'And *you* are, sir?'

'I am Christen Drachmann. *Dr* Christen Drachmann. I am visiting my cousin here for two weeks and I do not appreciate your tone of voice or your vulgar gestures. Now I ask you once again. What do you want?'

'Just a quick word with your cousin, doctor. It won't take long.'

I turn up the aggression a little. 'A quick word about what? She has done nothing wrong. You think you can just turn up at people's private dwellings with your fancy German car and walk in here like you're owning this place? There are crimes happening right at this second and you are here wasting time laughing and smirking and driving your fancy German car.'

DC Driscoll pipes up for the first time. 'We can go and get a warrant, sir, to come in and talk to your cousin if we have to. It's just…'

'Then that is what you are going to have to do.' I spit the words out. I know this will stress them. 'If I see either of you again, I shall be in touch with a lawyer. I am an important man. I have contacts here. I am now going to slam this door in your face. Good day.'

I slam it hard. Liva looks shocked, then starts laughing, her hand over her mouth. I place a finger over my lips to shut her up, though I'm finding it difficult to keep a straight face myself. I can hear them talking on the other side of the door but I can't make out what they're saying. They sound indignant. Two minutes later, I can hear them crunching their way out of the drive and getting into their fancy German car.

There're a few minutes of silence when I wonder what they're going to do, then I hear the engine turn over and they're off. But I think they'll be back. This was certainly a suspicious visit. Their reluctance to discuss what the whole thing was about confirmed that.

'What is happening? What is happening? Is this to do with that party? Am I in trouble?'

Is she in trouble? What could those two have possibly wanted? It's more than likely that someone was pulling their strings. But who? I have no idea. But she's right about one thing; it was almost certainly connected to the party/orgy/whatever. I can't let her stay here. It's not safe. And, more cynically, I still need some information from her.

'Listen, Liva. I'd like you to come with me. I have a flat in Covent Garden. You can stay there until I find out what's going on. I don't know what's happening, but I don't think you're safe here. Some bad things have happened to people involved with that party. I'll explain as much as I can to you, but…'

She becomes tearful once more. 'No! No. I'm not going to leave my house and my cat. Those men; they will come in here.'

'Not if they don't have a warrant.' I don't believe that even as I'm saying it. 'I don't doubt that they were genuine police officers, but who sent them here and *why* they sent them here is another thing altogether. They messed it up. They were too cagey. They didn't tell you which police station they came from and they didn't tell you what they wanted.'

'But they will look at my things. They will take my things. I love this house. And Katsumi, my cat. Please let me stay here. I'm frightened about what they will do. Katsumi will run away.'

I can't have her being distressed. 'If I can organise it so that no one will come into your house and Katsumi will be looked after, will you come with me?'

'But how will you do that?'

'Trust me. I'm a doctor.'

20

DECIMA

Liva is a fast, confident driver and her Alpine A110 is a smooth, swift ride. By the time we're crossing Chiswick Bridge, I've had to tell her to slow down six times. We *really* don't want to get pulled over for speeding. In one way or another, the police are after both of us now. Each time I ask her to decelerate, she laughs.

Shortly after the police left her house, I got her to pack an overnight bag and then called a company I've used several times before, though not quite in circumstances like this. Utterly confidential and discreet, dodgy staff. Perfect.

'Decima.'

'Hi. My name's Daniel Beckett. Platinum account. Code number 86958697.'

'Hold on, please.'

I can hear Liva singing upstairs. I'm glad she's not taking this too seriously. She's singing "More, More, More" by The Andrea True Connection. She has a good voice.

'Hello, Mr Beckett. How can we assist?'

'139 Fife Road, East Sheen, London SW14 0HE.' I can hear rapid typing on a computer keyboard. 'I need a lockdown ASAP. Police visit approximately fifteen minutes ago. If they're going for a warrant, it'll take two to three hours, maybe longer. Whatever happens, no one is to enter this property. Hold out for as long as you can. If you can't hold out, make sure you don't leave. Oh, and there's a cat.'

'Hold on, please.'

Liva comes into the sitting room and buzzes about by the bookshelf, choosing books. It's as if she's going on holiday. At least she's not wearing the robe anymore. She's changed into a long-sleeved black satin mini dress with red and turquoise flowers all over it, a pair of black suede Grenson hiking boots on her feet. Very chic. There's a big belt at the waist which she's tightened with predictable results on her upper body and on that pleasingly rounded ass. She's wearing perfume now. It's Bibliothèque by Byredo, just like Fenella. I don't know how much longer I can stand this. Thankfully, she runs back upstairs.

'Ten minutes,' says the voice on the phone.

'Thank you.'

While we're waiting, I call Francie.

'Hey, Superboy. So, what happened with Miss Hot Stuff?'

'I'm taking her back to my flat.'

'That was *quick*. You're such a smooth operator.'

'We had a police visit which I didn't like. It occurs to me that she may be in danger in the same way as the others, and we need her; at least at the moment. But it's taking time. By the way, THETA is a Swiss national, name is Jael Caspari.' I spell it out. 'Possibly from Neuchâtel. Keep working on her if you have the time. Might come in useful.'

'Sure thing.'

I hear a vehicle drawing up outside. Big engine. 'I have

to talk to some people now. I'll call you later.'

I open the front door. There's a gunmetal grey Range Rover Discovery parked outside. Nice choice, if intentional. Fits in with the neighbourhood. Two enormous Decima personnel get out. The driver, a good-looking black guy of about my age who'd be an asset to any rugby team, grins when he sees me.

'Mr Daniel Beckett, as I live and breathe! Do you remember me?'

We shake hands. 'Of course I do, Frank. It's been a long time. Come in.'

'Hair gone grey, I see.'

'Accountancy's a stressful job.'

'*I'll* bet.'

The other guy, a dangerous-looking, Spanish-sounding fucker called Héctor, nods at me and follows behind. He has a big handlebar moustache and he's carrying an oversized olive green Filson duffle bag. I don't ask what's in it. When he sees Liva, his eyes widen. He points and is about to say something. I stop him.

'I know. Be cool.'

'Who are you?' she asks them. 'Who are these men?' she asks me.

'It's OK, Liva. Both of these guys are from an utterly trustworthy private security company.' This comment gets a raised eyebrow from Frank. 'They're going to make sure that nobody comes inside your house while you're gone. If the police manage to get a warrant, these two will remain here and make sure that none of your things are touched or broken.' And God help anyone who tries it.

Katsumi reappears, takes an appraising look at Frank and leaps up into his arms, rubbing her head against his chin. Frank strokes her.

'Oh, look!' says Liva. 'She likes you!' She places a hand to her mouth and laughs. She's like a teenager. I make the introductions. Both Frank and Héctor shake hands with her. Héctor looks overawed and can't meet her gaze. I turn to Frank.

'You've got my number. Anything unusual, call me immediately.'

'The *wind* direction changes and I'll be in touch.'

'I have to put you in the picture. The police that came here seemed to be the real thing, but there's a possibility that they were not. You never know. Expect the unexpected.'

'Don't worry. I'll use my sixth sense.'

'I'll show you where the coffee things are,' says Liva to Frank, as if he's come here to babysit. 'And I'll show you where Katsumi's things are and when to feed her. She will miaou when she wants to go out, but not when she wants to come back in, so you have to leave the back door open.'

'Got it,' says Frank, who then starts talking to her about cats in general to put her at ease. His suit is getting covered in cat fur. Héctor starts checking all the windows while looking at a small, black electronic device in his left hand. I've no idea what he's doing.

Just before we leave, Liva gently places a hand on my arm. 'Don't forget your books.'

We drive in silence for a while. The route she's taking to the West End is insane and she can't stop herself overtaking other cars. By the time we're driving along Bayswater Road she decides to ask for directions. 'You said Covent Garden, yes? Where do I…'

'There's nowhere you can park near where I live, and I want your car to disappear. Do you know Cavendish

Square underground car park?'

'Oh, yes! I park there when I go shopping in Oxford Street. I like driving down that ramp.'

'We'll go there. When we hit Marble Arch, go straight into Oxford Street and take the first left that you can.' It suddenly occurs to me that this particular car park has an automatic registration recognition system which has the potential to be hacked, but no one has any idea where we're going, so I think it'll be OK to take the risk. Famous last words.

Apart from the general stress, driving along with her like this is actually quite pleasant. I take a sly look at her. She's absolutely lovely. Elegant, long fingers and well-manicured red fingernails. Her lips are pursed as she concentrates. I watch her leg muscles flex as she changes gear. She catches me out and laughs.

'*What?*'

I decide to tell her she's pretty. I can't help myself. It's insane. I need help. Besides, she's having a rough, unsettling time and it may get rougher. I decide that's a good enough excuse. I shall do it now. And I'll do it in Danish to sound suave and civilised. '*Du er meget smuk, Liva.*'

She smiles, then laughs out loud. '*Oh! Tak. Du er mest venlig. Jeg kan lide dig.*'

We both laugh like a couple of sophisticated multilingual people and turn into the car park.

I get her to make a note of her parking bay number before we leave. I can't tell when we'll be coming back to get this car, and there's nothing worse than forgetting where you parked in a place this size. She writes it down on an old receipt and stuffs it in her bag.

I also ask her if she wouldn't mind tying her hair up

until we get to my place. If anyone's looking out for her, she's way too conspicuous; her height alone makes her much too noticeable. She picks something purple out of her bag and does it in about two seconds. With her hair tied back she looks even more beautiful. She sees me looking at her and I get a quick frown which morphs into a mystified smile.

Once we're at street level, we run across Henrietta Place and walk straight through the large John Lewis department store into Oxford Street where I hail a black cab and get it to take us to the top of James Street in Covent Garden. The whole area is totally packed with tourists, which is a good thing.

Liva wants to go power shopping in Covent Garden Market, but I manage to dissuade her and after several rapid visits to assorted overpriced food shops, we get a load of stuff for lunch, plus a bottle of chilled champagne which cost over a hundred and fifty pounds, and head to my flat via a tortuous route taking in Maiden Lane, Bedford Street, the Strand and Maiden Lane again. She keeps thinking that either we're lost, or I've had a breakdown of some sort. 'How can you not know where you live?'

After she's had a good look around my flat, we sit at my kitchen table. I let her eat and drink. This champagne is pretty good. It's called Abysse. The bottle's covered in bits of marine stuff: worm casts, mollusc shells and sand. Gets aged 200 feet under the sea, apparently.

Liva looks up and smiles at me from time to time. I can tell she's feeling relaxed. Good. Once the champagne's finished, I make coffee for both of us and just look at her. I want her to start this off. I hope the champagne loosens her tongue. When she speaks, she sounds a little bit tipsy.

'It's nice here. I'd never seen this little road before. Right next to the market and right next to the Strand. And I'd never seen it. You are a bachelor?'

I laugh. 'I guess I am.'

'Me, too. I'm a bachelor girl. My house *will* be OK, will it?'

'It'll be fine. You mustn't worry about it. It's in safe hands.'

Or dangerous, malevolent, crafty hands; same difference. She stretches and runs the tips of her fingers down the small of her back. I look away for the sake of my own sanity.

'I'm kind of trying to remember what we were talking about before those policemen came,' she says. 'I didn't like them *at all*. They said my name as if it was a joke name or something, you know?'

'I know they did. I caught that as well.'

She lets her hair down and shakes it back into shape. 'I don't like the police. Anyway. Yeah. Funny little beard guy. Did I tell you that? He wanted Venus Temple for this party. But she's gone now. Scotland. Or Ireland. No, Scotland. Have you ever been to Scotland?'

'How did he get in touch?'

'Venus gave him my mobile number. He told me the sort of show he wanted, and I was cool with that, so I contacted Jael and she said yes. It was very short notice and it almost clashed with something else that Jael had going on. But we thought it would be good and we'd have a ball. But it turns out to be a little, er, *syg*, you know? Bad. But once we were there, you know, we had to see it through. All the guys there were creeps. I kept thinking of the money.' She shrugs. 'I've done worse.'

'So, what was his name, this guy?'

'Francen was his last name. Constantijn Francen. Very funny name. Sounded kind of French. His surname, I mean. But Constantijn is like *Dutch*, I think. It was almost like it was a made-up foreign name, you know? A bit of everything. But he sounded English to me. Not English with a little European accent. Just English. This is lovely coffee.'

'Thanks. It's Zimbabwe Chipinge. Just trying it out.'

'Can I make some more? Would you like some? We should have bought some chocolates.'

'Sure. That would be good.' While she has her back to me, I text both Francie and Doug Teng with the same message.

Constantijn Francen. UK resident. Anything you can get ASAP.

Getting closer to you, my friend. Got the goatee beard, got the girl, now I just need a tad more triangulation. I'll mention the piano and take a gamble that it won't occur to her that I shouldn't know about it. 'And you said he played the piano.'

'Oh, yes. Did I?' She places the coffees on the table 'Classical music. That's what he played. I don't like classical music unless it's very, very, very quiet as background noise. Like in a lift. Or maybe on a radio in the next room. Like tinted silence.' She sits down facing me and drinks some coffee. 'We should get some chocolate. You said I was pretty in the car.'

'I meant it. You are.' And as if it's just occurred to me: 'Oh! That's what I was going to ask you. The party was, what, five days ago?'

'Ah, yes. That's right.'

'And you said it was short notice. Can you remember

when Constantijn called you?'

'Oh, I don't, um–' She snaps her fingers. 'Oh yes. It was a Saturday night because he apologised in case he was spoiling anything I was doing. I said it was OK. I don't do anything, you know? Saturday night, any night.' She wrinkles her nose. 'It's always been like that. You kind of…people are very nice or hitting on you or whatever, but they don't really want to be friends with you, you know?

'Even other…actors, you know? I've made a lot of money – well, you saw my house – but you kind of have no one to share it with. All the stuff you buy with the money. It is not the case for everyone for sure, but it is for me.' She rests her chin on the ball of her hand. 'It sure is. Jael says I am too much. My looks, you know? Too, er, *iøjnefaldende.*'

'Conspicuous? Eye-catching?'

'Yes. That's it. Conspicuous.'

'Would you like to come out to dinner with me when this is all finished?' I'm a complete bastard.

'To dinner? With you? Oh, yes please. That would be delightful. Do you know good restaurants?'

'I know a few. Tell me, Liva. How many days before the party did he call you?'

'It was four days. Yes. Four.'

'And did he call you on that mobile?'

I point to a Samsung Galaxy Fold 5G that's on the table.

'Yes. That's my phone.'

'Can I take a look?'

'Of course.'

I open it up. There's a big purple and fuchsia butterfly pattern in the middle. I find what I think I'm looking for and show it to her. 'This number here. Is this him?'

'Yes. That's it. It was just before eight o'clock.'

I tap the number into my mobile and call it. I have absolutely no idea what I'm going to say if he replies. But it's dead. Oh well. Probably a PAYG which he's binned. Does he use a different phone for every single call he makes? Either he's a smart cookie or someone's advising him. I start pacing the room, just like Francie.

"How did you get to the party?"

'He met us both in a pub.'

'Which pub?'

'The Dove. You know? That little pub by the river. Hammersmith, I think. It's very small. He told us that Charles II and Nell Gwyn used to dine there. I didn't like it. It was too old-fashioned and quite cramped. It smelt like they hadn't cleaned the floors properly.

'You could go outside, but I didn't really like all the people who were there. Jael felt the same. Everyone kept staring at us. We weren't dressed up. We had some clothes in our bags, but he told us that he had some clothes for us at the party.'

Nell Gwyn again. Three days ago, just before I met Polly. That blue plaque across the road from the café on Pall Mall. Nell got around.

'So, did he arrange to meet you in the bar?'

'Yes. At seven o'clock precisely. He greeted us as if we were his nieces or something, you know? A bit of air kissing. Quite, er, *overdrevet*?'

'Exaggerated.'

'Yes. Yes. Exaggerated behaviour. As if it was for show. As if for people who might be watching. As if he was trying to be a regular guy, you know? Or what he thought a regular guy was like. Jael said that he squeezed her bottom. He didn't touch me, though. She said that it was not a sexual squeeze. Does that make sense?

'He was wearing a very smart blue suit and a red tie with blue stripes. Oh, and a red handkerchief in his breast pocket. I didn't like his clothes. They were too young for him, but at the same time they were old-fashioned, yes? That little beard.' She laughs. 'Jael said she thought he looked like a magician.

'He bought us both a drink and bought one for himself. He seemed very ordinary. No. Not ordinary. I think you would say he was a bit posh. That's how Jael described him. Posh. I wondered if he was going to buy us something to eat, but he said there'd be food at the party that we could have. He said there would be plenty of food and plenty to drink.'

'Did he ask for your home address for any reason?'

'No. Yes. Yes, he did. He was originally going to pick me up from my house, but something happened, and he decided it would be easier to pick Jael and me up from one location. That was the pub. Jael was staying in Swiss Cottage, I think, so the journey would have just been too much for him. Something like that.'

This links him to the police visit. I could be mistaken, but, like Francie, I imagine that Liva would be pretty difficult to track down, even for the police.

'So, you had a drink. Then what happened?'

'We walked up the road to his car. I remember the name of the road that it was parked in. Weltje Road. Unusual. Like a German name. I asked him about it, but he had no knowledge. He seemed disinterested in anything I said to him. Now we were out of the pub he was *afvisende*, er, dismissive. Jael felt that, too. It was as if he didn't have to pretend to like us anymore. I thought he was a bit high and mighty, you know? Snobby.'

'What was the car?'

'Oh, a big one.' She smiles at the memory. 'Very fancy and very old, I think. Jael and I looked at each other when we got in. It was fun. There was a lady in the back. She was very dark. Very beautiful, I thought. She said her name was Seraphina. She told us that her name came from the Seraphim, who were very powerful angels.

'There was a little cabinet in the back, and we all had champagne. Lovely champagne glasses by Villeroy & Boch. Champagne was Taittinger. Not icy chilled, though. But not warm, either. Just OK. I felt it was like we were going on a hen night, you know? No one's ever invited me to a hen night, but I thought it might be a little like this.'

'Was Constantijn in the back of the car with you?'

'Oh, no. He was driving.'

'So, where did you go?'

'Well, I wasn't really sure where we were. Seraphina kept talking and talking. Later, Jael said she thought that Seraphina was trying to distract us so that we couldn't remember where we were being taken or how we were being taken there. She talked about a statue she'd seen with a seraphim and Saint Teresa.

'She talked about Saint Teresa's spiritual orgasm as the angel is about to penetrate her heart with an arrow. She talked about how Saint Teresa wrote of being repeatedly penetrated by an angel, causing her to moan in ecstatic bursts of pain and setting her on fire. I thought it was very interesting and romantic, but it made Jael jiggle.'

'Giggle.'

'OK.'

'Tell me more about Seraphina.'

'Mm. She was in her forties, I think. A very sexy woman. She kept very good eye contact and kept crossing and uncrossing her legs. She had good legs and small, sexy breasts, from what I could see. She wore a very short green skirt and a tight-fitting white shirt/blouse thing.

'I started to wonder if she would be joining us in the entertainment and what that would be like. I have to say, the thought excited me, even though she was not my type, you know? Physically, I mean.

'I think she might have been Indian, now I come to think of it, but when she spoke, it was as if she came from Surrey, or somewhere like that. Or Kent. One of those sorts of places. Quite a hard woman, I think, but that made her quite *sexet*.'

Seraphina sounds like a groovy chick. This is all rather mystifying. I find I'm getting a little stressed from all the time this is taking, but when I look at my watch, I realise we've only been back here for twenty minutes. I smile at her and she smiles back. Smiling helps to allay anxiety. 'So, then you arrived at the house.'

'Yes. Like a little castle. I didn't know where we were, but I think it was quite close to that pub in Hammersmith. Not *that* close, but fairly close. We probably only drove for ten to fifteen minutes. Something like that. The car was very quiet. You could hardly hear the engine at all.

'We went through some gates and then we got out of the car and went into the house. When we got out, Seraphina tapped the little ornament of the lady on the front of the car with her finger. She laughed and said it was like a seraphim. She said it was called the Spirit of Ecstasy.'

So, it was a Rolls-Royce. Not really helpful. There are

a lot of them about in London.

'So, we didn't really see the man, Constantijn, after that for quite a while. Jael and I went into this lovely big bedroom and had some food and something to drink. After that, Seraphina dressed us. She made us both stand naked in front of her for a while first. She examined us. She talked and talked about our bodies and faces and how lovely and attractive they were.

'She was very appreciative indeed of our bodies and kept touching us both. I could see that this was affecting Jael – making her excited, I mean – and I think she was a little embarrassed. We all laughed and talked about nothing. Then she fetched the things she wanted us to wear.

'She put this amazing silver chain thing over me. The metal was very cold. It made me shiver. And these beautiful shoes. Silver, as well. They were my size, which surprised me.

'She put these pearls on Jael and they looked fabulous. They weren't real pearls, though. Jael told me how she knew. You rub them across your teeth or something. Jael also wore gold heels and a kind of leather corset thing around her waist. Oh, and this lovely headscarf.

'We were able to keep everything, Seraphina said, which was a pleasing bonus. She said there would be things going on and we weren't to worry about them. All we had to do was to hand out these pills and serve the champagne. Be nice to everybody. Be welcoming. Be gracious.

'Some younger people would come in and we were to greet them and smile at them and then ignore them. Then we just had to perform for a while. Not for too long, but about five or six times over the evening with rests in between.

'We both knew what to do. We'd done it before, though Seraphina had some suggestions. Things she'd like to see. She said that she would like to do what we did. She had thought about it a lot, she said. But she was too shy. She said that we were not to worry. None of the men were allowed to touch us. We were just the floor show. I have done erotic cabaret, you know? And private parties at houses. Did I tell you?'

'What were the pills?'

'I don't know. I just assumed they were things like Viagra. Cialis. Sex pills. I don't know. As it turned out, it was Jael who dispensed the pills, not me. So, we did all that. Constantijn had changed his clothes and he played the piano. It was grating to me. Jael said it was Chopin. I couldn't stand it. I wished I had ear plugs. I like trip-hop. All these kids there. It was very weird. Afterwards, Jael said she would probably never do this again and so did I. I think we both found it a little *usmagelig*, er, distasteful. But…you know.'

'Who took you both home?'

'They ordered a taxi for both of us. A minicab. It was about five in the morning. We were exhausted, as I'm sure you can imagine. I thought that we might go back in a nice car, a limo, but no. I slept until one the next afternoon. Jael stayed with me. She slept on for another two hours. She kept the corset thing on while she slept. A cincher. That's what those things are called. I remember now. She was very pleased with that, I think.

'Before I went to sleep, I hung the silver body thing up in my wardrobe, so it wouldn't get damaged. I will show it to you when we go back to my house. I don't think it was real silver. I hope it doesn't rust. I like it.'

I suddenly realise that I'm getting used to all this stuff. It doesn't seem anywhere near as bad as when Polly was describing it to me. It's become normal. And Liva's blasé, bemused, digressive attitude isn't helping at all. I don't think she's in denial or anything like that. I think she's become inured because of her background and just lives in a different world from everyone else.

My mobile rings. It's Doug.

'Got him.'

21

AN ERROR OF JUDGEMENT

'Well, that was a bit of a strange job, Mr Beckett. Interesting, though. Oh, by the way; a thousand OK with you? Not that I'm giving you a chance to haggle or anything. This isn't a medieval fish market in Baqiqi.'

'Yeah, Doug. Sure.' What's he talking about? Where's Baqiqi? I stand up and stare through the bars of the kitchen window at the brickwork on the side of the Lyceum Theatre. A sparrow is making a nest in the guttering.

'Okey doke. Some of this is coming up on my screens as we speak, so that's why I'll sound hesitant from time to time. Constantijn Francen. This immediately struck me as some sort of fake ID. Nothing obvious, but you get a feel for these things after a while, yeah? This guy has a timeline which goes back sixty-three years. Place of birth, date of birth, parents' names; all kosher. Grandparents, too.

'I didn't go back to great-grandparents as I reckoned I'd be wasting my time and yours and I'm not bothering with schools and all the rest. A lot of it gels. His National Insurance and tax details; all the dates on those make sense. Oh, hold on – just got something from DVLA. Driving licence registered forty-two years ago, complete with penalty points for speeding, two AC10s and five AC30s.'

'What are they?'

'An AC10 is failing to stop after an accident and an AC30 is undefined accident offences. All phony, I would reckon, the driving licence equivalent of artificially aging a fake passport. Anyway, the strange thing is that all the relatively unimportant stuff like house purchase, Amazon account, library membership, PayPal – did I tell you I take PayPal now? – electricity and so on and so forth you name it seemed to come out of nowhere a little over three years ago.

'Now, any of those things looked at individually wouldn't set alarm bells ringing, but as a group, they're pretty suspicious. I don't think whoever did this was expecting anyone with the sort of wherewithal we have to look at this in any detail and to look at it in quite this *way*. Sloppy, but there it is, man. All the major stuff is watertight. Everything was in its predicted place, which is why it didn't take me very long to crack it open.'

'Do we have an address?'

'We have two. Address on that driving licence is 69 Watermore Lane W3 9TL and there's another address that comes from, among other things, a house purchase agreement made three years ago and an active Amazon account from almost the same date. If you're going for a bit of the old midnight visit, I would ignore the driving licence address.

'The one I think you want is 44 Vicarage Gardens, London W8 0HT. Got it? Everything else is registered at that address. Right next to Kensington Church Street and a convenient thirty seconds' stroll from the Japanese Gallery, if you're a fan of *ukiyo-e*. I'm still working on getting a telephone number for Mr Francen. There hasn't been a landline at that address for eight years and I'm still carving my way through all the mobile companies. D'you want me to continue?'

'Don't worry. That's great, Doug. I'll thank you and your new basque-wearing girlfriend in person as soon as I get a chance. What was her name again? Haizea? She sounds lovely.'

'I'm emigrating.'

So, it looks as if Francen/van Cutsem isn't domiciled in Richmond after all. I'm rather annoyed that Polly didn't give me the address of that place; though at the time, of course, it didn't seem to be necessary.

I sit down opposite Liva and take her hands in mine as a sort of sincere gesture. I'm astonished that she hasn't asked me to explain in detail WTFs going on. Maybe she doesn't care. Maybe all of this is entertaining for her. Maybe she just likes my company.

'Listen, Liva. I've got to go out for a while. I don't know how long I'm going to be. I'd like you to stay here. I know there's nothing much for you to eat here and you may get hungry later on. If that's the case, you can go out shopping. But three things: firstly, if you go out, tie your hair back like you did before. Secondly, don't spend a long time at the shops. Try to keep it to half an hour at the very most. If anyone's interested in you, we want to give them as small a window as possible. Thirdly, please try and remember where this flat is. It's easier to get lost around here than you may think. I'll leave you my mobile number and write the address and location down for you. If you get into trouble, or if you get worried about anything, just give me a call.'

She looks momentarily tearful. 'But where are you going?'

'I just have to see some people and ask them some questions. I'll try not to be too long. Maybe we can go and get something to eat tonight if I'm back in time. Would you like that?'

'Oh, yes. That would be wonderful.'

'I'm going to give you some spare keys to this flat. Don't lose them. There is a moderately complicated locking system on the front door here. I use two enhanced Yale cylinder locks. You have to open both of them virtually simultaneously. If the second one isn't opened within three seconds of the first, the first one will lock itself again, OK? It's a kind of burglar deterrent.' I take her hand and indicate that she should stand up. 'Come on. I'm going to give you a quick lesson.'

'This is so exciting! Can I have a bath when you've gone?'

*

As I approach Trafalgar Square, I give Francie a call once more. 'OK. I've got an address for van Cutsem or whatever he's calling himself this week. Write this down in case I get bumped off. It's 44 Vicarage Gardens, London W8 0HT. Most of his traceable details only started three years ago which makes sense when we consider what you discovered.'

'There's another address on what's undoubtedly a fake driving licence; it's 69 Watermore Lane W3 9TL. You can probably keep that one on the backburner for the moment.'

'So, what now? Are you going to make a discreet

citizen's arrest or nail one of his hands to the wall?'

I wave a cab down and get in the back, asking the driver to drop me off in Kensington High Street. 'I'm getting a cab over there right now. I'm just going to knock on the door and take it from there.'

'What if he doesn't want to let you in?'

'I'll camp in his front garden and look miserable.'

'That usually works. Where have you parked the girl?'

'Still in my flat. If things go well, I'll get her to autograph a few of your Blu-rays.'

'Thanks. What's she like?'

'Very nice. Easily side-tracked.'

'Must be weird.'

'What must?'

'Meeting her in real life after…you know.'

'Yeah. It is. Your brain isn't computing that it's the same person. Hard to know what to make of it. I think she's tougher than she seems. She'd have to be.'

'Do you think they're going to send someone after her?'

'If I was these people, I'd view her as a weak link now. The other girl, too. I think it was a low priority that they've only just come around to considering. I just hope I can make sense of everything before the cogs start turning.

'I may get Liva to give Jael Caspari a call to see if she's OK, even though she's back, I assume, in Switzerland. But even as I'm saying that, I don't think it would be a good idea. If they can get police sent around to Liva's house, they may be capable of bugging her phone.'

'If you have that other girl living in your flat too, I'm leaving you.'

'My mother said you'd be the jealous type. But that

visit from the police this morning. I have to admit, that gave me a bit of a chill. This is getting more complex with each second that passes. I'll have to have a long think about this when I get some breathing space. Put myself in their place.'

'Be careful.'

'I didn't know you cared, Francie.'

'I just want the rest of my money, honey.'

The cab drops me off outside a branch of Gap. I cross the road and walk up Kensington Church Street. What happens next will depend on what van Cutsem knows. I can't waste any more time with this. Whatever I have to do to make him spill his guts, I'll do it. From what Liva told me, he seems to be in charge of part of the entertainment at these parties at the very least.

He books the girls, he meets the girls, he drives them to the house in Richmond with Seraphina distracting them in the back of the Rolls with bottles of champagne and tales of Saint Teresa. Then Seraphina, whoever the hell she is, takes over. She feeds the girls, she dresses them up, she briefs them on what to do.

Then van Cutsem appears again, tickles the ivories, schmoozes the guests and finally joins in himself. For someone with his tastes and his type of criminal record, the perks of a job like this must be deeply satisfying. Finally, he or Seraphina bundle the girls off in a cab and that's that; at least for a while.

This can only be conjecture at this point, but it's likely that someone else hires/organises/procures the kids, someone else hires/employs van Cutsem and Seraphina, someone else hires/owns the house in Richmond, someone else is able to manipulate the police into whitewashing what happened at Polly's flat and paying

Liva an unsettling visit.

And someone else, in case I forget, hires the ill-fated Salo triplets and their cousin to wipe out Polly and possibly Culpepper and Vanchev.

I have to assume that Polly didn't know who van Cutsem was, but Culpepper did. Culpepper conceivably made the mistake of telling that mysterious *someone else* that van Cutsem was still alive and in doing so, signed his and Polly's death warrants.

Vanchev was collateral damage. He had to go because once he was dead, the OFRP assignment could be shut down and the whole thing buried. I suspect that his death had to seem like natural causes so as not to alarm the other guests at the orgy, who didn't want to think that being murdered came as a complimentary addition to their fun evening out. Or something like that.

It's also a possibility – but only a possibility – that Vanchev died because his future behaviour might engender another, further investigation into his activities and then the whole thing would start over again, assuming that the Richmond event wasn't a one-off for him.

Vicarage Gardens is a leafy, moneyed, busy road with resident parking, fake Victorian lamp posts and big trees. The houses all look the same: white, three storeys, basements, concrete front gardens, shrubs in pots, iron gates. Some are obviously alarmed, some not.

Five or six bedrooms and each house worth around a million, I would guess. Lots of cars: Jaguars, Range Rovers, Volkswagens, BMWs, Porsches, Lamborghinis, a Nissan Rogue, a Citroën MPV; all upmarket automobile life is here.

I walk past number 44 allowing my peripheral vision a

quick glance. This house looks cleaner than the others, as if the exterior has been recently decorated. Can't see inside; blinds in the way. Strong-looking, grey front door. No security cameras anywhere in sight, but a blue Honeywell alarm box flashing away above the door. Two locks; an ordinary Yale and a Kingfisher ABS Cylinder Lock.

There's a red Audi A6 parked outside, though it may not belong to the house. I keep going, wondering what I'm going to do if he opens up and he's got a door chain on. Can I somehow talk my way in? What can I say? I turn on my heel, go back the way I came, open the gate, walk up the path and ring the doorbell. I'm sure I'll think of something marvellous in the next couple of seconds.

But no one answers. I count to twenty and try again. Still nothing. I get a feeling that the house is empty. I realise that I can't be seen too clearly from the road thanks to the slightly indented front door, the shrubs in the front garden and the tree outside. Would it be worth trying to break in?

I look at my watch and let thirty seconds go by, counting the number of people who walk past in that time. Four. None of them glance in my direction. I ring the doorbell once more and listen. No footsteps, no nothing. This is frustrating, but I've still got Lothar working on locating Eemil Salo, so if this lead comes to nothing, there's always that.

I put my latex gloves on and attack the cylinder lock first. Kingfisher are pretty good. Reputedly anti-drill, anti-pick and anti-bump, but they still have a basic pin-and-tumbler design. The correct key will push the pins up and allow you access. If you don't have the correct key, a pick and a tension wrench will usually do the trick. I have both tools on my keyring. I don't bother looking nervously behind me, even though I can hear footsteps approaching. I just attempt to become invisible; it's always worth a try.

I push the tension wrench into the keyhole and turn it very slightly to the right. Someone is now walking right past the house. Their speed remains the same. They're talking on a mobile to someone called Geraldine who isn't listening to reason.

Keeping the pressure on, I slowly slide the pick inside until I can feel the pins being lifted up, one after another. Click after click until they're all pushed up into the housing, then another turn to the right and it's open. So much for this company's anti-pick claim. Hi, guys.

The Yale is like a holiday after this and two seconds later I'm inside. I engage the night latch to discourage visitors. There's an alarm keypad to my left flashing red, which I disable using a trick that the manufacturers use; press the asterisk button three times, the hashtag button once, then any four number buttons. For an adrenalin-producing two seconds, nothing happens, then the green light under 'ready' comes on and all is well.

I take a deep breath and stand still. Just because no one responded to the miniscule noises of my break-in, it doesn't necessarily mean that the house is empty; they could be asleep, they could be drugged, they could be not switched on, they could be hard of hearing. I breathe slowly and, without any concentration, try to sense the presence of another person or persons. Nothing.

I give the big rooms downstairs a quick once-over then go upstairs, taking the steps two at a time and as quietly as possible. I check the bedrooms and bathrooms. All clear. Then up to the second floor; all clear again. Just as I'm on my way downstairs, I hear a loud crash which makes my heart leap, but it's only the post. *Condé Nast Traveller*, *The World of Interiors*, *Vanity Fair* and a Damart catalogue were responsible for the noise.

I take a look around a large sitting room. A lot of money has been spent on this place. All the furniture is very modern and very glam: two big Fendi Casa sofas, three glass-topped circular coffee tables of different sizes huddled together and covered in art books, an eight-foot-square antique mirror leaning against the wall and a terrible painting of a fox's face over the Edwardian cast iron fireplace. The frame is nice, though.

He's got a big Marantz stereo system connected to two fuckoff Fyne Audio floor-standing speakers that look like they could blast a hole in the wall. I take a look at his CD collection. Lots of harpsichord music: Handel, de Chambonnières, Scarlatti, Clérambault, Bach and a huge amount of classical piano. No surprise there. There's a Kawai baby grand piano with sheet music on the rack: Piano Concerto No. 4 by Michael Finnissy. No television. No computer.

I run a hand across a section of bookshelf and look at the spines: *Journey to the End of the Night* by Céline, *The Afterlife of Piet Mondrian* by Nancy Troy, *The Garden of Evening Mists* by Tan Twen Eng. A lot of books on nude photography: *Addicted to Nudes* and *Erotic Sessions*, both by someone or something called Dahmane, *Nus vénitiens* by Lucien Clergue, *Nudes* by René Groebli; all relatively tame stuff, more arty than erotic.

I look around for…something. Something that will help me move this onto the next stage. If I can't interrogate van Cutsem in person, I can at least see what I can glean from his possessions.

But there's nothing. Anyone making a casual search of this place would assume they were in the home of a well-to-do, cultured, wealthy individual with an interest in interior design, art, photography, literature, music, upmarket magazines and thermal clothing.

I go back up to the second floor and work downwards, giving myself two concentrated minutes' search in each room, but there's no joy. He doesn't have a safe, he doesn't have any locked desks or filing cabinets. I've spent enough time in here and decide it's time to go. I let myself out leaving the security measures as I found them.

Back on the pavement, I take another glance at the cars, embedding them in my brain in case I spot one of them again somewhere. I was half expecting to see the Rolls, but there's no sign of that. Of course, it may not have been his car.

About ten yards ahead, a well-dressed black guy in his forties is getting out of a brand new very cool-looking yellow and black Jeep Wrangler. I keep getting junk mail for these. They have heated seats, apparently.

As I approach him, I can see him glancing at a chunky black watch on his wrist. Looks like a Breitling Avenger. Worth about four thousand. He frowns and taps it twice on the face with an index finger. Oh well. Everything breaks down sometimes, no matter what it cost.

He looks from side to side and then spots me. 'Excuse me, mate. You don't happen to have the time on you, do you?' Brummie accent. Polite smile.

'Sure. It's…'

It's a terrific, practised, surgical punch. Exactly the right spot. An uppercut that strikes my solar plexus so hard that it almost lifts me off my feet. I wonder if my internal organs are OK. I almost feel concussed with the impact.

As I bend double with the pain, I raise my hands in front of my face to prevent whatever he's going to do next. In the second that it takes me to decide how I'm going to retaliate, I feel a hard, hammer fist strike at the base of my neck. Another inch to the left and I'd be dead. So, there are two of them and they're pros. I feel as if I'm going to throw up.

In the next couple of dizzying, disorientating seconds, whoever was behind me grabs my jacket collar and virtually throws me into the jeep. I hit my head hard on the far passenger door and feel momentarily stunned, with a side helping of tinnitus and nausea. Not good.

He slides in next to me, cuffs me, hoods me, then pushes me down onto the floor of the vehicle and presses his knee against the side of my neck, the full weight of his body behind it. I'm totally helpless, feel as if I'm suffocating and barely notice that we've driven off. The whole thing took less than three seconds.

I calm my breathing, attempt to ignore the pain in my stomach, head and neck and try to think clearly. Who is this? Is it the police? Unlikely. So far, the police have just been *used*, and so far as that's the case, they've been keeping to protocol, despite being a bit snotty at Liva's place.

Even if I was some dangerous criminal, that behaviour was unnecessary and well over-the-top. I feel such an idiot. I was distracted and just wasn't expecting that punch. I must up my game. I can't afford to get sloppy.

Was it someone watching van Cutsem's house? At the moment, no one knows who I am, certainly not van Cutsem, and the only people wanting my head on a plate so far will be Eemil Salo and the Metropolitan Police Homicide & Major Crime Command. Not to mention the two cops in the builder's yard.

The pressure on my neck doesn't let up for a second. My head is spinning. Occasionally, the jeep takes a sharp turn or goes over a bump which only serves to make things worse. I'm steadily breathing through my nose trying to stop it, but it's no good; the nausea gets the upper hand and I throw up inside the hood.

There isn't that much vomit, but it's enough to make this wonderful journey slightly more unpleasant. Am I concussed? I feel confused and lightheaded, so possibly. I wonder about the risk they took doing this in broad daylight. Did anyone see? Did anyone call the police? Maybe people saw it and thought it was part of some affluent gangland war and best ignored.

I think of the guy that punched me. The expensive chunky watch. The suit; was it a Briani? The jeep's worth forty thousand plus. All expensive stuff. What is he? A successful businessman with vigilante tendencies? A top of the range millionaire criminal?

Then I think of the hooding and the cuffs. Military? Have they got the armed forces involved in this now? Is there no end to their ingenuity? I'm shivering and it isn't cold. Never a good sign. Apart from the vomit, it smells of fresh natural rubber in here. New vehicle; possibly a rental.

After what could be ten, fifteen or twenty minutes, we stop. I've no idea where we might be. I'm dragged out of the jeep and made to stand up. I feel dizzy once more. I need a holiday.

I can hear someone fiddling with a set of keys, having trouble getting them in a lock. Apart from the close-up bouquet of my own vomit I can detect burning oil and damp iron oxide, and hear the shrill rasp of some sort of industrial saw about two hundred yards away.

Then someone grabs the centre of the handcuffs and pulls me forwards. This is the second time I've been handcuffed in two days and I can't say I like it much. I'm also sick of having two-against-one altercations with strange men. At least this time, the cuffs aren't behind my back. Whether I can make use of that lapse yet, I can't tell.

Despite the hood, I can sense that the light has changed and it's marginally colder. We're going inside somewhere. I don't know what this is, but I do know one thing; just like Salo's boss, these two have made a catastrophically stupid error of judgement.

22

CHUNKY WATCH/INFANTRY JACKET

I hear a metal chair being dragged across the floor and slammed down just behind me. There was anger in that action. Anger is good. Anger makes mistakes. A hand on my shoulder pushes me down into a sitting position. It doesn't look as if they're going to tie me up. They must reckon the beating, the hood, the cuffs and the two-against-one are quite enough at the moment. Perhaps they're right.

The hood is yanked off my head, taking some of my newly dyed hair with it. They like being rough, these two, and they're enjoying showing me who's boss. Chunky Watch sees the vomit over my face and neck and looks disgusted, as well he might.

'Oh, for fuck's sake. Chuck some water over him. He fuckin' stinks of puke.'

I get a good look at the other guy. Older. Late fifties. Short white hair. Hard. Big build like Chunky Watch. Wearing a green M65 Infantry Jacket. But not military issue. Wrong sort of lining, for a start. I can hear a bucket of water being filled. Well, this is going to be fun.

'Get that shit off him,' says Chunky Watch, who, despite being the younger man, seems to be in charge here.

Infantry Jacket comes back and he's grinning. I get the

entire contents of the bucket full in the face. It's cold. I tighten my muscles to prevent the inevitable shivering. It doesn't work.

Once the water is out of my eyes, I take a quick look around. It's a warehouse. Not very big. Lots of glass doors and windows stacked against the walls, big, dirty sheets of glass everywhere; some double glazed, some laminated, some reinforced, some cracked, some shattered. Everything's covered in dust and other crap. This place doesn't look like it's been used for at least a year.

There are windows, but they're all high, perhaps fifteen to twenty feet up the corrugated walls. There's a small office with big glass windows, most of which are damaged. Toilet next to the office. The door is broken. OK.

The two of them are getting ready for their big thing, whatever it is. Chunky Watch is pressing his fist into the palm of his other hand and twisting it around. These two aren't police. For starters, they haven't even searched me. I wonder who they think I am?

'Do you know who I am, you piece of shit?' says Chunky Watch. He's barely restraining himself from attacking me, though I can tell it won't be long. He's struggling with a white-hot rage. It's all rather baffling.

I look down at the handcuffs. Solid steel, nickel plated, pretty robust. Police issue, but not from this country. If I can somehow get hold of the tools on my keyring, I can get out of these pretty easily, but not, presumably, while these two are watching me and it's unlikely they'll help. Perhaps I can bet them a grand I can do it in less than thirty seconds and see if they go along with it.

'No, I don't know who you are. Should I?' I'm

surprised that my voice sounds normal. 'Are we friends?'

His rage spills over and he gives me a swift taekwondo kick to the chest which knocks me and the chair onto the floor. The kick and the fall are quite a combination; I feel dazed and punchy. My head hurts. Infantry Jacket pulls me and the chair up and makes me sit down on it again. He's as angry as Chunky Watch, whose face is now an inch from mine. He's been eating chocolate.

'We've been waiting for one of you to show your face for three fucking days,' he says. I didn't see that jeep before I went into the house. Where was it? Were they cruising around the block until someone came out of van Cutsem's house? Unlikely. I don't understand this at all.

Infantry Jacket reaches in his pocket and pulls out a retractable baton which he flicks out to its full length. Oh, good. 'Who do you think I am?' I ask.

This gets me a stinger across the thigh with the baton. Wow; there's going to be a bruise there after that. Infantry Jacket hisses into my face, 'You'll speak when you're spoken to.'

It's just like school. I turn and look at him. 'Is this what it was like in the army, sweetheart? Two against one but only when they were handcuffed?'

I get kicked hard in the side by Chunky Watch for that. Floor again. Picked up again. My brain feels as if it's come loose. So, they're army, or ex-army. I know that baton swipe didn't break my leg, but it feels as if it did. My tongue is tingling. I need some painkillers. Now Chunky Watch has produced a Victorinox Hunter Pro and is waving it in my face. Nasty little knives, but very well made.

'You and your mates ripped us off, man. I want to know where my fucking son is, or this knife is going straight into your throat. Understand?' His spittle is all over my face. Infantry Jacket slaps the baton into his open palm again and again.

Suddenly it all starts to fall into place. The kids at the orgy. My theory about them being victims of abduction. This guy has to be one of the parents. Well, he may not know much, but I may be able to extract *something* useful from him.

'Do you think I'm someone called Simon van Cutsem? Or Constantijn Francen?'

I catch a small, mystified glance between Chunky Watch and Infantry Jacket. 'What are you talking about? You must think I'm fucking stupid. I'd fucking kill you without any hesitation, you piece of crap,' says Chunky Watch. 'Go on. Just give me an excuse. I know he's probably dead by now, so I don't fucking care. I'm going to slit you open and pull your fucking guts out and piss on them.'

That's actually quite good. I must remember that one.

'Let me have a minute with him, Aaron,' says Infantry Jacket.

Aaron. Cute. 'I *do* think you're stupid, Aaron,' I say. 'Take a look at my wallet. Left jacket pocket. You'll see ID. I'm a private investigator. I'd just broken into that house. I don't live there. You're making mistake after mistake, sonny. And you're sloppy. Your anger's getting the better of you.' I thought 'sonny' was a good touch as he's at least a decade older than me.

'A private bloody *investigator*?' jeers Chunky Watch, or Aaron as I must now think of him.

This gets an incredulous laugh from Infantry Jacket. Then I get a big punch in the face from Aaron for bullshitting him. It's turning out to be a really bad day. At least I didn't fall to the floor that time, but I can taste blood in my mouth. This has to stop. I do some deep breathing to extinguish the adrenalin, then decide on a course of action while sensing their energy and attention.

Chunky Watch gives an almost imperceptible nod to Infantry Jacket. He grips the baton rightly in his right hand, ready to use it if I produce a submachine gun or nunchaku. Cautiously, he inches towards me and then his hand is in my pocket. The wrong pocket, as it happens.

'That's the pocket on *my* left, not *your* left, you total idiot. You need to get better help, Aaron. A trained cockatoo could do better than this.' God knows what that's going to get me in a few minutes, but it has to be done. I have to keep their anger level up.

I can feel my heart racing. I clasp my fingers together as much as the cuffs will allow. Infantry Jacket leans forward and the second his hand is in my pocket, I launch myself upwards and simultaneously swing hard to my left, catching him under the chin, whipping his head back and knocking him to the floor. He grunts with the impact, but he's still conscious. I'll get back to him.

Before the look of shock is off Aaron's face, I turn and kick the chair at him, catching him in the face and forehead. He bats it out of the way and comes at me with the knife. I grab the baton from the floor and in the same movement stamp on Infantry Jacket's balls.

I swipe the baton through the air a few times as if I'm holding a baseball bat, getting used to its weight and making Aaron keep his distance so I can work out what I'm going to do next.

'I'm going to kill you now, mate,' he says, coldly. I like the 'mate'. Nice touch. Makes everything not so bad.

He approaches steadily, professionally, focussed,

forearm protecting his neck and face. I can sense movement behind me, so I step back and bring my foot down on the side of Infantry Jacket's knee. I hear the crunch and the scream. I de-focus my vision so I can pick up the slightest telegraphing from Aaron. I'm going to forget the baseball bat technique and use the baton as if it's a *bokken*, or wooden training sword.

I turn my body side-on to him and edge forward a few inches at a time. Then he screams and rushes at me. I step to the side and bring the baton down hard on his right forearm, then whip it around, strike the left side of his torso twice, then attack his collarbone with as much ferocity as I can manage.

The pain makes him inhale sharply. That'll be two cracked ribs and a fractured clavicle at least. Breathing will be painful now because of the rib damage. His eyes water. While he's pondering all of that, I ram my shoulder into his chest, knock him to the floor and pick up the knife, kicking him on the side of the head once I've straightened up.

As he groans and hyperventilates, I run about twenty feet away from both of them so I can get these damn handcuffs off without interference. Getting my keyring out of my pocket was more difficult and painful than I'd imagined, but in five or six seconds the cuffs are picked and lying on the floor.

Infantry Jacket is up on his feet again. It must hurt like hell to put his weight on that knee, but he's a tough old bird and I'm sure it's probably no more painful to him than a butterfly alighting on his nose. What's he going to do now? I wish he'd just give up. Aaron coughs and hyperventilates and coughs. He tries to get up a few times but fails.

'I'm going to gut you like a fucking pig,' says Infantry Jacket. He's really pissed. I can tell.

Another knife; this time, it's an evil-looking MAC Shark M Tactical Military Knife. One of those goes inside you and it drags your insides with it when it comes out. I really don't like it here. He dances about like a washed-up ballerina, attempting to confuse me as the knife disappears behind his back and then reappears, but not in the hand you were expecting. So, he's got knife skills. I don't bother to do battle with him or use the knife I took off Aaron. I just wait to see what he's going to do.

He's deathly pale and perspiring with the pain of his knee (and the crunched balls), which is something, but I should have finished him off while I had the chance. The knife slashes through the air again and again. Sometimes it seems to disappear. I'm starting to feel that I'm not up to the concentration required for this and I'm starting to get the shivers.

Then he charges at me, holding the knife high above his head. Just when he feels he's in the right position, he drives the knife downwards towards my left subclavian artery; a killing blow. I block his hand with the side of my wrist, simultaneously jabbing him hard in both eyes with the rigid index and middle fingers of my right hand.

He cries out. His hands cover his face. He drops the knife and staggers backwards, falling through an enormous sheet of plate glass. Lots of blood, but unfortunately, it's only from superficial cuts. Before he can work out what's going on. I get a grip on his jacket, lift him to his feet, grab his shoulder and deliver one hard uppercut to his balls and another to his chin. Out cold. So much for gutting me like a pig.

As I head back towards Aaron, I try to make sense of

what he said:

We've been waiting for one of you to show your face for three fucking days.

You and your mates ripped us off, man. I want to know where my fucking son is.

I know he's probably dead by now, so I don't fucking care.

After the last couple of days, only an idiot would not realise what he's talking about.

1. He presumably thinks I'm van Cutsem or an associate but doesn't know that name or the name Francen. Perhaps he doesn't know what van Cutsem looks like. But he doesn't like him one tiny bit.

2. He has a son who may or may not have been involved in one of van Cutsem's 'entertainments'. But he doesn't know about this. He suspects his son may be dead.

3. He's been 'ripped off' in some way by van Cutsem and has been waiting for him to return to his house so he can exact revenge.

Not much to go on, but he's about to fill in the gaps for me. He's lying on the floor, holding his left arm, his breathing shallow, his face a mask of pain. I seize the shoulder of his jacket and pull him up to a sitting position.

'Hey. *Hey!*' I kneel down next to him and slap his face. His eyes are unfocused. If that baton strike didn't fracture his arm, it would have hurt like a bastard and the cracked ribs and collarbone pain won't help. He glances at Infantry Jacket and appears dumbfounded. He looks up at me. He doesn't believe what's just happened. 'OK, princess. You two can give each other some TLC in a minute, but I need some information from you first. Who are you?'

His head drops down. His eyes are tightly closed. He holds on to his arm and rocks backwards and forwards. Then he starts rubbing his collarbone. I do hope he's not going into shock.

'Staff…'

'Staff? *What?* What's that?'

'Staff Sergeant Aaron Quennel.'

I knew it. I can see Infantry Jacket has recovered and is attempting to get up. I point a finger at him. 'Stay where you are. Lie on your back. Don't even think about trying to get up.'

He squints at Aaron and does as I say. He's definitely not well. I thought I'd punctured both of his eyeballs but can only see blood and vitreous humour oozing from one of them. 'Who's your friend, Aaron?'

Now his eyes are open, but they look dull. 'Vernon Dansey. Former Warrant Officer Class One.'

'Which regiment are or were you both in? Quickly.'

He looks puzzled that I should ask. 'Mercian Regiment. I was stationed in Cyprus when it happened. Akrotiri. My fucking *arm*.'

He throws up. Over my shoes and new black jeans. A shame. This day was going so well. At least I've got two new knives.

23

ANGER AND HATE.

I drag Quennel and his moaning pal over to the wall next to the office and manhandle them into a sitting position a few feet away from each other. Quennel's head is slumped forward onto his chest, but at least now he's breathing a little more deeply. Hopefully he won't vomit again.

Dansey looks really sick, but then he's suffered a lot more damage than Quennel. That's OK; it's Quennel I want to talk to. Dansey keeps holding the palm of his hand in front of his eyes and waving it from side to side.

'I can't see. I can't fucking *see.*'

I want him to shut up and be a good boy. I take a risk and grab his chin, taking a quick look at each eye. The left one is totally fucked, but there's still hope for the right. 'Your right eye is fixable, but you'll have impaired sight in it for the rest of your life. You need urgent medical attention. Stay still. Don't speak. Do anything to piss me off and you won't get an ambulance. Understand?'

'You bastard.'

'You tried to kill me, Vernon. You're lucky you're still alive. Now; do you understand what I just said to you?'

He looks miserable and nods his head. Then he's sick over himself. His vomit is pale yellow. Has he been drinking snowballs? I grab the chair that I was being beaten on a few minutes ago and position myself in front of Quennel.

Taking a look at his face, I get a sudden flash of recognition. Do I know him? Then it hits me. I recognise his features. It's the grey eyes and the distinctive dead straight eyebrows. It was one of the kids at the orgy.

Lighter skin than Aaron, six or seven years old, dressed in a fancy green velvet kaftan top, being pawed by a dribbling DELTA, the obese Aleister Crowley lookalike. I get a sudden wave of nausea from the memory. I consider getting hypnotherapy to erase that and all the other scenes from my head forever. I might suggest that Francie does the same. It's not just that it's all horrific, it's also deeply depressing, like a constant unwanted reminder of what some men are really like.

'Come on, Aaron. Overcome the pain. You're a soldier. You've had worse than this.'

'What is it? What do you want…what do you want to know? I don't get it. I don't get this.'

'Yeah, yeah. You said something happened when you were in Cyprus What was it?'

'I should have been at home. If I'd been at home, it wouldn't have happened. I could have done something. Fuck it, man.'

'When what happened, Aaron? Tell me what happened? Was it your son?'

'Yeah. It was my kid. Ronny. Aaron. Aaron junior. He's seven.' He has a big sigh. He's calming down a little and for the first time he looks straight at me. 'It happened three weeks ago. He was abducted. We assume he was abducted. Yeah, he was abducted.'

'How was it done?'

The anger and hate in his eyes are making him look

crazy. 'Linda. My wife. She took him – he was *seven*, man – to this water park. Indoor water park. This place he went to. Been going there for years. Leyton Leisure Lagoon. His favourite place. Always packed. I never liked it because of the crowds. She went to get him a drink and something to eat. He liked those Fruit Shoots. Peach and mango are his favourite. She comes back, he's gone. She looked everywhere.'

'Did she call the police?'

'Yeah. Well, she called me first then called the police.' He has a brief coughing jag. 'She was hysterical. Just...out of it. I caught the next plane back. You've broken my ribs, man. Hurts when I breathe.'

'So, you left the army to find the people who took him.'

He looks confounded then shakes his head. 'No. No. I didn't quit. I'm still serving. They gave me compassionate leave. I'd have quit if I had to, though.'

'And your friend here? You said *Former* Warrant Officer Class 1.'

'We were in the same regiment, but he retired a year ago. Got his own business now. I told him what had happened. No. He *saw* what had happened. It was on the news. He got in touch and said, you know, anything he could do. We did an appeal on the TV. Me and Linda. The police said it would help things, but nothing happened.

'It wasn't happening fast enough, you know? With the police, I mean. They said...they were doing everything they could and to leave it with them. But there's a time limit with these things, you know? Every second that goes by there's less chance of finding them. The kids. And then this guy calls me on the phone. It was three days after the appeal, the TV appeal.'

'What did he want? Did he give a name?'

'He said he was called George Hawkins. Yeah. George Hawkins. It seemed like a fake to me. Something in his voice when he said it. Like he thought it was a ridiculous name or something. Sounded too posh to be called George Hawkins. He said Ronny...he said that he had Ronny, that he was unharmed, and he wanted fifty thousand to return him.'

'He called you on your mobile?'

'Yeah.'

'Was your number given out by the police? Was it part of the TV appeal? How do these things work?'

'Er, no. I hadn't thought of that. No idea how he got it. Only the police had it. They had my mobile and my landline. I just...I don't know. Had a lot on my mind and then the chance to get him back appeared. I had to take it. I had to. Linda, man; she's not well. She...she was smashing her head against the wall and stuff.'

Three days or less to track down a private mobile number? Not impossible, but tricky. 'Have you tried to call that number back?'

'No. Yes. I called him back on it to confirm the meet. Haven't used it since.'

'Get your mobile out. Show me the number.'

I copy it onto my own mobile and call it. Dead. Just like the mobile he called Liva from. This is so annoying.

'Did you tell the police about this?'

'Are you kidding? He said not to. He said he'd know. Hawkins, I mean. He said, like, he said he knew people...in the police who would tell him. He said he'd kill Ronny if he found out I'd called them. He said he'd torture him to death. He said he'd take his time. What the fuck would you have done? Fuck, man. Who the fuck are you?'

This is going too slowly. 'So, you got the money together and presumably you met him somewhere to hand it over.'

'Yeah. Blacknest…Road. Right next to Virginia Water. It's a long road. No houses or pedestrians. You can see the lake through the fencing. Not a busy road. It's pretty deserted. He said to stop by the Roman ruins.'

'Roman ruins? In Virginia Water?'

'Yeah. Don't ask me why they're there; they just are. He said to look it up so I could find it OK. He said I'd see the columns. He was right. You couldn't miss them.

'So, we got there. Nowhere to park, really, but there was an off-road dirt track just before the ruins where you could pull over without interfering with the traffic. He wanted to meet at seven-thirty in the evening, which I thought was a bit strange, 'cause it would still be light, but he said if the police happened to go by and saw a couple of cars parked there at eleven at night or something, they'd probably stop and take a look. Seven-thirty was better. Not too busy, but still a fair amount of people going home from work.

'We got there at exactly seven-thirty, just like he said. I took Vernon with me for moral support. He didn't say that I had to be on my own. Hawkins, I mean. I might not have been able to drive for all he knew. Vernon would be handy if there was any funny business. Besides, he knew I wouldn't try anything. Er, Hawkins, that is.

'We took his jeep. Vernon's jeep. The one you were in. Two minutes later, a roller appears and parks in front of us, facing us, headlamps full on. About five yards away. We were dazzled by the lights.'

Now we're getting somewhere. 'A Rolls Royce? Did you get the registration?'

'No. What? That was the last thing on my mind, you know? Besides, Vernon noticed that the registration plate at the front was covered in mud or some other shit so it couldn't really be read. It was a new-looking Rolls-Royce Phantom. Silver.'

'Who was in the Rolls?'

'Two men. One in the driver's seat who looked like he could have been police.' He closes his eyes as a surge of pain courses through his body. 'Tough-looking. Couldn't see his face too clearly. White, though. Middle-aged. Another guy in the passenger seat. I thought this must have been George Hawkins.'

'Describe him.'

'Tall. Maybe six two, six three. Hundred and eighty pounds or a bit over. Running to fat a little bit. Not too bad, though. Grey hair. Hard to tell his age. Maybe fifties or sixties. I've never been good with guessing people's ages. Never. Nondescript grey suit. Expensive tailoring, I would say, though. Poncy. Little beard. Like a goatee beard, they call them.'

Well, surprise, surprise. This begs the question, what the hell did van Cutsem think he was doing? I'll have to think about this later. Vernon keeps moaning. He's really annoying me. Quennel shakes his head to bring himself back into the room and continues.

'So, George Hawkins, or whoever he really was, gets out of the car. Now I could see Ronny.'

He suddenly switches off and stares vacantly at the floor.

'Come on, Aaron. Keep going.'

'Yeah. Ronny. He was sitting in the back, on the back

seat, looking straight ahead through the two front seats. He was looking straight at me, but it was like…' He stops for a brief sob. He rubs his eyeballs with a finger and thumb to clear the tears. 'It was as if he didn't know who I was. Like I was a stranger. Just didn't recognise me. Not even a bit, yeah? He just stared at me with this sort of empty expression. Totally blank. I reckoned he must had been drugged or something. I thought maybe they'd given him downers so he wouldn't run away.

'I got out and stood by the side of the jeep. Vernon stayed where he was, holding the money in this leather bag. It was his money. But I told him I'd pay back every penny, every single penny.

'Hawkins said something about the fact that I could see my son was perfectly alright, so all I had to do was get the money, place it in front of the jeep and then Ronny could get out of the car and I could take him home.

'Vernon handed me the money and I placed it on the floor where Hawkins could see it, then I looked up and he had a fucking gun aimed right at the centre of my head. I just couldn't believe it. He swung the gun across and aimed it at Vernon as a warning, then it was back on me again. He was grinning. Really pleased with himself. That…face. I could have killed him, man. Without any remorse. Made it really bad for him.'

'What sort of gun was it?'

'It was an FN FNS. A semi-automatic. American. God knows where he got that from. I was stunned. I didn't know what to do. We just weren't expecting it. I've got a piece at home, you know? An illegal. A P226. SIG Sauer. But it never occurred to me to bring it.

'He kept the gun on me, walked over, picked up the bag and went back in the Rolls. I could still see Ronny.

He was still, like, zombified. Like he didn't know where he was or what was going on.

'Hawkins leaned out of the Rolls window and kept the gun on me. Told me that we should stay where we were, or he'd kill Ronny. He said he'd shoot him in the gut, so it was slow. The driver, whoever he was, was looking straight at me and smirking. Then they just drove off. What could we do, you know? What could we do?'

I remember Polly using the term 'zombied out' when referring to the kids at the orgy, so there's not much doubt now that Ronny was one of them. I've no idea what the fate of the kids at events like these might be, but this kind of thing sounds as if it doesn't and can't happen very much.

Quennel said his son was abducted three weeks ago, so that may indicate that it doesn't take that long to program them, brainwash them or whatever the hell they're doing. 'So, what did you do?'

'What *could* we do? We went home. I had to go and see Linda. I felt pathetic, humiliated. She knew what I was doing, so I had to tell her what had happened. It was terrible, man. She's falling apart. She's gone to stay at her mother's for a while. We had to call the doctor to sedate her. I didn't tell her about Ronny's behaviour. How could I? But on the way back, we started to think of how we could turn it around. Something that Vernon had spotted.

'Our headlamps were lighting up the back window of the Rolls a bit when it drove off and he saw a symbol on the back. Like a big crown, a big red crown. Looked like a rental car symbol, he reckoned. There were words underneath the symbol, but he couldn't read them. And the car was new looking, you know? Spotless. Didn't look like it was a car that someone owned, know what I mean?'

This doesn't sound like the car that Liva had travelled in. Her impression was that it was old. Perhaps van Cutsem is just a Rolls Royce fan, or maybe both Quennel's and Liva's descriptions are inaccurate.

'We went through all the car hire places. Took ages. There're loads of them. We tried upmarket car hire, wedding car hire and still nothing. We widened our search out of London and looked at places in Surrey, Middlesex, Essex and still there was nothing with a logo that looked like that crown.' He winces again from another pain surge. 'I began to think we'd made a mistake; that it wasn't a hire car after all.

'Then just by chance, I was coming away from a meeting with the police and saw a Bentley Mulsanne parked across the road. Vernon was with me and he spotted it straight away. It had that logo on the back window. The same one as the roller. It was a company called Majestic in Runnymede by Windsor Park. Small place. Not that far from Virginia Water, as it happens.'

And less than half an hour's drive from Richmond.

'Vernon said it was best if I didn't show my face. He went there on his own. Asked the guy to tell him who'd recently rented a Rolls-Royce Phantom. Guy wouldn't play ball. Client confidentiality and all that. In a fuckin' car hire company of all things. Vernon threatened him. He can be quite intimidating if he wants to be.' He chuckles to himself. 'When we were in the army together, he...'

'Yeah, yeah. And that's how you got the address in Vicarage Gardens, yes?'

'S'right. The car was rented to one George Hawkins.

Two days' rental, paid in cash. Almost three and a half thousand. Can you believe it? We've been checking it out since. Early mornings, late at night. Sometimes we'd park for a few hours, other times do a drive-by. Sometimes we'd use Vernon's jeep, sometimes we'd use my car. Maybe we'd just knock on the door, though Vernon argued with me about that. Didn't think it was a good idea. We didn't know anything about this guy, and he might get the police onto us. Anyway; nothing. The roller was never there, but we didn't expect it to be. Not really.

'Then you came out. Thought our luck had changed. We guessed you *had* to be something to do with it. We thought you might be helping him. I don't know. You were the only chance we had. Whoever you were, we thought we might be able to beat something out of you. Maybe find out where Hawkins was. How we can get to him. Kill him. We were clutching at straws, man. And now all *this* shit.'

He punches the floor in anger. Well, pretty good detective work, I have to say. I had to use Doug Teng to get that address and these guys got it through simple legwork. I'm almost jealous. He starts sobbing again.

Van Cutsem is either addicted to risk or he's just plain crazy. He's sprung from prison, given a new identity, gets back on the orgy circuit and *still* he can't stop himself doing something like this. Anything could have happened when Quennel turned up. Van Cutsem *must* have known that Quennel was armed forces.

He brings a pretty good semi-automatic with him, but Quennel could have brought an anti-tank gun and a couple of frag grenades. Maybe van Cutsem was just having fun. Maybe he was short of cash and was doing a bit of moonlighting. Maybe he's just a sadist and is currently having a gloat to himself somewhere. I can't even begin to think what's going on with the kid. My various injuries start begging for attention once more. I must get some painkillers.

'Listen, Aaron. Look at me. I'm going to tell you some stuff now and you're not going to like it. I'm relying on you to keep your mouth shut about some of this. Don't forget that you and your visually impaired pal here both tried to kill me. That's attempted murder, Aaron. I have a lot of contacts in the police, *real* contacts, and I'm pretty sure that the last thing you want is to be arrested and sent to prison, because that is surely what will happen. I will *make* it happen. And then you'll never get your son back. You will never see him again. Understand?

'You said that you knew that your son was probably dead by now. I don't think that's the case. And here's why.'

I tell him about Constantijn Francen aka Simon van Cutsem aka George Hawkins. I tell him about the orgies. I tell him what happens at the orgies and who they are for. Not surprisingly, this breaks him in two. With his head in his hands he seems much smaller.

'Oh, Jesus. Oh, no. Oh, please no. Oh, fuck, man. Fuck.'

I let him cry it out for almost five minutes. He punches the floor again and again until his knuckles bleed. He wails like a child and for a moment, I begin to think he's having a complete meltdown. But it stops, so I can start again. He stares straight ahead like he's OD'd on lithium.

'I told you before. I'm a private investigator. I had a client who was murdered by these people and I'm tracking down whoever it is that's behind it. I'd got as far as van Cutsem and that address in Vicarage Gardens. Unfortunately, it seems like a dead end.

'But I am not going to stop. Once I've located van Cutsem, I'm going after the people who hired him. These are the people that *you* should be after. Van Cutsem's a big part of it, but I'm pretty sure he's not the one running it.'

Regrettably, he's not taking all of this in. Understandable under the circumstances.

'Just so people can make *money*?' he says. 'All this shit? I'm going to kill them all, man. All of them. Every fuckin' last one of them. I don't care if they're men or women. I'll gladly go to fuckin' prison. You fucking find them. You fucking send them to me. I'll rip their fucking brains out of their heads.'

'Yeah, yeah. Give me your address and your mobile number.'

'What? 26 Gainsborough Road, E1. 077708 605998.'

I type it into my mobile. 'And your wife's away for how long?'

'What?'

'You said your wife had gone to her mother's. How long for? Quickly.'

'Couple of days. Maybe more. She's…'

'Stay at home. Don't go anywhere. Don't do anything. I'll be in touch. I don't want you doing something stupid that'll fuck up what I'm doing, understand? I'm going to help you if I can, but you've got to help me.'

'How am I going to do anything, man? I'm fucked. I need to go and see a doctor.'

'Never mind that. You want to kill every last one of them? Well, maybe you'll get a chance if you do as I say. Maybe I can deliver one of them to you. Maybe more than one. Maybe you can get your pal here to help you if he's capable. Maybe I can get your kid back in one piece, maybe I can't, but get in my way and I'll neutralise you, and you won't get anything done and you won't see Ronny again. Think of your wife, Aaron. Think of Ronny.'

Bullshit, of course. I just want him out of the picture and not interfering. But he may come in useful. I don't know how yet, but I'm keeping all my options open. His expression has changed. He's starting to trust me. He sighs. Vernon whines.

'You better not fuck me over, man,' he says.

'You wait for my call, *man*. You leave this to me. And don't forget I can have both of you done for attempted murder.' I click my fingers. 'Just like that. Now. Where is this?'

'What? Where?'

'Where we are now. Where is this?'

'It's the old O'Keeffe Glassworks. Membury Road NW10. It's Harlesden.'

I chuck him his mobile. 'Here. Treat you and your mate to an ambulance. I don't know what you're going to say to the emergency services, Aaron, but I'm sure you can make something up. Just keep me out if it, understand? Keep thinking about Ronny. You better lose the weaponry. Say you were taking a look around this warehouse and a madman appeared and attacked you. Speak to your pal. Get your stories straight. Remember, I'm after the same people you are. I'm taking your jeep. Where are the keys?'

The traffic is awful. It takes me almost forty-five minutes to get back to the West End. I dump the jeep in Betterton Street in a permit-only area, throw the keys and knives down the drain and walk back to my flat. A few people stare at my dishevelled, soaked appearance. I'm beginning to suspect that van Cutsem and his pals are not very nice people. When I get out of the jeep and stand up, I feel a little faint, as if my blood pressure isn't working properly, but it soon passes.

I'm walking past Drury Lane Gardens when I get a text from Frank.

Carmin Red Renault Grand Scenic K7363 F118 parked outside 3 mins ago. 2 males. Forties prob. Smart dress. Not police. One blonde & tall, one bald & medium height. Muscular. Verminous. Rang bell. I answered. Asked for Heidi Savage. Told them she ws working abroad. Not impressed. Tough looks all round. Sat in car for 12 mins then left. Pics courtesy of Héctor and modern science.

There are two photographs of each of these guys, each one from a slightly different angle and obviously taken through glass, but super hi-res. Tall Blond looks like a dead-eyed, inflexible, order-obeying thug, whereas Bald Medium has a trustworthy, intelligent face. He could give a good impression of being a cop, but I doubt if he is one. Both are tall and stocky, but Bald Medium is running to fat.

Interesting. The police knew Liva's real name, but whoever these two are only knew her by her professional name. All this tells me is that it was a good idea getting her out of there.

When I get inside my flat, she's sorting out shopping in the kitchen.

'*Oh, Gud og Jesus!* What has happened to you? You are soaking wet and your *face!*'

24

COVENT GARDEN LADIES

I lie in a hot bath and think about van Cutsem and what could have happened to him. The orgy that Polly filmed was six days ago now. He could, of course, have gone on holiday. Stranger things have happened. I'd have him down for a sex tourist; a regular visitor to Brazil, Malaysia, Kenya and the like.

I consider the idea that he's been bumped off like all the others, but it doesn't hold water. After all the trouble they've gone to, to cover up the fact that he's still alive, that would be an insane waste of time and resources. Unless the people I'm after *are* insane, which is always a possibility. At the moment, the only other possible lead is that W3 address on the driving licence that Doug dug up.

Quennel's little venture was interesting. I'm almost jealous that he managed to track down van Cutsem before I did, but then we were coming from different directions and, of course, it was van Cutsem who got in touch with *him*. And that slip-up with the Rolls Royce; if I was using van Cutsem for anything, I'd view him as an incompetent loose cannon. Maybe that's his appeal.

When I got back, Liva didn't stop fussing. Her main concern was the red swelling on the left side of my face where Quennel had punched me and the resultant dried blood around my mouth and over some of my teeth. At least I don't seem to have a black eye.

Usually, after a series of events like that, I like to give myself a quick once-over to make sure that all the damage is containable and/or fixable. But this time, it looked as if I was going to have company.

'It's OK, Liva. I've just been in an altercation with a couple of people. It's part of the job. Nothing to worry about. I've just got to go and sort myself out.' I realise I sound out of breath. I can see little white spots swimming about in front of my eyes.

'You smell like you've been sick! Have you been sick?'

'Yeah, well, I…' I feel suddenly faint and put a hand on her shoulder to keep my balance. 'I'm OK.'

She huffs impatiently and hustles me into the bathroom. 'Unquestionably you are not! *Rend!* Get those clothes off. Don't worry about me. I have seen many naked people. It is part of *my* job. You need me to help you.'

Getting wet clothing off is always a bit of a pain, but with Liva's assistance, it's over quickly. The most painful area is still from that initial punch in the guts from Quennel, though apart from a little redness, there's barely any sign that it happened. There is, though, a big graze and a patch of broken skin in the same area from his taekwondo kick.

My head still hurts from being thrown into the jeep by Dansey, but, as yet, there's no sign of swelling or inflammation, though I was aware of a little double vision when I drove back.

The strike from the baton across my thigh is a different matter. There's an ugly, dark, six-inch bruise which looks like it's going to be around for a while and a constant, painful throbbing. No bones broken, though.

There's also livid bruising and a medium-sized laceration just beneath my left armpit where Quennel kicked me and a nasty friction burn on the side of my neck. Liva's fingers lightly touch each damaged area until she gets to Lothar's handiwork. Even in her bare feet she's only a little shorter than me.

'What is this?'

'Some stitches I had put in yesterday morning. Just a cut.' I decide it's probably OK to take the dressing off now. It's been over thirty-six hours. I remove the bandage and take a look in the mirror. Still not healed, but a lot better and no sign of infection.

'You should have a long soak in the bath, but you must have a shower first. Get in there now. I will clean you. You are too weak to do it yourself and I will be more delicate.'

I step inside the shower and watch her as she strips; the satin mini dress folded neatly over a chair, a black strapless bra and matching thong placed next to it. She ties her hair back and the action raises her breasts. Her body is magnificent, but then I already knew that. All I need now is another unexpected visit from Priscilla.

She steps into the shower, closes the door, turns the water on and squirts some Penhaligon's Halfeti shower gel into her hand. 'Turn around.'

I do as she says. She lightly massages the gel into my neck, shoulders and back, barely touching the areas where the injuries are visible. She starts work on my arms, avoiding rubbing gel into the stitching, but allowing the hot water to moisten it a little and remove some residual dried blood.

As the gel starts to effervesce a little more, the heady fragrances of amber, vanilla, patchouli and artemisia mix with the steam. Out of the corner of my eye I can see her looking at the bottle.

'Oh, I love this. I have not heard of this. So many scents in the air. I shall remember. Turn to face me.'

More gel. This time the graze from Quennel's kick gets her attention. Despite her soft touch, I flinch as her fingers make contact. She smiles.

'*Undskyld!*'

'That's OK, Liva.'

She rubs the gel into the bruise on my thigh. This is not as painful as I imagined it would be.

'You have very well-defined muscles. Do you do the weights?' she asks.

'Not that much. Sometimes. Mainly swimming, punchbag, other things.'

She runs a hand over one of my deltoids. 'Yes. Swimming. I can see. I did quite a lot of shopping when you were out having your adventure. I shall show you afterwards. I have bought you some gifts.'

I watch the water drip off the full breasts. Her body is becoming pink from the heat. She glances at me and I get a brief, curt little smile. I imagine grabbing her shoulders and kissing her neck, her mouth, watching her body respond. 'You shouldn't have, Liva.'

She smiles at me again, but rather shyly. The eye contact combined with her proximity and nakedness is astonishingly exciting. As she concentrates on cleaning me up, her expression is both intimate and querulous.

She discovers older scars and runs her fingers across them. This is both perplexing and highly erotic at the same time. I'm still not sure about her and find her difficult to read. I'm beginning to suspect that someone has hired her to drive me insane. Whoever you are, it's working.

'Yes, I *should* have,' she says. 'You have been nice to me. I am not used to it. I was frightened, but with you I am not frightened. I see now your hair is dyed. Will it be OK if I shampoo it?'

'Should be fine. If my face starts turning grey, let me know immediately.'

'*Sjov.* When you were out, I was thinking about how you said I was pretty,' she says, as I'm treated to an almost professional scalp massage. I close my eyes and enjoy it. 'In the car, you know? I'm not naïve. I know you were trying to calm me down; to relax me after those police. To make me feel at ease with you. So that I could help you. But it was still a nice thing to say and it made me happy.'

'It was true then and it's still true.' What am I doing? I feel like some gauche schoolkid practising his suave and ingratiating chat-up lines.

'Most people just say I'm hot or sexy.'

'Really? That never occurred to me.'

I get a charming, sceptical smile for that. 'Hm! Your body is telling me otherwise.'

Once the shampoo is rinsed out, she turns the shower off, takes my hand and leads me over to the bath. She turns both taps on and pours some Thymes Goldleaf into the water.

'Go on. Get in. Relax now. As hot as you can take it. Don't be sick in the bath. I shall make you some coffee. I have put your plastic ducks in there to cheer you up. I like that they are different colours!'

I watch her bottom as she walks out of the bathroom. She looks over her shoulder at me, giving me a practised, sexy smirk. 'You are a bad, bad boy.'

'It's your fault. You're too voluptuous.'

She flicks her hair back and laughs. 'Hah!'

I stare blankly at the ducks bobbing up and down in the suds. She returns about ten minutes later with a coffee and a box of Cubotti Chocaviar chocolates. She's wearing a powder pink La Perla silk robe. Either she brought it with her, or she's just bought it.

She purses her lips and smirks at me. 'I see you have calmed down a little now.' She laughs. 'You men. You are all the same! I have these chocolates for you. That shop Venchi Chocolate and Gelato. Have you been there? It is marvellous. You should see their range. It is excellent.'

She unwraps a green cube, leaning forward and torturing me with that deep cleavage once more. Her skin is goose pimpled and I can see the stiff nipples against the thin silk. 'This is pistachio cream. Open.'

I open my mouth and she pops the chocolate inside. Hi, fifteen-year-old self – what d'you think of *this*?

'I know I said I'd take you out to dinner tonight, but…'

'No, no, no. I understand. You are injured. Even now you look pale and your eyes tell me you are in pain. But no matter. I have bought a lot of food and some wines. I will make us dinner.'

She eats one of the chocolates and rolls her eyes with pleasure as she allows it to melt in her mouth. She sees where my eyes keep going, smiles, and wipes a ball of foam from the side of my face with the back of her hand. 'I like you looking at me,' she says, softly.

There's something that's been nagging at me and I think now would be a good time to bring it up. I just hope it won't seem like I've been looking into her private affairs. 'Can I ask you something, Liva? You don't have a work permit or a visa for the UK, do you?'

She shrugs. 'No. Just, you know, it sort of, two weeks went by, then six months, then a year. No one ever approached me or asked for anything. I am paid cash usually. I have a bank account and they don't ask. International driving licence. All the rest. I am like a ghost!'

I put a laugh into my voice. 'I just thought you might have someone influential helping you out. Some VIP in the government!'

'Oh, no! Nothing like that. Jael is the same. She said that there are so many people in the world, coming and going, that you may travel and work and if you are lucky, no one will notice. Jael says they are sloppy with the visas. Maybe one *day*, you know. Then I shall be in prison!'

'I'm sure you'll be very popular.'

'*I'm* sure I shall be, as well. In fact, that theme was intensely explored in *Lust Behind Bars*. We should watch some of my films together, Daniel. I mean with you sitting next to me, while we watched, you know? I have never done that with a man. It would be intriguing and novel. I think you would find it intoxicating.'

Gulp. 'I've no doubt, Liva.'

So much for that line of enquiry. The idea that she was being abetted by someone high up in the Home Office was an appealing one, but I didn't really expect it to hold water. Still, it was worth asking.

I get out of the bath and Liva carefully and delicately pats me down with a couple of warm towels, then wraps another around my waist. 'I think you get injured on purpose. I think you like me spoiling you like this.'

'You may be right.' She closes her eyes as I kiss her

once, on the mouth.

She makes me a double vodka with ice and lime and insists that I watch television while she makes dinner. I watch a documentary about deep-sea jellyfish with the sound off. Before that, we sat in the kitchen and she showed me the rest of her shopping. Despite my well-intentioned warning, I'm pretty damn sure she was out for more than half an hour.

'I shall show you what I have bought you.' She hands me a Waterstones bag. 'This book looked very interesting and as you live here, I thought you would like.'

It's called *Harris's List of Covent Garden Ladies* or *Man of Pleasure's Kalender For the Year 1788*, an eighteenth-century guide to local concubines, complete with their addresses and a guide to their looks and specialities.

The descriptions of the girls are something else. How things have changed. I flick open a random page and look at the résumé of Miss Betsy H—st—ng of No. 22 Charles Street, Covent Garden.

Cheeks from whence the roses seek their bloom,
And lips from whence the zephyrs steal perfume.

'Thank you, Liva. I have seen this in bookshops but never got around to buying it.'

'Well now you have it. And there's this!'

It's some gift-wrapped raspberry, camerise and lemon macarons from Ladurée. I also get a yellow and black checked scarf from Urban Outfitters, a bottle of Orange Sanguine cologne from Atelier Cologne and a large bag containing ten different types of coffee bean from Whittards. I'm touched, I really am. It makes me laugh.

'It's like Christmas!'

She laughs delightedly and kisses me on the cheek. 'Just wait until you see what's for dinner! And I bought myself some perfume. What do you think? It's called *Mémoire d'une Odeur* by Gucci.' She sprays it on her neck and onto her wrists, rubbing them together and holding one of them out for me to smell. It's interesting; hints of bitter almonds and jasmine.

'It suits you, Liva.'

'Men or women can wear it. It has Indian Coral Jasmine in it and Roman chamomile and musk. I love musk. It is animalistic. Here.' She sprays some onto her fingertips and rubs it into both sides of my neck. 'Now we smell the same.'

She's cooked a delicious *Rigatoni e Scorfano* in a tomato, garlic and basil sauce. God knows where she found the scorpion fish around here. It's excellent; she's a really good cook. She also bought two bottles of Louis Latour Chardonnay.

Just as we're finishing the Limoncello Ricotta Cake she made for dessert, her mobile rings. She looks at her phone and looks at me, shaking her head from side to side to indicate she's not expecting anyone to call her.

I grab a V5 and a Kastner & Ovens takeaway menu, sitting right next to her so I can eavesdrop. Unknown caller. Forced cheeriness in the voice.

'Hello! Is that Heidi I'm speaking to?'

'Yes. Who is this, please?'

'It's Constantijn, remember? Constantijn Francen! How are you? We were very, very pleased with you the other day. And your associate, too. What was her name? Jael Caspri was it?'

'Jael Caspari. That's right. How can I help you, Mr Francen? Is it about more work?'

Very good. I nod my head at her. If Doug Teng was sitting right next to me with all his gear, we could get an immediate location trace on this, but unfortunately, he's not.

'Well, not quite, my dear, but it's related to the last job you did. The one in Richmond.'

'I had not been to that part of Richmond before. It is a lovely area.'

'What an evening that was! A good time was had by all, as they say. Enhanced by your own superlative skills, of course.'

'Thank you, Mr Francen!'

'Well, the people who organised that were so pleased with your, er, performance, that they'd like to give you and Miss Caspri a little bonus. Cash, of course. It was, er, something they were going to do a few days ago, but somehow it got overlooked. You know how it is. Busy, busy, busy.

'Seraphina – you remember her? – was *very* impressed with both of you. She thought you were both *delightful* ladies. Would the two of you be able to pop round to my pied-à-terre tomorrow some time?'

'Oh, I think that Jael has gone somewhere in Europe. She didn't say where. I think she said she was going on holiday.'

'Ah-*hah*. No matter. Perhaps we can reach out to her another time. Do you have any idea when she'll be back?'

'No. She didn't say. I don't know where she's going or for how long. Sorry.'

'Ah. Right. Well, never mind. I shall give you my address and we can arrange a time. Just the two of us. Do you have a pen?'

'One moment.'

I raise a hand and count to ten before allowing her to reply, to give this some realism. Being this close to her perfume is driving me insane. Or maybe it's coming from my neck. I nod my head to indicate 'now'.

'OK. I have a pen now. I couldn't find it! It's always like that. Give me your address, please.'

'It's 287 Regent's Park Road. NW1.' I write it down on my takeaway menu. 'Shall we say tomorrow afternoon? Around two?'

I scribble *No. Can we make it morning? Perhaps eleven? I have appt in the afternoon.*

'Oh, I can't really do tomorrow afternoon. I'm so sorry. I have a dentist's appointment. A root canal filling. I hate them. Could it be in the morning? Maybe eleven o'clock? I am afraid I may feel ill after my appointment.'

'Ah. Um. Yes. I don't see why we couldn't make it earlier. Alright, Miss Savage. I'll see you tomorrow morning at eleven.'

'Thank you. And thank you for calling me, Mr Francen.'

'My pleasure, my dear. Look forward to seeing you.'

She clicks him off. We look at each other. She looks worried.

'What does he want?'

'I don't know, but I doubt that he's going to be plying you with champagne and caviar. Good detail with the dentist, by the way.'

'Why did you say the morning and not the afternoon?'

'I didn't want you to seem too keen; to readily agree with what he wanted. I didn't want him to get suspicious. Also, I want to get all of this over with as soon as possible. You won't be going to that address, of course. I will.'

If this is tidying up loose ends in some way, why didn't he try to get Jael's address and phone number out of her?

Maybe he intended to do that tomorrow. Or maybe he has other methods up his sleeve. I can't worry about that now.

I'm just getting the spare bedroom ready when she appears at my side. 'There is no need for this. I will sleep with you in your bed tonight. After your exertions, you will need the comfort of a woman's body next to yours and I will sleep better as I will feel safer.'

'Are you sure?'

'Of course.'

Once in bed, I perform a rapid inventory of the various pieces of damage to my body. The baton strike to the thigh is currently top of the pain charts, followed closely by Quennel's punch to the solar plexus, which is producing an agonising throbbing that I can feel, for some reason, in my teeth. I'm still aware of the ricochet wound, but it's not too bad at the moment. The rest of it comes and goes.

I don't know what I'm going to do when I visit van Cutsem tomorrow, but I have to keep in mind that he'll quite possibly be armed. Quennel identified his gun as an FN FNS. Semi-automatic with a trigger safety like on a Glock. That might give me a millisecond's advantage in an emergency situation but not much more. I also don't know whether he'll be alone. It would all depend on what he had planned for Liva. Whatever it was, I can't imagine it would have been good.

While I'm hatching a clever plan, Liva appears only wearing her powder pink silk robe. She undoes the belt, lets it drop to the floor and slides in next to me, her head on my shoulder, her arm across my chest, her right thigh resting on mine.

'Rest your hand on the small of my back.'

I do as she says. We just lie there for about ten minutes, neither of us speaking. Eventually, she moves away and turns on her side to look at me, a perplexed expression on her face. I try not to look at her breasts. I fail.

'I don't know what you must think of me,' she says, softly.

'I don't think anything of you. It's as if you don't exist.'

She punches me on an undamaged area of my arm. 'No. I'm being serious. I mean about what I do, what I've done. You've never referred to it and it worries me. I am afraid you are, er, *bebrejdende*, you know?'

'Disapproving? Reproachful?'

'Yes.'

'Liva, it really doesn't bother me in the slightest.'

There's a long pause. I can hear her quiet breathing and begin to think she's fallen asleep. 'I've done some lousy things, you know?' she says. 'Or, at least, some people might think that. I've had sex with a lot of people. Many people. Men and women. I can't even recall who some of them were. I don't mind, you know? I can't complain. I'm not ashamed. I'm proud of what I have done and what I have achieved.

'But they just become a blur of anonymous faces and bodies. It can become a bit soulless.' She adjusts her position so she can look at my face. 'I can't remember the last time someone actually made love to me. To *me*. Not to some fantasy character.'

'I can't believe that.'

'It's true.'

I turn towards her, running a finger gently down the side of her body. She inhales sharply as her hips jerk forward and her stomach muscles clench. She gasps and places a hand on my shoulder. There are tears forming in her eyes.

'Will you make love to me?'

25

QUESTION TIME

On my way to Regent's Park Road, I get the cab to make a stop at Goossens & Provoost, a safety wear supplier in Mornington Crescent. I buy a hi-vis yellow bomber jacket, a weighty yellow hard hat and some safety goggles, plus a black PVC clipboard.

The bemused guy behind the counter gives me some sheets of scrap paper for my clipboard. Once back in the cab, I sling the goggles around my neck, get the jacket on and weigh the helmet in my hand. The driver stares at me in his rear-view mirror, deciding it's best not to say anything. I think I look really good.

I get dropped off in Regent's Park Road outside a pub called The Queens. This is Primrose Hill; a villagey, upmarket area a little north of Regent's Park and the zoological gardens. Van Cutsem's place is directly opposite the pub, next to a house with a Friedrich Engels blue plaque. Too many shops, cafés, hair stylists, delis, pubs, boutiques, tea rooms and people around, so I'll have to be quick and careful.

I order an Americano, sit outside the pub and look at my watch. Twenty minutes past nine. He won't be expecting Liva for an hour and a half. It's quite a relief to sit down. I still don't feel too good and the bumpy cab ride didn't help. For a moment I feel as if I'm going to throw up, but some deep breathing and a caffeine blast makes the feeling go away.

It's a fair-sized three-storey Regency townhouse with a basement, a stained-glass Rennie Mackintosh front door and a lit-up Victorian carriage lantern above the lintel. Bike stands, newly planted trees, bags of dumped rubbish and anti-parking bollards on the pavement.

No apparent movement from any of the rooms. White French blinds on all of the windows except on the ground floor, where they're replaced by charcoal crushed velvet curtains. Can't see much of the interior; a couple of black bookcases, a large painting with a dark blue swirl on a white background and a silver uplighter floor lamp. The Victorian carriage lantern gets switched off. Someone's in.

I start wondering about the house in Vicarage Gardens. How many fashionable London addresses do you need? Unless, of course, this house is not his. It could be a place where people like Liva are disposed of. I'm interested in what he was going to do to her. If Jael had arrived, would he have needed help? Even now, is help on the way? That's one of the reasons I got here well before Liva's appointment.

I finish my coffee, put my hard hat on and jog across the road, while slipping on a pair of latex gloves. I ascend four steps and push the doorbell once, immediately reversing down, removing the hard hat, looking up at the second floor and scratching my head. I have no idea what I'm meant to be doing, but it feels convincing and hopefully looks that way, too.

With my peripheral vision, I can see someone looking cautiously out of a downstairs window. I pretend not to notice. I check my clipboard, look at the house again, go up the steps and push the doorbell once more.

Through the stained glass, I can see a tall shape approaching the front door. It's him. I'd recognise that smartly coiffured grey hair and cute beard anywhere. He opens up and looks down his nose at me, a horrified and supercilious expression on his face.

'Yes? What is it? How can I help y...?'

I swing the hard hat upwards with as much force as I can manage and catch him squarely beneath the chin. I can hear his teeth click together from the impact. He staggers backwards, attempts to support himself on a wall, fails and falls heavily onto his back. I take a quick look outside and close the door. He moans, holds his chin and looks up at me; stunned, utterly bewildered. I don't want any conversation yet, so I stoop down and punch him in the face.

I can see a large kitchen down the end of the hall. I grab his collar, drag him along the black and white tiles and dump him in front of the fridge. He's heavy, maybe two hundred and thirty pounds; a little bulkier than Quennel's estimate.

There are three antique iron kitchen chairs around a small glass-topped dining table that'll do nicely. I pick one of them up and place it directly beneath a row of spotlights on the ceiling. I adjust the spots, so they're all aimed in the general direction of the chair; I can fine-tune later if need be.

I hoist van Cutsem up and sit him down. He drools, looks delirious and I have to stop him sliding to the floor twice. I can smell his sour body odour. Nerves, probably.

I dump the hat, goggles, clipboard and jacket on the floor and attach him to the chair with four zip ties: two attaching his ankles to the front legs and two binding his wrists to the arms. Inexplicably, I start thinking about Priscilla.

I fasten another couple of ties around each wrist and tighten them until the skin around them turns white. I make myself a cafetière of coffee and pour it into an elegant Villeroy & Boch honeysuckle pattern mug. The coffee's OK. Nothing special.

He slowly recovers and starts to struggle. He coughs. He coughs again. His voice sounds thick and sluggish. His eyes bulge. He shakes with nerves, but the contemptuous manner remains.

'Now listen here. Is it money? Is that what you want? I'm asking you a question. Do you understand me? Do you even speak bloody English?'

I don't bother replying. I find a large cotton hand towel, soak it in cold water and then drape it over his nose and mouth, holding it in place with my hand. The spluttering, choking, panicked breathing and hoarse guttural sounds start almost immediately. I won't start the serious stuff yet; I want him to be able to speak. I count to thirty while I let him stew in it, then take the towel off. I drag over one of the other chairs and sit down opposite him. His eyes look wild.

'I'm talking to you. How *dare* you not reply to me,' he croaks. 'You will *pay* for this, believe you me.'

He's trying to be domineering, but his heart's not in it. 'That didn't feel very nice, did it, Simon? Felt like you were drowning.'

He takes a second to gather his thoughts. 'Who – what are you talking about? Who's Simon? You've got the wrong person. You've come to the wrong bloody house. You bloody idiot. You stupid bastard. Get these…ties off me this instant.'

'Please don't waste your breath. You're Simon Randwijck van Cutsem. The one who hanged himself in a prison cell three years ago. Ring any bells? How's the neck? Is there a heaven? Now, if you want to talk like an adult, we can just get on with it. If you don't, you get the wet towel treatment again and this time I'll be pouring water onto it from your smart Mason Cash measuring jug over there. Which is it going to be?'

His eyes narrow suspiciously 'Who are you? Who sent you? Did *they* send you?'

I don't say anything. I just look at him. His heart rate will increase, and his mouth will become dry.

'Listen. Listen to me,' he says, licking his lips. 'If you have any sense whatsoever, you'll untie me and let me go. I won't call the police. You can just walk out of here and nothing will happen. If you don't, you won't believe what will come crashing down on you, you really won't.'

I soak the towel again, fill the jug and deliver on my promise, dribbling water onto the towel from about a foot above his face. He coughs and retches and gags and coughs. I know from experience that this feels terrible. It could be worse. He could be lying down. I take the towel off his face and sit down again, watching as he vomits some water over himself. His eyes are bloodshot.

'You're quite a piano player, aren't you, Simon. It's one of your great loves, I suspect. You'll notice a couple of zip ties around your wrists. That's apart from the ones attaching you to the chair. Your hands will already be feeling uncomfortable. Soon, the tingling will start and then the feeling will begin to go.

'In a few hours, cells will start dying and your hands will start swelling. It varies from individual to individual, of course, but in six or seven hours–' I shrug my shoulders. 'Well, I'm sure you get the picture. Even if someone called an ambulance for you at that point, there would be nothing any medic could do for your hands. They'd have to be amputated. *Unsalvageable* is the word they use, I understand.'

I've got his full attention now. He looks crazed. I take a couple of sips of coffee. 'But *without* an ambulance, *without* a medic, which may well be the case here, your hands will eventually get infected and you'll die of blood poisoning. Tied to a chair. On your own. In your kitchen. Not the nicest way to shuffle off that mortal coil, I suspect. Perhaps I could put some music on for you to ease your passage. Any requests?'

He looks fearful, goes pale, recovers, then gets angry, speaking and panting in equal measure, clenching his teeth in anger. He struggles against the ties, but it's hopeless.

'I don't know who the hell you are, but you really, *really* have no idea who…'

I raise a hand to stop him. 'I get it. I *really* have no idea who I'm dealing with. But at the moment, I'm just dealing with you and you're just dealing with me. I know you're scared, Simon. I know all these things are rushing around your head: how to escape, how to get hold of your gun, how to contact your friends who I *really* have no idea about. But I'm still not going to let you go. Look at me. You're my prisoner.'

'Cunt,' he whispers under his breath.

'You have no idea, Simon. Now, I'm going to ask you lots of questions. I want quick, accurate answers. Believe me when I tell you that I'll know if you're lying or embellishing or prevaricating and you'll be punished for it.

'Keep thinking about your hands, Simon. Try to imagine what life might be like without them. You'll have to think about another musical instrument to master; perhaps kick drum or theremin.

'Or maybe meditate on that lonely, painful, awful death from sepsis; the agony, the fever, the confusion, the despair. Look at me. You know I'll let it happen. I just haven't decided which way to go, yet. Amputation or death. It's one hell of a choice, isn't it, Simon. But if you play ball with me, I'll cut those ties, leave and you can get on with your life. Things will go back to the way they were before you opened the door to me. That's the deal.'

He starts to say something, but just sighs.

'Now. First question, Simon. Are you expecting anyone to turn up here this morning? I'm sure you understand that I want you all to myself.'

He shakes his head. 'No.'

He gets the towel and the water jug again. This time I get behind him and tilt the chair back forty-five degrees. The effect is much worse. He coughs, gasps and splutters. He struggles so hard that for a moment I think he's going to break the ties.

I can hear the water in his lungs. He's frenzied. His face is red. A little mild asphyxiation; no brain damage yet. After twenty seconds, I return the chair to its original position.

'That was the wrong answer, Simon. I told you; I'll know if you're lying and you were lying just then.' I shove the jug in his face. 'Are we going to have to go through all of this again?'

He sniffs and shakes his head. I get him a glass of water. I'm kind like that; almost saintly. He drinks. I start thinking about Mrs Gardiner. A very pretty, distinctive face. I wonder if I've seen her in anything. Television, maybe, or a film.

'So, Simon. Are you expecting anyone to turn up here this morning?'

He nods. 'Yes. In about an hour and a half. A lady friend. She'll be alarmed if I don't answer the door, though. She'll be worried about me. She'll call the police. She's friendly with some high-up police officers. She could get them here in minutes.'

I tilt his chair back again and give him another twenty-second cascade. I wait until he recovers. I finish my coffee and place it slowly and delicately on the glass-topped dining table, to demonstrate sensitivity and possible insanity.

'We both know that's total nonsense, Simon. I'm trying to educate you. I'm trying to educate you not to lie to me. Things are bad enough for you as it is, Simon; they will only get worse if you lie.

'You have to understand, Simon, that I don't care what I do to you. You're nothing to me. I know who you are, what you are and what you've been doing. Piss me off enough and I'll just get rid of you. I'll dump your corpse in a skip. Don't forget, Simon; you're already dead. No one will miss you. Now; are we going to have an adult chat?'

He looks downwards and sniffs. 'Yes.'

There are so many things I want to ask this prick that I can barely think of where to start. It'll have to be the prison break; everything else should follow organically. If the police were involved, it'll be a useful piece of information to pass on to DI Bream, who'll be well pissed that a fellow officer helped a scumbag like this escape justice, particularly as she was in on the arrest.

I have to weigh up the risks of contacting her. She must have seen my media coverage by now. Maybe she hasn't. Maybe she's too busy. But she's probably my only hope of getting the police off my back.

I won't lie to her; I'll just have to be economical with the truth. I'm beginning to forget exactly what I've been telling everybody. If only I could be honest for once instead of giving everyone a slightly different version of events. It's exhausting. I should keep notes.

'OK, Simon. Your breakout from prison. Wormwood Scrubs, wasn't it? Tell me how that happened. I want names. Try and keep it precise. Keep thinking about your hands. The seconds are ticking away.'

'Just, um…listen, do we really have to talk about that? I…'

He gets another session with the towel and water jug. This is how they should interview politicians. He wheezes like a TB patient. He flexes his fingers. The feeling will be ebbing away by now. All this will certainly be placing a few deposits in his nightmare bank.

'Who organised it? Quick answers, Simon, or you'll be punished again.'

His voice is resentful, embittered, disdainful. 'I was in my cell and the prison officer said I had a visitor. Then he took me down to the healthcare room, healthcare suite or whatever it's bloody called.'

'What time was this?'

'About two in the morning. Something like that. Perhaps a quarter past.'

'The prison officer's name. Quickly.'

'Patrick Thomas.'

'And who was the visitor.'

'It was a police officer. Detective Chief Superintendent

346

Michael Small.'

'Which division?'

'He didn't say.'

'Were you alone in the healthcare room with him?'

'Yes. The prison officer departed immediately. He didn't come in the room. He waited by the door until the detective came in. Then he left.'

'Did this police officer show you a warrant card?'

'No.'

'Had you ever met him before?'

'No.'

'Any proof apart from his word that he was a police officer?'

'None at all. One assumed. He said that he'd been sent by an acquaintance of mine.'

'Name of the acquaintance.'

'He didn't say.'

'What happened then?'

'He said I was to leave the prison with him immediately. He had two bags with a change of clothes for me. A suit, shirt and tie, shoes and a black woollen scarf. Very conservative. Not my style at all. I got dressed and we left the prison. I only saw two other guards on the way out, but neither of them looked in my direction. One of them I knew…'

'Name.'

'Oswald Walsh. I didn't know the other one, but there was nothing unusual about that. It seemed quiet despite the time. I hadn't been in that part of the prison at that time of night before, but…'

'Forget that. Keep going.'

'We just walked out of the front door and through the gates. There was a Jaguar XJ parked across the road from the prison. In Du Cane Road, I mean. It was dark green. The engine was running. There was a driver. A rather, er, *portly* gentleman. Very short ginger hair. Fat neck. Wedding ring. Black suit. Rimless glasses. Another policeman, I suspect. He didn't look at me or speak. I sat in the back with Michael Small, and we drove out to Berkshire. Fast driver. Fast car. The speed gave me anxiety.

'They had Classic FM on the radio. We listened to Brahms and then Mascitti and then Telemann. I saw a sign for Finchampstead at one point, but I wasn't precisely sure where we were. Lots of country roads, then a stop. The driver got out and opened a very wide gate. There was a name at the front. It was called Antler Farm. It wasn't a farm, though. Just a big house. There might have been a farm there once; who knows?'

'And you'd never been there before.'

'No. First time.'

'What was the house like? Give me your impressions. Quickly now.'

'Big. Dull décor. 1950s. A little dusty, I felt. Furnishings eclectic but in a bad way. Five bedrooms at a guess, but it didn't feel like someone's home, if that's what you're asking. It smelt mouldy, dank, like a place that was left empty and unattended for long periods of time. Tedious prints on the wall. Awful, cheap ornaments scattered around the place. Horses, dogs, that kind of thing. Vulgar.'

He has a coughing jag which lasts for a minute. This sounds like spook stuff and Antler Farm sounds like a safe house. There seem to be a lot of police involved in all of this. Some aware, some not. That driver had a distinctive appearance, which may come in useful.

'Who was in the house?'

He doesn't like this question. He's looking shifty.

'The, er, the two police in the Jaguar left. I heard them drive away.'

He's afraid. I can feel it. He's weighing up which would be worse for him: keeping stuff from me or protecting his pals, whoever they may be. He stares straight ahead. His expression is blank, but tormented. I've seen that look before; he's trying to disassociate himself from what he's about to tell me, as if it's not his fault that he's spilling his guts.

I sigh impatiently. 'Who was in the house, Simon?'

'Two people. One of them was a man I knew as Gabriel White. I'd known him for six years or so.'

'You don't think that's his real name.'

'No. Firstly because that's what people like him are like, secondly there was, I suppose, a twinkle in his eye when he first gave me his name, understand?' He coughs again. 'Like we were both in on the fact that it was an alias.'

'So, he's some sort of intelligence officer. Who does he work for?'

He starts to say something, but stops himself, closing his eyes. 'I – I don't want to be vague with you, but I have no choice. From what I've been told and from what I gather, he's either with MI5 or with the NCA. It could be that he *was* in MI5 and then got moved, as it were, to the NCA. Or vice versa. I'm truly not sure. He may be in both. He may be in neither. It isn't something he can be drawn on.

'It doesn't really make any difference. Not to me, anyhow. I suppose you could say that I work directly to him whatever organisation he happens to be in. People like him get moved around, or they involve themselves in long term liaisons with other departments. Just my impression. Who *are* you? Are you with MI5?'

The NCA or The National Crime Agency is mainly concerned with organised crime. The British FBI, as some call it. It's pretty new; principally law enforcement as opposed to intelligence. From what I can recall, its major concerns are cybercrime, human trafficking, weapons and economic crime. Works closely with MI5. Economic crime. That would link it, via MI5 or not, to the OFRP. Human trafficking? Could they conceivably be *involved* in it as opposed to preventing it? Are the dots getting joined up?

'Who was the other person at the house?'

'A woman. I'd never met her before. She was introduced to me as Mrs Margaret Carter. At first, I thought she must be some kind of senior police officer or some sort of bloody spook like Gabriel White, but, um, something he said…'

'What did he say?'

'It wasn't when I got to the house, but later on. They were laughing about something. They were in the hallway or the kitchen. He said something like "This would set the cat amongst the pigeons at the DIT".'

'What does that mean?'

'DIT? Department of International Trade.'

'Was Margaret Carter another alias, did you think?'

'Yes. Certainly. It didn't occur to me for a minute that she was really called Mrs Margaret Carter. They were very affable, but I never felt they were being one hundred per cent honest with me. Par for the course. I am au fait with their world, I am proud to say.'

Lothar mentioned that the OFRP was partially

subsidised by UK Export Finance and the DIT. So now we have world trade thrown into the mix. Is there a link? I'll keep it in mind. Van Cutsem hasn't given me that much yet, but it's already a little overwhelming. I need to get a framework and hope all the pieces will slot together.

He starts wriggling and rubbing his fingers together. The tingling sensation has started. If he had any doubts about what I told him would be happening to his hands, they'll be fading now.

'OK. So, we have White and Carter in the house. What happened next?'

'They told me that I would be given a new identity. I was to disappear for two months while they made some arrangements. There was a cottage in Bury St Edmunds where I was to stay. They gave me a car and some money. It was a very nice cottage, but the DVD selection was a disaster.

'When I returned, I would have a new house to live in and all my identity papers would have been sorted out. Everything would be back to normal. My hands are feeling odd. Could you untie me now, please?'

'This was the house in Vicarage Gardens. And now you're Constantijn Francen.'

'That's right.'

'What was the address of the cottage?'

'Ah. Um. Foxgloves. Sicklesmere Road. Postcode was IP something. Can't remember the rest of it. Had a three in it, I think.'

'Tell me about that driving licence with Watermore Lane as the address.'

He sighs and shakes his head. 'That was a...not a mistake exactly; it was what you might call a false start or a trial run. It was something that was going ahead and then was never pursued. I never found out why. I'd never been to that address. Someone changed their mind, I suppose.'

'Why go to all that trouble to get you out of prison? You were in for pretty serious stuff; procuring, sex with a minor. It must have been important to someone. Was it White that was behind it all?' He nods his head. 'You said you'd known him for six years. How did you know him? Give me your history with him. Keep thinking about your hands, Simon.'

He sits up as well as he can, his demeanour suddenly haughty, proud and pompous. 'I'd been organising sophisticated sex soirées for a UK elite for a little over fourteen years. Judges, politicians, bishops, police, celebrities, royals; the usual suspects. The best people. The highest people. Then I…then I expanded, as it were, to include important people in business, diplomats, foreign dignitaries. It happened naturally. I didn't plan it.'

'So, when did White get involved?'

'About six years ago, as you said. Someone had been…talking. To this day I don't know who. White had me arrested, dragged in for a chat; whatever you wish to call it. I thought I was for the high jump. But he seemed interested in what I'd been doing and the people I'd been doing it with. He seemed to know everything. He wasn't threatening me exactly, but it was definitely coercion of a sort.

'He said that he had had me checked out and that I had quite a reputation. He said he would subsidise me and aim me in a different direction. He would decide who my guests would be. Very important people, he said. People who were of great value to this country. It would be my patriotic duty. He knew what my speciality was.'

'Children.'

'Yes. I was reluctant to lose my older clients, but the money offered persuaded me that it was worth it.'

'How much do you get paid?'

'Half a million a year, though I'm due a raise. It's peanuts, considering how much money my activities help to bring into the country.'

'Do you procure the children yourself?'

'I offered my services, but no. White has someone who does all that, but I have no idea who. Someone with superior contacts to me, I suspect. Maybe a wider reach. I suggest the type and the numbers required. I am a consultant!'

'Who does the behavioural programming, or whatever it is?'

'What? Oh, yes. All of that. Once again, no idea. Not my area of expertise. Sorry. How do you know about all of this?'

'Then three years ago you fucked up and went to prison. What happened? Did you go crazy? Multiple counts of sex with a minor, procuring, administering a substance with intent, facilitating the commission of a child sex offence; were you moonlighting? Couldn't White and his pals have prevented you going to prison? It would have saved a lot of trouble.'

He shakes his head. 'There was nothing White could do once the legal wheels were rolling. That's what he said, anyway. Perhaps he thought a short, sharp shock would do me good. My fault entirely that I was so abruptly incarcerated, and I was sad I'd let everyone down. I'm impulsive. Devil-may-care. I was indiscreet, but indiscretion can be such an enticement. I can't help myself. We can't always be perfect. You may think that those entertainments were enough for me; for my tastes, for my urges. Well, they weren't.'

'Why didn't he just throw you to the dogs? You'd become a liability.'

He sniggers to himself. 'To keep the bloody show on the road! It was all going so well. They'd never find anyone else like me. They didn't want to lose me. I know how to fine-tune the events to the clients. I know what they want and what they like. I can take them to places where the exciting and unimaginable reside. I make them feel special. Then I can join in and show them what can be done; what the possibilities are. I can show them how to truly enjoy themselves.

'It's highly skilled work. I give the entertainments an artistic touch, a personal touch, a unique touch. But it's more than that. Much more. I don't think I'd be exaggerating in this context to say that I'm like a god. I control. I debauch. I debase. And it is a god-like power that is *unimaginable* to ordinary people. And I exude it. It pours out of me. I can transmit it to others. To the men who attend those parties. It makes them more *virile* to be in my presence. More powerful than they already are. It *oozes* out of me.'

'And presumably the regular guests, if there were any, would keep your resurrection to themselves.'

'Of *course* they would. Who were they going to tell about it? The bloody police? Don't be obtuse. Anyway, it was as if I'd never been away. Just a trifling tarriance in prison and a short sabbatical in Suffolk. The slight inconvenience of a name change.'

'Give me the address of the place in Richmond where you had the orgy a week ago. Yes, I know about it. Address and owner or you'll get a couple of zip ties on your ankles, as well. Imagine the consequences of that, Simon.'

He looks seriously mystified when I mention the orgy. For the first time he makes sustained eye contact with me. It's frightening and perplexing for him and it's intended to be; but there's no going back for him now.

'Langston Road. Casquatel. That's the name of the house. Casquatel, Langston Road, London TW9. Don't know the rest of the postcode. H something. I've organised many entertainments there. It's not…no one lives there permanently. Well, they might do, I was never very clear about that. It's been owned by the government since the 1940s, I think. Perhaps even before that. Didn't seem very lived-in to me, but then it's a big place. Please take these ties off.'

'And this place we're in at the moment. Is this owned by the government, too?'

He nods his head. He looks sad now. 'Yes.'

'And what were you going to do to Heidi Savage when she got here?'

He looks up and frowns; things get more bewildering with every second that passes. 'I was to keep her here. I have a telephone number that White gave me, though he can't be contacted on it. I was to call in if and when she arrived. You can never be sure that people like that will be reliable. I have a gun.' He pouts. 'But you knew that, of course. I would keep her here, I would restrain her, and call in. I don't know who's on the other end of that line. It's an automated…a recorded voice. Electronic. I just leave a message. Works very well, though. Someone would come here and take her away.'

'Have you called them yet?'

'No. Really. No. I was going to wait until she turned

up. I didn't want to make the call if there was a chance she wouldn't attend. I didn't want to waste their time. Like I said, people like her can be unreliable.'

'White told you to do this? To come here and do it?'

'Yes. He said that he had someone else working on it, but wanted to be sure she was, er, apprehended. Belt and braces, he said.'

'What would have happened to her?'

He shrugs like he doesn't give a fuck. 'What do *you* think? She's nothing.' He sneers contemptuously. 'No one would miss someone like that. They're the flotsam and jetsam of the world. I don't know why they left it this long. With that girl, I mean.

'There have been other peripheral personnel in the past and they're usually dealt with fairly quickly. They can't be trusted. Perhaps my people were busy. But in this case, there seemed to be something else going on, so things were slowed down. I have no idea why. I never know about unnecessary matters. I am not to be bothered with such trifles.'

'Give me the number you call.'

I save it on my mobile under BG for 'bad guys'. He wants to talk now; to show off. They always do, once you've given then enough of a shake. But it seems that there's no way that I can get to Gabriel White through him.

I've heard a lot of useful stuff, but it's becoming clear that this guy is a dupe and something of a dead end. But he will have his uses. I'm getting bored listening to him, so as soon as he gives me a physical description of White and Carter, I'm going to curtail our little chat.

'So, let me get this straight, Simon. To the best of your knowledge, Gabriel White, or whatever he's really called, coordinates these orgies. He selects the guests, gets the children from somewhere, chooses the government-owned venue, then gets in touch with you to organise and choreograph the entertainment, schmooze the participants and give off divine vibrations.'

He winces at my mockery. 'I suppose that's about right. Now will you get these ties off my hands, please?'

'No. Use your god-like power.'

As I leave, I can hear him crying.

26

SO MUCH FOR HYPNOSIS

I made a couple of identifier sketches of White and Carter until van Cutsem was satisfied that they looked like the real thing, then photographed them with my mobile.

White looks about fifty, toad-like facial features, with bushy eyebrows, blubbery lips, piggy eyes and a chin so weak I genuinely wonder if he has a lower jaw. Carter is in her forties, moderately attractive, short black hair with a little grey, big, surprised eyes, thin lips, firm jawline.

I found van Cutsem's gun and I also found what had to be Quennel's fifty thousand in a big leather carry-on bag. I took both with me. I also took the front door keys. While searching his bathroom, I discovered a box containing a dozen 10mg ampoules of diazepam and a handful of disposal syringes, presumably to dope up Liva until the bad guys got there.

Predictably, he didn't have any idea how to get in touch with Gabriel White and I believed him. It was White who would get in touch with *him* and it was not possible to contact White directly through his emergency telephone number.

This is all very smart, efficient and frustrating with its various cut-outs and ever-changing official and non-official personnel, not to mention the using and dumping of mobile telephones. The closer you get to these people, the further away they seem to get. Also, like van Cutsem, I don't believe for a minute that White and Carter are their real names.

Once again, the collusion of the police seems to be a factor here. It's happening so frequently now, sometimes in an arbitrary way, that I'm finding it difficult to keep it all in my head. In fact, I'm finding it difficult to keep *anything* in my head at the moment. I should get a pad and a pen and write it all down, or dictate it into my mobile.

The police were definitely involved in the reporting of Polly's murder to the media, they'd *have* to have been, but I have no names so have no idea which officers were involved. Hooper and Taylor, who arrested me, were acting on a tip-off from a member of the public, but their behaviour was odd, and I still can't work out where they were taking me.

Moss and Driscoll, who called on Liva, also seemed genuine, but, once again, their behaviour was unusual. And what did they want with Liva? What would have happened if I wasn't there and she'd let them in?

Then we have Detective Chief Superintendent Michael Small and his portly driver who escorted van Cutsem out of Wormwood Scrubs and took him for a mysterious drive in the country. Someone, perhaps the same person, was pulling all of their strings, whether they were aware of it or not.

Just as I was leaving van Cutsem's, I got a text from Frank at Liva's house.

Red Renault appeared again 20 mins ago. Parked three houses down on far side of road. prob same two males. Sat and stared then drove off. Nothing since.

Then…

BBC news just now. You with dark hair. Suspected murder still hot stuff. Now serious assault of two police officers in the mix. Apparently yr v.v.dangerous & not to be approached. Decima have some vacancies if yr interested!

Then…

Héctor still in shock after meeting Heidi Savage. Unable to speak. Will slap him.

That episode with the police was almost two days ago. Why the delay before the media got it? Did someone have to have a couple of meetings? I sit back in my cab and look out of the window. Two police cars, blue lights flashing, overtake us as we drive down Albany Street.

I check my watch. It's still only 10.17 and, strictly speaking, this is only the beginning of day three of my investigation. Despite that, I still feel uneasy and it seems that things are not progressing quickly enough. That's not necessarily my fault, but it feels as if it is.

I decide to bite the bullet and make a call I've been reluctant to make. But at least now I've got some leverage. And I need to get van Cutsem sequestered from his spooky pals. I don't want them to know about our conversation/threat session and I don't want them to know I'm coming for them.

'I just saw the news. Are you turning yourself in? Because that's the only conversation I'm going to have with you.'

I have to smile. I just love listening to that attractive, husky voice with its hint of Yorkshire. I've known DI Olivia Bream for a couple of years now and I like to think she'd probably still be a detective sergeant if it wasn't for the odd spectacular morsel I'd tossed in her direction from time to time.

This is in all likelihood untrue, but I still like to delude myself that it is. Still, she's my only contact in the Met and she may be able to help with some of the missing pieces of this increasingly complex jigsaw.

It's going to be a tricky negotiation: I give her van Cutsem (with certain conditions she won't like) and in return she attempts to get the police to drop me as a suspect in Polly's murder. I can't have my time being wasted by being arrested again. She may also give me a few more clues as to what the hell's going on. It's a kind of unequal, shameless and unethical tit for tat.

'I have to speak to you, Olivia. Just give me a half hour's time out.'

'Time out? What? Are you kidding? Do you think this is a film or something? You're wanted for murder and assaulting two police officers. I shouldn't even be talking to you on the phone.'

'Simon van Cutsem.'

Two seconds' silence. 'What about him?'

'He's not dead.'

'He – what?'

Got her. 'Do you know the Hard Rock Hotel in Great Cumberland Place?'

'Of course. It's just around the corner from here.'

'Meet me there in fifteen minutes. Go to the Rock Royalty Lounge. I'll be waiting.'

'Don't you have to be a guest to go in there?'

'Go to reception. Tell them you're meeting me. Someone'll escort you in.'

'Good God.'

The Hard Rock Hotel is the Hard Rock Café gone mega. Hasn't been open long. We sit in a pair of comfortable turquoise Scandi-style chairs with David Bowie and Amy Winehouse peering down at us from the wall. I place the leather bag containing the money and gun by the side of my chair. I just hope she doesn't ask what's in it. Not yet, anyway.

It's just before eleven now and too late to order breakfast, but Uberto, the manager, makes sure we get fresh coffee and a basket of warm croissants. Uberto was a client of mine. Blackmail. His past as a drug dealer was coming back to bite him and he needed it to stop. It stopped.

He grins at me as he places our food and drink on the small table. 'You've picked the worst possible time, Mr Beckett,' he says, looking over his shoulder at the empty lounge. 'We're rushed off our feet. Chaos! Pandemonium!' He laughs at his own gag.

'I can tell. Thanks, Uberto.'

'My pleasure, Mr Beckett,' He glances at Olivia and then at me. 'Mid-morning date? None of my business, of course, but I simply must know.'

'Yeah. This is only her coffee break, but she was desperate to see me. She said that an hour without me is like a decade for her.'

'Ha! You must treat her well. She has a mouth made for the longest kiss in Christendom.'

DI Bream rolls her eyes and takes her leather jacket off with that slow, exaggerated body stretch that I like to think I'm the only recipient of.

She's wearing a long-sleeved grey cotton top which emphasizes her gorgeous and, dare I say it, impudent breast shape. Her hair is longer than when we last met. She takes a good look at the swish, modern décor. I can tell she likes it.

'It's a nice place. Very cool. I always fancied having mirrored tiles on the wall in my bedroom,' she says, smiling.

'I've heard they can come in useful.'

'Making the room look bigger?'

'Something like that.'

'So,' she says, sipping her coffee. 'Are we going to talk or are you going to stare at my breasts all morning?'

'I think I'll go for the latter option, if that's alright with you.' This makes her laugh. Good. 'And I'd be grateful if you wouldn't use the b-word in such a brazen manner. We are in a public place, after all. Your hair's longer. You look good, Olivia.'

'Yours is grey, Daniel. New image?'

'I'd heard women go for older men.'

'You heard wrong. No stamina.'

'Is that an important factor for you, detective inspector?'

She blushes and she knows I've spotted it. 'So, tell me about van Cutsem,' she says, recovering.

'Can we start with me being a murderer first? The whole thing'll make more sense.'

'If you wish.'

'I can't tell you everything because I don't know everything, and I guarantee it'll get frustrating. But, you know, client confidentiality…'

I'm harpooned with a *this had better be good* look from those arresting blue eyes.

'First of all, is there any way you can get all that shit about me off the media? I'm innocent, I tell you. It's a stitch-up!'

She laughs and shakes her head. 'Out of my hands, I'm afraid. I could only intercede if you could deliver the actual murderer or some useful piece of evidence like the murder weapon. If we were not having a time out session, my next step would be to inform the Met Homicide gang that I knew who you were.'

'But you'd only do that if you were one hundred per cent certain of my guilt.'

'That's right.'

'Which you aren't yet.'

She purses her lips. 'I'm thinking about it. I have to say, though, that I'm a pretty good judge of character, and you don't strike me as someone who could or would kill someone in cold blood.'

'You're very perceptive.'

'Particularly a woman.'

'I'm flattered. That aside, if I started murdering people who came to me for help, it would be terrible for my professional image.'

'I can see that it would be a poor business model. Has someone beaten you up recently?'

'My bank manager.'

'Again? So, what happened? With the murder, not the bank manager.'

I'm getting warm now, so I take my jacket off and drape it over the back of my chair. The action makes my ricochet wound ache and the dizziness I felt yesterday returns for a few worrying seconds. Olivia looks at me with concern.

'Are you alright?'

'I'm fine. Have you got a notepad like ordinary police have? You may need to write a few things down.'

She reaches in her messenger bag and produces an A5 notebook with flamingos on the cover and a Cross Bailey black ballpoint. 'Ready.'

'And do I have your word that this is off the record?'

'You have my word.'

There are very few people who can say that and you'll

believe them. DI Bream, thankfully, is one of them. My hope is that she'll look into some of the cop issues and give someone, somewhere, a bit of a scare.

'There's a lot of stuff, so I'll try to make it as clear and brief as I can. The woman in the flat in Devonshire Street was my client. The police report said that they suspected she was the victim of an aggravated burglary. Beaten to death while she slept. Possibly with a baseball bat. No murder weapon found at the scene.'

'I saw. But that's not what happened.'

'No. She wasn't asleep. She was awake. She was shot in the head...' for the first time since it happened, the perturbing image of that moment re-enters my consciousness. I bat it away '...she was shot in the head by an unknown intruder. That intruder had an accomplice. Both, I believe, were professional killers.'

'So, the murder weapon was a gun.'

'Yes. But there's a problem with that. Even if, by some unusual circumstance, I was able to produce the murder weapon – the *real* murder weapon – it may not be of any use if the body they have was killed by blows from a baseball bat or other blunt object.'

'You're suggesting that the real body was disposed of and another with relevant trauma put in its place.'

'Strong possibility. Then they adapted the statement to fit in with its physical condition.'

'If you could produce the body – the real body – that would help to exonerate you. It would contradict the official statement and the cover-up would start to unravel.'

'I know. I'm working on it.'

'So, you saw this happen? The actual murder, I mean?'

I swerve away from that question. 'The description of

me that was given to the police was purportedly from a neighbour who heard a suspicious noise at around four-thirty a.m. I don't think that neighbour existed. You may want to look into that. One of the intruders was shot and killed, the other was incapacitated.'

I keep eye contact with her. I know what she wants to ask. I'm going to hypnotise her telepathically, so she doesn't mention it.

'So, who gave the police your description? The incapacitated intruder?'

Working well so far. 'It would seem so.'

She places her hands over her face and rubs her eyes. 'God almighty, Daniel. So, who shot the intruder? Was it *you*? Did you have a firearm? Who incapacitated the other one?'

So much for telepathic hypnosis. 'It would make it too complicated for me to answer that at the moment. You'll just have to bear with me. I'm sorry. I don't fully understand what went on in that flat yet. It was pretty dark. Everything happened incredibly fast and it was confusing to work out who was firing at who.

'The guy that shot Judith Hart tried to shoot me, but accidentally fired four shots at his colleague. I think that's what happened. I heard eight shots altogether, including the two that killed my client. He was panicking and shouting and that gave me the opportunity to incapacitate him and get out of there.'

She nods. Her expression is serious. I think she bought that. Eemil Salo would beg to differ, of course, but that's a problem for another time. I'm quite pleased with the credible, sincere way that distorted bullshit was delivered. I should take up acting.

'This is hard work,' she says. 'It's giving me a bloody

headache. Can we back up for a second? You were in the flat when all this happened, yes?'

'My client was concerned for her safety. We went back to her flat to pick something up from her safe.'

'In the early hours of the morning.'

'That's right.'

'Why would she be concerned for her safety?'

'She'd accidentally stumbled onto the fact that Simon van Cutsem was still alive.' That's not strictly true, of course, but it's the truth's best school pal. I'm confusing *myself* now.

'This client of yours. Who was she? I know her name. I mean who was she *really*?'

'That would muddle matters at the moment and I'm not sure I can give an accurate answer.'

I'm getting irrational anxiety from this type of calm, relentless questioning. I can't imagine what it would be like being interrogated by her if you were a conventional criminal. 'I went in first to make sure it was safe. She was jittery and insisted. It seemed OK. Then we both went in and all hell broke loose. But this is just reiterating. Can we move on?'

'I may be destroying my career here, but I'm going to have to trust you. Keep going.'

'Someone called the police to that flat. I have to assume that before they arrived, someone *else* paid it a visit. Whoever they were, they'd have almost certainly been called by the surviving intruder. In a matter of hours, they got him to safety, cleaned up the mess and removed two bodies.

'They couldn't leave the woman there. The cause of death they had planned to sell to the media wouldn't match up. Like I said, if anyone saw the body, they'd know immediately that the official cause of death was a lie.

'That PortraitPad impression of me; I don't know who did it, but I'll bet anything that it wasn't the police. Maybe that fact will come in useful, maybe it won't. Maybe you could check all Metropolitan Police PortraitPad use in the last seven days or something.

'That's it in a nutshell. I will now take questions. My question to you, however, is: how could this be done so fast and with the apparent collusion of the police?'

She sighs, nibbles at a croissant and looks up at David Bowie, as if for help. 'OK. The surviving intruder has some sort of direct line to the Security Service. God knows why or how. Maybe he works for them directly or indirectly.

'The Security Service contacts the local police – possibly – gives them a rough sketch of what's happened, tells them that it's their baby and they're in charge as it's a security matter. The local police are able to cordon the place off, but they can't go inside.'

She shrugs. 'That's a possible scenario, but it would be pretty unusual. If it was me, I'd insist on going inside and taking a look. I wouldn't allow myself to get pushed around by a bunch of Security Service personnel, especially in a murder case.'

'And once inside, you might expect to find it crawling with SOCOs dusting for fingerprints and wiping all the blood off the walls.'

'Indeed. They'd have been called out immediately in a case like this, had the police got there first.'

'But no one apart from the *real* police would have been able to put out a statement to the media like that. So, they were obviously being given their brief by the Security Service.'

'A strong possibility. Was your client connected with the Security Service?'

No point in lying. 'Yes.'

'You have some interesting clients, Daniel.'

'Thank you. So, the first thing here is you've got a big cover-up going on. The second thing is that the investigation was deflected away from the real perpetrators by using the police and pointing the finger at me.

'Someone told the police to do this; to set me up, even though they had no idea who I was, and they *still* don't have any idea who I am. So, the police are in on this whether knowingly or unknowingly.'

She stares into space for a few moments. I look at her mouth and imagine kissing it. She'd close her eyes, I think. 'So, they were given an accurate description of you from a non-existent witness, the description really originating from one of the perpetrators of the murder.' She scribbles something in her notepad. 'Someone would have written a report saying they *had* interviewed the mysterious neighbour and it was left at that. We just had to take their word for it, whoever they were.'

'Could that happen?'

'Unimaginable in a murder enquiry. This is fishy.'

'Bent?'

'Not yet. Just fishy at the moment. I'd go as far as saying it was *very* fishy. It could be that an officer or officers had pressure put on them from on high.'

'From the Security Service.'

'Possible. OK. What happened next?'

'After I was all over the news, I was reported by

someone who recognised me from the PortraitPad likeness. Bad luck, really. I didn't see it coming. I was arrested by Detective Inspector Christopher Hooper and Detective Sergeant George Taylor. Hooper in his fifties, Taylor in his twenties. Rapid response. Dark green Ford Mondeo, OX65 DSW. Got handcuffed, read my rights, and off we went.

'The nearest police stations with cells would have been Charing Cross, or, at a pinch, Savile Row, but I don't think that's where we were headed. I think they were genuine, but something didn't seem right. Just a feeling. But I could not let them detain me. I had a feeling that once I was stashed away in a police cell, I'd never get out again, and I was in a hurry. They didn't ask me for my name, and they didn't search me for ID.'

'Very curious.'

'I think they had instructions on what to do if I was detained. I don't think it was a straightforward ride to a local police station. I think there was a universal protocol on what to do if I was apprehended and it very likely came from the intelligence services.'

She shakes her head and scribbles in her notebook. 'I don't know Hooper and Taylor, but I can find out. It sounds like they weren't quite doing things by the book. Are we any nearer to van Cutsem yet?'

'Getting there. In the course of my investigations, I interviewed a woman who was connected to van Cutsem. While I was at her home, two *different* police officers turned up. Detective Sergeant Peter Moss and Detective Constable Roland Driscoll. Moss in his thirties, Driscoll in his twenties. Dark blue Audi A6, HY55 VVJ. Wanted to come inside. No reason given. Didn't say where they came from. Convincing ID but no warrant. Surly. Bad attitude. I slammed the door in their faces. They left.'

'What did they want with her?'

'No idea, but I don't think it was good. Through her, I managed to get to van Cutsem.'

'Were you sure it was him?'

'Absolutely. I found him at 287 Regent's Park Road NW1 7AH, but he doesn't own that place. But that's where he is as we speak. Attached to a chair with zip ties, soaking wet and shitting himself.'

She sits up in her seat, her eyes both alarmed and excited. She keeps scribbling.

'It's government owned, so I'd make sure your warrants are in order if you're going to bother with them. Van Cutsem has a permanent address – possibly – at 44 Vicarage Gardens, London W8 0HT. The night he was thought to have hanged himself, he was escorted out of Wormwood Scrubs at approximately two a.m. by Detective Chief Superintendent Michael Small. No division given, no warrant card. Van Cutsem had never seen him before.

'There was a dark green Jaguar XJ parked outside the prison. We don't have the registration. Driver probably another cop, described by van Cutsem as portly. Rimless glasses. Fat neck. Very short ginger hair. Black suit. Wedding ring. Classic FM on the radio.

'Two identifiable prison guards witnessed all of this: Patrick Thomas and Oswald Walsh.

'He was then taken to what sounded like a safe house where he was met by two probable spooks. Told to lie low for a few months and given a new identity. He's now called Constantijn Francen.' I spell it out for her. She scribbles away. 'There's a lot more to all of this, but we'd be here all day, and not all of it is reliable. All I can say is that if you're going to do something about this, you should be pretty damn careful.

'Oh, and there's a driving licence in the name of Francen with a different address: 69 Watermore Lane W3 9TL. I think that can be a low priority; some sort of fake ID they didn't pursue.'

Her scribbling gets faster. She's having trouble keeping up with this information overload. 'Could you slow down?'

'That's the opposite of what you said the other night.'

She laughs. It makes her look beautiful. She runs a hand through her hair. 'My tastes would surprise you, Mr Beckett.'

I give her some breathing space. She looks a little stunned. She drinks some of her coffee, which has to be cold by now. 'I'm not stupid, Daniel. I know you're only telling me a version of the truth. I've always had my suspicions about you and where you came from. And you're putting your own interests first.

'OK. Firstly, you're going to have to give me something – and it's going to have to be something good – that I can use to get the heat off you. Until you do that, I can do nothing to help you. Secondly, I assume it'll be useful to you in some way that I arrest van Cutsem and take him into custody.'

'Yes. It will. But I would suggest that you don't use his real name or his new one when you're checking him in. I would also suggest that you don't allow him his phone call or give him access to a lawyer.'

'But I can't…'

'I know it goes against everything you stand for. But if you let him have *any* of those rights, he'll be out on the street before you can bat an eyelid, and I *guarantee* it'll put your life in danger; maybe other police personnel as well. Think of all the future crimes that won't get solved if you're no longer around.'

'That sounds like emotional blackmail.'

Talking of blackmail, Uberto reappears and clears our stuff away. 'Is there anything else I can get you, Mr Beckett?'

'Some more coffee would be good, Uberto.'

He nods and leaves.

'Is there anyone you know who can help you pull this off? Someone in the Met you can trust? Someone who'll bend the rules in the cause of truth and justice?'

A little resigned sigh escapes from her mouth. 'Yes. There is. Perry Cook.'

Cook. I saw that surname in the article Francie and I found about van Cutsem's arrest. 'Where is he? What is he?'

'He's...' She waits until Uberto has delivered our coffees and left. 'He's a superintendent at Bishopsgate now.'

'City of London police.'

'That's right. He thought that they should throw away the key with van Cutsem. He was furious that he was placed in solitary for his own protection when he got there. If he finds out that his suicide was faked, and all that work was undermined by some fellow officers...'

'Get in touch with him. Do it this morning. Tell him what I told you. Say it was an anonymous source.' I place van Cutsem's front door keys on the table in front of us. 'These will get you into the house at 287 Regent's Park Road. He's in the kitchen. He's immobile. I suggest you take a pair of scissors with you. Remember; don't let him near a telephone. He'll likely threaten you, but you'll have to ignore the threats. Like I said, once he's officially booked into the system, he's as good as free.'

'I don't understand. Do you need him to be out of circulation for some reason?'

'Yes, I do. I need to speak to some people, and I want them to think everything's OK with van Cutsem. I don't want him getting in touch with anyone at all. Is there any way that you can put him on ice once you've lifted him?'

'How long for?'

I think I'm only saying this to be dramatic, but it'll act as a spur at the same time. 'Thirty-six hours. Then you can go to the press and be famous and get promoted again.'

'Alright. But not a minute longer. We'll have to think of some way of convincing him that everything's normal. It may not be easy. Bringing a successful conviction against someone like that when you've held them for a day and a half without their rights could be problematic.'

'Kill the electricity in the police station. Disable the telephone lines. Create some emergency that will delay his processing. Knock out the computer system. Set fire to part of the station. Pretend you have a migraine.'

'Thank you for your suggestions. And how do I explain away the presence of Superintendent Cook, assuming he'll go along with all of this?'

'You and he are both bright, experienced, senior police officers. Have a brainstorming session. I'm sure you can come up with something smart between the two of you. Tell your bosses or whoever that you felt morally obliged to let Cook know that van Cutsem wasn't dead because of his history with the case. Believe me, this *has* to be done, whatever the consequences might be. The alternative is that van Cutsem slips through your fingers again and you'll have whoever is behind all of this on your tail.'

She sighs. 'OK. I'm sure we can think of something.'

'And another thing. Van Cutsem is now involved in kidnapping. He tried to hold an abducted child to ransom only three weeks ago. I'm not sure he did the actual abduction himself, but the thing backfired on the parent and he got away with the ransom money and the kid.

'He has a gun, or should I say, he *had* a gun.' I reach down into the leather carry-on bag and pull out van Cutsem's FN FNS, which I've wrapped in a Bees of Kew Gardens tea towel. I place it on the table between us. 'This is that gun. His prints are all over it. Definitely unlicensed. Find out where he got it from. When the dust settles, I may be able to put you in touch with the father of the abducted child. I'm one hundred per cent sure that he'll want to press charges.'

'When the dust settles. Jesus Christ. And I thought today was going to be a quiet day. I'll do what I can.' She gingerly picks up the weapon and places it in her messenger bag.

'Thanks, Olivia. He's a bit potty, isn't he? Apart, you know, from being a prize-winning perve.'

'Van Cutsem? Yes. I should say so. I read all the interviews. NPD at the very least, I would say.'

'What's that?'

'Narcissistic personality disorder. Lack of empathy, exaggerated sense of own importance, need for admiration.'

'Sounds accurate. I don't know what his previous prison arrangements were, but I think when he goes back inside, it would be a good idea to let other prisoners have access to him. I'm sure the police can arrange that sort of thing if they're motivated enough.'

'I think Perry Cook would agree with you there. Last time, he wanted him to be sharing a cell with a rabid psychopath. Two rabid psychopaths. Of course, he wouldn't pull any strings to make that happen. That would be prejudicial to the good name of the police and the prison services.'

'Of course.'

'Well, thank you for the coffee and croissants. And allowing me to see what it's like in here. And thank you for van Cutsem. I'll see what I can do about your problem, but I'll need something substantial. In an ideal world, your identity would have to remain a secret and the investigation deflected away from you, whoever you were.

'We'd have to have the real culprit, irreproachable forensics, and you'd have to remain a man of mystery for evermore. That should make you feel right at home. I'll keep you up to date on what's happening. What are you going to do now? Continue your investigations, whatever they may be?'

'I thought we could get a room here. It is a hotel, after all.'

This makes her laugh. 'Unfortunately, I have to get back to work. We've had a report of a severe terrorist threat, so I've got a couple of meetings to attend.'

'What about your lunch hour?'

'You think an hour would be enough for me, Daniel?'

'I've no idea. Would it?'

She leans over and whispers in my ear. 'Nowhere near enough.'

I watch her as she sashays out of the door, her jacket slung over her shoulder. The hairs on my forearms are standing on end. Fuck.

27

HITTING THE JACKPOT

I head back to the flat to pick up Liva, and after ten minutes of passion, we get a cab to Francie's office. I've done my best to make her look inconspicuous, but she only seems to own sexy designer clothes.

This morning she's wearing a black, body-hugging crêpe minidress with dark green four-inch D&G stiletto heels, which may have been the reason we got a cab that another four people were trying to hail.

I made sure she tied her hair back and she added to the disguise by wrapping a dark blue bandana around it and wearing a huge pair of Dior sunglasses. And now she looks like an incognito film star, which I suppose she is. Try as I might, I can't stop looking at her legs. She looks at me, smiles, and gives my thigh a quick squeeze.

I'm trying to work out what to do next. The obvious route would be to track down Gabriel White and Mrs Margaret Carter and have a gentle word with each of them while they're pumped full of ketamine. The only problem is that those are certainly not their real names.

This means, for a start, that I can't use Doug Teng. It would be a major operation, involving hacking every single government department including the DIT, MI5 and the NCA until, if we were very lucky indeed, we came up with a photograph or photographs that matched the identifier sketches that I'd made at van Cutsem's place earlier this morning.

Then we'd have to find out their real identities, where they lived and so on and so forth. That's assuming that van Cutsem's guesses were correct and they work for the government in the first place. Plus, his descriptions would have to be impeccable, and my sketches photographically accurate works of art. It gives me anxiety thinking about it and it certainly couldn't be done in twenty-four hours. I also don't think I could afford it.

Francie's software is fine for identifying photographs or, in my case, stills from an HD film, but to do it from sketches drawn on a couple of junk mail envelopes with a biro would be a waste of time.

I'm going to discuss this with Francie and see if she has any inspired ideas. As for Antler Farm near Finchampstead in Berkshire, it may be worth checking out, but it just sounds like a run-of-the-mill safe house and I can't imagine Gabriel White and Margaret Carter make a habit of hanging out there in their spare time.

Then there's the problem of helping DI Bream clear my name. I have the actual murder weapon in my safe covered with Eemil Salo's fingerprints, even though he actually didn't fire it, but that's no problem. He also has matching gunshot residue on his clothing and skin. All well and good, but the official cause of Polly's death was not a gunshot wound.

At the moment, the only way that gun can be linked to her demise would be by discovering where her body has been stored and matching the bullet wounds to the weapon, if it's not already too late. I'm assuming that both her body and that of Wolfert or Redolf would have been taken to the same place. I could be wrong, in which case having that gun in my possession is not going to be much help.

Both bullets would have passed straight through Polly's head and embedded themselves somewhere behind her, though I didn't have a chance to check. If that's the case, they'll still be in good condition, still have striations and could be linked to the gun, assuming that someone doesn't make them disappear and repair the damage they made.

It shouldn't make a difference, though. Residue in her body would be enough to make the match. Why does everything have to be so complicated?

As soon as Francie sees Liva, she shrieks.

'Oh my *God*, I am *so* pleased to *meet* you!'

She strides over and gives Liva a bone-crusher of a hug. Liva laughs and looks at me with an amazed expression on her face. If she was shorter, Francie would have lifted her off the floor.

'Would you like a coffee? Tea? Coke? Dr Pepper? This is just fuckin' unbelievable. Heidi Savage in my office.' She's walking around in circles, flustered and blushing.

'You can call me Liva. Coffee will be great. Thank you.'

'Oh God. Sorry. Yeah. Hi, Liva. I'm Francie. I just – you know – I am *such* a fan of your movies. *Castle of Sin, Spank Me, Juliana's Promise, Ride me to Hell* – shit. And you look, just, really gorgeous in real life! You're just amazing looking. Totally ravishing. You're so tall. Wow! You take milk? Sugar?'

'Milk with one sugar, please. A sugar lump if you have it,' says Liva, looking around the office. She turns to me. 'Why don't *you* have an office like this? I could be your receptionist!'

'The idea has suddenly become tempting.'

She gives Francie an appraising look as she's bending over to make the coffee. 'Oh, my God! That's why! I forgot. He told me yesterday. Yesterday seems so long ago. I thought you looked familiar, then I just looked at your ass and it's the same! The same shape. You look just like her! You look *just* like your sister! You look just like Shelley! Shelley Saint! Oh my *God*! I must give *you* a hug now!'

Francie puts the coffee making on hold. They hold onto each and jump up and down for a while. I don't know where to look. That's a lie. A tiny devil appears on my shoulder and whispers poison into my ear.

'It's incredible,' says Liva, looking at Francie's face and softly patting her cheekbones with the tips of her fingers. 'You are different, but you have the same face shape, the same cheekbones, the same dark eyes and the same widow's peak. And your figure.' She holds Francie's hips and looks her up and down, then explores her curves as if she's measuring her for a dress. Francie is almost purring with the attention. 'Yes. Yes. Your hips are wider, and you are a little taller, but wow. You have bigger breasts, too. I bet you look great in the sexy lingerie. I bet you are a knockout like your sister.'

Francie can't stop herself laughing. 'You better believe it, honey.'

'I *do* believe it, my darling. Maybe leather. I don't know.'

'Leather lingerie?'

'Yes. Black leather. I think so. Big women like us, it is a good look. Very powerful. Like a Günter Blum photograph. Very dangerous. The body feels like a weapon. It is like a sex gun. *Meget erotisk*. It is a look to make the mouth water; to assault the senses with our ferocious voluptuousness. We should do a photo session together. Both in tight black leather. Can you imagine? People would die! It would melt their coffee tables like erotic nuclear waste!'

She starts laughing at what she's said, as does Francie.

'Sorry to interrupt. I think I'm having a heart attack,' I say.

Liva giggles, walks over to me and rests a hand on my shoulder. She smiles at Francie. 'Daniel and I made love last night.'

Oh, Christ.

'Oh, *really*!' laughs Francie, shaking her head incredulously. 'I wondered why he had those dark rings under his eyes.' She walks over to me and takes a squint at my face. 'In fact, you're looking pretty peaky as a whole, honey. You feeling OK?'

'Never better, Francie.'

Liva laughs, takes the bandana off and unties her hair, flicking it out with her fingers until it looks normal again. 'It made me feel *so* good. When I awoke this morning, I felt fully satisfied. I had that warm feeling, you know? I was glowing. I so rarely reach my crisis when I'm working.' She walks over to Francie and whispers something in her ear while looking at me.

'Oh, *did* he! This *morning*!' says Francie.

'Yes. He did. It was sensational. I had such a convulsion. I thought I was going to faint. Luckily, he held me up, so I did not fall onto the kitchen floor.'

'Yeah,' says Francie, nodding her head sympathetically. 'Kitchen floors are the worst.'

'Shall we sit down and have a chat?' I say, trying unsuccessfully to focus my thoughts. I must get a full medical check-up when all this is over.

We sit on the sofas, Liva and Francie sitting opposite me, Francie smirking at me and trying not to laugh.

'I'm sorry, Liva, but Francie and I have to talk about the case we're on. It shouldn't take long. You're kind of involved, so if you want to add anything please feel free. In a nutshell, this is what has happened.'

I tell her that Constantijn Francen is really a criminal called Simon van Cutsem, that he went to prison and his death was faked so he could get out and organise the parties/orgies again.

It was a big secret, but someone accidentally filmed him and was killed for it. Then someone else was killed for it. Then someone else. I don't mention the decimation of the Salo clan; that would make it all seem too scary and mad.

I tell her that whoever is behind this is manipulating the police and that's why they called on her yesterday. It's also the reason that van Cutsem wanted her to go to his place this morning. Until this is over, she'll have to stay with me or Francie. I don't tell her about the other guys that turned up at her house yesterday, whoever they were. No need and I don't want to alarm her, but I'll have to give those two some thought when I've got a minute.

'So, will he come after me? This van Cutsem and his policeboys?' she asks, frowning slightly.

'No. I spoke to a friend of mine who's in the police this morning and she's going to make him disappear for thirty-six hours as a favour to me. Then he'll be officially in police custody and fast-tracked back to prison. I'm now trying to find out who he works for.' I look at Francie. 'When they busted him out of jail, he was taken to a house in Berkshire.

'There were two people there; a guy called Gabriel White who is either MI5 or NCA or both or neither, and a woman called Mrs Margaret Carter, who possibly works for the Department for International Trade. I don't think that those are their real names. That means it's going to be difficult to locate them.

'I was hoping that getting hold of van Cutsem would seamlessly lead me on to the next link in the chain, but if these people are as circumspect as I think they are – as I think they'd *have* to be – then we may have to face the fact that we've reached a dead end here and try tugging on another thread instead.'

'What about that house?'

'It was called Antler Farm. Van Cutsem said it was a big house and was somewhere in the vicinity of Finchampstead. That's in Berkshire. Nearest big town probably Wokingham or Bagshot.'

Francie gets up and heads for her computer. 'OK. Well, let's check those names first, just for the hell of it. If they're fakes, they're fakes. If that doesn't turn up anything, we'll have a look for Antler Farm. House names are nowhere nearly as duplicated as house numbers, and that's a pretty unusual name. Or is it? I'm a foreigner here. I don't know what the fuck I'm talking about.'

'We've got nothing to lose by taking a look at it, but from van Cutsem's description it sounded like a seldom used safe house.'

I sit next to her as she pulls up the website for the Department for International Trade. There are five ministers, each with a mugshot. Two are women, and neither of them fit the description of Mrs Margaret Carter.

Beneath that section are the names of the managers,

eleven of them, four of them women. This time there are no photographs at all. I write down their names and positions. One of the women, Alana Tancred, is the permanent secretary. We Google her. Her name crops up pretty frequently, but there are no photographs.

We Google the names of the other three women with and without their job descriptions. Only one of them, Emma Wentworth-Shields, a non-executive board member, yields a photograph, but once again, it bears no relation to van Cutsem's description of Margaret Carter.

I need a break on this, and I have no idea where it's going to come from. Well, at least we've got a couple of fake names and we know that one is male, and one is female.

While Liva excuses herself to go to the ladies' room, I have a quick word with Francie.

'I told you the police paid a visit to Liva's place yesterday. They weren't the only visitors. Another couple of guys turned up at her house asking for her. They used her professional name whereas the police used her real name. They were there again this morning, but they were just parked outside. I've got some guys in Liva's house keeping an eye on it and reporting anything suspicious to me.'

'Some *guys*? What – some *blokes* you met down the pub?'

'That's right. Anyway, they left after a few minutes and didn't visit the house again. I don't quite understand who they were. Liva, as you surmised, has been living and working here for five years plus without any of the required paperwork, visas, work permits and the rest. Almost certainly hasn't been paying tax.

'She's been under the radar and has been pretty lucky

so far, but that visit by the police, whatever it was about, is a sign that her luck is running out.

'What I wanted to ask you was if you have any friendly lawyer contacts among your classy clients who could sort her out. Keep it discreet. Pull some strings. Sprinkle fairy dust over the situation. I'll pay for it. It's probably best if she doesn't know.'

'You got it. I know exactly who to hit up. He'll do anything for me. Let's see if we have any luck with Gabriel White.'

While Francie taps away, I sit down and call Doug Teng. It's clutching at straws, but I give him the registration number of the red Renault that's been haunting Liva's house. I try to focus on who the inhabitants of this car might be, but my mind keeps wandering. I feel as if I'm coming down with something.

Liva returns. She sits down opposite me. Her hair looks bigger and her perfume is more noticeable. I get a charming, warm smile from her.

'Have you seen *Naked Witch Sabbath*?' she asks Francie.

'Oh, Jesus, baby. You looked fabulous in that one. So pale and seductive. No wonder Satan wanted you so badly.'

'I have a few on Blu-ray at home. I can autograph one for you if you like.'

'Wow, that would be so great. I've got a few more you can autograph, too, if you'd be so kind.'

'Oh, certainly. It is always nice to meet genuine fans of my work.' She giggles. 'And of course, you're almost like family!'

I was going to say something to Francie, but it's gone. For a millisecond, I experience an odd sensation, as if my spirit is trying to leave my body, then it passes.

'Would you like another coffee, Daniel?' asks Liva, suddenly sounding as if she's a hundred miles away.

'It's OK, Liva. I'll do it.'

I stand up quickly and walk over to the coffee area. For the first time, I notice the metallic brown head of a Native American on the one arm bandit. So that's why it's called a Bronze Chief. I forget why I'm standing here. Of course; the coffee. I look down at the cups and the coffee jar and the Morphy Richards coffee maker as if they're alien artefacts.

'Plenty of Gabriel Whites,' says Francie, her voice thin and remote.

My peripheral vision crashes. I feel suddenly weak, inhale sharply and grab the lever on the side of the one arm bandit for support. But it's no good. I slide down the machine onto the floor. The last thing I'm aware of is being hit on the face by dozens of coins and Francie shouting, 'Son-of-a-bitch!'

28

UNKNOWN, UNKNOWN

I'm sitting outside a café with Polly in the centre of Amsterdam. It's past eleven; a little late for breakfast, but we're both having coffee and typical Dutch breakfast food. Polly's having smashed avocado and smoked salmon on toast and I'm going for the healthy option of choco-banana pancakes with a mega-drizzle of chocolate syrup. The coffee is amazing. I'm surprised Polly's eating avocado. She hates it.

This is the café where the Provos used to meet in the 1960s. Provo was a kind of Dutch pacifist counterculture thing; free white bicycles, the taxing of air polluters, contraceptive advice to women and girls, anarchic demonstrations against the royal family, non-violent provocation of the police and getting arrested for smoking fake cannabis.

It all seems pretty normal now, but at the time, the authorities viewed it as radical and dangerous. It's a fresh, spring morning.

Polly's wearing a black leather biker jacket over a bright pink cotton dress and a pair of Converse turquoise glitter trainers. Her blonde hair is dyed black and tied back into a cute ponytail and there's a pair of Dolce & Gabbana round scallop sunglasses perched on the end of her nose. She looks like a funky, affluent student. She watches me eat.

'Are you OK? You look a little peaky.'

'I'm fine. You're the one who's been doing all the hard work.' I don't know what I meant by that. Why did I say that? 'It's interesting that this was a meeting place for the Provo movement.'

'This place? You're making a mistake. You're thinking of d'Vijff Vlieghen in Spuistraat. We're in Eggerstraat. And d'Vijff Vlieghen is a restaurant, not a coffee bar. Nicolaas Kroese started it. He was like a patron saint of the Provos.'

'So, what's this place?'

She gives me a strange look. 'De Drie Graefjes. It's like an American bakery. Look behind you. It's on the windows. Are you sure you're OK?'

I turn and look. There's nothing on any of the windows. Nothing at all. I shrug and start wondering why we're here. I really can't remember. This has to be the first time we've been in Amsterdam at the same time.

'They've got red velvet cake inside,' I say. 'It's on a blue and white plate with a peacock. Is that canal over there the Rokin? That must be the old peat market over there.'

'Well, of course it is. How can you not know that?'

'Which hotel are we staying in, Pol?'

'What? The Toren. You're in the Royal Suite and I'm in the Garden Cottage.'

'Have you seen *Naked Witch Sabbath*?'

'What the fuck are you talking about? Have you been hitting the coffee shops again?'

I sit up sharply with a massive inhalation that people must be able to hear a mile away. I'm in a room. There's a woman standing a few feet away from me. I look at my watch. It's gone.

'Do you…what time is it? What day is it? Where is this?'

She turns to face me. She's a nurse. Thirties. Dark blue tunic. Curvy. Black hair cut in a straight bob. Striking green eyes. She looks down at her fob watch. 'So, we're back into the land of the living, are we?' European accent. Czech? 'It's two forty-five precisely. And it's still Tuesday.' She laughs. 'I'm Zuzana Závodská. I'll be your nurse this afternoon.'

I'm disorientated. I look around the room. It's very cream. I'm lying on a hi-tech bed, there's a pale blue pulse oximeter on my right index finger. I'm attached to an ECG monitor, there's a saline drip in my arm, I'm wearing a blue hospital robe. There's a green chair and a small table. Antiseptic smell. And Polly's dead.

'Which hospital is this?'

'You're in the University College Hospital, Euston Road. You'd collapsed in an office in Bedford Square. Your colleague called an ambulance. She thought you'd had a heart attack. You hadn't had a heart attack, in case you were worried.

'There's a plaster on your left forearm. That's where I took some blood, you understand? Don't pick at it. We're still waiting for the results. All laboratory technicians are lazy. A monkey could do their job. It is all machines. If they can send a chimp into space, you know?'

'I've got to get out of here.' I start to undo the tape that's holding the drip in place.

Her voice becomes mock-severe. 'You'll do no such thing and you'll leave that drip in your arm there. You'll wait until Dr Ts'ai sees you. I don't know who you are or why they've put you in here, but you're not getting me into trouble by running away.'

'Put me in where?' I shake my head from side to side. 'I've got white spots in front of my eyes.'

She rolls her eyes impatiently. 'Perhaps it's snowing in here, yes?'

'Why am I in this room on my own?'

'You must have influential friends, yes? Maybe you are a VIP?'

'You're very beautiful, Zuzana.'

'Hm. And you can stop *that*, as well.'

She turns away. I can tell she's smiling. I'm going to ask her out as soon as I get a chance.

'How long have I been here?'

'Almost two hours. Lie down. Don't move. Don't speak. Don't breathe.'

'Where's my mobile?'

'*What* did I just say? Are you *deaf?*'

I watch her exaggerated wiggle as she exits the room and closes the door. This is all I need. I'm almost certainly here due to that prick Quennel and his pal. I'll be patient. I'll find out what's wrong with me and then I'll leave. I try to remember what we were doing. The last thing I remember was Francie attempting to check out Gabriel White.

We'd hit a dead end with Mrs Margaret Carter at the DIT. I can't concentrate enough to work out what we should do next. Am I on some sort of medication? I look at the writing on the drip; just 500ml of saline.

Dr Ts'ai is a tall, fit-looking Chinese guy who's probably somewhere in his mid-forties. He's wearing a dazzling white shirt and a loud red and green tartan tie, which I hope was a gift from a grateful patient. Beige slacks and a stethoscope slung around his neck.

He closes the door behind him. He smiles at me, then, to my surprise, leans forwards slightly and presses the fist of his right hand into the open palm of his left, the four straight fingers then covering the fist. This is a traditional Chinese greeting called *Bao Quan* or fist wrapping. Now I get why I'm not in a public ward.

'Mr Daniel Beckett. I am so pleased to meet you. I am Dr Xiong Ts'ai, and I am an accident and emergency consultant at this hospital. But first things first. When the ambulance brought you in, I happened to be on duty and heard your American colleague give one of my junior doctors your name.

'I took over immediately, transferred you to this wing and booked you in as an 'Unknown, Unknown'. Anyone now querying your presence here would collide with a brick wall, as they say. I hope that is alright with you.'

'Of course. Thank you. What is it that's…?'

'We took the liberty of taking a blood sample. The results should be available soon. I examined you briefly. There are signs of injury all over your body. You will have to tell me what has happened to you, then I can advise you on how to proceed. I shall be totally discreet, of course. Nurse Závodská told me you were keen to leave. We shall see.'

I run through the various assaults of the last few days: the ricochet wound, the stitchings, the booze, the amphetamines, the painkillers, the mild solvent inhalation, the bad-tempered punch to the solar plexus, the strike to the neck, the head into the jeep door, the miscellaneous blows, kicks and hammerings, the lack of sleep, the work-related stress like the events at Polly's flat. I'm almost beginning to feel sorry for myself.

Dr Ts'ai's eyes widen as I float each sordid detail past

him. I leave out Szonja, Fenella, Priscilla and Liva. I don't want to unduly alarm him. I realise all their names end with the letter a. Is this a thing for me, I wonder?

'So, can I go now?'

'Do you remember what happened just before you passed out?'

'I hit the jackpot.'

'Ah, yes. Your American lady colleague mentioned that. Good luck can come in many guises.'

We find out whether I know where I am, the day, the month and the year and I pass with flying colours. The nurse had already told me where I was, though, so that was a bit of a cheat.

'Do you have double vision or a headache?'

'Always.'

'Hah!' He turns my head from left to right. He shines a small torch in my eyes. 'I understand you have met my cousin, Mr Beckett.'

'Is that a male or female cousin?'

'Female.'

'What's her name?'

He allows himself a brief chuckle. 'She has many names.'

'Oh. *That* cousin.'

'Could you stand up, please, Mr Beckett? Close your eyes. I'd like you to raise your arms in front of you and walk on the spot. Imagine you are a sleepwalker in a movie.'

I do as he says, aware that I probably look really stupid.

'That's fine. You can sit down now. Do you need anything for nausea?'

'I don't think so. No.'

Nurse Závodská returns with a green printout which she hands to Dr Ts'ai. He glances at it and hands it back to her. I manage to catch her eye. She quickly looks away.

'Bloods are quite fine, all things considered. Lactate is raised on your blood gases which reflects your recent alcohol consumption. I think the major culprit was that blow on the head when you were thrown into the vehicle.

'It is my opinion that you collapsed due to cumulative trauma and delayed mild concussion. Hardly surprising. My advice to you is to have a least twenty-four hours' complete rest.'

'Thank you. I can't do that. I know you'll understand. I have to leave right now.'

'As you wish. The nurse will help detach you from everything and discreetly escort you off the premises when you are ready. Your clothes are in that cupboard and your personal effects are in this drawer beneath the table. I turned your mobile off while you were asleep. Take it easy as soon as you can. No exertions. Drink plenty of water. Glad to meet you, Mr Beckett.'

'And you, Dr Ts'ai. Thanks for everything.'

'You are most welcome. Oh, and take this.'

He hands me an embossed business card covered in Hanzi characters with a telephone number at the bottom.

'That is a direct telephone number. Maybe for emergencies. I also practise traditional Chinese medicine. This is my card for that service. Don't worry; I won't make you eat deer antlers or caterpillar fungus.'

'That's what they all say at first.'

He laughs, though it's more a sort of enhanced grin. Zuzana stands and looks at me, her arms folded. 'Is there anything you would like? Tea? Coffee? Breakfast? Lunch?'

'I'm fine. What sort of restaurants do you like?'

*

'I don't fuckin' believe it.'

'I'm sorry, Francie. It wasn't intentional.'

'I've been dreaming of hitting the jackpot on that damn machine for six years and you do it while you're passing out. Are you OK? What did they say at the hospital?'

'It's twins. I'm over the moon. Where are you?'

'I'm in a cab like I can hear you are. I've parked Liva at your place. I took your keys while you were comatose, just in case, and she had your address on a piece of paper in her bag. I offered to take her to mine, but she said she felt safer at yours. I had a nose around. Great place, but you need your hall floor looking at. Who's the smokeshow in that oil painting in your bedroom? Jesus Christ, she's stacked.'

'Just a friend.'

'Big girl.'

'Finnish.'

'One of the seven deadly Finns?'

I laugh. 'Certainly finished *me* off.'

'I've run out of salacious Finnish wordplay. I wish I had tits like that. Holy shit. And what a mouth! I'm about half a mile away from the office. Liva wanted to wait until you came round, but the doctor said you shouldn't have any explicit satanic stimulation or hardcore three-way lesbian action.'

'Ha ha. Where did you tell her we were going, if anywhere?'

'I said we were following up a lead. She said she couldn't believe that I was a PI.'

'Neither can I.'

'Shut up.'

'I'll see you there in five minutes, Francie.'

*

She's already tapping away at her computer by the time I arrive at her office. The images of ALPHA, BETA, DELTA, EPSILON and ZETA are projected onto the wall. She hasn't bothered displaying Vanchev or van Cutsem. She's obviously hoping that something will leap out and solve the deadlock we're in.

'Any luck?'

'I've given up on White and Carter. As you say, they're probably false names, so it was at best a shot in the dark. I'm looking for Antler Farm just for the hell of it. Your pal may have thought he was in Berkshire, but he could have been mistaken.

'Taking that assumption, I'm looking for anywhere called that in the south of England. So far, there's an Antler Farm on the Isle of Wight, another near Sevenoaks in Kent and a third one out near Dover. It could be, of course, that the sign outside that house was a fake.'

'Possible. It's the sort of spiteful thing that these people would do.'

'Liva thought you had died, by the way. She got really distressed. She was crying. She thought it was her fault. I said most men could only *dream* of dying after a night with her. Or a morning with her in the kitchen. She thought that was funny. She giggles a lot, doesn't she? I really like her.'

'Did you tell her not to go out?'

'Yeah. She knew the drill from staying at your place

yesterday. What d'you think those guys wanted with her? Not the police, the other guys?'

'I'm not entirely sure. I was a bit concerned about the way van Cutsem talked about her. Called people like her the flotsam and jetsam of the world. Someone who wouldn't be missed. He said that people like her – he called them peripheral personnel – are usually dealt with fairly quickly. But this time something else was going on.'

'That has to be the business with your client.'

'It's possible.' I start making both of us a coffee. 'But what if whoever's behind this has an agenda, a *policy*, if you like, of eradicating all of those peripheral personnel; people like Liva and Jael for starters,' I say. 'People who, for one reason or another, are out of the loop in this country, are non-persons in some way. People who, like van Cutsem said, wouldn't be missed.'

'Hey. Maybe that's why he hired those two, you know? Both foreign nationals. Both here illegally, or at least working here illegally.'

'Could be. You couldn't go on running this sort of thing indefinitely. Eventually, there'll be an increasing number of people out there who know exactly what's going on and who is involved. Neither Liva nor Jael had done this type of thing before, so there must have been others. It would just be too much of a risk. You'd be on tenterhooks; waiting for the day that one of them blabbed to the police or the media.'

'Or tried to blackmail you.'

'Exactly. Throwing money at them might solve the problem in the short term, but…'

'I got you. Maybe that's who the guys that turned up at Liva's house were. Could they be some sort of clean-up squad? Does that always happen, or is it just *this* time because your client compromised Simon van Cutsem? *He* didn't know what Liva's real name was and neither did they, for whatever *that's* worth. And what about the kids at these frikkin' things? Jeez.'

Is there a two-tier clean-up squad system in place? The recently decimated Salo clan deal with recalcitrant intelligence operatives and the red Renault suits deal with the flotsam and jetsam? Are *they* who van Cutsem speaks to? Almost certainly. I can't imagine him having access to Eemil and his bros, however indirectly. Are the two tiers connected? Do they take orders from the same person? Are they even *aware* of each other? And which of them dealt with Culpepper and Vanchev? Unlikely to have been Salo and his wankstas, but I'm keeping an open mind.

'I've already given that some thought,' I say. 'More than ever now, I'm pretty sure that these are all abducted kids. So, they had already ceased to exist in some way. What happens to them after the orgies? Do they participate in more than one? It's likely; my client described them as 'professional'. She said they seemed to know what to do. But a time must come when they outlive their usefulness in one way or another. What happens then?'

'They ain't going back to school, that's for sure.'

We sit on opposite sofas and look at each other, so numbed by the implications of all of this that I spill my coffee when my mobile starts ringing.

'Hi, Doug. What have you got?'

'Okey doke. Carmin Red Renault Grand Scenic K7363 F118. That registration smelt like a phoney when you called, but I gave it a hammering anyway. Not a crumb. Over the last five years, there have been approximately two to three thousand of these cars produced every day.

Ran every single one through a programme that looked for unusual/atypical/anomalous registrations. Then went back another five years. Couldn't specify colour unfortunately, so it took a bit longer than I'd have liked. Nothing, man. Fake plates. Has to be. Sorry I couldn't be more helpful.'

'Thanks, Doug. I'll be in touch.'

'Sure, man.'

Francie raises her eyebrows at me, and I shake my head. A second of silence then it's my mobile again. Doug?

'Ah, Mr Cambridge. Fortuna smiles and frowns according to a timetable surprising even to herself! I have good tidings concerning the execrable Eemil Salo. Do you happen to have a quill and ink pot handy?'

29

SOME MORAL DECAY

This is it. I can feel it. My main fear was that the surviving Salo triplet would get the next available jet out of the country. This would be normal behaviour after a hit; but as Lothar correctly surmised, this one almost certainly has revenge on his mind.

Basically, he's going to want to find me and kill me, even though, at the moment, he has no idea who I am. It's also possible that he'll want to hand me over to someone else who can do it for him.

It's also conceivable that the people who hired him want him to stay in the country and do a few more chores. Things have got out of control. Someone (me again), is creeping around on the outskirts of their operation, pushing people in front of black cabs and eliminating their hitmen. And they'll soon discover that van Cutsem has vanished off the face of the earth, courtesy of the Metropolitan Police.

'OK, Lothar. Let's have it.'

'The address you require is 43 Onslow Gardens, SW7. Not too far away from yours truly, which is a tad chilling. Makes sense. Just a short walk to South Kensington tube station and a straight run on the Piccadilly line to Heathrow Airport.

'This property is owned by a company called Castle

Harbour Investments, Castle Harbour being in Bermuda, as I'm sure you're aware, which could indicate absolutely anything. Some vulgar offshore financial scam, I'll wager, run by rich, grubby tax-avoiders who like having street lighting but don't want to pay for it. The house is probably worth something in the region of three million, so someone's in the money.

'It is my thesis – and you may argue with it if you wish – that a little group like this would not stay in separate hotels or rented accommodation. It would be an unnecessary expense for whoever hired them and would create unrequired administration burdens. And as they're family, I'm sure they'd want to share the same bed.

'Anyway, the late Redolf Salo celebrated what we must assume was the predicted success of his ultimate job by hiring not one but *three* call girls from my good friend Trinette Boisclair. She covers the area, so I thought a quick call, a smidgen of flattery and a bung of five hundred quids was required. Are you acquainted? She is an exquisite beauty and delightfully bestial.'

'No. When was this?'

'Five days ago. The girls, who had to be of a *very* specific body type, hair colour, age and speciality were booked for one a.m. Redolf paid by credit card. When the girls arrived at that address, no one answered the door.

'As far as they could tell, there was no one there. They waited for half an hour in their vehicle, then called Trinette and explained the situation. She told them to go home. They would still be paid, of course, as the credit card payment had gone through.

'Rather sloppy, paying with such an identifiable card, but then he had no reason not to. At that point, he didn't know his hours were numbered or that we would now be discussing him in this way. Sloppy, also, having his sexual peccadillos in the public domain, as it were. Amateurs, basically, despite all their success and notoriety.'

I'm about to interrupt him, but he bulldozes on.

'And just a thought: it could well be that he arrived in this country on a false passport, but still kept his financial paraphernalia in his own name. People like this often do. If they're cocky enough, they'll assume they're not going to get stopped at customs and have their credit cards minutely inspected. Can be a mistake, though. Do you remember Johanna Kruger? That's what happened to her. Lovely girl. Beautiful eyes. An avid galactophile, if memory serves.'

This would have been a short while after the first attempt on Polly's life. Redolf, I assume, wanted to celebrate. That means Polly killed Jitser Vonk and Redolf Salo, which means I killed Wolfert Salo. Well, at least we've got that small detail cleared up. Presumably there was no one in as they were either dead or attempting to find out what had gone so disastrously wrong at the safe house.

'So, Mr Cambridge, we now have a feasible location for our little survivor Eemil Salo,' continues Lothar. 'It is possible, of course, that he is not at that location, but I think it would be prescient for you to check it out, so to speak. Case the joint, as they say. If he's not there, you could perhaps attempt a little forced entry and hide in a cupboard. If he is there, politely introduce yourself and request an informal chat. Oh, there is also a landline telephone number: 020 7899 7266. Give him a call. See if he's free for high tea.'

'I think I'll pay him a surprise visit rather than warn him first, if that's alright with you.'

'Excellent! I mean, er, that is exactly the course of action that I would have taken in my younger, more reckless days. If, of course, that turns out to be a blind alley, I shall resume my quest. Just let me know. Good luck, Mr Cambridge.'

'Thank you, Lothar. Good work. I have a few other matters to deal with first. I'll pay him a visit in about two to three hours.'

I click my mobile off and take a deep breath. Francie raises her eyebrows at me, a querulous expression on her face. 'So, what was that all about?'

'I think it might have been the lead we're looking for. Or at least it'll move things on a little. Remember all the A, B and C stuff? There was a four-man hit team involved in all of that. Three of them are dead now and I've just acquired a possible address for the surviving one. This may give us a better route to the two people that van Cutsem spoke of.'

'Did he kill your client? The surviving one, I mean?'

'No. But he was involved. It's his employers I'm interested in.'

'So, what are you going to do now?'

'I've been given an address in Kensington where at least one and probably all of that hit team were staying. There's a good chance that the survivor is still there. His name's Eemil Salo and he's from Frisia.'

'Where the hell's that? Forget it. I don't care. I'm coming with you.'

'I can't let you come with me, Francie. It's too dangerous and unpredictable. There's a good chance we'll be walking into a trap.'

'Are you fucking kidding me? What sort of person d'you think I am? I've been in on this almost since the beginning. I've got to see it through. This looks like it's going to be the most exciting part! You can't do this to me. I'm not in frikkin' telesales or managing a cupcake shop. I'm a private investigator like you. Plus, you're paying me.'

'That was for identifying the people on that film.'

'Oh, come *on*.'

'This guy is a world-class assassin. A tough bastard. A psychopath. Served in the Netherlands Marine Corps. They're nicknamed the Men of Steel and the Black Devils. They have a really scary reputation.'

'Oh, *do* they. What about the other three?'

'They served in the same unit.'

'And – please remind me – where are the other three *now*? Oh, sorry. I forgot. They're in the frikkin' *morgue*. For a moment there I thought they were totally invincible bulletproof samurai ninja warriors from outer space.'

'OK. There's a good chance this guy will be armed. He's…'

'What is this? Some sort of "I always work alone" macho bullshit? You're not Superman. You just got yourself delivered to hospital in an ambulance. I'll bet anything your doctor told you to take it easy for a couple weeks. You still look as pale as a frikkin' corpse.'

'This is all about me hitting the jackpot on your fruit machine, isn't it?'

'Shut *up*. I take it you want this guy alive. Presumably it's not going to be easy. What happens if you get injured or pass out again? That'll be it, won't it. Finito. Whatever it is that you're trying to do here will just grind to a halt.'

'But…'

'You'll need brains and strategy skills for something like this and I'm smart, you know? I've read *The Book of*

Five Rings and *The Art of War*. And I can take care of myself. I did Muay Thai for six years. OK, I haven't practised properly for maybe two or three years now, but it stays with you. Listen. I was attacked by a couple of teenagers four, five years ago. They must have been seventeen or eighteen years old? Big guys. Vicious. Jocks. High as kites. Attempted mugging.'

'OK. I get the picture.'

'One of *those* guys won't be passing on his seed to future generations, I'll tell you that for nothing.'

'Well, don't say I didn't try and stop you.'

'And the other one'll be on a dialysis machine for the rest of his life. What? What did you say just then?'

'It's OK. You can come.'

She looks stunned for a moment, then recovers. 'I'll have to get changed.' She indicates her dress and heels with a quick sweep of both hands. 'I'm in Lancaster Gate. We can stop off at my place on the way there. I know what I'm going to wear. It'll take maybe ten minutes off the journey. I mean, we've waited this long…'

I check my watch. Just after four. It'll be getting dark in about two hours. I know Onslow Gardens. Houses on one side of a fairly narrow road, tree-heavy private gardens on the other. Streetlamps every hundred yards or so. I want to get there in that twilight zone where people are starting to return from work, it's not quite dusk, and the streetlamps will just be warming up.

I put my fake glasses on. I have to keep remembering that I'm still wanted by the police. But I don't bother with the summer suit and shirt. No need. Just jeans and a t-shirt will do for this. 'Sure. Lock up and let's go. We don't have to get there for a couple of hours, so you can select your *kunoichi* outfit at your leisure.'

'What the fuck's that?'

*

'You live in a church?'

We've just got out of a cab in Lancaster Gate and are walking into what looks like the entrance to a nineteenth-century gothic tower topped with a spire that's maybe three hundred feet tall.

'Ha ha. Yeah. Used to be a church. Christ Church, I think it was called. S'called Spire House now. Pretty cute, huh? So *English*. The whole thing became unsafe in the sixties or seventies and was demolished. They just kept this bit. This development was built onto it about thirty-five years ago. Twenty apartments and three penthouses.'

I take a step back and look up at the apartments. The new building doesn't really match the old tower, but it still looks OK; plus, the whole thing is in its own gardens. An expensive place to live, I would think.

Francie sticks a card into a cute little concrete security station and types five numbers into a keypad. The glass entrance door clicks, and we go inside. A porter nods and smiles at her. She says hi. His name's Robert. The way she says it makes it sound like a cool name. Her apartment is on the third floor. We get the elevator. It smells new. Someone's been wearing Flowerbomb in here. Her apartment door has three security locks.

'Coffee?'

'Please.'

I take a look around. This place is enormous. We're in an open-plan kitchen/dining/living area. There's a long breakfast bar with a Swiss cheese plant on top and a smoked oak dining table which seats six.

Antique pine flooring. Only one print visible: a big monochrome photograph of Isabella Rossellini, probably by Helmut Newton. You can see Kensington Gardens from the window. Good view.

'This is an incredible place.'

'Thank you, Mr Beckett.'

She places two coffees on the breakfast bar, and we sit down.

'So, why the delay? Why not go round there straight away?'

'You had to get changed.'

'Yeah, yeah.'

'I wanted to get there at a time when the lighting was not too good and when it was maybe a little busy with commuters. I don't know yet if we're going to have to break in or not. I'm going to play it by ear. There's never an ideal time for this sort of thing. You just have to use your intuition.'

'I'm not going to change into anything crazy,' she says. 'I just thought, you know, if I had to defend myself, or run, or be quiet, or whatever the fuck, then this stuff I'm wearing now would not really be appropriate.'

'Sure.'

'I wouldn't want to ladder my stockings.'

'I know the feeling.'

'So, what happens when we get there?'

'I honestly don't know. Once again, I just do what feels OK at the time. Sometimes, walking up to the front door and ringing the bell can seem like the right thing to do.'

'And what happens if this guy answers?'

'No idea. Maybe he'll ask us in for coffee.'

'Would I be at the front door with you if you did that?'

'I don't know yet. Don't take any ID with you. Only cash and your keys.'

'Would you mind if I had a shower? I want to psyche myself up. Then I'll pick out some clothing.'

'Of course not. I'll just wander around looking at your personal effects and inwardly criticising your taste in everything.'

'Thanks. I appreciate it.'

Once she's gone. I text Liva.

Remember not to go out. No shopping unless absolutely necessary. I'll be back later tonight. Not sure what time. Francie and I are working. Don't answer the door under any circumstances. I'll text you shortly before I return and again when I'm right outside. D

I have to wait for a few minutes before she replies.

Are you alright? I was so worried. I am watching Un Coeur en Hiver. *I am afraid it will not end well.*

I'm OK. Just moral decay from my night with you. Recovering slowly.

You are so funny!! I shall be waiting with some more moral decay…

I finish my coffee and hear the sound of the shower being turned off. I can hear Francie padding around. I get up and take a look at what could be some sort of sitting room. It's almost as big as the room I just left.

Two big abstract prints on the walls. Artist fond of turquoise. A couple of brand-new brown velvet sofas which look like no one's sat on them. A black hanging basket seat right in front of the sixty-five-inch Smart TV. Another Swiss cheese plant. A fierce-looking cactus which is so tall I wonder how she got it in the lift.

Books on a black circular coffee table: *The Complete Claudine* by Collette, *A Complete Guide to Forbidden Books* by

Henry Spencer Ashbee, and a slim volume called *The Merry Order of St Bridget* by Margaret Anson York. Another fine view over Kensington Gardens.

There's a smart-looking oak veneer cupboard next to the television. I open it up and take a look inside. It's full of hardcore porn DVDs and Blu-rays. Rough estimate: two hundred, maybe two fifty. I pull one out. It's called *Raw Kinbaku.* There's a profile shot of an attractive Japanese woman in a black and green silk kimono. There are hemp ropes tied above and below her breasts and her wrists are tied behind her back. I look at the other side of the DVD case but it's all in Japanese. I wonder how many of these discs feature Liva? Has she got more stashed away in another room?

'Hey! Where are you? Come here for a moment.'

I quickly replace the DVD, shut the cupboard door and try to locate where her voice came from. Somewhere to the left of where I am now. I pass one bedroom which is full of unopened cardboard boxes, then go into the next one. This is pretty big, with a large ensuite bathroom.

Francie is spreading clothing on a king-size bed. Two pairs of identical-looking black jeans, some sawn-off red Levi's, a black t-shirt, a dark red t-shirt and a charcoal hoodie. She's wearing a short pink and blue silk robe. I get a flashback to Liva opening the door to me in a similar item. I can smell shampoo and/or shower gel. I can't help but stare at the shape of her body and keep thinking of Liva's professional appraisal of it earlier on.

I bet you look great in the sexy lingerie. I bet you are a knockout like your sister.

She makes eye contact with me, then breaks it and looks down. 'I wasn't sure, you know? When I was working in the States, I usually wore jeans, t-shirt and a leather biker jacket if I was doing field work, but I don't know if that would look a little conspicuous here. Am I too old for that look here? I'm not sure.'

My mouth is dry. 'Too *old*? No. Um.'

She runs both hands through her hair to dry it. This action opens the robe slightly and reveals a substantial amount of cleavage. Intentional? She looks shorter and younger standing there in her bare feet. Her legs look great. She can see I'm looking at her breasts. We stand and stare at each other for what must be a full minute without saying anything. The atmosphere is electric.

'Can I tell you something?' Her voice is soft and subdued.

'Sure, Francie.'

'I found it…weird that you'd made love with Liva.'

'In what way?'

'Well, you know, I've seen her in lots of films. I've always found her very, very attractive. I'd seen her doing things; well, you know what I'm talking about. I've been thinking about it since this morning. And, of course, she was at the orgy. So, everything got a little mixed up. It was like fireworks in my head. And it was like, I knew you, and then I met her, and she knew my sister and she'd acted with her. Is *acted* the right word?'

'I think so.'

'And then Liva was talking about my figure that way in front of you, remember? It was…I don't know what it was. It was overpowering. It was like she was describing my body to you for your…delectation, I guess. And what she said about you and her in your kitchen.' She shakes her head from side to side. 'She's kind of unconsciously *blatant* and she doesn't realise the effect it has, I don't think.'

'You found it exciting.'

She looks down and swallows. 'Yes. Very exciting. Whatever it was. Incredibly exciting. Overwhelming.' She rubs her right shoulder with her left hand, pushing the robe to the side so I can see the bare flesh. Her breathing has become rapid. 'You have to…you have to tell me what to do. Do you understand?'

'I understand, Francie.'

'I knew you would.'

30

SET-UP

'I hope this won't affect our professional relationship.'

'Of course not.'

'And don't think I'm going to take orders from you like some frikkin' sub when I'm working.'

'It would never occur to me.'

'I'm embarrassed now.'

'You don't have to be.'

'This changes everything. It's like some life-changing reveal in a movie. Did you know as soon as you met me?'

'Yes. I consulted my spirit guide.'

'Am I that obvious?'

'Stop talking.'

'That was the hottest session I've ever had. Really. I saw God. I think he saw me, too. Heard me, as well. We're going to be pen pals.'

'Comments like that are allowed.'

It's a little past six. We're walking up Selwood Terrace towards Onslow Gardens. We left our wallets and phones at the flat and only carry cash and keys. It's overcast and I can feel small spots of rain on my face. Francie finally decided on the second pair of identical black jeans, the red t-shirt, a well-worn black leather jacket and a pair of multi-coloured Vans trainers.

In less than ten minutes, seven passing guys and two

women have given her appraising looks and/or made complimentary comments. She can't stop grinning. She looks a little conspicuous but doesn't look like someone who's on their way to confront and/or capture one of the world's most dangerous assassins, so that's OK. Of course, it may be Salo who'll be doing the capturing, and that's fine, too. I just hope that Francie comes out of it all in one piece.

Five minutes later, Selwood Terrace seamlessly becomes Onslow Gardens, so I start checking the house numbers. The light is just as I like it. The streetlamps have just come on and several of the houses have turned on their porch lights. I thought there'd be more people around, but that doesn't really make a great deal of difference. Everything feels OK.

I get her to link her arm around mine, press close to me and slow down. We've got all the time in the world, wherever the hell it is we're pretending to be going to.

'Talk to me about nothing as if we're a couple.'

She laughs. 'You've made me forget all the other men I've been with, and, believe me, there have been many. Only now do I truly know what it's like to be a woman. I'm your slave. Command me.'

'A little more realistic, if you don't mind.'

'I don't know why you're inviting Graham and Lisa around for dinner again. All he ever talks about is his job. And Lisa smells.'

'Graham happens to be one of my oldest friends.'

'Perhaps you should pick your friends more carefully.'

'At least I've *got* friends.'

'I've got *plenty* of friends, thank you very much.'

'People you have five seconds' conversation with in the gym changing room don't count as friends, Tracey.'

'Perhaps I'm not talking about them, Rupert. Perhaps I have other friends you don't know about. Men friends. Real men. Men who know how to treat a woman.'

We walk slowly past number 43. I take a quick glance. Most of the houses here have internal lights switched on, but not this one. Doesn't mean there's no one inside, though, and lights in rooms at the back of the house may not be visible from the street.

We keep walking as I try to figure out what to do. I visualise the front door. Wooden and sturdy. Three steps up from street level, Doric columns either side, visibility from the street good but not brilliant. Two locks: an Abloy Protect2 Deadbolt and a Yale BS8621 Nightlatch. Abloy at the top, Nightlatch two foot beneath. The Abloy is problematic and time-consuming.

'Was that it?' asks Francie.

'Yes. We'll keep walking. I have to think.'

We walk for ten yards and take a right into Sumner Place. I want to look at the side of these houses and see if there's any way in from the back that avoids climbing up walls and clambering over roofs.

I can see a potential solution at the rear of the last house of the row, but it's right next to a streetlamp and I'd have to take a running jump at it from the other side of the road. Even at night, that would be too risky, noisy, and there's no guarantee I'd be able to reach the top of the wall, which is about nine foot high. It's going to have to be the front door.

As we're walking along, I find my burglar's tools and also a small wheel pick, which I've rarely had to use, but will almost certainly be the best way to bypass the Abloy. This time, I've remembered to bring a pair of latex gloves and slip them on, handing a spare pair to Francie.

'What are you going to do?'

'I'm going to have to go in through the front door. We'll be a couple visiting for dinner. I'll ring the bell first; see if anyone answers.' I keep forgetting that Salo may not recognise me with grey hair and glasses. Doesn't really matter. He gets the drop on me or I get the drop on him; the end result will hopefully be the same.

'If it seems like there's no one in, I'll pick both locks. Hopefully, it'll only take about three minutes, but it could be longer. While I'm doing that, I'd like you to stand at the top of the steps, facing the street, arms folded, slightly hunched posture, looking impatiently from side to side as if you're waiting for someone who's late for an appointment. Don't ham it up. I'll say "OK" when I'm finished. Then you follow me inside.'

'Gotcha.'

We talk excitedly as I ring the bell. Nothing. I leave it for thirty seconds and ring again. Still nothing. I listen for any sign of activity from the interior. Quiet as the grave. I look at my watch, let a full minute go by then ring again.

Saving the easiest until last, I start work on the Abloy. It's pretty resistant to normal lock-picking because of the way it's made. Unlike a Yale, for example, this one has sixteen disks inside which all have to be rotated at the same time before it opens.

I use a slim burglar's tool and the wheel pick. I close my eyes and attempt to intuit my way into the housing, turning the pick as carefully as I can. It's fiddly and not easy. All my focus is on this, but it's taking too long.

I'm trying to feel the moment that the security bar drops down, but nothing yet. I can feel perspiration dripping down the side of my body. Then something happens, but it's not what I was expecting. The whole

415

housing has come out and about twenty small pieces of metal clatter onto the floor.

I don't bother to pick them up, I just kick them onto the pavement. Francie ignores this. Good. Now I just turn the wheel pick and the lock opens. I remove the pick. The security bar falls out onto the floor. That took three minutes, but it felt like three hours. God knows what happened there. I hope they don't ask me to pay for a new one.

The Yale is much easier as five-pin locks always are. A basic pick into the base, a little anti-clockwise tension, then a quick turn with a medium hook and it's open.

'OK.'

I push the door and Francie follows me inside, carefully closing it behind her. The hall is cold. There are no lights on. I place my mouth next to Francie's ear and whisper.

'I'm going to check upstairs. Take a look down here and out the back. Don't speak.'

'Can you say *you've been a bad girl* in that voice?' she whispers back.

'You know what you're asking for, don't you?'

'Mm. I sure do.'

I decide to start on the third floor and work my way down, moving as quickly and as silently as I can. I can feel a faint presence up here, maybe more than one, but intentionally ignore it. The bedrooms all look as if they've been used fairly recently. They're mainly untidy with clothes strewn everywhere.

In one of them, there's a full ashtray, though no one's been smoking in here for a few days. There's a half full bag of Zware Shag tobacco on the floor and an empty pack of Rizlas. Zware Shag is a strong Dutch tobacco, so

I'm in the right place.

I take a look in the wardrobe. Assorted shirts, t-shirts, slacks, jeans, coats, shoes and there on a hanger, the black mission clothing that all four of these guys wore during their two attacks on Polly. Impossible to tell whose room this is, but it hardly matters.

The other three bedrooms tell the same story. The only bedroom on the first floor smells like it's been more recently occupied. There's a small dressing table with three drawers. I can feel something's not right here, but I'm letting it go; I want to make it easy for them.

I'm just about to open the bottom drawer when something makes me stop. I feel the hairs on the back of my neck stand up and feel my heart rate increase. I turn around and look at the door. It's Salo, with a gun pointed at my head.

'Hello, Mr Cambridge. Looks like your luck has been run out.'

And it looks like my high-risk gamble worked. Good old Lothar, the duplicitous bastard. Well worth the money.

*

As instructed, I place both hands behind my head and turn to face him. He has a contemptuous sneer on his face, but it's mixed in with annoyance. He knows he can't kill me, as much as he undoubtedly wishes to. It would piss off his bosses, who, I suspect, badly want a word with me. Almost there, Polly, almost there.

'Nice to meet you again, Eemil. How's the family? I hear there's been a cull.'

'Hands behind your head. No funny actions.'

I try to remember why the left side of his face is so red and swollen, then realise that's where I'd kicked him twice and pistol-whipped him. I think that makes us close. Dammit, we're almost engaged. Was that really three days ago?

When he speaks, I can see that he's missing a couple of teeth on that side. Good. I hope the dental appointment was a bastard. I hope his smile is impaired. I hope they fleeced him.

'They will give you to me when they have finished with you,' he says quietly. 'Then you will not laugh with the smart comments. I will gut you. I'll torture your ass until you scream for your whore mother. I'll pull your fucking eyes out.'

'Oh, stop being so cryptic, Eemil. Give it to me straight. Let your real feelings flow.'

His eyes almost pop out of his head with rage. 'You fucktwat,' he hisses. 'I'm going to torture you every day of your fucking life. I'll keep you alive. I'll get doctors. I'll pull your fucking nerves out of your body and stamp on them. You will pay for what you did to my family. You will scream even when you are in Hell, you antfucker.'

'Why don't you just pull the trigger, Eemil? Before you do, any messages for Wolfert, Jitser and Redolf in the afterlife? I promise I'll pass them on.'

Even after that, he's not shooting me or damaging me in any way. He's had instructions and he has to obey them and he can't stand it. Maybe it's financial. You have to admire him, in a way. He's a real pro. Antfucker?

I can hear Francie downstairs. She's yelling at someone to get their hands off her. I wonder who that can be? Not a Salo, as they're now an endangered species. Eemil sneers and waves his Grand Power K100 Whisper at me and indicates that I should go downstairs. Is he curious about what happened to Wolfert's gun? Can he guess that it's covered in his fingerprints and safely ensconced in my safe? Probably not.

When we get downstairs, Eemil takes a salacious look at Francie. The guy who has her in a painful looking arm lock is the one I called Tall Blond; one of the creeps who turned up at Liva's house in the red Renault Grand Scenic. Still looks like a dead-eyed self-important thug. Well, at least this confirms which stone those two crawled from under. He's packing; I can see the bulge on his left hip.

'You always bring women with you? Perhaps I shoot this one, as well,' says Eemil, now getting cocky as he's in charge of the situation, or so he thinks. He presses the suppressor right against Francie's temple. 'I'll blow her brains over the wall. Just like your pretty girlfriend, huh? Just like blondie, you fucking ballsack. That was her name, eh? You going to cry? Boo-hoo.'

Francie's doing pretty well with this, all things considered. She's not shaking, she's not talking, she just looks straight ahead.

'You gonna answer me, Mr Cambridge? I'm asking you something.'

I shake my head as if my train of thought has been interrupted. 'Sorry, Eemil. I was just thinking about the look of terror on Wolfert's face before he died.'

Eemil spits in my face. He keeps well back and resumes pointing the gun at my head. He knows what happened when he got too close last time.

I smile at him. 'How did you know I'd come and visit you today, Eemil? Did you plan this all on your own? Or did you have help? Are you going to take all the credit so you can suck up to your boss and get a pat on the head?'

A ripple of suspicion flits across his features. He shrugs it off and has a little laugh to himself. 'You think you're very smart dude, Mr Cambridge. Not so smart now, yeah? Just wait. We have fun.'

Tall Blond has a green leather holdall. He unzips it and produces a pair of yellow polycarbonate plasticuffs. These are one-time restraints with a roller lock retention system. Very simple to get out of; all you need is a pin. A little more difficult if they're behind your back, but still not too bad. Either they can't afford proper handcuffs or they're just plain dumb. Hardly matters; I have no plans to escape. Not yet, anyway.

He looks at Francie. 'Hands behind your back.'

She does as he says, raising an eyebrow at me as the cuffs go on. Then it's my turn. Tall Blond manhandles both of us so we're leaning with our backs against the same wall, close together for convenience's sake. Salo keeps the gun trained on my head, occasionally waving it in Francie's direction.

I have to wonder what they're making of Francie. I'm pretty much an unknown quantity to them, but I certainly don't think they were expecting her. Still, they're not hurting her or being rough with her, so that's something.

We're both expertly searched. Before we came out, I told Francie that neither of us should carry any identifying material, so Tall Blond doesn't have much joy with any of my pockets. He takes out my keyring and money and puts it in his jacket.

Then Francie gets the same treatment. Once again, all she has on her is cash and a set of keys, and Tall Blond pockets those as well. For a moment, I wonder why she has so many keys on her keyring, then I remember the three locks on her apartment door and, of course, her office. Tall Blond gets his mobile out and presses something on it.

'Ready. There are two. A woman. What? I don't know.'

Francie turns to look at me. 'What sort of a date d'you call this?'

'I'm sorry. The agency said they were sending a couple of girls. I've no idea who these two are.'

'I bought special lingerie.'

'Really? What did you get?'

'Just a La Perla string thong. Oh, and some seven-inch heels. I didn't think I'd need anything else.'

'Well, I mean, that's hardly *buying lingerie* is it. Heels aren't lingerie.'

'Depends how you define lingerie.'

'That doesn't make any sense at all.'

'Hey, shut up,' says Salo, now getting a little irritated. He points the gun at Francie, then points it again at me.

'*You* shut up,' replies Francie. 'Get these cuffs off me and put that gun away. I'll show you *shut up*, you monobrowed freak.'

He's about to hit her across the face, when the noise of a car drawing up outside stops him just in time. I wonder who this is, and I wonder where they're going to park. I didn't see any free spaces when we arrived. I hope they don't get a ticket.

'OK,' says Tall Blond to Salo. 'Keep the gun on them. I'll take a look outside and let you know when you can come out.'

He opens the door and leaves. Unfortunately, I can't see what's going on from where I'm standing, so I decide to goad Salo a bit more while I'm waiting.

'They don't trust you anymore, do they, Eemil? You've screwed up too many times. How are things in Leeuwarden, by the way? I was thinking about going there on holiday when all this is over and you're lying in a morgue somewhere having the top of your skull cut open with an autopsy saw. Any recommendations? Isn't there a Dutch pottery museum?'

He doesn't say anything, but his expression has darkened. How did I know about Leeuwarden? How did I know the names of his brothers and cousin? Who am I? I'm trying to unsettle him. I don't know why, or whether it'll benefit me in any way, but I'm still doing it. Why not?

'They still talk about you in Minsk, you know. That bank job. What a cock-up. You're a laughing stock there, as well. You and Wolfert. Wolfert just wasn't cut out for this line of work, was he? It's your fault, Eemil. It's your fault Wolfert's dead. You goaded him into joining you and he simply wasn't up to it. You killed him. Whatever would your mother have thought?'

Now I've hit a raw nerve. His eyes blazing, he grabs the gun around the barrel and is just about to bring the butt down on my face when Tall Blond reappears and just stares at him. He stops immediately, the weapon about an inch from my left cheekbone. Now I know who's in charge here.

Tall Blond looks at Francie. 'You go in first. Back seat. Driver side. No funny business. Quickly.'

Then it's my turn. 'You in second. Back seat, middle, next to the woman.'

I turn to Francie. 'You're a *woman*? I want my money back.'

He looks at Salo as if he's a scorpion. 'Salo. You go in third. Back seat. Left hand side. Keep the gun on this one at all times. We do this quick when I say.'

'Quickly,' says Francie. 'We do this *quickly*, not we do this *quick*.'

Thankfully, he ignores her. He takes a look out at the street and then walks down to the pavement. Francie and I are now a foot in from the front door. He nods at Salo and we all troop into the car and settle into our allotted positions.

Salo pushes the gun into my left side, a little more forcefully than is necessary, but then he does hate my guts. I can see why they got Francie to sit on the right; they didn't want me behind the driver.

Once Tall Blond is in the passenger seat, we take off immediately. The driver is Bald Medium, the other red Renault dude; the one with the trustworthy cop face. He doesn't look at us and he doesn't speak, though I can see him clocking me from time to time in the rear-view mirror. He's wearing a cologne I don't recognise which is seriously polluting the atmosphere. Neither Francie nor I are allowed seatbelts. I'll complain about this in writing at a later date.

Francie turns to look at me, an incredulous smile on her face. She leans over and whispers in my ear. 'You *knew*. You set yourself up.'

'Hey. No talk,' says Salo.

'That's *no talking*,' says Francie. 'Not *no talk*. Jeez.'

It's a grey Mercedes E-Class Estate in a fetching dark metallic blue. Brand new, at a guess. Smoked glass windows, comfortable leather seats and very cool blue ambient interior lighting. Good acceleration, smooth ride. How much are cars like this? Forty thousand?

The deeper I fall down this particular rabbit hole, the more I start wondering about the money involved and where it comes from; the cars, the houses, the sinister personnel – this can't be a cheap operation by any means, and it's largely because Polly spotted van Cutsem. Francie is looking out of the window as if she's disinterested in the whole thing. When this is over, I want to have sex with her again; I've got the hang of her now.

We drive up to the Cromwell Road and head west. I wonder if we're going to Antler Farm. But then we pass through West Kensington, Hammersmith and Chiswick, bear left at The Hogarth Roundabout and then over Chiswick Bridge, so my guess is we're heading towards Richmond. Tall Blond takes a call on his mobile. He says, 'Ten minutes', so I think my guess is correct.

Pretty soon, we're driving past Mortlake Cemetery. There are a lot of flats on the opposite side of the road. I wonder if the view of the cemetery makes them more expensive or less expensive. Probably OK if you want an existentialist experience or a memento mori episode when you open your bedroom blinds in the morning. Then we're on the outskirts of the town, zooming past fire stations, megastores and huge storage facilities.

I stop taking in the view and narrow my focus, going into what Polly was amused to call 'operational mode'. I forget about the who-did-what problems regarding Polly, Culpepper and Vanchev. I forget about all the manipulated cops, buzzing around like flies. I forget about van Cutsem and his pompous bullshit. I forget about Quennel and his kidnapped kid.

I take a look at Salo and the charmless monkeys in the front seats. They don't realise it, but they're working for me now, delivering me to my target, in chauffeur-driven luxury.

31

THE CASTLE ON THE HILL

Now we're heading up Richmond Hill, so there can be no doubt where we're going. Francie gasps at the view, an impressive and breathtaking vista which takes in parks, palaces, fields, wildflower meadows and the meander of the Thames.

'Will you look at *that!*' she says, her voice animated. 'Must cost a packet to live up here. What a fantastic view. I've never been here before. Look at it!'

'Shut up,' says Salo, helpfully, in one stroke obliterating any hope of being a London tour guide.

'Yeah,' I say, to piss him off. 'This view is actually protected by an Act of Parliament. Mick Jagger and Jerry Hall used to live up here.'

'Did you know them?'

'Intimately. I was their kitchen maid.'

'Interesting work?'

'Gruelling. A twenty-hour day. No pay. I had to pay *them*. They were slave drivers. Totally without mercy.'

'I said shut *up*,' says Salo once more.

I turn and look him in the eye. 'Hey. Don't take your bereavements out on me, Eemil.'

He fumes and gives me the mother of all tough looks. 'You will scream,' he whispers. We take a left turn and then I can see the house. I can understand why Polly described it as being like a castle, but it's closer to the Disney version than some primitive Norman fortification.

It's surrounded by trees and tall shrubs, just like she said, but they only partially obscure the building itself. Much bigger than I'd imagined. Five stories, definitely; old-fashioned but less than a century old. A striking piece of work. We turn into the entrance; the driver's window slides down and Bald Medium says 'Harker' into a slick-looking entry system. The gates open and we drive in.

'Hey. Driver,' I say. 'That was pretty mysterious. Harker. What does that mean?'

He ignores me, of course. Is Harker his name? Francie chuckles. Tall Blond turns and gives me a needlessly menacing look. We seem to be driving down the left-hand side of the building and heading to the back. A shame; I was looking forward to making a grand entrance through the thick black oak door at the front, with its massive lion head cast iron knocker.

I look up at the side of the building as well as I can. The front wasn't a one-off façade like you sometimes see; the design of the whole thing is pretty consistent, with cute medieval windows and multiple arrow slits.

Despite this, it doesn't really look like anything that actually existed in any era; it's more like a romantic novelist's idea of what a gothic revival castle should look like.

The car crunches to a halt outside some more magnificent wooden doors. There are two big terracotta pots flanking the four steps that lead up to the entrance, and each one contains a tall, bright green cryptomeria. There's a wooden coat of arms inset into the bricks above the door, featuring two griffins, a swan and some red roses. No idea what this indicates.

One of the doors opens and a young, smartly dressed woman in dark red power clothing runs out and opens the driver's door and then the passenger door. I can't imagine who or what she must be. A PA? A car park attendant? A software developer?

There's a red Motorola walkie talkie hanging from her waist. She has medium-length black hair, severe good looks and is much too thin in a way that's pretty sexy.

Height five feet, weighs about ninety pounds, pale complexion, dark red lipstick, powder blue eye shadow, four-inch black stiletto heels. Not carrying a weapon. No ID badge, so I can't discover what her name is. I bet she's got a single, significant tattoo somewhere on her body. I can always tell. It's a gift I have.

'Is she not going to open your door, Eemil?' I say. 'Are you really so low down in the pecking order here that you have to open your *own door*?' I turn to Francie. 'When I say the word, we make a break for it. Ready?'

Tall Blond reacts much more quickly than Eemil. He produces a Grand Power K100 Whisper from somewhere inside his jacket and aims it at Francie's head. Do they all have these guns? Bald Medium looks startled and is about to do the same thing, but Tall Blond stops him with a hand on the shoulder. Bald Medium looks straight at Francie and leers at her. So that's three guns so far. Bald Medium uses a shoulder holster which is under his left armpit.

Francie and I get out and stand by the car, waiting to be told what to do next. Salo doesn't take his gun off me for a second. What's the problem here? Are they frightened of me? I'm flattered. It's only now that I notice an enormous dog standing by the side of one of the terracotta pots. It's so immobile, that for a half-second I think it's a statue. But it's not a statue. It's a Tosa Inu or Japanese Fighting Mastiff. I've heard of this breed but have never seen one in real life.

It's a massive brute; three-foot-high, two hundred pounds and muscular. They're bred in Japan and I think their ownership is banned in over a dozen countries; too aggressive, too mean, too intimidating.

It's not a young dog, and there are lots of scars over its body, mainly around its face and neck. As one of these would eat most other dog breeds as a light snack, I can only assume it's been used for fighting.

It turns to look at me and Francie and its jaws slowly open in a silent snarl, showing its razor-sharp teeth. Salo looks uncomfortable, his eyes hate-filled. Bald Medium snaps his fingers once and the dog approaches him, licks his hand and sits down.

Now I remember; Polly mentioned she'd heard a single, deep bark coming from inside this house during her stakeout. Must have been this guy. Her description of the animal that made it was *not a Chihuahua*. Well, she was right there.

I imagine it's called something like Saxon or Terminator. It seems to know everyone here apart from us. I can feel its coiled belligerence and I get the feeling it would only need a single finger snap from Bald Medium to leap up and tear my throat out.

'Well, aren't *you* a cutie!' says Francie to the dog. It shows more of its fangs to her. 'Roll over!' she says. It shows even more fangs and growls. Bald Medium just points at it and it stops.

'I don't think it's into that sort of thing,' I say.

Bald Medium and Tall Blond walk up three steps and stand either side of the doors. The dog stays where it is, never keeping its baleful gaze off us for a second. Red Motorola stands a few feet away from Bald Medium and stares at me incuriously. Salo waves the gun at the doors.

'Inside.'

I decide to ignore him and hit on Red Motorola. 'Hi. I know this isn't a particularly appropriate time, but would you like to come out to dinner with me next week? There's a fantastic sushi bar called Hot Stone in Islington. It's meant to be the best sushi in London.'

She looks at me as if I've just announced that I'm the King of Neptune. *'Inside,'* repeats Salo. Oh well. It was worth a try. Once we're through the doors, she, Bald Medium and the mastiff disappear and we're left with Salo, his brooding malevolence, and Tall Blond.

We're ushered into a big room at the end of a long corridor. Sunflower oak flooring, matching bookshelves covering two walls, a couple of big, soft, comfortable-looking leather sofas with plenty of cushions. Like an academician's study, but much bigger.

There are books and magazines on two big glass-topped coffee tables. Recent copies of *MoneyWeek*, *What Investment* and *The Economist*. A book called *Africa* by Leni Riefenstahl and another called *Gaudi. The Complete Works*. A smart wood and chrome dining table that seats eight. A glass cocktail cabinet groaning with expensive booze. A big bowl of pot pourri that's making the room smell of cloves and cypress.

There's a large antique executive desk, which supports a green banker's lamp, black wireless intercom and a Lenovo desktop computer. Tall Blond reaches in his jacket pocket and slaps down our keys next to the intercom. He's keeping our money, the bastard. I'd have done the same.

Behind the desk is a big barred stained-glass window which looks out onto a small garden with a concrete Buddha and a bird table. Some indifferent art on the walls in expensive tacky frames.

Salo indicates that we should sit down on one of the comfy sofas. Tall Blond nods at Salo, who makes himself comfortable on a dining chair, positioning it so that he can keep aiming the gun at us. Tall Blond sits at the dining table and places his gun on it, about six inches away from his right hand, the safety off. It's very warm in here. Or maybe that's just me.

I take a quick look at Francie. She's warm, too; small beads of sweat appearing just beneath her hairline. She wriggles uncomfortably. Despite the softness of these sofas, sitting down when you have your hands tied behind your back like this is very uncomfortable, particularly on the shoulders. She whistles at Salo.

'Hey. You. Frida Kahlo,' she says to Salo, who doesn't get the joke. 'Can you get these ties off our wrists? They're really uncomfortable and my shoulders are aching.'

'You shut up and sit there,' he replies, pointing his gun at the centre of her head. 'You wait.'

Francie sighs with frustration. She turns to me. 'So, anyway. That was pretty damn hot earlier on. Were you shocked that I had all that stuff?'

'Not at all. I'd have expected nothing less. Most of it seemed new. Was it?'

Despite having her hands tied behind her back, she's sitting in that straight backed, closed posture I'd noticed when I first met her. She looks downwards. 'It was. I haven't had a chance to use it since I've been here, but I keep on buying it, you know? It's just like, you know, 'click' and next day the postman shoves it through the letterbox. I open whatever it is like a frenzied madwoman; shredded wrapping paper flying everywhere. I get a buzz out of it, know what I mean? Ordering it. Opening it. I think of it as erotic CBD.'

'Good name.'

'Anyway; even now, with the circumstances being as they are, having my wrists tied like this is...'

'Hey. I tell you no more. Stop with the chatter,' says Salo. Tall Blond allows himself a grim half-smile.

'This is something I'd like to explore with you, if you'd be interested,' she continues. 'With zip ties. Or maybe something else. Solid bar handcuffs. Hemp rope.'

'I tell you one more time,' says Salo, his voice starting to crack. 'Stop with this talk.'

She winks at me. She's doing this intentionally to wind him up. 'That feeling of utter helplessness,' she continues. 'The humiliation. The shame. It can be exhilarating. But it needs the right kind of man to control a scene like that.'

Salo gets up and points the gun directly at her left temple. 'You shut up now, harlot. You shut up with that.'

'Eemil,' I say. 'We're just having a civilised conversation about this young lady's desire for consensual restraint. What's the matter with you?'

'And who the hell says *harlot* nowadays?' says Francie. 'You living in the fourteenth century or something? Harlot yourself, punk.'

Before this exchange can go any further, the door opens and a busy man with too much to do and not enough time to do it breezes in. I recognise him immediately and am quite pleased that my sketch from van Cutsem's description was so accurate. I really must consider a career in art.

The snotty, supercilious expression, the chinless, rubbery face, piggy eyes, bushy eyebrows. He's serious. He's angry. He's also a little worried. This is Gabriel White, or whatever his real name is. Dark blue Brioni wool suit, black tie with a white polka dot print and highly polished brown leather brogues.

I don't know what it is about some men, but it all looks wrong on him, as if someone told him *you'll look really cool, smart and sophisticated in this suit,* but they were joking, and he was too dumb to realise it.

He takes a quick look at me and Francie, then sits at his desk. He has a buff folder in his hand, which he places in front of him. He switches the computer on. While it's booting up, he pulls some papers out and starts reading as if there's no one in the room. I hate people who do this; insecurity for beginners, disdain for dweebs.

'What's your first name, Mr Cambridge?' he asks, still not looking up.

'Before we begin,' I say, and he slowly raises his head indignantly at the impolite interruption. 'The young woman in the dark red suit who was out there when we came in. Do you have her name, by any chance? I'd like to ask her out to dinner. A telephone number would be good, too.'

I count to ten while he stares at me. 'Was that meant to be funny? Are you trying to be funny? Because, believe me, Mr Cambridge, you are not funny, and you are not in a funny situation. I'll ask you again. What's your first name?'

Now here's a conundrum. Mr Cambridge doesn't have one. The 'Mr Cambridge' appellation only existed in regard to Lothar Koch. There was no need for a forename under the circumstances of its creation and there never has been. I have a quick think.

'Oliver.'

That sounds OK. Oliver Cambridge. That sounds quite cool, actually. Sounds like a handsome, upmarket antiques dealer who drives a Ferrari 458 Italia and gets married women pregnant. I imagine Francie must be a little confused, but by this time she's probably getting used to it.

'And you?' he says, nodding in Francie's direction, but not making eye contact with her.

'Luigiana Sciarra. What about you, handsome? Got a name? Or are you above that sort of thing. No. Don't tell me. Your mother didn't give you one because she was going to get you adopted anyway. No one likes an ugly baby.'

He ignores this. 'We are aware that you are a dangerous individual, Mr Cambridge. As you can well imagine, Mr Salo here, who so skilfully ensnared you, is more than ready to put a bullet in your head if you try anything. The same goes for your lady friend. Mr Milne over there will also respond accordingly, so I would strongly advise against any foolish or impetuous actions. Am I understood?'

'So why don't you take these damn ties off our wrists?' asks Francie. 'With all your firepower here, what the hell are we going to do? Are you *that* afraid of us? Are you *that* much of a pussy? And while I'm at it, I'd like a coffee. Black. No sugar. Cup, not mug.'

White has a little smirk at this outburst. She's called his bluff and his ego will have to respond. He's weak. 'I don't see why not. Mr Milne; if you would be so kind?' He looks at us and smiles coldly. 'We're not barbarians, Mr Cambridge, Ms Sciarra, and a stress-free atmosphere can be conducive to information gathering.'

Salo shifts in his seat and readjusts his focus on me. Milne, Tall Blond as was, produces an SOG Arcitech folding knife and opens it with one hand. Francie and I lean forward in turn as he cuts through the plasticuffs and puts the remnants in his pocket. Are there no bins in here? We both rub our wrists at the same time. I think of van Cutsem.

Milne returns to his seat and places a hand flat across the side of his gun. So now that's three guns and one knife. White speaks into the intercom. 'Jane. We'd like three coffees, please. Get one of the residents to bring it in.'

'Jane? Is that her name? The one in red?' I ask. 'What's she like?'

'I'm going to lay things out for you, Mr Cambridge. I'm going to ask you some questions and I want quick, truthful, detailed answers. Be in no doubt of the seriousness you find yourself in. I am a senior member of the Security Service and one way or another,' he pauses for dramatic effect, 'I intend to find out who and what you are, exactly what you've been up to and exactly what you know. How you respond will determine your future and the future of your, your *girlfriend* there.'

'Am I your *girlfriend?*' asks Francie, in as cute a voice as she can manage. 'Just wait 'til I tell my mom.'

'You'll only be my official girlfriend when you let me get to first base.'

'That won't happen until we're engaged, buster.'

I want to get White talking. The worse everything seems, the more confusing/frightening/out of control it appears to be, the more he'll start to spill the beans without realising it, each droplet of information giving me the answer I want.

I have no idea what I'm going to say; I don't have a plan, and that's always the best plan. I hope Francie keeps it together. I have no idea how she'll react to all of this, but she's doing OK so far. She'll be used to guns, at least.

'So, what about the two gorilla-men here? Don't they get a coffee?' I ask.

'First of all,' he says, ignoring me. 'We know you took apart the surveillance team on that young woman. The description that I received of you was generally accurate, though I can see you've changed your hair colour. And your eye colour. Probably very wise.' He smirks at me. 'I understand you've had a little trouble with the police.'

'I admire and respect your subtlety and humour.'

His face becomes grim and serious. 'Those were Security Service professionals with over fifty years of experience between them. Shall I tell you what became of them?'

'No. I'm not really interested. Can we talk about Jane?'

'One of them died this morning, Mr Cambridge. Hit by a black cab. He was twenty-seven years old. He had a young family.'

'Shocking. Did you not tell him he was involved in potentially dangerous work at his interview?'

'One of the other officers suffered a crushed windpipe. It was such a severe injury that he will have to have a permanent tracheostomy tube in place. He also had a cracked sternum. He was lucky that there was no damage to his heart. The third member of that team suffered a ruptured spleen and spinal injuries. Both officers will be spending a considerable amount of time in hospital.'

'Do you want me to send flowers? Is that what this is about?'

Not amused. Whatever he is, he's not an interrogator. All this guilt-tripping about families and injuries; just a waste of time.

There's a single knock on the door and it's carefully pushed open. A young girl, no more than eight or nine years old, enters the room holding a tray. She looks oriental and my first thought is Vietnamese, though I could be mistaken. Dead straight jet-black hair, very pale skin and a hint of pink makeup around the eyes.

She's wearing a charming ethnic-looking gown: dark purple and asparagus green with a long, wide, brick red and green belt around the waist. Expensive. I catch a familiar smell. Bitter almonds and jasmine. My God; she's wearing the same perfume that Liva bought for herself.

She carefully places two cups of coffee on the table in front of us, along with a small porcelain jug of milk and a matching bowl containing both brown and white sugar cubes.

She looks up and makes brief eye contact with me, smiling as an adult would. Then she places a coffee in front of White. No milk, no sugar. Francie and I turn to look at each other.

We're both thinking the same thing.

White sips his coffee and smiles to himself as the girl leaves. Constantly aiming that gun at my head must be killing Salo's arm. Do either of these monkeys know what goes on here, I wonder? My guess is that they don't. I think they're both need-to-know guys. Salo, for example, would have no idea why Polly had to be killed. Their focus on me and Francie never lets up for a millisecond.

'So,' he says. 'I'd just like to know who you are and

what you think you're doing. Then we can move on. We know that you shot and killed an associate of Mr Salo here, and we know you took a memory stick from Ms Hart's safe. You waved it in Mr Salo's face. I want that memory stick, Mr Cambridge. You can either tell us where it is voluntarily, or we'll force you to tell us.'

I wonder how much Lothar told Salo about me. Bare minimum, I imagine. An anonymous telephone call, a quick exchange of information and money with no elaboration and damn the consequences.

Now I'll mix a version of the truth in with a few blatant lies, a couple of surprises and see where that gets me.

'I can see you're confused,' I say. 'The truth is that I'm a private investigator and so is Ms Sciarra here. We were both hired by the late Judith Hart. She was in fear of her life – quite rightly as it turned out – and contacted us by telephone four days ago. I think she wanted us to hide her somewhere. That's what we were going to do.'

He writes something down on a sheet of paper. 'Why you, of all people?'

'Because we're so damn attractive.'

'So, you then arranged a rendezvous by the Crimean War Memorial.'

'Correct. Before I made contact with her there, I had a look around. I could see that she was being observed. Considering the seriousness of her fears, I decided that the best course of action was to neutralise the surveillance team.'

'And kill one of them.'

'Accidents will happen. Turn me over to the police if you're that worried about it.' And now I'll give his feathers a quick ruffle. 'Perhaps you can give Detective

Sergeant Peter Moss and Detective Constable Roland Driscoll a call. I'm sure they'll be delighted to pop over. I understand they work locally. I believe they were in East Sheen only yesterday.'

Now he looks slightly more perturbed and there's maybe thirty seconds of silence while he attempts to factor in this alarming, baffling news.

He laces his fingers together, rests them on top of his head and frowns. How could I possibly know about those two cops? Unless they've been used in some other way relating to this mess, I could only know about them through their visit to Liva's. Have they got back to him regarding my terse Danish relative impression? Obviously not. Is he expecting a call from van Cutsem regarding Liva's fate? Hard to say. I just know he's got an icy hand gripping his guts.

'I'm not familiar with those two officers,' he says.

'Of course you're not. How could you be?'

I smile at him as I watch his face. I've got him on the back foot. He's still quick to respond, but not quite as quick as he was five minutes ago. He taps away on his computer for a few seconds. He changes the subject. 'What's the name of the company you work for?'

'There is no company. We have a good reputation and get work by word of mouth.'

'Who recommended you to Miss Hart?'

'We didn't get around to discussing it.'

'Do you have a business card?'

'I have a dozen of them on me right at this moment. Obviously, I thought it was a good idea to carry a shitload of ID when breaking into Mr Salo's house. Have you got any questions that might *not* have come out of the mouth of a chimp?'

'Don't get clever with me, Mr Cambridge.'

'It's such an easy thing to do, Mr...*what* was your name again? Why don't you ask me how I knew where Mr Salo lived? How I knew his name? You're useless at this, aren't you?'

He ignores this and takes a sip of coffee, his eyes never leaving my face. He looks indignant and tense. This persistent denigration is starting to work.

'I'll tell you what pisses me off, though,' I say. 'We start work on her case and then she goes and gets killed. I'm sure you'll understand that this was not a good move as far as we were concerned. Financially, I mean. If I could find out the name of the prick who ordered her death, I'd make him pay up. Someone has to. We're not a charity.'

'I'm not sure I believe your private investigator story, actually. Your skills are too specialist. What would happen if I had you checked out, I wonder? I mean *really* checked out. Mr Salo said your response to the situation at Ms Hart's flat was fast and expert.'

'Eemil, you're making me blush.'

'So?'

'You can believe what you like. There was one thing that confused me, though. Ms Hart told me about the incident that led to her hiring us. The incident with the two incompetent assassins? She was pretty sure she hadn't been tailed, but when I caught up with her near the Crimean War Memorial...'

He snorts proudly. 'We had people on her the whole time. There were two backup units. Belt and braces job. Not that it's any concern of yours. I wouldn't expect you to understand.'

That explains it. Like everything else, Polly just wasn't

expecting that sort of cover. There was no way she could have foreseen it. Two backup units? They must have been soiling themselves. Either that or they didn't have much confidence in Jitser and Redolf for some unknown reason. He shouldn't be telling us stuff like this. It means he's going to kill us.

'Did you hear that, Eemil? He didn't trust your little family group. If I was you, I'd kill him right now for putting Redolf and Jitser in such danger. Go on, Eemil. Do it. You're holding a gun. You could take him out in a couple of seconds. Just visualise him with blood spurting out of the side of his neck. Good, isn't it?'

'You shut your mouth,' says Eemil.

'You're a chickenshit, Eemil. Just like the rest of your useless family.'

Eemil starts to stand, but Milne shakes his head. I like Milne; he's cool, calm and collected.

'I must say, Mr Cambridge; we're a little stumped by what happened in the safe house. We read Ms Hart's file. There was nothing in there to indicate that she'd be capable of such a brutal act or acts. Perhaps you can enlighten us.'

''Fraid not. A safe house? Is that what you call it? Can't have been *that* safe, can it? Maybe there was someone else there. Who knows? Ms Hart didn't elaborate. Why should she? I mean, this is just you not knowing what the hell's going on, isn't it? You're not focussing. I'm not sure what your job title is, but you're plainly floundering here. Asking me about Ms Hart is a foolish waste of time. I knew her for less than twenty-four hours.'

He's getting pissed. 'We're dawdling. Where the memory stick? This is your last chance to tell me. If you don't, we'll be forced to extract the information from you by other means. And if that's not successful, we'll start on Ms Sciarra here. While you watch. Some forms of torture can be far worse for a woman than they are for a man. I'm sure you know what I'm talking about.'

I make him wait for five seconds. 'Memory stick? You mean memory *sticks*. I made a copy for myself. That makes things a little worse for you, doesn't it? Where can they both be? God almighty. Imagine if one of them had been sent to the media. Have you got a good lawyer? I think you might be needing one.'

He looks at Salo, then looks at me. His expression hasn't changed, but his vibe has. I just know he's thinking *shit*.

'Something's puzzling me, though,' I say. 'I may be just a dumb private detective, but I don't understand who gave the order for our client, Miss Hart, to be killed. It can't have been Mr Salo or any of his morgue-dwelling compadres; they were just guns-for-hire.

'Please tell me it wasn't Jane in the red dress. OK, it would make her more sexually interesting, but I don't really want to start a relationship with someone who'll shortly be going to prison or worse.'

'It can't have been you, because you so obviously don't have the intelligence or balls to organise something that ruthless or complex. I must admit; I'm at a loss.'

Francie starts laughing. She points at White. 'Can you imagine? It'd be like discovering Spongebob was responsible for the Kennedy assassination.'

'Yeah, but Spongebob wasn't around when Kennedy was alive, so that doesn't really hold water as an example.'

'OK, smartass. It would be like discovering that the Taliban was run by Ren and Stimpy.'

'Oh, God.' I can't stop laughing. This is terrible, but what the fuck. It might work. 'That would explain everything.'

'Or finding out that Mr Meeseeks was doing PR for your royal family,' Francie continues. 'I mean; this guy hasn't even got the balls to tell us his fuckin' name. He's coming on like this big 'I'm Judi Dench but I'm a man and I have some serious questions for you and I'm a ruthless spymaster in a faggy pot pourri sitting room with art books by Nazi photographers on the coffee table in my fake bouncy castle', but he looks like a guy who still lives with his mom when he's forty and collects tea towels with puffins on them. And that frikkin' dog. Guys with small dicks own dogs like that. And why is it so warm in here? Did your mommy not want you to catch cold, Mr Whatsit?'

Both of us laugh. White's face goes a deep shade of crimson. Now all the irritation and frustration of the last ten minutes of prodding and disdain is floating to the surface. His eyes are watering. His expression brings a new meaning to the word 'malignant' and an even newer one to the word 'murderous'.

'And another thing,' I say. 'I didn't want to mention this, because, you know, obviously we're in a bad situation here with Patty and Selma pointing guns at us and all the rest of it, but interrogation really isn't your forte, is it? Your questioning of me is all over the place. You're hopping from one topic to the other, babbling about your dead staff and you're missing the really interesting and important stuff, stuff you should have picked up on, but haven't. This is much more complex than you can comprehend, isn't it?

'And then we have your two tame cops, Moss and

Driscoll. How do I know about them? Just think about that for a moment. Have they reported back to you yet about what happened at Miss Søndergaard's place? Thought not. This is sloppy work. When I first saw you, I thought it was pretty unlikely that you gave the kill order, but now I realise it's laughably impossible. You couldn't order a Domino's.'

Francie laughs. 'Oh, shit!'

Whether it was the pizza reference that changed things between us, I have no idea. Whatever, he gets up from behind his desk, walks over, grabs me around the throat and squeezes. This is unpleasant; he's stronger than he looks, and he knows the right pressure points. But I let him do it, despite the fact I could instantly crush the bones of his hand. He bares his teeth.

'You fucking don't speak to me like that. You have no *idea* what I can do or what I've done in the service of my country. Ordering a hit on some troublesome minor intelligence operative like that girl was nothing to me, do you understand? It took one telephone call and it was all set in motion. You piece of shit. You moron.'

Excellent. That's all I needed to know.

He pushes me back into the sofa and storms back to his desk, mumbling, 'I've fucking had enough of this.' I swallow the saliva that's gathered in my mouth. I can feel Salo and Milne relax. He speaks into his intercom through gritted teeth.

'Rebekah. Could you pop in here, please? As soon as you can. Thank you.' He turns to me. 'I've tried to make this civilised. Now we'll see how reticent you are, Mr Cambridge. Now we'll see what a big man you are.'

'Hey, John Merrick,' says Francie to White. 'Any chance of another coffee?'

32

MYLA GIRL

'*Vous m'aimez, monsieur?*'

Pain experienced under torture has to stop sometime. It can't go on forever. I don't mean that eventually either you or the torturer will die of old age, though that, of course, is true. I mean that it's counterproductive.

'*Que puis-je faire pour vous, monsieur?*'

The torturer usually wants something from you. Of course, it can be that you're being tortured as a punishment. You may be being tortured because someone wants you politically re-educated. They might want to make you do something that you don't want to do. They might want to annihilate your dignity. They might want to intimidate or coerce. There are many reasons for torture.

'*Is there something I can do for you, sir?*'

Some people, of course, get pleasure from torturing others. Some people like to watch torture for their own gratification, sexual or otherwise. It could be that both types of individual are simply mad.

'*Iskam da vie napravya shtastliv, sŭr.*'

But if it's some sort of information they're after, what they don't want is you passing out or dying from the pain before you've given it to them. So, they have to stop at a certain point. They know that there'll be a danger of you babbling nonsense just to get them to stop. Or maybe you'll be babbling nonsense because your mind's starting to go. It's why they say that information acquired from torture can be false or misleading.

'Jeg vil være din spesielle venn, sir.'

A professional, competent torturer will know this, of course, and will give you a well-deserved rest from time to time. They'll often try to become your friend. Hopefully, you'll feel a kind of love for them each time they walk into the room for another session.

If pain is their weapon, what they're doing will become almost predictable. There will be peaks and troughs. You can make minute adjustments to your concentration from second to second. You can stop it breaking you. But, eventually, it *will* break you. One way or another.

'Do you like me, sir?'

But if it's an inexperienced child doing it, it becomes something else. They simply don't have the skills. I've heard about this happening in African countries and elsewhere. All those dead-eyed little soldiers who want to be the Big Man. They can inflict permanent damage, both mental and physical. They can accidentally kill you because they don't quite know what they're doing. They'll make you have fond thoughts about some enhanced interrogation executive from the CIA taking over and getting the electrodes out.

'Kayf yumkinuni alturfiuh eunka?'

And on top of that, there's the scary disbelief you're experiencing. The horror. The fear. The repugnance. The dismay. The unreality of a child asking you brainless cocktail party questions in multiple languages because they're not sure where you're from or what language you speak. The fact that they look and sound zombied/drugged out and are not really 'in the room'. What was it that Polly said about the kids in the orgy?

A bit Village of the Damned. *Like they weren't children anymore. Like their childhood had been surgically removed.*

I throw up again. Then, thankfully, I begin to pass out.

'Can I get you something to drink, sir?'

*

I was a little disappointed that the woman called Rebekah wasn't Mrs Margaret Carter. No resemblance at all to my sketch. It didn't really make much difference; I just like things to tie up, that's all.

It's all irrelevant now, of course. I can only assume that Mrs Margaret Carter was more involved in the remake/remodel of Simon van Cutsem than she was in organising forbidden entertainments for wealthy and influential men of the world.

Whoever Rebekah is, she seems to be on equal footing with White, if not his superior. Once White had regained his cool and called her in, things seemed to move very quickly. I noticed that Milne stood up when she entered the room. Whether that was from politeness or that she was his boss, I couldn't tell.

Salo didn't stand up but gave her a miniscule nod of recognition, getting a frosty smile in return. I'm gradually getting a picture of the pecking order here, but it's still a tad nebulous. I'm sure things will become more unambiguous as time goes on. Or maybe they won't.

'Hello, Rebekah. We're going to have to move this on to the next stage and we'll need some proper persuasion,' White looks at Francie and me. 'This gentleman is Mr

Oliver Cambridge and the woman is Ms Luigiana Sciarra. They are both private investigators, or so they say. Neither have ID. Their client was Judith Hart. Mr Cambridge tells me that there are two extant copies of the memory stick; the one made by Judith Hart and one that he made himself. He is reluctant to reveal the location of either.'

I take a quick, appraising glance at Rebekah. She's Indian, I think. Mid-forties or early fifties. Handsome rather than beautiful; a hardness in her eyes that makes them fall short of being pretty, but somehow makes them seductive. Great figure. Fantastic legs. Small sexy breasts. Long black hair, very shiny; probably an expensive dye job at some exclusive and upscale salon. Long, blood red fingernails. Left ear used to have three piercings on the lobe.

She's wearing a dark blue short-sleeve dress, with white floral patterns. It clings to her body. Killer heels. Immediately, all eyes in the room are on her. She smiles to herself. She likes the attention. She's sexy. I can feel my pulse rate rise just from looking at her. Then I realise who she must be. What was it Liva said about her ride with van Cutsem?

There was a lady in the back. She was very dark. Very beautiful. She said her name was Seraphina. She was in her forties, I think. A very sexy woman. She kept very good eye contact and kept crossing and uncrossing her legs. She had good legs and small, sexy breasts.

'Also,' continues White. 'He knows about Moss and Driscoll visiting the girl's place.'

Rebekah nods her head and looks at me with a delightfully knowing smirk. She already knows all the answers. It's one of *those* looks. The piercing, concentrated, full-on eye contact of someone who's terrified of another person putting one over on them. It's a raging insecurity stare. I'll bet anything she's panicking inside; I mean *all of the time*. I wonder if there's any way I can sleep with her. I think it would be a fiery experience.

'We still haven't heard back from those two,' she says to White. 'I thought Moss would have called you.'

'Tame cops acting up, Seraphina?' I say. I get a slight eye twitch in response to my use of that name. 'You just can't get the help nowadays, can you? It's been like Euston station at Liva's place, not to mention van Cutsem inviting her around for tea. I advised her against that little tête-à-tête; I hope you don't mind. Rude of me, I know.'

The mention of van Cutsem doesn't go down at all well. I wonder if they'll try to call him. So, now I'm definitely doomed. But that's OK. All these dribs and drabs of what I know and what I don't know are like groundbait when you go fishing; toss them in the water and see what turns up.

'She's a popular girl,' I continue. 'One tiny slip-up: your detectives referred to her by her real name, whereas Milne here and his buddy asked for her by her professional name. Or maybe it wasn't a slip-up. Maybe it was intentional and clever, but I somehow doubt it. I don't think we're dealing with the brightest bulbs in the chandelier here.'

'Where is she?' she asks.

'She's safe.'

I get a glacial smile for that. A *don't worry; we'll get it out of you sooner or later* sort of smile.

The door opens and another kid comes in. This time it's a boy of about fourteen. For a second I thought he was wearing cricket whites, but it's just a floppy cotton shirt and matching baggy trousers, so I won't start bowling off spins at him just yet. He collects the coffee debris. He looks at me as he clears my cup and saucer away.

'*Marhabaan.*'

I must look momentarily nonplussed. He changes tack. 'Hello.'

'Hi.' I take a look at his eyes. Pupils dilated, focus a little off; as if he's talking to someone who's sitting on my left shoulder. *Marhabaan?* Arabic. Do I look like someone you'd speak Arabic to?

Rebekah walks over to where White is sitting and leans against the desk, folding her arms. 'Adonis,' she says to the boy. 'When you have finished your chores, I'd like you to fetch Baba and Jaheem. Tell them that I'd like to see them. In here. Perhaps in ten minutes. Do you understand?'

'Yes, mistress,' replies Adonis, which I'm pretty damn sure isn't his real name. She makes him repeat his instructions back to her. I can see why; he looks and sounds zombied out.

Just as he's leaving, Francie holds his wrist in her hand. White is about to intercede, but Rebekah shakes her head. 'Honey?' she says. 'Do your folks know that you're here?'

He turns and looks at her, his smile vacant and robotic. 'How can I please you?'

'What?'

'Not now, Adonis,' says Rebekah. 'Off you go.'

He doesn't reply. He and the coffee things leave the room without a word. I take a look at Salo and Milne. They look disinterested in all of this. Rebekah glares at

Milne. She's a little irritated.

'Were these two not tied up or anything?'

'Their wrists were tied,' replies White. 'Milne cut the ties off.' He says this as if it was Milne's idea and not his. Milne's expression stays the same, but I'll bet he didn't like that.

'Get some cuffs on them,' she orders. 'Proper cuffs. We don't want any more fatalities.'

'Yes, ma'am,' replies Milne. She's definitely his boss, then. There's a black leather attaché case resting on top of a small chest of drawers. He clicks it open and produces a pair of lightweight aluminium hinge handcuffs. I try to see what else is in there, but it's too high up. As he's walking towards us, Rebekah puts a hand out to stop him.

'Get them down to their underclothes. We don't want to have remove the cuffs once they're on or cut through their clothing later.'

'Certainly, ma'am.'

I don't like the sound of this. I wonder what's going to happen later.

'You heard her,' says Milne. 'Stand up and strip.'

I look at Francie. 'It's OK. Do as he says. It's pretty warm in here, anyway.'

Rebekah looks at Salo. She pouts. 'Salo. You don't have to keep aiming your gun like that. It's giving me anxiety. Hold it if you must. I'm sure your reflexes are fast enough to take these two down if need be.'

Salo doesn't reply, but he lowers his gun and rests it on his thigh, never keeping his eyes off me.

As we undress, I can see Rebekah taking a good look at both of our bodies. By the time Francie is down to her bra and briefs, Rebekah strolls over for a closer look and lightly runs her finger down the entire length of Francie's left arm. 'Maison Lejaby. You have good taste in lingerie, my dear. That bra, in particular, suits your curves. I'm more of a Myla girl myself.'

Francie is not fazed. 'Myla. Really,' she replies. 'I was browsing in their Brook Street store just last week.'

'Did you see anything you liked, Luigiana?'

'Their Elm Row collection rather took my fancy.'

'Mm. Yes. I can imagine that. I can imagine it on you, I mean. I'm wearing Columbia Road at the moment. Cobalt. Cuffs behind the back, please, Mr Milne.'

She watches as Milne pulls Francie's wrists behind her back and attaches the handcuffs. She smiles as she observes the predictable effect this has on Francie's upper body and breasts. 'Ooh. That's quite an appealing look, Luigiana. Being cuffed obviously suits you, my dear.' She pinches Francie just underneath her left armpit. Francie raises a bored eyebrow. If that hurt, she isn't showing it.

Rebekah turns her attention to me, placing her right hand flat against my stomach. 'Such muscle definition. So many men are out of shape nowadays and particularly ignore the abdominals. How old are you? Mid-thirties? A little younger?'

'That's a nice perfume you're wearing, Seraphina,' I say. 'Blackcurrant, cinnamon, rose, patchouli; is it Portrait of a Lady by Dominique Ropion?'

She looks surprised. 'Very good. I like it. It's quite an intimate thing, when a man recognises the perfume you are wearing, Oliver. It's as if you've discovered one of my darkest secrets. I feel as if I've been unexpectedly penetrated. It's invigorating.'

'It's very decadent. I can't imagine you wearing anything else.'

She places a hand on my right shoulder and pulls it

forwards, so she can get a good look at my ricochet wound. Her face is a few inches from mine. 'That looks nasty. Did it hurt?' she whispers.

'It's just a scratch.'

'How brave you are. But it's a little more than just a scratch, isn't it? It looks like a burn mark. Quite deep. I've seen superficial bullet wounds before and that's what this is, isn't it? I wonder where you picked that up?'

She nods to Milne, who places the other pair of handcuffs on my wrists. Like Francie's, they're behind my back. He's being rough, and I flinch as they catch the skin on the side of my hand.

'Oh, he didn't hurt you, did he? We can't have that.' Her face is now about an inch from mine and I can feel her breath inside my mouth as she speaks. She's been eating something with lime and chili in it. I must ask for the recipe. I can see White watching all of this and he's pretty uncomfortable with it. I would dearly love to see the job descriptions of these two. If either of them is really high up in counter espionage, this country's in big trouble.

She takes a step back and I think she's finished with me for the moment, then she turns quickly and savagely jams all the fingernails of her right hand deep into my chest, her grip fierce and strong. It's excruciatingly painful and it makes me gasp, but more with the shock than the pain. For a second it seems as if she's going to try to rip a chunk of pectoral muscle out. She grins and stares into my eyes. She looks, I have to say, a little crazy.

'What do you think of that? What do you have to say?'

'I want to know if I should call you Rebekah or Seraphina.'

Her voice is trembling, breathless. 'Ha. Which would

you prefer, Oliver?'

'Seraphina. It suits you more than Rebekah. It's enigmatic and alluring.'

'Then Seraphina it is.' She tightens the grip. The muscles in her forearm flex with the effort. I clench my teeth together. I can feel my eyes start to bulge. Then it seems as if she loses interest and lets go. I look down and watch the blood trickle down my torso from the five small puncture wounds. Well, that was a first. I'm dying to know what she's like when she makes love. I imagine you'd end up in a hospital emergency department.

Milne places two dining chairs about three feet apart from each other and indicates that Francie and I should sit. Seraphina stands and looks at us, her arms folded once more.

'So,' she says, back in business mode. 'First things first. I'm sure you can understand why we want those memory sticks. I don't really understand why Miss Hart made a copy, to be honest, but I'm beginning not to understand Miss Hart.'

'You want my theory?' I say. 'She had a fear that something that hot and career-ruining might vanish into thin air.'

She looks nonplussed. 'Fair enough. You've watched the film, I take it? Both of you?'

Francie looks at her with contempt. 'Too frikkin' right we have. What sort of people are you? Who organises that shit? Did *you* organise it?'

'I'm proud to say I did, along with my colleague here. It's a complex operation. The logistics can be a nightmare sometimes and, as I'm sure you'll appreciate, the security has to be more than watertight. It has to be infallible. Our clients have to trust us absolutely. Of course, what you've seen was not the *only* event, as it were. There have been plenty of others. Different strokes for different folks, as they say. What you observed is the tip of the iceberg, believe you me.'

Francie glares at her. 'But they all involve the kids.'

Rebekah sighs. 'You're not one of these bleeding heart snowflakes are you? Where are you from, Luigiana? In America, I mean?'

'Raleigh. North Carolina. What's that got to do with anything?'

'Raleigh. The City of Oaks, I believe it's called. Hm. Well, it's an affluent place. An affluent place in an affluent country. But the UK is not an affluent country and hasn't been for some time. Not really. And now it's worse. This is a failing territory, Ms Sciarra. We have to do business with whoever we can and give them whatever they want.'

'Yeah, yeah. Who are these kids? Where do they come from?'

Rebekah looks at White, smiles at him, then turns back to face Francie. 'There is no pat answer to that question, Luigiana. Too many sources to name, I'm afraid. Some are abducted, some are from countries where they'll gladly hand their children over for the right price.

'We have representatives who will source suitable material. It's sad, really. Many of them think that they're giving their children a better life in a richer, nicer country. I suppose in some ways they are, but not quite in the fashion they imagine.

'We have standards, though. We don't accept just any material. The children have to be of a certain quality. Looks, I mean. Age, obviously. Intelligence, too. But not *that* intelligent. If they're too bright, they're less susceptible to our programming.

'And we don't directly solicit from traffickers, if that's what you're thinking. We're not unethical. They will…' she shrugs. '…do what they do, and if they have a property that they think will appeal to our operations here, they will get in touch. It's an international business like any other, that is all. And, of course, that means we get a wide variety of nationalities. It's not just the usual sources like Albania, Vietnam or Romania. We cast a much wider net than that. We have to, because of the tastes of our clients.'

'So, let's cut to the chase here,' says Francie. 'You're involved in trafficking children to suck up to some of the biggest scumbags in Christendom, just so you can get some business and big bucks flowing your way.'

'Yes. But with the blessing of the government. We're not criminals. We're just civil servants. The government knows roughly what we do and lets us get on with it.'

'So, you're making a big damn fuss about modern slavery and child trafficking, but you're actually practising it yourself? God almighty.'

'No. That's government policy that makes the fuss, not us. We're part of the intelligence services. Honestly; who else would be capable of this? The police? We use them when we need to, but they're just half-baked foot soldiers following orders. We follow orders, too, but in our case they're government directives.'

'*Secret* government directives. *Illegal* government directives. Including murder.'

'How can it be illegal when it comes from the very top? This is outside legality and illegality. Beyond good and evil, to quote Nietzsche. Besides, what the government say and what they do are two different concerns, as I'm sure you're aware. It's just that there are some things that the public are not ready to know about. Some things that they're simply not *bright* enough to know about.'

'I'll bet. Like springing that piece of crap van Cutsem from prison.'

'Exactly. No one wants to know how the judicial system can be manipulated in that way. It would cause outrage and mistrust. You wouldn't believe the staggering number of cover-ups we've been involved with. You can doubtless guess at many of them.

'Technically we're counter-espionage, counter-terrorism and security, but in reality, we protect the worst people this country has to offer. In its way, that *is* security. We deal with people like van Cutsem so that other people don't have to. If *we* didn't do it…'

'Yeah, yeah, yeah. *Somebody else would.* That feeble bullshit argument. Shifting the blame. But that doesn't make what you're doing *right*, does it? You're meant to protect people. This is so messed up.'

'You call it messed up; I call it a success story.'

White laughs at Rebekah's quip, then strolls over and takes a closer look at Francie. 'You're a very attractive woman, Ms Sciarra. From your name, I take it you have Italian blood. I can see it in your face and in your figure.' He takes one of her bra straps in his fingers and pulls it down, so it hangs off her shoulder. The look of loathing and contempt on her face is priceless. I keep hearing an intermittent, quiet, very high-pitched bleep and wonder if I'm imagining it.

'What woman doesn't covet diamonds?' he asks. 'A stupid woman. It's one big cycle, you see. Business. Wealth. Those are the important things. Those are the things that make the world go round. The best life has to offer. The finest wines. The finest jewels. To facilitate that business, that *important* business, certain sacrifices have – *have* to be made. We have to give the businessmen – the movers and the shakers – something that they want. Something that they hunger for.'

'You fuckin' piece of shit,' says Francie, who in many ways was just asking for the backhander that White gave her across the cheek. She runs her tongue inside her mouth to see if he's drawn blood.

'It's true, Luigiana,' says Rebekah. 'Powerful men want – no – *need* – powerful sensations. The best sensations. And the sensations that taste the best are forbidden sensations. I've looked into your eyes, Luigiana. I know that you understand what I'm talking about. I can feel it.' She grabs a handful of Francie's hair and grips it firmly in her hand. 'Look at me.'

'Go fuck yourself.'

'And that's what we supply,' says White. 'Forbidden fruit. Fruit you can gorge on. Fruit that you can sink your teeth into. To savour that unthinkable juice as it runs down your chin.'

'The first taste,' says Rebekah, still looking straight into Francie's eyes and tightening her grip on her hair. 'The anticipation. The saliva flooding the mouth. You know that feeling, don't you, Luigiana? And it's better. Better than you could have dreamed. Something that stirs the chilled blood of the most blasé connoisseur. They never tell you this. It's as if you can see for the first time. *Really* see, I mean. Pure power in your veins. You feel like a god. You *are* a god. Omnipotent. Transcendent. Every thirst slaked.'

She's beginning to sound as potty as van Cutsem. Francie's mouth is half open. Her breathing has changed.

457

It's deeper, slower. She has blood on her lower lip. Rebekah smiles at her. 'You have a lovely mouth, Luigiana. Beautiful, full lips.' She snaps her fingers at Milne. 'Handkerchief.'

Milne gets up and hands her the white pocket square from his suit jacket.

'Is this clean?'

'Yes, ma'am.'

'It better be.'

She moistens it with her tongue and goes to work on Francie's mouth, delicately patting the blood away. 'Lovely,' she says. 'I've tried not to damage your lipstick.'

'That's more than considerate.'

'Chanel Rouge Allure, is it not?'

'You're one frikkin' lipstick connoisseur, honey.'

Rebekah tosses the handkerchief in Milne's general direction. He catches it in mid-air and stuffs it in his pocket.

'So, these kids that have been serving the coffee,' I say. 'Is this what they do when they're not entertaining your exclusive and sophisticated clientele?'

Rebekah looks annoyed, as if I've spoiled her atmosphere. 'What? No. Well, it hardly matters now. Some of them we call *residents*. They have been or are still involved in the entertainments but also have an aptitude for menial tasks in this house. There are not many who do this.'

'So, when you have no more use for them, some of them become tea ladies. What happens to the others?'

White starts to explain. 'When we have no more use for them, well…'

Rebekah turns sharply and hisses at him. 'Say it!'

'When we have no more use for them, we do them a

kindness,' says White, smiling to himself. Francie's eyes darken.

'I've got to know,' I say. 'How are they controlled? They can't be doing all this stuff voluntarily.'

'You're asking a lot of questions, Mr Cambridge,' says Rebekah. 'But that's OK; you won't be passing on the answers to anyone. We have medical staff who deal with that side of it. Consultants. Top people. It's an accelerated process. Very scientific. Behaviour modification. Drugs. Hypnosis. Methods that would have seemed space-age half a century ago are now commonplace. It's quite remarkable. We can get these children to do virtually anything and we can do it quickly.'

A smile spreads across her face and she looks over at Milne. 'Get Mr Cambridge and Ms Sciarra down to the basement. I think it's time we gave them a little demonstration. Where are Baba and Jaheem? If Adonis forgot to tell them...'

Milne walks over and gives us his hard-man stare. Salo gets up and points his gun at us again. It's funny; I'd almost forgotten he was in the room.

'Stand,' says Milne.

Just as Francie and I get to our feet, the door opens once more, and two children come in. One of them is a pale, blonde girl of about eleven with a vacant, masklike expression on her face and the other a good-looking dark boy with grey eyes and distinctive dead straight eyebrows. I don't have to guess at his age. He's seven years old.

Hi, Ronny.

33

CHILD'S PLAY

Now I finally realise why this place is so warm.

We're marched down a long underground corridor which leads to a large, wide basement room with a pretty high ceiling. It's difficult to work out the proportions of this house; this room seems to be too big to be in the basement, but there it is.

Despite the heat, there's a damp, mouldy smell which permeates everything. I can taste it on my tongue each time I breathe in and it's irritating my sinuses. From what I can tell, the floor and walls are made from handmade Victorian bricks. It's lit by about a dozen halogen bulkhead lights.

Not a great deal of furniture; just some chairs and a big oak wardrobe with a mirrored door on one side and an electronic keypad on the other. Whether intentionally or not, the whole effect is rather cool and fashionable, apart from the fact that there are no windows. Stick a few prints on the walls and it would be a classy pad if you were nineteen.

In the centre of this area, which must measure about forty by fifty feet, there's something that at first glance looks like a miniature, windowless house, made from the same handmade bricks. It has a thick, rusted iron door, five foot high, which is currently wide open. To the right of the door there's a sizeable control panel which is an ugly mix of old-fashioned brass piping and modern digital displays.

It's the residual heat and faint smell of burning that gives its use away. This is some sort of incinerator, and the pipes that travel from its sides into the walls make it obvious that it was designed to heat the whole building at some point in the past.

I close my eyes and visualise the room we just came from; there was an electric wall radiator behind the executive desk and another to the right of the dining table, so it's unlikely that this is still utilised for domestic heating. So, what is it used for? I have my suspicions, of course, but my brain is telling me to forget about it and focus on my current problems. I remember Polly telling me about everyone sweating, *glowing* during the orgy, as if the heating was jacked up to the max.

I take a look at Ronny, who Rebekah just called Jameel. I don't quite understand what's going on here. How on earth did van Cutsem manage to spirit him out of this place for a cynical extortion shakedown with Quennel and his pal? Was it with the blessing of White and Rebekah? Did they know? Were they going to share the fifty thousand? Perhaps they're not here all of the time and he was able to organise it in their absence.

How long would it take to drive from here to Virginia Water? Thirty minutes? Less? Van Cutsem gave the impression that he wasn't a frequent visitor and was a little vague about the layout of the house and who lived here, but he could have been prevaricating. Still; hardly important at the moment. The name Jameel is nagging at me, then I remember that Polly's female colleague in the

OFRP was called Jameela.

Ronny is dressed in something that looks like an orange toga; obviously going for the casual Buddhist priest look. He doesn't wear sandals, though, just a pair of dark red Skechers trainers which, frankly, ruin the whole conceit.

His hair is held in place with some sort of sparkly gel. There's a big circular badge on his chest with what looks like a Sanskrit symbol on it. I have no idea what this indicates. Perhaps it has some sort of resonance with one of the guests.

So here we are: me, Francie, Milne, Salo, Rebekah, White, Ronny/Jameel and Baba. I wish I knew White's real name; it's really bugging me. Milne and Salo stand next to each other watching all of us; alert, but not as alert as they were fifteen minutes ago. I keep watching, waiting, working out who is in charge of who, who is weak and who is strong.

Milne drags out three upholstered dining chairs and a black faux leather office swivel chair.

'You may want to sit, my dear,' says Rebekah to Francie, indicating one of the dining chairs.

But Francie ignores her, walking over the incinerator and looking inside. Salo makes a move towards her but Rebekah raises a hand to stop him.

Francie stands and stares for about a minute while I'm tied to the office chair, cuffs still behind my back. Milne is very quick and professional. He's using silver duct tape and uses almost half the roll to attach my forearms to the arm rests. That's all he needs to do for my upper body; I can't get up and I can hardly move. It's incredibly painful and uncomfortable due to the cuffs behind my back; both of my shoulders are being pulled downwards and feel as if they're being very gradually dislocated.

When he's finished with that, he wraps the rest of the tape over the tops of my thighs and underneath the seat. I'm more concerned about what it's going to feel like when the tape is ripped off than I am about the fact that it's going to cut off my circulation in a few hours. I look around to see if I can work out where he got the tape from but can't see anywhere obvious. He certainly didn't seem to have it when we were upstairs.

Francie turns to Rebekah. 'What have you been burning in there? What's all that white ash?'

Rebekah glances at White who gives her a cute little eyebrow-raise.

'Do you know, Ms Sciarra,' he says. 'How many people have ever lived on earth? I'm talking about *Homo sapiens*, of course. We've only been around for fifty thousand years or thereabouts. You'd think it would be longer, wouldn't you?'

'It's chinless ugly geek quiz time,' she replies.

'One hundred and eight billion people,' he says, ignoring her. 'Over the last fifty thousand years. Only an estimate, of course, but it's the best the experts can do at the moment. Quite a number, I'm sure you'll agree. It's such a large number that it's difficult to *get your head around it*, as they say.'

'And your point is?' says Francie.

'My point *is*, Ms Sciarra, that human beings are much more dispensable than you might think. To say that the disappearance of one individual – their *discontinuation*, if you like – is a drop in the ocean, would be a *monumental* understatement.'

He's not expecting it. Francie, her face distorted by an angry scowl, runs straight at him, using her shoulder to

463

knock him to the floor. Milne is quick to stop her, but before he can, she's kicked White hard in the head three times with her heel, and despite her bare feet, or maybe because of them, he's bleeding profusely from the mouth. What was it she said she'd studied? Muay Thai? Ouch.

Milne grabs her around the waist, lifts her off the floor, then spins around and hurls her into one of the brick walls. She hits it hard and it knocks the wind out of her. The frustration I feel from not being able to do anything about this is irritating to say the least. She looks stunned. Rebekah squats down beside her and strokes her hair.

'Oh, Luigiana, Luigiana,' she says. 'I thought you were worldly. I thought you'd be more mature about this.'

'Get these cuffs off me and I'll show you how worldly and mature I am, you sick fuck.'

Rebekah nods at Milne, who again picks Francie up as if she weighs nothing and dumps her on one of the dining chairs. He produces another roll of his mysterious supply of duct tape and quickly immobilises her. I would guess that Francie weighs around a hundred and fifty pounds, which means that Milne is pretty strong. Might come in useful, might not.

I'm worried about what White might do. He slowly gets up, touches the side of his mouth and looks at the blood on his hand. He looks stunned and shocked. Whatever his job is, he's a stranger to any sort of combat; you can see it in his eyes, which are a tiny bit tearful.

And I reckon it's considerably more humiliating for him that his attacker was a woman, and a woman with both hands cuffed behind her back. He glances towards Rebekah but can't meet her gaze. Is he embarrassed?

He reaches a hand up towards Salo, who jerks him to

his feet. Rebekah's face is serious, and she watches White like a hawk.

'Don't do anything stupid, Caspian. We still need her in one piece,' she says.

Caspian? Really? What were his parents thinking? He should sue them. Well, at least I've got a name for him now. He walks slowly over to Francie and places his face an inch away from hers. He runs a hand through his hair, but it's still a mess after that little incident. He hisses at her. 'Don't you *like* that idea, Ms Sciarra? People being dispensable? Shall I tell you what happens here? Shall I tell you in detail?'

'Did you clean your teeth this morning, Caspian?' she says, smirking at him. 'Or does your breath smell like an open sewer 'cause you're so full of shit?'

A violent slap across the face for that, but she was expecting it. I notice that she's got a swelling appearing on her forehead, probably from her squabble with that brick wall.

Caspian jerks his head towards the incinerator. 'Your guess was correct. About the incinerator, I mean. What we've been burning in there. We had a few alterations made, of course; lined it with refractory bricks, had a dual exhaust system attached.

'The temperature required to cremate a human body is tremendous; up to around eleven hundred degrees Celsius, and it can sometimes take two hours. Heats this house up for a long time afterwards. Because of their size, of course, we can process them two at a time.'

He takes a long look at Francie's face, noting her disgusted expression. He leers at her. 'You're obviously a very smart woman.' He grabs her shoulders, drives his mouth down on hers, then immediately shrieks and jerks backwards. I can't see what's happened, but I can guess. She's bitten one of his lips.

He goes a bit crazy and starts repeatedly hitting her around the head. Rebekah gives Milne the nod and Milne pulls him off her. Caspian stands there, panting. I feel this day is getting worse and worse for him, which can only be a good thing. A lot of people involved in this operation are getting rattled, damaged or snuffed out in one way or another. Since Polly and I got involved, it's escalated quite a bit.

They're acting relaxed and in control, but it has to be a front. It's all going sideways. They're panicking. Caspian's lower lip is bleeding, and the cut looks bad. Three stitches? Four? He's lisping a bit when he speaks now. He's trying to ignore the pain he must be in to look like a cool cat in front of Rebekah.

'You've seen what happens at those entertainments, Ms Sciarra. In our line of business, you have to be pragmatic. Let's face it, once any of those assets – those *children* – are past their sell-by date, they're no use to man nor beast.

'We can't let them go – too much of a risk – and none of them are really going to grow up, meet someone nice, settle down and raise a family, are they? They're fucked. Fucked in more ways than most people can imagine. Like I said, we're doing them a kindness. Sure. We keep some of them as residents, as you've seen, but eventually even those will have to be dealt with.'

Francie turns her head to look at Baba and Ronny. They're immobile and expressionless. If they understand what he's saying, they're showing no obvious signs of it.

'But we're not without feeling,' he continues. 'Once they've come to the end of the road, they're anaesthetised, given a lethal injection – usually potassium cyanide – and once we're sure cessation of life has occurred, they're popped in the oven. There's no struggle or distress. They're quite pliant due to their conditioning. Like putty in our hands.'

Despite the residual rage in Caspian's voice, this is told so matter-of-factly that everyone's quiet for almost thirty seconds. It's as if what they've been doing here has been properly shoved in their faces for the first time and overridden their denial. Rebekah is the first to snap out of it.

'Baba. Come here, my dear.'

Baba walks towards her. I'd guessed her age to be eleven, but now I'm not so sure. Maybe a little older, but not by much. I can see now that her blonde hair is dyed. Good, regular features, with eyes as dead as ashes.

She's wearing what I think is called a djellaba; a long, loose-fitting robe with a big hood which rests on her shoulders. It's pretty striking; diamond patterns in yellow and black and a bright orange trim on the long sleeves. Is this Moroccan dress? I can't remember. I think that Polly described some of the clothing she saw as Moroccan or Egyptian. How long ago was that? Four days? Five days?

'Baba. Go to the magic wardrobe and open the doors,' says Rebekah.

Baba does what she's told. She presses the keypad and there's a loud click. When a wardrobe like this one opens, you'd expect to see clothes hanging up, but this one has been customised and contains a lot of the sort of junk you might see in someone's garage. Now I know where Milne stores his duct tape. There are a lot of tools, some unfamiliar, which I'm guessing are connected to the maintenance of the incinerator. Without trying, I can spot a dozen potential weapons.

To the right, there are three shelves groaning with basic first aid kit stuff; bandages, plasters, cotton wool, scissors, tweezers, syringes, creams, pills, packets of sterile gloves, ampoules of God-knows-what and bottles of pure medical alcohol. Baba stands still, waiting for instructions.

'Baba. Do you see the little pair of scissors next to the big bottle? Take it out, please.'

I make a note of the fact that Rebekah says this child's name first, before giving her orders. This smacks of trigger words or *anchors* used in behaviour modifying hypnosis. Baba takes out the scissors. Rebekah walks over to her, holds her hand and then approaches me. Both of them stand a little to my right. Baba stares at me but she's not fully in the room. I experience a little surge of adrenalin as I realise what's probably going to happen.

'This man's name is Oliver. He has had an accident. Say hello to Oliver.'

'*Bonjour, Oliver. M'aimez-vous?*' says Baba. OK. She's done it. I'm creeped out and lost for words. The way I've been taped to the chair makes my ricochet wound easy to get at. Rebekah and Baba take a look at it.

'He has a cut on his arm. Can you see the little stitches, Baba?'

'*Oui, madame.*'

'Baba. I'd like you to cut through each stitch with the scissors. It looks as if there are ten stitches altogether. Be careful, dear.' She leans forwards, her face bright and friendly. 'This is a very fiddly job!'

'*Vous m'aimez, monsieur?*' says Baba. I decide not to reply.

Rebekah smiles at me as I listen to the scissors do their work. It feels as if she and I are colluding on something that Baba knows nothing about. If nothing else, this is a unique experience and one I'll always treasure. It's pretty painless, though, so at least that's a plus.

Milne looks disinterested. Salo has moved closer to get a better look. He's grinning. Caspian keeps touching his lower lip and looking at his fingers to see if the bleeding has stopped. It hasn't. Ronny moves closer to us but stares straight ahead as if someone's left him on standby. Francie, wisely, decides to keep silent.

I look at nothing while Baba cuts through each stitch with quite admirable delicacy. Rebekah keeps trying to look into my eyes, but I'm not playing. I'm trying to keep calm, but I feel my heart rate increasing with each second that goes by. Rebekah runs her hand over the puncture marks she made on my chest, then stops when she sees that Baba has finished. Baba stands to attention.

'Good girl,' she says. 'Jameel. Come here, please.' Ronny snaps out of it and turns to face her. 'Do you see the cut in the man's arm, Jameel? It's a long cut, isn't it?' Ronny nods his head and gives her a big, wide smile. 'I'd like you to pull that cut apart a little. It got wider when Baba cut through the stitches. Now you must make it wider still. Off you go!'

Ronny leans forwards and inspects the wound like a normal kid would look at a ladybird on a leaf. Then his small fingers slowly prise the wound apart. Now this *does* hurt. I close my eyes tightly and breathe deeply, trying to block it out.

There's a chill in the pit of my stomach. If my right hand wasn't trapped behind my back, I'm pretty sure it would be shaking. This is probably unfair, but I'm starting to take a major dislike to Aaron Quennel and his family. After a minute, Ronny stops.

'Well done, Jameel!' says Rebekah. 'Now go to the magic cupboard and find the big scissors. Good boy!' She turns to me. 'Now, Oliver Cambridge, private investigator. I'd like you to tell me where both memory sticks are.'

'It's not going to happen, Seraphina. I do hope that prison food won't make you put on weight. It would be so unfortunate if you lost your figure.'

'Such a shame, Oliver. Such a shame. Jameel. Come here please, dear.'

Jameel walks over to her, a pair of large, heavy duty Murrena kitchen scissors in his hand. She takes the scissors and hands them to Baba. 'These are much bigger scissors, aren't they, Baba!'

For the first time since I've seen her, Baba smiles. She nods her head excitedly as if she's being given a birthday treat and takes the scissors from Rebekah. Do these kids have birthdays? Are they here long enough? Do these scumbags even know when their birthdays are?

'Baba. I want you to hold the scissors like *this!*' Rebekah mimes a tight psycho grip. Baba imitates her. 'That is excellent, Baba. Now we're going to help Oliver with his cut once more.'

Baba stands by my side and smiles at me.

'Que puis-je faire pour vous, monsieur?'

Rebekah smiles indulgently. *'Baba. Essayez l'anglais, ma chère.'*

'Is there something I can do for you, sir?'

'Good girl. There *is* something that you can do for Oliver to help his cut. Let's see how long it is, shall we? I think it's five inches long, or thereabouts. That's about twelve centimetres, isn't it? I'd like you to make it a little deeper. Stick the scissors into the top of the cut and drag it down to the very bottom. Off you go!'

This time I have to take a huge inhalation through my nose to counter the pain. I can actually hear the flesh ripping and I can hear the duct tape squeak as I strain against it.

'*Iskam da vie napravya shtastliv, sŭr,*' says Baba, cheerfully. Bulgarian. She wants to make me happy. Nice. Maybe I should suggest repeatedly stabbing Rebekah in the neck; I'd be overjoyed. I wonder if she learned that phrase for Vanchev's benefit. Vanchev. I'd almost forgotten about him. I wonder how his wife's doing. What was her name? Lilyana?

'Look, Baba. Can you see the blood? Does that shade of red remind you of anything? It's like your pretty quilted skirt, is it not?'

Baba doesn't react. I take a quick look at my arm. Well, she's certainly got the blood flowing. It's pouring out of the wound and dripping off my elbow onto the floor. I'm starting to feel nauseous. My breathing has become a little shallow. I hope I'm not going into shock.

'So, Mr Cambridge. The location of both memory sticks, please.'

'Listen, Seraphina. I don't know if you're with anyone at the moment, but I'm sure you're aware of how attractive you are. I was wondering if you'd care to come on holiday with me. I was thinking maybe Florence or somewhere like that?'

In reply, she gives me a hard, open-handed slap on the wound. Now that was pretty bad, and for a second, I think I'm going to pass out and/or throw up, but I take a deep breath and I'm still here. Out of the corner of my eye I can see Caspian silently chuckling to himself.

'The memory sticks, please.'

I shake my head. The movement brings on a wave of nausea and I throw up.

'Baba. Take the scissors and stab Oliver's cut in the middle. Do it as hard as you can, my dear. Keep the scissors in the cut.'

Jeg vil være din spesielle venn, sir,' says Baba as she drives the scissors, just once, into the centre of the wound and holds it there. For some reason I start thinking about Priscilla. Why is that? Oh, yes. Florence. We went there together and stayed in the Hotel Orto de Medici for three nights. Great rooms. Our bedroom was overlooked by the hotel across the road and she wanted to keep the blinds open the whole time so people could see in.

'What are you smiling at? You think this is funny?' says Rebekah. 'Baba. Twist the scissors around in the cut. Do it now.'

This time I can't stop myself crying out. I'm shivering and sweating. 'Do you like me, sir?' says Baba, smiling and turning the scissors from left to right, as if she's using a screwdriver on a particularly stubborn screw. I start wondering about the damage this will do to my arm. I start thinking about the blood vessels in that area. The nerves. What's there? The radial nerve? I can't remember. Brachial artery? No. Wrong part of the arm and I'd be spurting blood in Baba's face by now. I try not to look at Francie, but it happens anyway, and our eyes meet for a second. She looks pale.

Kayf yumkinuni alturfiuh eunka?' says Baba. There's no hope for her; no way back from this. Her mind is gone. She's like a malfunctioning, unrepairable piece of software spouting phrases she probably doesn't even understand in every language known to man. She's got a facial tic by her left eye, which makes everything a little more eerie.

'The memory sticks. Tell me where they are, and this will stop. Do not be foolish.'

I smile at her, but now attempt to sound more fucked than I am. 'So, Florence is a no-no? Stop beating around the bush, Seraphina. Tell me straight. I can take it.'

This time I get about half a dozen fierce open-handed slaps on the wound from Rebekah. She's losing it now and perspiring. An amateur. Desperate. Her hair is dishevelled. It's a sexy look. She'd love Florence.

'Can I get you something to drink, sir?' says Baba.

Now it's Ronny's turn with the big scissors. Baba hands them to him, but there's no sign of any communication between them, either verbal or facial. Unlike Baba, Ronny never speaks, but I notice a puzzled expression flash across his face for a millisecond.

I wonder if they use different techniques on different kids. Everyone has a unique response to behaviour altering procedures. Children even more so, I imagine. Do they keep experimenting until they get the required result? Rebekah strokes Ronny's head.

'Did you see what Baba did to the man's arm, Jameel? To Oliver's arm? She turned the scissors around and around and around. Would you like to do that? See if you can get them in deeper than Baba!'

Ronny nods his head. She hands the scissors to him. He rests a hand on top of my shoulder and stabs as hard as he can. God almighty. This is real eye-rolling agony. I close my eyes tightly and blaspheme loudly for a few seconds. I hope no one here is religious.

Ronny is smaller and younger than Baba, but then he's a boy and maybe played rough games with his mates, good practice for an occasion such as this. Didn't

Quennel say he swam? Wasn't he lifted in a pool somewhere?

My heart rate is about 120 bpm. I feel light-headed and my tongue is tingling. Then Ronny imitates Baba's screwdriver action, twisting the scissor blades from left to right. I start thinking about Liva and her gifts, then throw up and pass out.

Almost immediately, I'm slapped back into consciousness by Rebekah, who's getting impatient now. Ronny has stepped back a little, as if awaiting further instructions, but he's still holding the scissors in my arm. It looks like the blades are in about two inches, maybe more. Feels like more. Bit of a weird angle, so it's difficult to judge. Still, I've had knives penetrate more deeply than that. I raise my head to see Salo looking at me. He's still grinning.

Then Rebekah grabs the embedded scissors in both hands and impatiently twists them from left to right. She looks angry. She looks malicious. She looks mad. This time I have to scream. It's not the worst pain I've experienced, but it's certainly in the same ballpark. This phase is coming to its conclusion now and it's time to let her have what she wants. She pulls the scissors out and hands them to Ronny, who seems to be on standby once more. I let my head drop down. She grabs a handful of my hair and jerks my head up so she can look into my eyes.

'Running out of smart comments, Mr Cambridge?'

I shake my head from side to side, make my breathing shallow and place a hint of delirium into my voice. 'I wish I'd never taken this fuckin' job. All this; it's nothing to do with me.'

She attempts a sympathetic expression. It's difficult for

her. 'This can all stop, and you know how to stop it.'

'If I…' I mumble.

'What? What did you say there?' says Rebekah eagerly. 'If I? If I what?'

'There's a…guy we work with. Computer expert. I gave him the memory sticks. The copy I made was different. I put a menu on it. Told him to make copies and to encrypt them, which I didn't know how to do. I asked for twenty copies of each. He said he wouldn't have time until next week. Thursday. Friday. I can't remember. What day is it today?'

I can see Francie looking at me with horror. I can't tell whether it's faked or genuine. 'What are you *doing*?' she says. 'Shut *up*.'

'No. *You* shut up, Luigiana. Where is he? Give me the address.'

I make my voice sound weak. 'They'll both be in his safe. They're in an orange flash drive case. BUBM. That's the make. It's in white letters on the front. But he won't…he won't let you have them.'

'Oh, *won't* he? What's the address?'

'There's no point. He won't let you in. He's a really suspicious guy. He does a lot of illegal stuff.' I allow myself a couple of seconds of panting. 'Paranoid. He won't…'

She snaps her fingers at Caspian who hands her his mobile. 'What's the number? You're going to tell him to expect a visitor.'

I try to look defeated. '077708 605998. But it won't get you anywhere.'

'Where is he?'

'Whitechapel.'

She taps the number into the mobile and holds it next

to my face. 'No funny business. Act naturally. Make it sound like nothing's wrong. Tell him I'll be there in an hour to pick the sticks up. Think of a convincing reason. Use the name Seraphina. Tell him I'm a friend. Pep yourself up, Oliver. I don't want you sounding sick.'

'It might be more than an hour, ma'am,' says Milne, checking something on his mobile. 'There's a bomb gone off in W1 this morning. Marble Arch. No specific time given, but it's certain to cause disruption. We'll have to go via South London.'

'Yeah, yeah.' A look of concentration appears on her face as we wait for a response. She wants to hear everything. Not an ideal situation, but I'll have to work with it. Marble Arch? When did that happen? That's quite near to the police station that DI Bream works out of and not too far from the Hard Rock Hotel where we had coffee. I seem to recall she mentioned something about a severe terrorist threat. I hope she's OK. After about thirty seconds, the call is answered.

'Yes?' A sick-sounding, exhausted voice.

'Hi. It's me. Sorry for the intrusion. I'm going to send someone round for those two memory sticks. I know you haven't had time to encrypt and copy them yet, but it's no problem. I can bring them around again next week. Ronny can give me a lift.'

Silence. Let's hope the penny drops. The longest five seconds in history goes by. 'I'm sorry, man. I've just been up to my eyes in it.'

Well that's a relief. And now I'll take a gamble and assume that Rebekah didn't know about van Cutsem's ransom scam.

'It's a friend of George's. You remember George. Best behaviour. She's very attractive. Just your type. Name's

Seraphina, would you believe. Just give her the flash drive case. We can sort out the copies another time. She'll be there in about an hour, maybe less.'

'I guarantee she'll get a warm welcome. We must meet up for a drink again sometime.'

'Good idea, mate. Bricklayers Arms like before?'

'Sounds fine.'

'OK, pal. Later.'

She stops the call. 'Address? This is the third and last time I'll ask you.'

I give her a big tragic sigh. '26 Gainsborough Road, London E1. Guy's name is Aaron Quennel. You're not going to hurt him, are you?' Let's hope his reactions are up to scratch and his P226 is fully loaded.

She turns to Milne. 'You're coming with me. Are you still armed?'

Milne opens his jacket. His Grand Power K100 Whisper is in a brown suede holster on his left hip.

She looks at Caspian. 'I'm taking the Citroën. Get these two unwrapped before they soil themselves. You'll have to handcuff them in the front but be damn careful. Get Salo to put both of them in one of the cells and make sure it's properly locked. We'll get the information regarding the girl when I come back. Maybe we can get Hannibal to give them a savaging they'll never forget.'

She turns her attention to me once more. 'Have you met Hannibal, Mr Cambridge? A handsome animal. But very ill-tempered if he doesn't know you. He can go into a bit of a frenzy. It's not very pleasant to watch. He's a little bloodthirsty. He always goes for the throat. He's been trained well. He's an extremely useful associate to have in certain types of interrogation. Fear of large, aggressive dogs is deeply ingrained in many people, and also in children.'

Hannibal. Well, it had to be something ridiculous like that. Perhaps he rides elephants.

Then something odd happens. Baba starts looking around the room as if she's just woken up from a bad dream. She looks at each person in turn as an expression of extreme distress passes across her face. She starts walking towards Francie, smiling, her hand held out.

'Mummy?'

34

PEOPLE IN GLASS HOUSES

Francie looks dismayed and tearful. Rebekah looks irritated. She quickly puts both hands on Baba's shoulders and redirects her towards Ronny.

The expression on Baba's face reminded me of something. That's it. It's when I was looking at the contents of the memory stick in my flat. That same upsetting, confused expression of anguish and terror occasionally appearing on the children's faces, as if, for a second, they remembered who they were and wondered what was going on. Didn't I spot a flash of confusion on Ronny's face a few minutes ago?

I try to remember when Quennel said Ronny was abducted. Was it three weeks ago? How much conditioning would he have had in that time? The orgy was almost a week ago now. It seems to be effective in the short term, but do the subjects require regular repeat treatments? Top-ups?

'Jameel. Take her to her room,' Rebekah says to Ronny. 'Sit with her until she feels better. Give her two spoonfuls of her blue medicine and wait until she goes to sleep. You and she have done very well today, my dear. I am pleased with both of you. You shall have a reward.'

Ronny smiles, nods, puts his arm around Baba's shoulder and leads her out of the room. I'll say one thing for these kids; they're really versatile.

Rebekah inspects Caspian's face. 'You're going to have to get that lower lip looked at. I think it'll need a couple of stitches. Maybe give Niels a call.'

'I can deal with that, Miss Giri,' says Salo. 'I have advanced field medical training. I have dealt with much worst.'

Caspian nods his head. 'Well, that'll save a bit of time.' He looks at Rebekah. 'How long will you be?'

'This time of night? An hour there, an hour back. Maybe less. Probably less. Oh. Damn. I forgot. That bomb in the West End. Never mind. What we have to do will only take a matter of minutes. Take a break. We can start again when I return, though I doubt if the residents will be up to it.

'I think Baba will need a little R&R and I noticed Jameel was looking a bit jumpy. We'll have to do it ourselves.' She glances at Francie. 'Maybe have a session with the rather gorgeous Ms Sciarra. I think you'd enjoy that, Caspian. I know *I* would.'

Caspian nods his head and leers in Francie's direction. 'I'll feast upon her,' he says, without humour.

'Come on, Milne. We're going to intimidate a computer nerd!'

They both laugh as they leave the room. Well, good luck with that, you two.

Caspian looks at Francie, then he looks at me, then he looks at Francie again. He goes to the magic cupboard and produces a Stanley knife. He leans over Francie and places the blade flat against her cheek.

'You will regret what you have done, Ms Sciarra,' he

lisps. 'You will bitterly regret it. I am not a man to forget such things.'

'You're a *man*?' asks Francie. He spits in her face. There's a fair amount of blood mixed in with his spittle. It looks gruesome. I just hope he doesn't have infectious hepatitis.

He cuts through her tape and allows her to stand up. The cuffs must be killing her wrists by now. With Salo keeping a careful eye on proceedings, they're removed and then reattached in front of her body. She stretches and turns her head from side to side. Then Salo does the same to me, only using a Mac Coltellerie Z08 combat knife, obviously the duct tape carving implement of choice for Messrs Salo and Vonk. As my handcuffs are transferred, I consider trying something, but decide against it. Not yet, not yet.

When it's all been cut away, I rotate my shoulders to alleviate the pain caused by the way I was attached to the chair. I can stand up but have lost feeling in most of my right leg. It'll pass, but I don't like being this unsteady on my feet.

Francie and I both need to get our clothes back on. I assume they're still in the upstairs room where we removed them. It's very warm in this house, but it's the psychological disadvantage of being in your underclothes that I'm concerned about.

For some, it's not a big deal, but it can make a miniscule difference to the way you react to problems and the way you solve them, and we don't need that sort of handicap at the moment.

Francie is looking pale and dishevelled from her ordeal. I try to catch her eye, but she's too busy glowering at Caspian.

Salo isn't speaking to me, but I can tell his mouth is watering in anticipation of getting me to himself when all the interrogations are over and I'm expendable, but that won't be happening quite yet. Perhaps he doesn't want to signal his intentions to Caspian.

As Francie and I are marched at gunpoint down another underground corridor, I attempt to make polite conversation with Salo about his family, but it's useless. I can feel him staring at my back, though, and I know that he'd dearly love to put a bullet in it. What was it he said in the car? *You will scream?* Something like that. Still, I have to admire his professionalism. He's been employed to do a job by these people and he's keeping his personal feelings to himself as well as he can.

'You were a lot more garrulous in your house earlier on, Eemil. But I get it; you're afraid of these people here, aren't you? Tell me; do you get to keep the money that Wolfert, Jitser and Redolf got for that job? I'd give it to charity if I were you; you'll only feel guilty when you spend it on more funky black clothing for yourself.'

Nothing. I wonder if he's trying to think up a witty riposte. Francie takes a look at the ugly, bleeding wound in my right arm. 'Does that hurt?'

'Does what hurt? I'm so tough, I don't even know what you're talking about.' As I speak, I realise that I've got blood in my mouth, but can't work out why that should be. I've got pins and needles in my right hand. 'You look terrible, by the way.'

'Why thank you, kind sir. You, of course, certainly don't look like someone who belongs in a hospital ward on a drip.'

'Kids, eh?'

'Yeah. They're always up to some mischief or other.'

'Shut up and keep walking, pissfat,' says Salo.

Pissfat. I'm learning a lot from this guy. Before we left the incinerator room, Salo referred to Rebekah as Miss Giri. So that's Rebekah Giri. I'll try to remember that.

After a couple of minutes, we turn right and enter another big basement area which has been converted into what can only be described as residential cells. All the walls, doors and ceilings are made from some sort of grey-tinted reinforced glass.

In between each cell, the glass is green and moderately opaque, to give each resident a modicum of privacy, like the shower partitions at a gym. Each cell contains a bed, a small toilet area, two armchairs and a chest of drawers. Each door has a small digital lock with a chrome keypad. On each wall, a small unidentifiable black unit with a red flashing light.

In one of the cells is the girl who brought us coffee, the one with the straight black hair who I thought looked Vietnamese. She's sitting on her bed looking straight ahead, her hands folded on her lap. She has that standby look on her face that Ronny had earlier on. Her cell is locked or at least closed. When we walk past her cell she doesn't look up or react in any way.

There are two empty cells, then I spot the boy that Seraphina called Adonis. He looks ill. He's sitting cross-legged on the floor, playing some sort of game on an iPad. Like the girl, he doesn't look up when we pass.

Across from him is what must be Baba's cell. The door is open. She's lying on her bed staring at the ceiling. Ronny, still in his orange toga, sits at the bottom of the bed and fiddles with a small plastic item that looks like a Gameboy but isn't. He's concentrating on the game, but his eyes dart from left to right as if something's continually distracting him.

Salo stops and points to the cell opposite Baba's. 'In there.'

We do what he says. He never keeps his eyes off me as he closes the door and types a five-digit code into the lock. He gives me one final tough look, smirks and leaves.

Francie and I sit staring for about a minute. We have a lot to absorb. My arm hurts like a bastard.

'You OK?' she asks.

'Never better. Refreshed. Ready to rock. What about you?'

'Nothing that a five-hour soak in a Molton Brown bubble bath won't cure. So, what was all that about?'

'Which bit?'

'The bit about the guy who was copying the memory sticks. The one who lived in the East End of London. Aaron something.'

'Oh, yeah.' I keep my voice low. 'Well. You know the kid who was sticking the scissors in my arm? The boy?'

'Jameel.'

'Well, his name's actually Ronny. Ronny Quennel. He's seven. I sent Seraphina and Milne to see his dad who's a serving soldier. He and his mate lifted me after I went to that address in Vicarage Gardens. Thought I was connected to van Cutsem. They took me to a disused warehouse for a beating.'

'That's *such* a cliché. Does it always have to be a disused warehouse? I hope you gave them a piece of your mind.'

'I asked them if it could be a disused cathouse next time.'

'Far superior.'

I bring her up to speed on Ronny's abduction and the

mental state and intent of Quennel and his associate.

'Crap. What do you think he'll do when they get there?'

'I can't imagine. He's pretty angry with them all. I told him everything and he freaked. Worst case scenario for them is that he'll kill them first and ask questions later. I suspect he thinks he's got nothing to lose. His wife's losing her mind and he's getting that way, too. I just hope he can blindside them; they certainly won't be expecting the reception they're undoubtedly going to get.

'My intention was to get some of these people out of the way to make things slightly easier for us. Rebekah taking Milne with her was an unexpected bonus.'

'But what she was doing to you. Why did you wait so long? You must have been in agony.'

'I had to make her work for it to make it seem convincing. I kind of promised Quennel I'd try and get his kid back, too, so I gambled that he'd go along with whatever bullshit I told him over the phone.'

'So now what?'

'From what I can gather, there are only four adults in the house apart from us: Caspian, Salo, the guy who drove us here who I'm calling Bald Medium and the girl they called Jane, who we saw when we first arrived. I don't know where she is now, and I don't know *what* she is. We have to treat her as skilled, dangerous and hostile. She may have even gone; I don't know.

'Then there's the kids. We've got Ronny and Baba across the way, Adonis and that other girl with the straight black hair. But this is a big house. There could be other people here we don't know about.'

'Hey; and don't underestimate these kids just because they're kids, you know? You've already had a first-hand taste of what they're capable of. I don't think either of them had done that before. Those creeps can tell 'em to do something and they'll do it without question.'

'I've already thought of that.'

'Rebekah mentioned a Citroën just before she left,' says Francie. 'I saw that when we got here. It was a dark blue C5 SUV. So far as I could make out, there were no other cars apart from the grey Mercedes that brought us here, but I could be wrong.'

I stand up and take a look at the walls of the cell. I'm still not sure what the little black things with the red flashing lights are. Francie follows my gaze.

'They're Fleischer and Pabst motion sensor alarms. They won't go off while you're walking around, but if you try something tough, like kicking the door or the walls, a signal gets sent somewhere and an alarm will go off.'

'Does that mean there's someone here we don't know about sitting in a room watching monitors?'

'Probably not. It's unlikely we'd be able to bust our way out of here, so one of the goons would probably come down and tell us to stop it if they heard an alarm.' She places a hand against one of the walls. 'I think this is palladium-based metallic glass, so you'd be onto a loser even if you had a sledgehammer. Tougher than steel, they say.'

There are a couple of Sony Jupiter CCTV cameras in each corner of this area, but these usually have a tiny green pin light under the lens when they're operating. It could be that these cameras are only used when there are more people in here.

Handcuffs allowing, I pat my hands gently across the glass wall next to the door just to get a feel for the solidity and thickness. Nothing happens. With my shoulder, I attempt to push the door the wrong way, but it doesn't move an inch. I run a finger down the gap between the door and the adjacent wall. I shake my head in exasperation.

'What are you doing?' asks Francie.

'I don't know.'

Just as I'm about to sit down on the bed and decide what to do next, a small movement from across the way catches my eye. It's Ronny. He's standing up and is imitating my movements, running his finger down the side of his door, even though his is open. I place my hands high up the glass and slowly spread the fingers. He does the same thing. I waggle my fingers as if playing an invisible piano, and he copies that, too. I smile at him; he smiles back.

When we walked past the room that Adonis was in, I could hear the bleeps and explosions of whatever game it was he was playing, even though his door was shut. As far as I could make out, he was only using an iPad, so the sounds can't have been that loud even with the volume on max. I keep eye contact with Ronny. I raise my voice as much as I can without shouting and put a light tone into it, as if greeting an old friend.

'Ronny!'

He can hear me. The smile falls from his face. His expression becomes dead. I do hope he's not going to become catatonic. I have no idea what sort of conditioning he's been through but know enough to be wary of saying or doing something sudden/disorientating/weird.

He didn't speak at all earlier on. Why was that? I keep eye contact with him. His brow is furrowed. He's not blinking so tears start to gather in his eyes. I raise a hand.

'Ronny.' He's still not moving. I turn to Francie. 'Smile and wave your hands from side to side. Don't look crazy. I know it's difficult.'

She does it. I keep forgetting we're both in our underclothes, so this probably looks a bit crazy to him anyway, but I'll persevere. I point to Francie with my thumb.

'Do you remember Francie, Ronny?'

He looks puzzled, but at least his expression has changed a little. He squints at Francie, then looks back at me. I keep smiling. I probably look insane. I try to imagine I'm a children's television presenter. I must remember to keep using his real name as much as I can.

'Francie asked me something about you, Ronny, but I couldn't remember what the answer was. Can you help me, Ronny?'

His demeanour changes. He looks mildly suspicious, but his features have relaxed slightly, and his eyes have a little more humour in them. He nods his head. I beckon to him with a single finger. I exaggerate my mouth movements. 'You'll have to come over here, Ronny. I won't be able to hear you properly.' I tap my ear with a finger. Do the handcuffs look weird? He doesn't seem to notice.

He turns and looks at Baba, who's still prostrate and staring at the ceiling. He looks conflicted.

'It's OK, Ronny. Baba will be asleep soon. She told you to come over here and talk to me. Don't you remember, Ronny?'

He thinks about this for almost a minute. Then he leaves Baba's room and walks over. He stands in front of the glass wall and looks at us.

'Qanday qilib men sizga xizmat qila olaman?'

'What the fuck language is that?' whispers Francie. 'They should open a branch of Berlitz here.'

'It's Uzbek. I understand it, but I can't really communicate well in it. He wants to know how he can serve us.'

'I'd like a Dirty Martini.'

I wave at Ronny and speak as slowly and clearly as I can, always keeping a smile in my voice. 'You'll have to speak English to us, Ronny. We're not very clever. We don't understand many foreign languages. Shall I tell you what Francie wanted to know, Ronny?'

He nods his head and smiles suddenly. The smile doesn't reach his eyes.

'Francie wanted to know what your favourite Fruit Shoot was, Ronny. Your favourite Fruit Shoot. I told her it was pink lemonade, but I don't think I'm right, am I?'

He shakes his head. Good. Slowly prising him open.

'Peach and mango,' he says.

Thank God for that. 'I knew it!' I say, brightly. 'I knew it was something with two different flavours, Ronny. Because your mum bought one for you at the Leighton Leisure Lagoon. Do you remember, Ronny?'

He looks worried once more. 'Yes.'

'Shall I tell you what my favourite flavour is, Ronny? It's cranberry and apple.' I have no idea whether such a flavour exists, but he nods briefly as if he recognises it, so perhaps it does. 'I'll tell you what, Ronny. I'm really thirsty. I'd really like to have one of those to drink right now, but I can't get to the shops because I can't get out of this room. Have you ever been in this room, Ronny?'

'It's Izabela's room.'

'Is Izabela your friend, Ronny?'

He shakes his head. 'No. But sometimes I lend her my

game. She's gone now.'

'That's a shame. Did you come in here and lend her your game?'

He nods his head and presses five buttons on the chrome keypad. There's a loud click and the door opens. He walks straight towards Francie and puts his arms around her. Awkwardly, she hugs him and draws him towards her.

35

SWINGING SIXTIES GIRL

It took three awkward and painful minutes to break the pin off the back of Ronny's Sanskrit badge. He was reluctant to hand it over, so we had to use Rebekah's technique of saying 'Jameel' before giving him orders and thankfully it worked. This seemed to snap him back into his torpor, so we escorted him back to Baba's room and he sat down on the bed once more, engaging with his game console.

As soon as the pin was off (and had punctured my fingers three times), I was able to bend it into an L shape, use it to manipulate the pawl on one of the cuffs and release the ratchet.

In less than thirty seconds, both pairs of cuffs were on the floor and Francie and I were massaging the discomfort from our wrists. I kick the cuffs underneath the bed, as I can't think what else to do with them. If only I had pockets.

'OK. What do we do now? Run into the street in our underclothes and attempt to flag down a passing car?'

'Well, why bother with the underclothes? Let me think.'

I press my fingers into my eyeballs until everything goes white with accompanying psychedelic swirls.

'OK. Keep your voice as low as you can. We've got at

least two armed personnel running around in this place, one of whom is motivated on a number of levels to shoot us, or at least to shoot me. On the plus side, they're still quite keen on using us to locate Liva, and they don't really know which one of us can or will give them that information.

'I think there's been a serious communications breakdown regarding Liva; first a police visit using her real name, then Milne and his pal using her professional name, then van Cutsem trying to lure her to her doom, then Milne and pal parked outside her house again. I don't know what's going on and I don't think they do, either.'

'Why do you think they want her?'

'They'll liquidate her. Knows too much. She'd probably end up in that incinerator. They were hoping to kill two birds with one stone by catching Jael at the same time, but that didn't work out. Someone delegated that job to van Cutsem; it would have been the obvious thing to do as he knew both women and they knew him. It was just bad luck that I was in the room when he called Liva. The visits to her house were either crossed wires or incompetence or both.

'Normally, I think they'd have dealt with those two much more quickly, but they had all this other stuff going on and it slowed them down and caused confusion. That's how Jael was able to slip out of the country without them noticing.

'At the moment, I'm sure they're confident that they can track her down another time, maybe the next time she visits the UK. God knows how all of this will pan out but trying to lure those two to their doom is another thing that'll get van Cutsem a few more years' jail time, unless the other prisoners get him first.'

'Did this happen to other girls who'd been hired for these entertainments? Or other boys, for that matter?'

'Wouldn't surprise me at all. I doubt that it was the first time that they'd used performers like that. This whole thing could have been going on for years. We've got no idea what the casualty rate for a set-up like this would be. It's probably better to just block it out.'

'Shit.'

'Yeah. Think about it. You could never employ people like Liva and Jael for something like this and just hope there was no comeback.' I think of Liva's gentle, kooky personality and what these fucks almost certainly had planned for her. It makes my blood boil.

'First things first. I need to obtain a gun or other weapon and we need to recover our clothes or find someone else's. We're too vulnerable like this. Initially, we're going to make our way back up to the faggy pot pourri sitting room, as you so wittily called that study. Who knows; our clothes may be where we left them.'

'And ideally there'll be loaded guns all over the place and a chilled bottle of the finest champagne. Your arm's bleeding again.'

'I know.'

I look at my right hand; blood is dripping off the fingers onto the floor.

'Does it hurt?'

'Throbs a bit.'

'You look fucked.'

'Is that your best chat-up line, *Luigiana*?'

'Usually works, *Oliver*.'

'Also, I need a lot of information from Caspian. Whatever else happens here, I'm wanted for the murder of Judith Hart and I can't have that hanging over me. I need evidence to the contrary. I need to find out what happened to her body and I also need a shitload of names, ranks and numbers.'

It occurs to me that Polly's two OFRP colleagues could positively identify her body if I managed to discover where it was. Olivia could arrange it. That would be disastrous for the official fabrication, and the appearance of the real murder weapon with Salo's prints over it would be the coup de grâce.

'There are a lot of people involved in this who I'm sure would be of interest to the police – the non-corrupt police, that is,' I say. 'The more stuff I can give them, the more my part in all of this will be obliterated.'

'Until then, you're a fugitive from justice! This is super cool.'

We leave the luxury residential glass cell complex and turn left into the corridor which takes us to the traditional, Olde English incinerator suite. At least having no shoes on means that we can travel fairly quickly and silently. The corridor is fairly narrow. I ask Francie to walk a few feet behind me and two feet to my right. Just a precaution; if someone shoots me and the bullet passes straight through, then she won't get hit as well.

'They didn't mention your friend's boss,' she says. 'What was his name?'

'Culpepper.'

'Yeah. Or that Vanchev guy. I take it those two were Salo's work, as well.'

'Either Salo or the two punks that brought us here. They had no reason to bring it up and I didn't think there was any reason to mention it to them. None of that matters now. I'm where I wanted to be. Besides, I had to keep something in reserve in case I needed it. Turns out I didn't.'

'Jesus; this is going to keep the police busy for years.'

'If they find out about all of it. So, how are you enjoying this type of detective work?'

'I'm dying of boredom. It's like being trapped for all eternity in the worst sort of cozy mystery.'

There's a small room to our left that I didn't notice when we were being marched down here earlier. I raise a hand to indicate to Francie that we should stop and take a look. I stand still for a moment and listen. There's no noise and it doesn't feel as if the room is occupied.

I slowly turn the handle and open the door. The room is empty. It looks like a doctor's surgery in a health centre. There's a desk with a Hyundai laptop and a swivel chair that looks like an ergonomic model that people buy for back pain. Doesn't feel as if anyone's been in here for a while. Once Francie comes in, I close the door behind us.

There's a medical beam scale in the corner and a model of the human ear on top of a small wooden cupboard. There's a message board on the wall with no messages pinned to it and a stack of magazines on the floor.

I tackle the cupboard first. It's unlikely there's a gun in there, but I have high hopes of finding a scalpel or some other sharp medical instrument. The problem is, I have no tools I can use to get inside it. I take a look around the room. The computer? The scales? I just don't have the wherewithal to take them apart and look for the sort of bits I'll need.

'Francie. Could you stand with your back to the door, please? Arms spread out and legs wide apart. It'll muffle the noise a little.'

'You like this look? I feel like the Vitruvian Man.'

'But a little sexier.'

'Only a little?'

'Not even that.'

'You owe me for today.'

'You're still pissed about the fruit machine, aren't you?'

'Six years I've been waiting for that to happen.'

I stoop down by the cupboard and hit it just above the lock with the ball of my hand. The whole unit doesn't feel very strong and I'm hoping something amazing will happen and it'll open. It doesn't. I don't want to hit it too hard because of the noise.

For my second attempt, I pull the handle towards me while striking it above the lock once more. Still nothing. Well, at least I'm getting the measure of the lock strength and the thickness of the wood.

One last attempt. I hold onto the top to keep the unit steady and after making a couple of passes, ignore the pain in my arm, make a fist and punch it with as much force as I can on the strike plate side. The wood splinters and the door creaks open.

'Holy shit. That was pretty awesome.'

'I like showing off to girls. You can come in the room now.'

'I think I'll stay like this for a few more hours. I'm starting to like it.'

She walks in, takes a look around the room and shrugs. I pull the cupboard doors wide open, but there's nothing there I can use. A couple of piles of white hand towels, a roll of adhesive strapping tape, a sharps disposal kit, a big pack of single hand tourniquets in red, green and blue, a small blood pressure monitor and a stack of disposable vomit bowls. I could have done with one of those earlier.

'No bazookas in there?'

'Nothing. OK. Let's make our way upstairs.'

'Let me make sure the corridor's clear.'

She opens the office door and pokes her head outside. After two seconds, she slowly reverses in and gently closes the door behind her.

'What is it?'

'You know – I've kinda grown fond of this office. I think I'll stay here for a while longer.' She indicates the corridor with a nod of her head. 'Take a look outside. Slow. No sudden movements.'

I was half expecting to see all the kids from the cells huddled together in a sinister grouping, but it's worse than that. About ten yards to my left is Hannibal, our friendly neighbourhood Tosa Inu. He's not accompanied. He just stands and looks at me, his lips curled back in his familiar silent snarl. There's a long trail of drool hanging from his mouth. One thing's for sure; I'll be really glad to get out of this house. I close the door.

'OK,' I say. 'We've got two options. Either we stay in here with the door closed until someone realises we've got out of our cell and comes after us with a gun, or we go out into the corridor and deal with the dog.'

'*Deal* with the *dog*? How the hell are we going to do that? Have you got a steak on you or something? A stun gun? A kitten you can throw at it?'

I try to remember everything I can about this breed. Immensely powerful, bred as a fighting dog in Japan, much too dangerous to be a family pet. I'm sure I read that they're used in weight pulling contests and can pull some insane weight like three thousand pounds.

They're fast, they're heavy, they're intelligent, they have a high pain threshold and, unbelievably, they used to fight with Samurais.

As I noticed before, this one looked like it had been used in fights, and some of its scars looked recent, so that means it's active and fit. What was the other thing? Oh, yes. They're silent when they fight. It's bred into them. Something to do with the rules of dog fights in Japan. It's the only quality they have that might come in useful.

Like Polly said – *not a Chihuahua.*

I rest a hand on Francie's shoulder. 'I'm going to have to kill it. Will you be OK with this? I wouldn't want to upset you if you're a dog lover.'

'Kill it? You're going to kill *that* thing? What – with your bare hands?'

'There's a way. I have to get it to charge at me. Then I'm going to need it to leap up as if it's going for my throat, which I'm pretty sure it will. Rebekah confirmed that earlier on.'

'You can't do this. It's crazy. What if it doesn't do what you want it to? It might attack you in a way you're not expecting. What'll you do then?'

'It's a risk I'll have to take. This isn't some police dog that's going to grab your forearm in its jaws and politely wrestle you to the ground. These things will *always* attack. It's their nature. Don't worry. It'll be OK.'

'Don't *worry*? You're going to get a two-hundred-pound attack dog to go for your throat and you're telling me it'll be *OK*? What will you do when it attacks?'

'I'll use its speed, strength and weight against it. I'll wait until I can feel its breath on my face, then get my right forearm under its lower jaw and my left forearm against the base of its skull. Then I quickly rotate both arms and break its neck.'

I demonstrate the action for her. She looks nonplussed.

'I think you should go back to hospital. Psychiatric ward. Have you done this before?'

'Not with this breed.'

'Not with this *breed*? Do the RSPCA know about you?'

'You don't have to come. It's probably better that you don't in case something goes wrong.'

'I'm coming.'

I open the door as slowly and quietly as I can, half expecting Hannibal to be waiting outside, having listened to our conversation and worked out a way of thwarting my intentions, but when I poke my head out of the door, he's gone.

I take a look in each direction and try to listen out for any dog noises, but it's completely silent. I walk out into the corridor and indicate to Francie that she should follow me. She looks at me and raises her eyebrows.

'Where's it gone?' she whispers.

'Get back in the office.'

We go back the way we came, and I close the door behind us. Francie looks mystified.

'There was someone heading this way, medium speed, about fifty yards to our left. It'll be one of the three males. The girl was wearing heels, so it's not her.'

'She might have gotten changed into ballet slippers.'

'Yeah, I had thought of that. I'm also going to assume that it's likely to be the guy who drove us here, as he seemed to be controlling the dog. Plus, I suspect Caspian will want to keep Salo close, particularly if he's going to sew Caspian's mouth up.

'Whoever it is, I'm going to have to bring him down. I just hope Hannibal won't reappear and leap to his defence. If he does, well…' I open the door wide. 'Stand to the right of the door, your back against the wall. Don't speak. I'm going to have to surprise him.'

The fact that I'm only wearing a pair of briefs gives me a little cause for concern, but I'll have to swallow it. I try to visualise Bald Medium; tall, stocky, running to fat and alert. Perhaps two hundred pounds plus. He'll be able to handle himself and he'll be motivated. He was about to pull a gun from a shoulder holster in the car, so I have to assume that he's still armed. He was right-handed. Speedy reactions, but not as fast as Milne.

I take half a dozen steps back from the door, look at Francie and place a finger against my lips. I close my eyes and attempt to listen to his footfalls. He's about ten yards away from the door now.

'Hannibal.'

It's him. It's the same voice that gave the password to get in here.

'With those bloody kids again,' he grumbles. I can hardly believe what I'm hearing. They allow Hannibal to roam round and wander into the kids' compound? Ah well.

Five yards.

'Hannibal. Here.'

Three yards. I put my right foot forward and get into a semi-crouch. He's two feet away from the door. I have to time this so that I sprint towards him just as he enters my field of vision.

And there he is.

I hit him side-on with such force that he almost bounces off the far wall and knocks me onto the floor.

His first instinct is to reach for his gun, but I'm ready for this. I grab his wrist through his jacket, hit his elbow upwards with the ball of my hand, whip him down to waist height and smash my knee into his face.

While he's considering that, I slap a hand across his mouth to prevent the incipient scream and wrench his arm so high up his back that I break the ball joint of his shoulder. The pain brings him to his knees, so I'm able to deliver a powerful knife-hand strike to the side of his neck and he's out for the count.

I'm pretty seriously out of breath after that and have to steady myself with a hand against the wall for a couple of seconds before grabbing his jacket under the armpits and dragging him into the surgery/office. Francie gently closes the door behind us. The white spots in front of my eyes are back.

The first thing I do is grab his gun. It's a Heckler & Koch HK45; full magazine, ten rounds. I hold it in my hand to get the feel of it; new smell, nice ergonomic grip, weighs a little under two pounds. I place it on the floor a couple of feet away.

'We're going to get his clothes off. Give me a hand.'

It takes the both of us five difficult minutes to get him down to his underpants. He has a neat appendectomy scar and his left nipple is pierced. Francie takes his shirt and I take his trousers and, at Francie's insistence, his jacket. The keys to the Mercedes are in his left jacket pocket. His leather shoulder holster is too fiddly to bother with, so I lose patience with it and chuck it on the floor.

I smile at her as she runs a hand through her hair. 'You look like a swinging sixties girl in that huge shirt.'

'You look like someone who's suddenly lost two stone in weight.'

He starts to groan, so I punch him a couple of times in the face. I unwrap six of the tourniquets from the cupboard and use them to tie his wrists and ankles, using the remaining ones to hogtie him.

There are no scissors around, so I have to use the entire roll of adhesive strapping tape on his mouth, winding it around his head until it's finished. He looks ridiculous, but at least he won't be talking.

He'll find it difficult to do anything when he comes round, particularly with that damage to his shoulder, but just to be on the safe side, I break the handle off the door so it can only be opened from the outside. I pick up the gun, give Francie what I hope is an encouraging grin, and head down the corridor.

36

STITCH-UP

'What did he look like?'

We're standing a few feet away from the entrance to the study. So far, there's been very little evidence of any of the people we might expect to encounter. My main concern is that Hannibal is still roaming around somewhere and is now without his handler or handlers. I have no way of knowing whether he only responds to orders or will take the law into his own paws if necessary.

The other unknown quantity is Jane, who may or may not still be in the house. There might, of course, be other people present that we're not yet aware of. I have to assume that there are. I can hear Caspian talking to someone on the phone. I reckon Salo is in there with him. I'm waiting for some confirmation of that.

'Grey hair. Yes. That sounds like our chap. Danish, you say. That doesn't quite make sense. Why didn't you call earlier? Well that's just not good enough, Moss. I don't give a flying fuck about some bloody terrorist atrocity. You had all of yesterday. Yes, yes. You want to keep doing this sort of work? Do you?'

So that's one of their tame cops getting a bollocking. I stand side-on to the wall right next to the door, the gun aimed at the floor. I indicate to Francie that she should stand next to me but keep looking in the direction we came from, touching my arm if she sees or hears anything. This tousled-hair-wearing-a-man's-shirt look is distracting, and I can smell her sweat and perfume.

'Listen,' he continues. 'I don't understand how he turned up at her house in the first place. What time was this? Well, she couldn't possibly know about us. It must have been someone else. Don't think I won't be reporting this.'

This is a little confusing. Now I know that Moss and Driscoll were ostensibly working for Caspian here, it again raises the question of why Milne and Bald Medium turned up at her house today asking for her with her professional name.

Is it possible that Caspian doesn't know about their visit? Are they working for someone else? Rebekah, maybe? Interesting, but I don't think there's anything conspiratorial about it. Once again, I think things have got a little chaotic since Polly upset the applecart and I got involved.

I can hear an exasperated sigh as the call is finished. 'Alright, Salo. Let's get on with it. Is it too much to ask that I get a local anaesthetic?'

'No. No anaesthetic. Take a drink,' replies Salo.

Salo's going to stitch Caspian's mouth up. Francie heard this and realises. 'I hope it hurts like fuck,' she whispers in my ear.

I can hear the glass cocktail cabinet being opened and Caspian making himself a drink. He doesn't offer one to Salo.

'How long will this take?' asks Caspian.

'You stay still. You don't make fuss. Maybe five minutes. Maybe more. Maybe you have one more drink. It will hurt. But I do good job.'

'God almighty. You better.'

So at least I know that Salo's in there. It's quiet for a moment and I guess Caspian's gulping down his first drink and getting ready to prepare another. Sure enough, I hear the cocktail cabinet being opened again and more clinking of glasses. I wonder what he's drinking.

For a moment, I think I can hear a noise coming from the entrance hall. I hold my breath and listen, but it seems like it's a one-off. I nudge Francie and nod towards the direction the noise came from. She nods back. She heard it, too. I'll have to keep focussed on it, whatever it was. Might be the dog.

'Alright. Let's get on with it,' says Caspian.

A few seconds silence, then a guttural shriek of pain followed by harsh hyperventilating as Salo starts his needlework on Caspian's lower lip. I have to admire Salo in a way; stitching a nasty injury like that in a difficult location can't be easy. Caspian seems to have quietened down. Salo said it'd take five minutes. Now's the time.

I turn into the room and aim the gun at Salo's head. He's standing over Caspian, who's sitting on one of the dining chairs right in front of his desk. Salo's K100 is on the cocktail cabinet; out of reach, but it would take him a second to get to it.

He looks up, seems unconcerned and continues his stitching. Caspian, on the other hand, looks alarmed and slaps Salo's hand out of the way. There's a lot of blood pouring out of his lower lip and dribbling down his chin. The suture needle hangs uselessly, still attached by the thread.

'Salo! Do something!'

'Go on, Eemil,' I say. 'Your gun's three feet away. I can see you looking at it. Take a chance. You can do it. I believe in you.'

He looks into my eyes, nods resignedly, calmly steps away from Caspian and gets down on his knees, his hands behind his head. Good boy. I touch Francie's arm.

'Close the door, then grab one of those dining chairs and shove it underneath the doorknob. Our clothes are still over the sofa there. Get dressed as quickly as you can.'

'Going to make good your escape, Mr Cambridge? You idiot.'

'You really have got this all wrong, Caspian, haven't you? Get off that chair and get down on your knees like your pal here. Three feet away from him. Hands behind the head. If you *breathe* in a way I don't like, I'll put one in your gut.'

He sneers at me but does as I say. 'You are dead, my friend.'

'Never mind the amateur dramatics. What's your surname? Quickly.'

'Tennesley.'

I glance at Salo's face. It tells me that Caspian is telling the truth. Francie taps me on the shoulder, and I hand her the gun as I get dressed and transfer the Mercedes keys to my own pocket. She notices Salo's contemptuous smirk as she aims the gun at his head in a professional-looking two-handed grip. She smirks back.

'Sir Walter Gun Club, Creedmoor, North Carolina. NCCCH course. Use of deadly force and target training. Top student four years in a row. If either of you say one single word, I'll shoot the other one in the head. Nod once if you understand.'

Both monkeys nod. Well, that told *them*. I can tell that Caspian and Francie aren't going to be an item any time soon; all the head kicking, lip biting and now this. It's a terrible basis for an embryonic relationship.

Once I'm dressed, I let Francie keep the gun on them and stand a few feet away, fold my arms and stare. Before I take things further, I need some answers. I let a full minute go by before I speak. Caspian looks fearful. Salo doesn't want me to see the rage in his face, so keeps avoiding my gaze.

'OK, Caspian. I'm going to ask you a question and you may reply. Judith Hart and Wolfert Salo were both killed in that flat in Devonshire Street. Both bodies were removed, either by your bent cops or by one of your Security Service rodents. Where were they taken?'

'You're wasting your time. There is no way that…'

'I'm going to ask you again. If you don't tell me the truth, I'll nod once at Ms Sciarra and she'll shoot you in the leg, aiming at the femoral artery. You'll bleed out in approximately five minutes. It won't be pleasant. Now. Where were those bodies taken?'

'They were taken to the morgue at the Royal London, Whitechapel. There's a…there's a "morgue within a morgue" there called the Edith Cavell Room. No idea why it's called that. Only the police and the Security Service are able to use it. Even most of the staff at that hospital don't know of its existence, or its real purpose, I should say. Refrigerated, of course. It's been in use since the 1930s. It's used for cases where…'

'I don't need a history lesson. Are those bodies still there?'

'Yes. We…we were going to dispose of Judith Hart's body three days ago, in the sea probably, but events overtook us. I don't know what the arrangements will be for Wolfert or the other two. But that's where

507

they're…resting at the moment.' He looks at Salo, whose expression of contained apoplexy remains unchanged.

'The other two. You mean Redolf Salo and Jitser Vonk. So, all four of those bodies are in the same place, and they're there right now, is that correct?'

'Yes.'

I hear a quiet, very high-pitched bleep that's maybe coming from the direction of Caspian's desk. I'd noticed this earlier on and couldn't quite place its location.

'What was that?'

'I don't know.'

I look at Francie. She heard it, too. I'll disregard it for the moment.

'You're doing very well so far, Caspian. I'm very pleased with you. But keep in mind what will happen if I don't think you're playing straight with me. Now. Alistair Culpepper. Why was he killed?'

He looks dazed. 'You know about Cul…? OK. OK. He saw what was on the memory stick; *who* was on the memory stick. He flagged up the file on Simon van Cutsem. An alert on our system appears when that happens. I knew about it within five minutes.

'I'm sure you know this already as you seem to know everything else, Mr Cambridge. Culpepper's in charge of a minor intelligence unit. We set up their computer system for them. We know everything that they do, everything that they look at. It was just a matter of security. Nothing to do with all of this particularly, but…'

'But it came in handy this time.'

He nods his head. 'Culpepper actually called us to tell us about van Cutsem. He spoke to Rebekah. But he must have smelt a rat. Sixth sense, maybe. Something like that. Smart fellow. He got his girl to that safe house in

Mornington Crescent, but we picked that communication up, too, and got there first.'

'So, the Salo family were already in the country.'

'Yes. Another job. Nothing to do with this at all. It was meant to be a bit of harmless overtime for them.'

The small bleep sounds again. So quiet that I can't pinpoint where it's coming from. So quiet that you wonder if you really heard it. Only Francie's reaction tells me that it was real. For a panicky moment, I wonder if it's some sort of alarm; something that he has to respond to.

'Are you sure you don't know what that noise is, Caspian? Slow as you like, get your mobile out of your pocket and throw it on the floor in front of you.'

He fishes it out of his jacket pocket with two fingers and flicks it towards me. If it's his mobile, that noise'll be louder next time.

'You got any other tech on you?'

He shakes his head. Every time he speaks or moves, the suture needle, still hanging from his lip, swings from side to side. It's difficult not to laugh.

'Who set up the autoerotic asphyxiation red herring with Culpepper?'

A puzzled frown. 'That was Leckie.'

'Who's Leckie?'

'Oscar Leckie. The officer whose gun your colleague is holding.'

'Why that method?'

'Purely for variety. Confusion.'

'And Vanchev? How was that done and by who?'

'That was Milne. A new drug. Not traceable. Don't know the chemical ins and outs. Causes anaphylaxis, then results in heart failure. Something like that. It needed to be an innocent death. Natural-looking.'

'Why kill Judith Hart? She wouldn't have known who van Cutsem was. She wouldn't have been aware of his history.'

'That's true. She wouldn't have known. Not at that point. But she might have found out one day and looked into it all. She was clearly an intelligent woman. It's quite possible that one day she might have got Culpepper's job or even gone higher than that.

'She'd have been a ticking time bomb. Sometime in the future, she might have seen a photograph of van Cutsem and everything would have fallen into place. It was as simple as that.

'We had to have a purge and we were right to do it. Like you said, she'd made an unauthorised copy of the memory stick, so she was already sceptical. She'd seen everything. It was a huge security breach. She saw activities that no one should have seen. She suspected that this was serious.

'If we'd let Hart live, once she found out that Culpepper had died, it would have confirmed her suspicions that something was not right. You can imagine how the shit would have hit the fan if any of this got out.'

'So. Vanchev. Why did he have to die? Did he know about van Cutsem?' I give the gun a twitch to keep him on track.

'The name would have meant nothing to him, neither would van Cutsem's, er, history. He was a first timer and a useful asset. We were rewarding him for his work; keeping him sweet. He'd done a lot for the country financially that was off the books.

'But he was too high-risk. He had attracted the wrong sort of attention. He had suddenly become a liability. His actions led directly to Culpepper's discovery that van

Cutsem had not died, and that could never get out.

'Obviously, Culpepper had to be taken care of, as did Hart. But try and imagine what a serious, long-term investigation into Culpepper's death might uncover. Every single case he had been working on for the last nine years could be subject to the most detailed scrutiny. Whoever was investigating would doubtless start with the most recent cases and work backwards.

'If the Vanchev case was put under the microscope, it would only be a matter of time before someone got him in for questioning. He's a weak man. He would spill the beans, and then where would we be? But if he was dead that could not happen, so we cauterised the wound. He was in a vicious circle. Tough break.

'The remaining personnel in Culpepper's unit wouldn't be aware of the machinations. That's not how that department worked. All they'd know was that Hart had been murdered by an intruder, Culpepper was a grieving, Hart-obsessed pervert who finally went too far and Vanchev, if they ever knew of his existence, died of a heart attack. Bad luck. Coincidence. Both.

'If we'd thought those other two needed dealing with, we'd have done it. But it helps to allay suspicion that they're both still alive. We're keeping an eye on them, believe you me. And we'll replace Culpepper and Hart in due course. Or maybe have the unit shut down. We haven't decided yet.'

'Sounds to me like you panicked, Caspian. What's Milne's first name? Quickly.'

'Conlan.'

'You and Rebekah, Milne and Leckie. Where are you from?'

'We're all CPNI.'

Centre for the Protection of National Infrastructure; a high-up section of the Security Service that provides advice and protection to businesses and services that are important to the UK. It's all starting to fall into place. I'll let it sort itself out in my subconscious for a while and allow it to become more coherent at a later date.

If I pass all of this over to DI Bream at some point, she'll be able to follow the paper trail and bust fellow officers and recalcitrant spooks to her heart's content. I'm going to have to write all of this down before I hit her with it. It's just too confusing. There are a couple of other loose ends which almost slipped my mind. The more I can hand Olivia, the better it'll be, for a number of reasons.

'Mrs Margaret Carter. Real name and job, please.'

'Her name's Taylah Childe. She's an officer in the National Crime Agency. Modern slavery and human trafficking department. She helps us with procurement. Has excellent contacts. The best. She's close to van Cutsem and it was in her interest to protect him. They did good work together.'

'The two cops who picked van Cutsem up from the Scrubs and took him to Antler Farm. Van Cutsem told me that one of them was Detective Chief Superintendent Michael Small. Was that a fake name and rank? Something that was made up for van Cutsem's benefit?'

'Yes. How did you…it was Detective Chief Inspector Edward Pope. SO15. Counter terrorism command. I don't know who the driver was.'

'Is the fact that he was in counter terrorism relevant in some way?'

'No. The police we use are just the police we use. Contacts can be made in different ways and often go back years. It doesn't really matter where they come from or where they're stationed. Some do it to get on, some do it for the money, some do it because it makes them feel important.'

'Van Cutsem knew you as Gabriel White. What other names do you use?' I'm starting to get the white spots in front of my eyes once more.

'Adam Barlow, Zachary Chadwick, Julian Ellis.'

'Is that it?'

'Yes.'

'The girl here you called Jane. Surname.'

'MacInroy.'

'Is Jane MacInroy her real name?'

'Yes.'

'What does she do?'

'She's a physical security advisor.'

'What about Rebekah? Rebekah Giri. That's her real name, right?'

'Yes. She has no need for aliases. She only uses Seraphina – no surname – when she's helping out at the entertainments.'

'Is this helping out a regular thing?'

'Sometimes she'll prepare additional personnel. Tell them what to do, how to act. Sometimes, she and van Cutsem orchestrate the whole thing. Sometimes she'll participate, if what's going on is to her taste. She likes to use and be used.' He looks up at me. 'I don't agree with that. I think it's unprofessional. But she's very good at what she does, so we turn a blind eye. She's a…she's quite the libertine. She likes extremes.'

This fits in with what Liva told me. I wonder what ordinary taxpayers would think if they knew where their money was going. Once again, I think I can hear something on the other side of the door. I'll bet anything it's that bloody dog.

'Luigiana. Keep your focus on these two. I'm just going to check outside.'

She nods and keeps aiming the gun at them both. I can tell by their facial expressions that they have no doubt that she'll pull the trigger if they do or say the wrong thing.

I place one hand on the door and turn the handle with the other. I try to visualise what a two-hundred-pound dog leaping at the door would feel like and how much strength and energy I'd need to slam the door on it and keep it out of here.

Once I think I'm prepared, I pull the door wide open and find myself facing a SilencerCo Osprey suppressor which is attached to the business end of a Sig Sauer P320 pistol. She's still wearing the dark red power clothing and the four-inch stilettos.

There's no way I'd be fast enough to slam the door shut and she's too far away for me to be able to take her gun. I raise my hands. She indicates that I should go back into the study. I guess that date at the sushi bar simply isn't going to happen.

37

THE WOLVERINE

'What took you so long? Is everybody here totally bloody incompetent apart from me?'

'There's something wrong with the device. I think there's an echo on it that gives the OK response,' says Jane, who I still quite fancy despite everything.

'Oh, that's right,' says Caspian. 'Blame it on the tools.'

As far as Caspian knows, Jane just might have saved his life, but he just can't help being a dick.

So now I know what that barely audible bleep was. I should have realised. Something that Caspian had to respond to within a certain timeframe to let Jane know that everything was OK. Where was the source of that noise? Sewn into his jacket?

Why he'd bother with some gimmicky piece of tech like that under these particular circumstances is beyond me, but it certainly paid off. Perhaps he's paranoid. I'm angry with myself for not pursuing my suspicions. Too late now.

So, Jane is, at the very least, some sort of in-house security person. Now I can get a better look at her, I'd put her age at twenty-three or twenty-four. Healthy-looking, hits the gym, intelligent face, confident, eager to please, wears lenses. I'd guess she's MI5 graduate intake, double first in media studies or geography, on thirty grand a year. Is this her normal duty? Would she have actually shot me?

She has the gun trained on us in a steady, two-handed grip. Seven feet away; not too far, not too close. Her concentration is palpable, but I'm aware of an inflexibility that can come from a lot of training but no real experience. I'll keep watching her and assess her capabilities and motives from second to second.

Salo had his trusty K100 in his hand before I backed into the room, safety off as before. He nods at Francie. He wants Leckie's Heckler & Koch. Reluctantly, Francie flips the gun in the air so she's holding the barrel and hands it to Salo, grip first, who gives it a quick once over and sticks it in his jacket.

He makes Francie and me stand in front of Caspian's desk with our hands behind our heads. If I was him, I'd have got us on our knees, but I'll keep that to myself.

Caspian, suture needle still dangling, walks around in front of us and punches me hard in the face. Jane keeps looking at him, not sure how she's meant to react to this sort of behaviour. A round of applause, perhaps? 'What happened to Leckie?' growls Caspian. 'How did you get his gun? How did you get out of the cell?'

'I think you need a refresher course in interrogation, Caspian. Where's your little training centre? Rickmansworth, isn't it? Which question would you like answered first? Or shall I just pick one at random?'

He rapidly shakes his head from side to side without making eye contact, his voice low and harsh. 'You know you're never leaving here, don't you? Either of you. Certainly not after that little session a few minutes ago.'

'You mean the session where you spilled your guts about virtually everyone involved in this shitshow?' I say.

'You should have seen him, Jane. It was pathetic. I hope you don't end up like that when you get his job. Anyway, Mr Leckie is resting in that little medical room in the basement. I suggest you send Eemil or Jane here downstairs to untie him. Or maybe you could do it yourself.'

'Hey. Yeah,' says Francie. 'Shoot us, and then go down and sort your porky pal out. But you can't shoot us, can you, Caspian. You have to find out where we've stashed Miss Søndergaard. It could be that I know, it could be that Mr Cambridge here knows. Because if *she's* out there somewhere where you can't get at her, you're *never* safe, are you? And you're already up to your waist in shit.

'I think she's the type to go to the police. In fact, we suggested it to her. She's a wealthy woman. I think she's the type to get some fancy expensive hot-shit lawyer on your tail, no matter who you say you work for. I think she's the type to go to the media. She's very photogenic, very attractive. I'm sure she can cry to order. I can see it now. "The Adult Entertainer and the Security Service Sleazebucket." She'll hang you and your pals out to dry.'

'That's right, Caspian,' I say. 'Go and help poor old Oscar. He's in pain down there. But you won't. You're too shit-scared to go anywhere on your own, especially now that Rebekah's gone. What are you going to do? Have you heard from Rebekah, by the way? Or Milne?'

'Leckie can wait.'

'You see how he treats his staff, Jane? I'd get a job in television, if I were you. There's still time. The people are much nicer.'

Salo is six feet away to my right; three feet away from Francie. He aims his K100 at Francie's head. Caspian looks stressed and impatient.

'Salo. Put that bloody gun down and finish this blasted stitching. Jane; you make damn sure these people don't move an inch.'

'Yes, sir.'

Salo places his gun on the desk. I'm a little surprised to see that our keys are still there, but then what would they have done with them? Got them melted down and turned into a novelty commemorative ashtray? I'm surprised they haven't inspected the burglar's tools on my keyring more closely.

I watch with pleasure as Caspian grimaces, grunts and twitches with the pain caused by Salo's work. Now we have only one gun on us, though Salo has positioned himself so he can still keep us both under supervision. His gun is never more than two feet from his hand, and I know he's fast. I keep an eye on him but keep my main focus on Jane. She's blinking a lot. Nervous tension? Itchy lenses?

'What was your degree in, Jane? You must have at least a 2:2, am I right? Maybe higher.' I keep my voice low, hypnotic, mellifluous. 'You could be doing something useful to society now, instead of mopping up the mess that this bunch of criminal incompetents have created.'

I can see that Caspian wants me to shut up, but his mouth is indisposed at the moment. He glowers at me.

'The freak doing the embroidery over there. Do you know who he is, Jane? What he is? His name's Eemil Salo. He's one of the top assassins in Europe, possibly the world. Your boss hires him and people like him when he wants people killed. That guy's brother murdered a female intelligence officer just the other day. Could have been you, Jane. Could have been you. Remember his face. Not that you'll see him coming, of course. He might monitor your phone calls. One day you'll order a pizza. Half an hour later the doorbell will ring, you open it and bang! They call it slipstreaming.'

Jane doesn't say anything. Her expression hasn't changed, but her concentration will have. It's not the content of what I'm saying that counts, it's the fact that she's being directly addressed. She may not be listening, but she has to be hearing.

'Have you been to this place before, Jane? Do you know what goes on here?' I give her the lowdown on the scene that Polly witnessed. I don't miss out a single detail. I take a glance at Salo, who's still busy with Caspian's lip. 'Your boss is corrupt, Jane. All the people who work with him are corrupt. This means you yourself are corrupt. What about that, eh, Jane? All your hopes and dreams shattered. It's not me you should be aiming a gun at, it's Caspian Tennesley there. Go on. Pull the trigger, Jane. Do something useful for once. Spray his brains over the wall.'

I look at the distance between myself and Jane's gun. If I was quick enough, if I could *spark* enough, I could take two lightning fast steps towards her and get my hand around that suppressor in one or two seconds. Disable her, twist it out of her grasp or use her finger to squeeze off a couple of shots into Salo's head.

But I don't think I'm up to it. If it wasn't for Salo's watchful presence, incapacitating her would be a possibility, but even then…

Salo finishes up, tying off the suture and detaching the needle. 'That's enough from you, Mr Cambridge,' says Caspian, gingerly patting his lower lip with the palm of his hand, looking down and checking for blood once more. Then he stops suddenly. He looks baffled. He looks shocked. I follow his gaze to the door.

It's Ronny. And standing next to him is Hannibal, his upper lip curled in his usual friendly snarl. Ronny looks around the room. Once again, he has that bewildered, dismayed look on his face. He slowly places his hand on top of Hannibal's head, and pats it. Hannibal doesn't react; he continues to snarl. It was silent before, but now I can hear it, deep in his chest. Jane, who's side-on to him, keeps glancing to her right. She wants to keep her complete focus on Francie and me, but she can't.

Well, this is interesting. I attempt to assess how each person in the room is reacting. Jane is certainly concerned and fearful. Is this dog a danger to everyone here without Leckie to control it? Why is it nonplussed by Ronny's presence? I can't imagine it would allow *me* to pat its head like that; it would undoubtedly tear my hand off if I tried.

Is this connected to Ronny's programming? Is the dog docile in the presence of those other kids, too? Does whatever they do to them here remove all those antagonistic human traits? Fear? Aggression? Sudden movements? Does it make them appealing to dogs?

Caspian's eyes have widened, and I just know his pulse rate is up. Salo is assessing the situation calmly, as you would expect. He raises his gun slowly and starts to draw a bead on the dog's head, but Jane is in the way.

'You. Step back,' he orders her. 'Slow movement. No talk. Keep gun raised.'

She does as he says. I can see her gun is trembling slightly. My knowledge of these dogs is only theoretical; has she seen what this one can do at first hand?

'We don't want this animal killed, Salo,' says Caspian. 'It's a valuable interrogation tool. Miss Giri has plans to use it on these two. She will be angry if you shoot it.'

Salo sighs impatiently. 'Then tell child to take dog out of the room. Close door. I've seen dogs like that. I know them.'

Caspian doesn't like having responsibility bounced back to him. Interrogation asset? Seraphina's a real piece of work. I thought it was only US intelligence that used un-muzzled dogs to intimidate and frighten prisoners being interrogated, and only then in cultures where dog fear was at a premium. You learn something every day. I turn slowly and look at Francie. She isn't fazed by this development at all. After what has happened so far, I don't think anything can surprise her anymore.

Caspian calms himself down. 'Jameel,' he says. 'Take Hannibal out of the room and put him in his compound.'

'Are you happy with me, sir?' replies Ronny.

'Jameel. Take the dog away now. Take Hannibal away now. Thank you.'

'Kas olete minuga rahul, söör?'

Hannibal, for some reason, finds all of this irritating. He lowers his head, narrows his eyes and growls. He's shivering. He's looking at Salo and seems to disapprove. Didn't Lothar say something about Salo disliking dogs? Can Hannibal sense this?

'Jesus Christ,' spits Caspian at me. 'This is your fault. If you hadn't...'

'I'd keep your voice down if I were you, Caspian. He's getting cross. Look at him. Who d'you think he'll go for first? I think he'll go for you. You're the sort of person that dogs attack.'

He goes for a third attempt. 'Jameel. Take the dog into the hall and close this door behind you.'

No response at all this time. Salo aims his gun. Ronny looks tearful, turns, and hugs the dog's head, covering it completely. Stalemate. Salo edges closer and closer, all his focus on the animal and the boy.

'This child is not right in the head. He will not listen to you,' says Salo.

Even though it's muffled by Ronny's body, I can hear a loud, low, long growl coming from the dog. It doesn't sound good. Caspian tries one more time.

'Jameel.'

Salo aims his gun. 'Fuck this shit,' he says. He squeezes off five rapid shots through Ronny's back into the dog's head. There's a blood-curdling scream from the animal and I can see a patch of red spreading rapidly against the orange of Ronny's toga. Both of them slump to the floor at the same time, though the animal twitches and jerks for ten seconds before all is still. Five shots. That means Salo has ten rounds left.

Sometimes you can second-guess events in situations like this, but I really can't imagine what's going to happen next. I take a quick two-second look around. Francie's hands have dropped from behind her head and hang at her sides. Her mouth is open.

Jane is still holding her P320 at chest height, but now the gun is slowly descending until it's aimed at the floor and no longer pointing at Francie and me. She's as white as a sheet and her lower lip is trembling.

Caspian, not surprisingly, is speechless, his eyes bulging out of his head in shock. Things must have seemed so straightforward four days ago and now this. Salo does not look at anyone else and is unconcerned, a contemptuous snort escaping from his mouth as he watches for any further movement from his targets, his focus and his gun still aimed at Ronny's torso. I let my hands drop to my sides. Just as I do that, I can see a small movement to my left.

Before I can stop her, Francie takes two steps towards Salo and taps him on the shoulder. 'Hey! Fuckface!' He turns towards her, but before he can work out what's going on, he's on the receiving end of a swift, weaponised punch to the face. It's a second before I see the keys clamped between her fingers, but by that time it's too late. Two of them have punctured Salo's left eye and there's a third in his right. People's eyes are having a tough time of it lately.

He screams with the pain and frantically grabs Francie's forearm, holding her in place so he can raise his weapon and finish her off, but I can't have that. I grab his arm and push down on a point four inches below the wrist. The pain makes him release his grip.

I follow that up with two open-handed strikes to the face, smashing the keys further in. He drops his gun and his hands fly to his eyes. To be honest, I'm surprised that didn't kill him. Must have got the angle wrong, though his head and torso are twitching and jerking like something's seriously amiss.

'*Ik sil dy wol deadzje! Ik sil dy wol deadzje!*' he screams.

Leckie's Heckler & Koch is on the floor. I snap my fingers to get Francie's attention, point to the gun and then point at Caspian, who's still in stunned mode. She knows what to do. I hear her spit one word at Caspian: 'Down!'

I start to bend down to pick up Salo's gun when I get a knee in the face that almost snaps my neck and knocks me flat on my back. Instantly, Salo is on top of me, his full weight on my chest and his right hand around my throat; an incredible grip that almost makes me lose my vision. I have to keep reminding myself what I'm dealing with here. This is an Afghan veteran. A Man of Steel. A Black Devil.

The keys are still in his eyes, blood dripping from his face to mine. With his left hand, he locates my shoulder and feels his way down to the ricochet wound, forcing his fingers into it and pushing as hard as he can, screwing his three middle fingers from left to right. I didn't think the pain inflicted on that area could get any worse, but I've just been proved wrong.

'*Jo hawwe myn famylje fermoarde! Ik sil jo felle harsens derút sûgje. Ik sil jo holle neuke.*'

I try to resist his strength and mass and somehow get him off me, but it's impossible. He's just too big and powerful. He screams and curses and convulses. It feels as if he's having an epileptic seizure. His head keeps jerking to the left. I think he's dying, but he's going to finish me off if it's the last thing he does.

Through the fug of incipient oblivion, I grab the hand that's around my throat and attempt to break the ring finger by pushing it to the side and making it overlap his middle finger. It actually works, and I can hear and feel the snap, but it doesn't make any difference to him; he's barely noticed it. Not good.

I get a repeat of that feeling that I had in Francie's office, as if my soul is trying to leave my body. I suddenly feel as if I've become light, that if Salo let go of me, I'd float up to the ceiling. Then I hear two quiet gunshot cracks, the pressure on my throat stops and Salo's face drops onto mine, one of the keys narrowly missing my right eye.

I've got just enough strength left to push him off me and stand up. Just before I manage that, he delivers a weedy post-mortem vomit onto my neck, face and chest, to accompany the major blood squirt that's coming from somewhere inside his head. I must look awful.

Jane is standing a few feet away, shaking. So, the bullets came from her gun. A sudden attack of conscience? Who knows or cares? Francie stands three feet away from me, aiming the Heckler & Koch at Caspian, who's now lying flat on the floor, his hands on the back of his head. There's blood absolutely everywhere in here. Salo aside, most of it seems to have come from Ronny and Hannibal. I pick up Salo's K100.

'You know what they call that?'

'Call what?' replies Francie.

'When you stick your keys in between your fingers like that.'

'No idea. Bitch punch?'

'It's called the Wolverine.'

'Really? Shit. Yeah. I see that.'

'It's not a very good technique to use, though. Can damage your fingers.'

'Well, pardon me for living.'

'Bitch punch?'

'OK, OK.'

Jane is still standing and shaking. I still haven't heard a word from her. Shock? Or is she faking. I'll assume she's faking. I take the gun from her hand. I'm not feeling too good, so I'm having trouble deciding how we're going to clean this mess up; what stories we're going to tell. And I still haven't finished my work here yet. I turn to Francie.

'OK. She needs to be taken somewhere and disabled so we can decide what to do. I don't know what's going through her head at present, so keep the gun on her and keep her about six feet in front of you. Hold on.'

I open a few drawers and find a bunch of pink and

yellow tea towels. Pretty pathetic, but they'll have to do. 'Hands behind your back, please, Jane.' Using two of the towels, I tie her hands tightly behind her back, which is not easy when you're holding a gun. I hand three more of the towels to Francie.

'These are for her ankles. Could you take her down to that room where we've got Leckie tied up? No. Take her somewhere else. I don't want Leckie to see her. There's some sort of reception room across the hall. Go in there. When you tie her ankles, get her on the floor face down. She fucks around; shoot her in the head. Stay alert. We don't want any more surprises. I've got some stuff to do here; I'll be with you as soon as I can.'

'Sure thing. Come on, honey. Play nice and we'll get on just fine. Oh–' She turns to look at me. 'Can you take me out to dinner when all this clusterfuck is sorted?'

'It would be my pleasure.'

'Somewhere really frickin' expensive. Because I'm worth it.'

'Sure. Medium or large fries?'

'You're asking for a bitch punch.'

38

AN EYE FOR AN EYE

Prioritising in a situation like this is bad enough without all the added traumata of torture, nausea, mild shock and a splitting headache, but I guess I'll have to do my best.

I shove Jane's P320 into my belt and weigh Salo's K100 in my hand. He fired five shots into Ronny and Hannibal, which means there must be ten or eleven bullets left in the magazine. Feels about right. I give it a quick check to make sure everything's in working order and aim it at Caspian, just in case he has plans to try something amusing. I almost remove the suppressor, then decide to keep it on. You never know; there might be an Amazon delivery pending.

'You stay right where you are, Caspian, old pal, or I'll have to shoot you in the spine. Are we OK? Nod your head.'

He nods as well as anyone eating carpet could be expected to manage. I take a quick look around the room. The first thing I do is check Salo, aiming my gun at the base of his skull and taking his pulse from the neck. Definitely deceased. Two bullets at close range to the head is usually terminal, but there have been exceptions.

It was a neat execution, straight in the temple, and only looks like one bullet had been fired. Blood still seeps from the hole. I move his head so I can see the exit wound. It looks like hell on toast. It takes three sharp tugs to remove Francie's keys from his eyes. Once they're out, I put them in my pocket.

I do a quick body search. In his jacket, there's a spare magazine for his K100 and a wallet stuffed in his jeans. I look inside the wallet. Five hundred pounds in fifties, which I pocket, and two credit cards.

One is a British Airways American Express Premium Plus Card in the name of Mr Yoeri Weijts and the other is an ANWB Visa Classic Card in the name of Mr Pauli Hänninen. He's a lot more careful than Wolfert was. Nothing else of interest. I keep both credit cards. I was hoping for a passport, but that's undoubtedly back at the house in Onslow Gardens or in a safe somewhere.

Keeping an eye on Caspian, I open the cocktail cabinet. The only vodka they've got is an unopened bottle of Chase Rhubarb. Beggars can't be choosers. I twist the cap off and pour myself a triple with some ice, downing it in one. Interesting taste.

Next, I take a look at the gruesome mess that is Ronny and Hannibal. There's no need to check for signs of death here; they couldn't be more silent and immobile if they tried. Lots of blood. I wonder what happened when Seraphina and Milne got to Quennel's place. Whatever it was, I'm sure that Quennel will regret it hadn't been much, much worse when he finds out what happened here today, if he ever does.

All of the drawers in Caspian's desk are unlocked, so it doesn't take too long to undertake a quick search for anything interesting. Most of it is junk, unfortunately, but there are a couple of memory sticks still in their packets, so I unwrap one, switch on the computer and see what I can find under documents. As soon as the screen lights up, it asks for a password.

'Password for this computer, Caspian. Quickly, now.'

He says something like 'I'll rust the fella'.

'What? Stop necking with the carpet, Caspian. Say it again. Clearly.'

'I love Rebekah.'

'That's your password? Christ, how embarrassing for you. Are you eleven? Spell out Rebekah for me.'

I type it in, and it works. I download the entire documents file onto the stick. It takes three minutes. I've no idea what's on here, but it may come in useful.

Well, I think that's almost everything. I walk into the centre of the room and stand about seven or eight feet away from Caspian.

'OK, Mr Tennesley. You can get up now. Very slowly. Hands behind your head, look straight at me. I'm sure I don't need to tell you not to fuck around.'

He moves awkwardly to his feet. His lower lip is red and swollen. His face has mottled carpet marks all over it. I aim the K100 at the centre of his head.

'So, what's all this with Rebekah, Caspian? Does she know about your feelings for her?'

No reply, just a disdainful scowl.

'I suppose when you work with someone, organising orgies for the rich and powerful, bumping off people who get in your way, certain *feelings* are bound to develop. It's actually quite romantic; a genuine workplace love story. Does she feel the same way about you, I wonder? Somehow, I doubt it. Rebekah is or was pretty attractive and sexy, whereas you are a horrendous geek with a rubbery face.'

'What is it you want? Let's get it over with. Is it money? How much do you earn each year?'

'I don't want *money*, Caspian.'

'Listen. I get it. I get it. What you've seen here. What you saw on that damn memory stick. It's shocking, I know. Please don't think I'm not aware that ordinary people would be outraged if they knew about the things we did here. And I know – I *know* that using someone like van Cutsem then getting him out of prison was probably a little naughty. I understand that bypassing the justice system, giving him a new identity and all the rest was not the way people like to think their government operates or the way their tax money is spent. But people are stupid, Mr Cambridge. They just don't understand.'

'Did it hurt when Rebekah participated in the orgies, Caspian? Did you think "Why not me?" It must have cut like a knife.'

'Look. Forget Rebekah. Why are you talking about *her* all of the bloody time? What I'm trying to say is that we do a job that most other people would never want to do in a million years. This is the way the world works. Someone *has* to do this. It's not pretty. But it's essential. You should grow up. Let me ask you something. Do you drive a car?'

'You want a lift somewhere? Or are you going to bang on about how much I'll thank you when the petrol starts to run out?'

'Is it the children? Is it because of that boy over there by the dog? It's like I said before, they're a drop in the ocean. If you like, they've sacrificed themselves for the greater good.'

'You really don't get it, do you? Why I'm here. Why I've gone to all this trouble to track you down.'

A slight pause. 'You didn't track *me* down. We *captured* you. Salo captured you.'

'I had several lines of investigation running parallel to each other. Belt and braces, as you would put it. I knew Salo would be after me, so I took steps to make sure he caught me. It worked and he brought me here.

'Then you bragged about ordering the hit on Judith Hart and my job was complete.' My arm is starting to ache from aiming the gun at his head. Reluctantly, I'm going to have to bring things to a close.

'But how? And why would you want to put yourself in danger like that? It doesn't make any sense. We – we tortured you, for God's sake.'

'The woman you knew as Judith Hart. Her real name was Polly Greenburgh. And she was a friend of mine.'

'I don't understand.'

'I know.'

The impact of the bullet knocks him backwards and he almost flips over his desk and ends up in the seat. Almost, but not quite. By the time he comes to rest, he's sitting on the floor with his head leaning to the left, like he's inspecting some baffling modern art. I would go over and close his remaining eye, but I can't be bothered.

Over by the cocktail cabinet, there's an empty stainless-steel ice bucket with a black wine bottle napkin hanging over the side. I use that to wipe my prints off the gun and then get Salo's all over it. I'm having déjà vu. I'm sure we'd have a laugh about this if he wasn't dead. Then I pick up the gun with the napkin and drop it halfway between his body and Caspian's.

I can see the two P320 bullet casings from Jane's execution of Salo, both of which are about three feet from his corpse. I pick them up and pocket them. I'll deal with them and her gun later. I had considered wiping the gun clean and getting both Salo's and Caspian's prints on it to cause confusion but decided that it would look too contrived. Now that's sorted, I leave the room, stepping over Ronny and Hannibal, and meet Francie in the reception room across the hall.

'You done? What were you doing?'

'A bit of unfinished business.'

I look at Jane lying on the floor. Ankles and wrists tied, tears seeping from her eyes. I'll bet *this* is a day she'll never forget.

'Has she said anything?'

'Not a word. Sobs from time to time.'

'Come outside for a moment. I have to talk to you.'

'Are you going to ask me to marry you?'

'Is it that obvious, darling? Bring the gun.'

We step into the hall and I close the door behind us.

'We've got some complicated tidying up to do here. We have to assume that sooner or later the police may be involved in this and I've been creating a convincing if confusing crime scene. It could be, of course, that the police will never be involved as it's a security matter. But anyway. First of all, the guns.' I show her Jane's piece. 'Your friend in there used this one to kill Salo. This is going to disappear completely, as are the cartridges which I have in my pocket.

'The gun Salo used to kill the kid and the dog is still in there. I used the same weapon to kill Caspian.'

'OK.'

'Is that it? Just "OK"?'

'D'you think I'm completely dumb, Daniel? Did you think for a frikkin' millisecond I didn't know what all this was about? Well. OK. Maybe a millisecond. Maybe a — you know – a few hours. Couple days.'

'Right. Sorry. Salo's prints are all over that gun. It's on

the floor in there and that's where it's staying. It's going to look like he killed the kid and the dog and then shot Caspian. Now the gun that you've got that belonged to Leckie. That's coming with us. I'll get rid of it when I get rid of Jane's.'

'Gotcha. So, what about Jane and Leckie? What are we going to do about them?'

'OK. What have we got on them?'

'Well, um. Jane's committed murder.'

'What would you do if you were her, Francie? What would you want to happen after all of this?'

She stares into the middle distance for a couple of seconds. 'I wouldn't want to be charged with murder or manslaughter. I wouldn't want to go to prison because of what these people roped me into. But I'm not entirely without blame, either, even though I might not have known exactly what was going on.' She purses her lips. 'OK. What I did was necessary and was done under extreme stress after witnessing what Salo had done. I couldn't let him kill a third person/being. If anyone needed to be terminated, he did.

'But, bottom line, I still shot and killed another human, so I could be in some sort of trouble, despite this being spook stuff. Someone may want to blame me for everything. I'd go along with anything that would exonerate me. Anything. I'd also want to get the hell out of this life and get a job working in a pet shop.'

'That's good. Go and untie her and get her out here.'

'Why me?'

'Well, you tied her up. You'll know what you did and how to reverse it.'

'Ah. OK. I thought you were just ordering me around.'

'Not that you enjoy that at all.'

'Funny guy.'

A minute later, Jane is standing with us in the corridor. She contemplates the floor. She rubs her wrists.

'Jane,' I say. 'First of all, I have to thank you. You saved my life.'

She looks dubious. 'What are you going to do to me? I don't understand who you are.'

She's Scottish. What was her surname again? MacInroy? 'We're not going to do anything to you, Jane. But you may be in serious trouble for this. You know what the people you're working for are like now. There's a very strong possibility that someone may try and scapegoat you for murder and then you'll be screwed. You want to disassociate yourself from all of this as much as you can. We've got to get a story together. First of all, did you personally sign that P320 out?'

'No. No, it was here already. Mr Tennesley issued it to me informally. It's one of his spares, he said. He just…it was in a drawer and he handed it to me. I was just to be a kind of floating security presence.'

'Who else knew you had it? Did Oscar Leckie know you had it?'

'No. It was just me. I was going to ask for a shoulder holster, but I…'

'Right. Listen to me, Jane. I'm going to get rid of your gun and the shells. The only evidence of its use will be Salo's corpse in there. Oh, and Caspian Tennesley is dead. It will look as if Salo killed him, do you understand? That is what happened. The same gun was used. Apart from us, there is no one left alive who saw you fire those shots into Salo's head, and we won't be talking to anybody about it. It will be our secret. Understand? We will never mention it again.'

She nods her head. Her expression is sharp and focussed. She's decided to collude, as I thought she would.

'You did not shoot him. You never received that gun from Tennesley. You were not in the room when Salo was shot or when Tennesley was shot. You're going to have to think your way out of this and be on your guard, but initially I would suggest taking a long, thorough, hot shower or bath ASAP and getting rid of your clothes and your shoes. Gunshot residue. Just a precaution. Do you have spares here? Spare clothes, I mean? And shoes?'

'Yes. I was given a room to use on the third floor. I've got a holdall with clothes. I wasn't sure how long I'd be here. They were all a bit vague.'

'Good. That's where you were when all this happened. Tennesley told you to take a break or whatever. Think it through. We'll get rid of what you're wearing. Call this in in about an hour. Leckie is tied up in the basement in some sort of medical room and he doesn't know what's been going on up here, doesn't know you were in that room across the way, doesn't know you shot Salo. Have you been to this house before?'

'No. I was ordered here about five hours ago.'

'How did you get here?'

'A cab.'

'Good. You have no idea where Leckie is. You weren't even aware of the basement or that medical room, OK? Whoever turns up here in the next few hours will find him. You came down from your room to ask Tennesley what was happening, and then you came across the carnage and called it in.

'Leckie knows about us, but it's unlikely he knows exactly who we are. He drove us here; that's all. He's in deep shit, Jane. He's involved with murder, kidnapping, torture, trafficking and God knows what else. You don't want that rubbing off on you.

'If he has names for us, they'll be assumed names, but he may not have even have those, as he wasn't present during our interrogation. He may not even mention us, as it may incriminate him. If it comes to it, and someone asks, you saw us getting out of the Mercedes and going into the house. You didn't see us again after that. You had no idea who we were. You're suffering from mild shock at the moment. Remember what it feels like. Use it to your advantage.

'Also, there are a few more kids in some glass cells in the basement. All as zonked out as the one that Salo shot. Look surprised when you're told about them. If you're asked about Rebekah Giri and Milne, say you saw them drive away in the Citroën. You had no idea where they were going. Work out a convincing timeline for yourself while you're having a shower or whatever. Any questions?'

'I've got it. Thank you.'

'OK, honey. Let's get those clothes off, shall we?' says Francie. 'The blouse, the top, the skirt, the stockings, the shoes, the underwear; everything. Don't worry about this gentleman. He's seen it all before.'

'I promise I won't peek,' I say. I do, though. A fabulous, lithe figure. She has a small tattoo of an orange and black orchid just beneath her navel. I knew it.

'Thank you,' says Jane once more.

She heads off to where she's going, and Francie and I return to the study, Jane's clothing tucked under Francie's arm.

'What are we going to do about Leckie down there?

You going to shoot him?'

'What sort of person do you think I am?'

'I don't think I can answer that.'

'I'm going to go to that med room and have a discreet word with him. There's not much he can really do. Once this particular shit hits the fan, which it will, he's going to be too busy disassociating and covering his back to worry about what you and I have been up to. Maybe he'll try and blame us for some of it, maybe he won't. But like I said to Jane, any mention of us will be self-incriminating.

'We were always a troublesome side issue in all of this, and any inquisitors are going to be more interested in the whole van Cutsem orgy business, not to mention all the murders. We'll just leave him down there to suffer in his uncertainty. Wait here. Don't talk to any strange people.'

I think that sounded convincing. Five minutes later, we're in the Mercedes Estate and driving through Fulham on our way to the West End. I look at my watch: ten forty-one. I can hardly believe it was only this morning that I was in van Cutsem's place. Time flies when you're having fun.

39

SMØRREBRØD AND CHENIN BLANC

Our first stop is Francie's place in Craven Terrace so I can pick up my wallet and mobile and Francie can shower and grab a change of clothes.

I almost forgot to give Rebekah a call, just to see how things are with her. I find her number on Tennesley's mobile, but just get the 'no one is available to take your call' message. That's typical of her; always too busy to talk.

Thirty minutes later, we're parking the car in an NCP multi-storey on the Strand and walking towards my flat, binning Jane's clothes, the car keys and Tennesley's mobile on the way.

What with Leckie's HK45 and Jane's P320 bouncing around on the back seat under a newspaper, I kept my speed down the whole way over to avoid a pull by the police, who I'm starting to find a tad untrustworthy.

I call Liva and let her know we're on our way. She sounds excited. I make another call to Dr Ts'ai and ask him if he makes emergency out-of-hours visits. He does. I'm about to give him my address, but he already knows it. No surprise there, I suppose. He says half an hour.

When we get inside, Liva kisses and hugs both of us, then leads us into the kitchen where she's laid the table with a dazzling spread of traditional Danish open sandwiches. Apart from the food and wine, I'm pretty sure she's been clothes shopping again, as she's wearing a sexy floral pattern mini dress with a dramatic, plunging V-neckline that I haven't seen before. It also has an open back. I can't stop looking at her. Like Jael opined; she's too much. The crystal-embellished heels are new, too, I suspect.

She smiles when she sees my mouth is hanging open. I managed to slip both guns down the back of my chinos and I'll transfer them to a kitchen cupboard when she's not looking.

'I know you said no shopping unless necessary, but I thought you would both be hungry, so it was necessary, so I have made us some traditional Danish smørrebrød. Also, you can make your own, if you wish. Sit down immediately.'

We do as she says. She opens a bottle of chilled Chenin Blanc and pours us all a glass. I empty half of mine straight away.

'Hey, hey. Not so fast, please. Are you an alcoholic?'

'I'm beginning to wonder.'

'My uncle Silas Troelsen was an alcoholic and he once drove a car through the window of Salotto 42 in Copenhagen.'

She walks around the table pointing at each item and making suggestions. 'Three types of bread: dark rye, white and ordinary almond sourdough buttered toast. We have little plates of liver pâté, sautéed mushrooms, steamed plaice, meat jelly, salted beef, tomatoes, roast pork with crackling, chopped bacon, pickled cucumber, smoked salmon, shrimp, white herring and scrambled eggs. And that is dill and that is rémoulade and that is shredded horseradish and that is tartare sauce. You can mix up as you wish. There are little spoons and tiny forks to help.'

Whether it's relief, pleasure, stress, or a complete mental breakdown, I have no idea, but I start laughing and I can't stop. I've got tears in my eyes. It's infectious, Francie starts, too, and then Liva.

'Oh, God,' I say, attempting to stop.

'What is it?' asks Liva, still laughing. 'I don't get it. What is making you laugh so much? Do you not like the food?'

I try to control myself so I can speak. 'I'm sorry, Liva. It's not the food. It's marvellous.' I start laughing again. 'It's just the contrast between all of this and you and the wine and what Francie and I have been doing today. It couldn't be more…'

More laughter, especially from Francie, who, when Liva sits down next her, leans over and hugs her and kisses her face over and over again. 'Thank you, darling. You can't believe how great this is for us. You're fuckin' sensational.'

She likes this, even getting a little tearful, and shyly kisses us both on the lips.

Once we've finished eating, Liva disappears somewhere and returns with two gift-wrapped parcels. 'And I have bought you each a present.' she hands them to us. 'One for you and one for you. Go on. You can open them now.'

I let Francie open hers first. It's a black leather Bottega Veneta clutch bag. 'Oh, my God. Liva! These are so expensive. I…you…oh, thank you, babe.'

More kissing. Liva gets up and opens the refrigerator, producing one of two bottles of Armand de Brignac champagne, while I open my package, which is in a large rectangular box. It's a set of four beautiful Waterford champagne trumpet flutes.

'You did not have proper champagne flutes here, so I felt sorry for you. I hope they are OK. Put them on the table. We will christen them.'

'They're fantastic, Liva. Thank you.'

Just as she's filling the glasses, the entry buzzer sounds. Francie freezes, but I give her a reassuring shake of the head, get up and allow Dr Ts'ai to come in.

When he enters the kitchen, his eyes are out on stalks. 'Is this the emergency? You have four champagne glasses but only three people?'

Liva pours him a glass ('just the one') and he makes small talk with both women while helping himself to some of the smørrebrød. He has two big medical bags with him. After a few minutes, he suggests we retire to somewhere a little quieter.

I sit on the bed and take my shirt off so he can see the damage. My hand is trembling. He shakes his head from side to side and exhales softly.

'This is very serious. What happened?'

I explain about the torture. I don't mention that it was executed by children, as that's simply too insane and would be catastrophic for my image. I give him the details of Seraphina's vicious slaps and Salo's desperate poking around just before Jane euthanised him.

'How long ago did this occur?'

'Two, three hours ago.'

'Are you in pain?'

'Er, yeah.'

'Scale of one to ten.'

'Six. Sometimes seven. Occasionally eight. The grip of my right hand is affected a little; I noticed it while I was driving just now.'

'Where is the bathroom?'

He returns holding half a dozen dampened pads with some sort of pink stain on them and gently pats the dried blood away and cleans the wound itself as much as is possible. I can smell something antiseptic. Whatever it is, it stings. Then he produces an aerosol with Greek writing on it and sprays something directly into the wound for five seconds. This stings as well, but a little worse than the other stuff. It's also freezing cold.

He opens the second of his large bags and selects eight acupuncture needles. After he's swabbed down my right arm with alcohol, he gently taps each needle into different points along the length of the whole limb: hand, wrist, elbow, forearm, bicep, shoulder. Each needle produces a dull pain and I start to feel dizzy. Gradually, though, the discomfort from the wound starts to fade. Loud laughter from the kitchen, followed by intense whispering and then total silence. I can't imagine what they're doing in there.

'You have deep tissue damage here. It is also infected, which is not surprising, and it is still bleeding a little, which is not so good. Luckily, the radial nerve will not be damaged. I am going to give you a course of antibiotics which you must finish and a supply of powerful painkillers which may make you feel drowsy. No driving, no alcohol. I'm not going to re-stitch this wound at present. I'll leave it open with an antiseptic dressing on it.

'Tomorrow, you must come into the hospital and have it operated on. I will text you your appointment time. It will be treated as a high priority case. I will make that happen. I shall refer you to Ms Sherry Ahart as this is not my speciality. She is the best in London. Bring your medication with you.

'Once that is done, the wound will be closed once more. Then you will wait for four days, perhaps five days, and you'll be referred to a plastic surgeon for further surgery, probably Mr Danny Payne if he is available. You will need a month off after all of this and I most definitely mean a month.'

'Got it. Thanks for your help, Dr Ts'ai.'

He removes the needles and applies the dressing.

'You are most welcome. As you have had a tough day, you may go against my excellent advice and have one more glass of champagne. Wait half an hour, then start your medication. Don't get this dressing wet. And have a good night's sleep tonight.' He gives me an ostentatious wink. 'If that's at all possible!'

'How much do I owe you?'

'Mr Beckett. You should know better than to ask me that.'

I take a shower, wash my hair, then return to the bedroom, fire up the computer and start a new document. I can hear a lot of giggling coming from the kitchen. I've got to try to get some of this down for myself and for DI Bream before it starts slipping away. Some of it, like Salo's fake credit card numbers, will be of use to Interpol. It'd be good to speak to Olivia and get an outsider's opinion on this whole mess, plus I need to clear my name and get one final thing sorted. I decide to text her.

Blind Beggar pub Whitechapel Road tomorrow 11.30 am? I need a favour and the Met will be licking your boots when I tell you what I've discovered. Sexy clothing pls. xxx

I don't know where to start, so I outline the van Cutsem lift at Wormwood Scrubs. I told Olivia that the cop who picked him up was Detective Chief

Superintendent Michael Small, but that seems to be a fiction, and it was actually someone called Detective Chief Inspector Edward Pope. I'm sure she can see if that checks out. She'll undoubtedly check both names because I know that's what she's like. I also include a description of the driver. I'm going to leave describing the Richmond situation until last, as it requires a delicacy, concentration, creativity and slyness that I don't feel up to at the moment. My mobile pings.

11.30 fine, Looking forward. BTW — you are in a shitload of trouble. Checking wardrobe for tight miniskirt and one-size-too-small t-shirt. XOXO

'What are you doing? Are you *working*? Jeez.'

'Something I have to do for tomorrow, Francie. No problem. It can wait.'

'Come back into the kitchen. We have a surprise for you. Liva and I have been talking and plotting and conspiring and scheming while you were having your arm repaired. He's a nice guy, that doctor, isn't he?'

'Plotting? What sort of plotting?'

'You'll see. Come on. Don't bother putting your shirt back on.'

'The doctor said I can have one more glass of champagne, but that's it.'

As soon as I'm in the kitchen, Liva gets up, walks over to me, drapes her arms around my neck and gives me a long, passionate kiss. I can taste champagne, Chenin Blanc and pickled cucumber in her saliva. I hold the side of her neck and pull her closer to me, so that her breasts are squashed against my chest. She gasps for breath, her eyes wide.

'I've been waiting all day for this,' she says. 'This morning was such a long time ago. I have thought of nothing else.' She turns to Francie. 'I think you deserve a kiss from Daniel, too. You have had a tiring day just like him, not to mention what happened at your flat, you bad girl. Come here.'

I turn to face Francie, whose lips are on mine almost immediately. It's a slow, seductive, lip-nibbling kiss. She pulls back and Liva takes over once more, kissing my mouth and then my neck and then my chest. 'You have a difficult decision to make, honey,' says Francie, her voice low and flirtatious. 'Two desirable women, both wanting you. I don't know how you're going to resolve it. I really don't.'

'It is a problem,' says Liva, taking my hand and Francie's and leading us back to the bedroom. 'Come on, Francie. We will both help him to make up his mind. But I warn you both; it might take some time.'

Francie laughs. 'Well, sweetie; it's still early.'

'*Vi dræber dig,*' whispers Liva to me.

'Promises, promises,' I reply.

*

'They should demolish this place and build a nurse's hostel or police station on the site.'

We're in The Blind Beggar, a pub famous for being the location where one of a matching pair of East End gangsters offed one of their kind back in 1966. This place is still living off the fame, and there are plaques and framed photographs of the terrible two on the walls to remind you in case you'd forgotten.

I was looking at one of these photographs when Olivia Bream appeared behind me and made her observation, followed by another.

'There's a theory that talking about and looking at photographs of the Kray twins is used in psychiatry to cure impotence in insecure males.'

'Is that true? I must try that sometime. I've tried everything else.'

She laughs. 'But really; there shouldn't be shrines to people like that. They should just be allowed to fade into obscurity, not have fucking films made about them. It really pisses me off.'

'They loved their mum, apparently.'

'Really? Oh, well that's alright then. All is forgiven. Why is it all men in here? It's like the bloody 1950s.'

'Do you want to go outside or stay in?'

'Outside.'

We order a couple of Americanos at the bar and sit at a table under a big umbrella in the beer garden.

'Are you sure you don't want anything to eat?'

'Too early for me. You can take me to lunch afterwards if you can find a restaurant around here where no one was slaughtered.'

'Might be difficult, though I've heard there's a very nice Jack the Ripper themed bistro nearby.'

She looks at my attaché case. 'What's in there?'

'It's a gift for you, but you can't have it yet. What happened to the tight t-shirt I was promised in your text?'

'Sorry. Left it at home.'

'Shame. Maybe another time.'

'Maybe. Your roots are starting to show.'

'You're such a bitch.'

'Try me.'

A young guy places our coffees in front of us and asks if we'd like to see a lunch menu. We say no. Olivia takes a sip of her Americano and smiles at me, her eyes narrowing.

'So why am I in a shitload of trouble, DI Bream?'

'Well, it isn't official trouble. Not really. More like moral trouble. I just wanted to see your face when I told you.'

'That's OK, then.'

'Did you hear about that terrorist attack in Central London yesterday?'

'Yes, I did. I was worried about you. Marble Arch, wasn't it? Not far from Seymour Street police station.'

'Close. It was in Bryanston Street, so we were involved. Four cars destroyed, six shop fronts blown out, seventeen injured. No deaths, luckily. They still don't know who was behind it.'

'So…what? Do you think it was me?'

'No. It's just that when Superintendent Perry Cook and I went to Regent's Park Road to lift van Cutsem and take him into unofficial police custody, we got there about nine hours later than we might have done due to the explosion.' She raises one of her eyebrows at me.

'Ah.'

'Someone…had fastened zip ties around both of his wrists, cutting off the blood circulation. We took him to St Mary's under an assumed name. His hands had to be amputated. There was nothing they could do to save them.'

'Bad luck.'

'Wasn't it, though? He declined to tell us anything about what happened. He said that an intruder had broken into his house and threatened to kill him unless he told him where his money was hidden. Though why the intruder would have done that with the zip ties is

547

anybody's guess. I got the impression that he was rather – what's the word – *terrified* of whoever the intruder was.'

'I can't imagine who that would have been. When I spoke to him, he said he was expecting someone to turn up later in the day. Didn't say who. Seemed like a guy with a lot of enemies.'

'Some worse than others, obviously.'

'But you've still got him in incognito custody, yes?'

'Yes, we have. As you suggested, we concocted an excuse for not observing due process. That terrorist attack came in very useful. Had a devastating effect on the local electricity supply and that was just for starters. We're going public with him tomorrow. You can probably watch it on the news. Perry Cook was in seventh heaven, as I'm sure you can imagine.'

'Well, I'm glad I could be of help. I've put everything you need to know on a memory stick here. Took me two hours to type it all up this morning.' I take it out of my pocket and push it over the table to her. 'Some of it is still speculative and some of it won't make any sense whatsoever. Part of the point of all of this was to make everything as confusing as possible and it almost worked.

'And here's another memory stick. This one you may find disturbing. It's film of what van Cutsem got up to to assist various government departments. Don't say I didn't warn you. This is why they got him out of prison, so he could continue doing this stuff. It's why Judith Hart was killed, it's why an intelligence officer called Alistair Culpepper was killed and it's why a Bulgarian diplomat called Dragan Vanchev was killed. There have been a lot of killings and you may discover more. It's mayhem out there. I'll say it again: be careful, Olivia.'

'Thank you for your concern, Daniel.'

'Believe me, this lot will keep you busy for at least a year and you'll probably want to create a special dedicated team to deal with it. Get Cook to help you. You can't be too careful. My name won't be involved, of course. You can take all the credit yourself. Just say it was all delivered anonymously. Oh, and there's a third memory stick.

'It must be my birthday.'

'This is from the computer of an intelligence officer who was up to his neck in all of this. I haven't had a chance to look at what's on it, but I'm positive you'll find some interesting stuff; bent cops, major corruption, human trafficking, murder, slavery, unpaid parking fines, the lot.'

'What happened to the…what about the kid that van Cutsem attempted to hold to ransom? The father's address. Did you…'

'Unfortunately, deceased.'

'Jesus Christ. Was it van Cutsem?'

'No. Details are in my report. But you can still use that little spinoff against van Cutsem in court. Get him a few more years. You may or may not find out subsequent stuff about the father. Go easy on him.'

I'd love to find out what happened to Seraphina and Milne, but something tells me I won't. I'd like to think the police will find their bloated corpses floating in the Thames in a couple of days.

Olivia's about to say something, but instead places her fingers against her mouth and slowly shakes her head.

'I've identified some of the major players on the film, who you'll also want to bust and/or stop coming into this country again,' I say. 'And there's the address of a house in Richmond that you may like to visit. PDQ, I would imagine, but you may find that the MI5 clean-up people have already been there. But that's an incriminating act in itself, one could argue. More cans of worms. There's nothing much these people can do now without digging themselves a deeper hole, though I'm sure they'll try to lie their way out of everything.

'The place in Richmond is where van Cutsem held his entertainments for the great and good. Or some of them, anyway. Get ready for a shitload of smoke and mirrors. You may find one or two sets of fingerprints that you are unable to identify.' I smile at her. 'But I'm sure you're used to that sort of thing.'

'Have you come up with the weapon that killed Judith Hart yet?'

I slide the black attaché case under the table, so it touches her leg. 'It's in there. It's a Grand Power K100 Whisper. It's loaded, so be careful. You'll find that the fingerprints on it belong to one Eemil Salo. He's one of four assassins who were involved in this mess. It may well turn out that he owns two guns like this.

'He was the incapacitated intruder at the Devonshire Street flat. He was the one who murdered Judith Hart. He was also the guy that accidentally shot his colleague in Hart's flat and is responsible for a few more killings relevant to all of this. You should be able to check the veracity of those prints with Interpol. I'm sure they have a pretty thick file on him.

'You may also discover gunshot residue on some of his clothing, if you can find it. There's an address in my report where he and the other three assassins were staying. You might like to do a thorough search.' Mixing bullshit in with the truth is making my teeth ache.

'There were *four* assassins?'

'I told you it was complicated. Three of them are in

the morgue across the road in The London Hospital, as is the body of Judith Hart; the real Judith Hart. Forensics will easily be able to match this gun to the shots that killed her, and her former colleagues – names and location in my report – will be able to ID her. As will I, but unofficially. Shall we go?'

'I knew there'd be some smart reason for meeting me here. Come on.'

'Don't forget that attaché case. You know what they're like about guns in this place.'

40

ALL DONE

Olivia flashes her badge at the reception woman and asks for someone to accompany us down to the Edith Cavell Room. After three minutes a tall, serious, uniformed guy approaches us and just says, 'This way please, madam.' It's as if I don't exist.

We walk through the main part of the morgue. It's chilly, with a baffling combo of chemical smells. In about ten yards, there are a pair of double swing doors which we walk through until we see another door with 'Edith Cavell Room' engraved on a brass plate.

There's a blonde woman in some sort of green medical outfit sitting there writing and I wonder if she's a doctor or nurse or something else. Olivia flashes her badge again.

'Do you know what you're looking for, madam?' asks the woman.

'Yes, thank you,' says Olivia, and we're nodded through.

'What are we looking for?'

'Dates. Anything that came in here in the last four days, that doesn't have an ID or maybe has a fake one. One thing; where's the guy whose prints are on this gun? Is he in this place, too? You didn't say.'

'No. He's dead, though. I refer you to the highly complex subsection entitled "Richmond" on my well-written and diverting thesis.' I wonder how Jane's doing and if she's bearing up. I'm sure she is. My main worry is Oscar Leckie. Lying on the floor like that with his mouth taped up could easily lead to accidental suffocation if his remaining breathing channels were somehow blocked. A tragedy waiting to happen, if you ask me.

This section of the morgue is much more modern and hi-tech than the one we just walked through. Olivia inspects the labels on the sides of the stainless-steel drawers for a few seconds, then raps one of them twice with a knuckle.

'It's these four. Admitted here three days ago, three male and one female. Nobody since and previous residents were here three and a half weeks before that. Names are Radosław Czerwinski, Evan Forbes, Horvát Zágon and Alexandra Farrell. Nice variety. Shall we take a look?'

'Sure. Guys first.' I'm still not ready to see Polly. Maybe I never will be.

She tugs the drawers open, unzips the body bags as far as the neck and unwraps part of a small sheet from each face. We look down at the blank expressions of Wolfert and Redolf Salo and Jitser Vonk. Olivia points at them.

'Are these two twins?'

'Close. They're two-thirds of triplets. The other one's in the house in Richmond, unless he's already been scooped up. Their names are Wolfert Salo and Redolf Salo. I don't know which is which. Hard to tell. The other guy here is their cousin. His name is Jitser Vonk. They're all Frisian. Ex-military. All four are – were – one of the top assassination units in the world. Eemil Salo is the one who can't be with us here today, due to a prior engagement with the Grim Reaper. He's the one who accidentally shot either Wolfert or Redolf.

'They were all in the UK on some sort of job. I have no idea what that might have been. Could be on that third memory stick. Anyway, they were still here when Judith Hart caught van Cutsem on film and had to be terminated, so they were sent in to deal with her.'

'All four of them? After one woman?'

'Confidential?'

'Confidential.'

'You'll read about this in my thrilling narrative; but anyway. Vonk and Redolf Salo were sent to kill her. She was unarmed. But she killed *them*. So Wolfert and Eemil Salo were ordered, I assume, to finish the job. This time they got her, but Wolfert didn't survive the mission.'

Olivia looks up at me, willing me to give her more information about Wolfert's death, but it's not forthcoming. I look at her mouth. I imagine kissing her right now, in the morgue. It'd be really weird, but we'd always remember it.

'OK. Let's have a look at Judith Hart.' She suddenly turns and points a finger at my face. 'I hope you've damn well covered your tracks.'

She slides the drawer out; unzips and unwraps the head and I see Polly for the first time since that shoot-out at Devonshire Street. It's a cliché, but she looks like she's asleep. Only the entry wound in her forehead suggests that this may not be true. Olivia looks at her face.

'Is this her?'

'Yes.'

'I'm surprised. She's beautiful. From what you said, I'd expected…I don't know. Nothing like this.'

'I'll make the arrangements for her.'

'Of course. I'll go out and talk to the reception

woman. I want to find out exactly who brought these bodies in and precisely when.'

'OK.'

She turns on her heel and walks out, leaving me on my own with Polly. Very sweet of her, but there's really no need. For the second time in four days I gently run the back of my hand up and down Polly's cheek. All done, Pol, all done.

The text tone on my mobile gives two quiet trills. There's one message from Dr Ts'ai:

UCH. Tomorrow. Main Reception. 2.40 pm Ask for me. No breakfast. No lunch. Bring medication. Xiong.

And another from Priscilla:

Two nights ago. That must absolutely never happen again. I'm utterly mortified. Call me ASAP.

*

I can't remember the exact month that Polly and I were in Andorra la Vella, but I remember that it was incredibly hot. May have been late July, may have been early August. This was five years ago, though, so I can be forgiven for forgetting the exact date.

We're walking down the Avenida Meritxell, looking like a couple of tourists; Polly in a stripy crop top, cut-off blue Levi's and huge pair of Cee Cee mirrored sunglasses, me in khaki cargo shorts, black Sun O))) t-shirt and a pale blue baseball cap, a disposable Kodak hanging from my left wrist.

She's hot and thirsty, so we stop at a pavement café and order coffee and croissants. If you look down the street, you can see the Pyrenees. While we're waiting, she nudges my arm and indicates that I should look across the road.

'A Jo Malone shop right in between a Superdry and a Tag Heuer outlet. We could be in Guildford.'

I nod at the mountains. 'Difficult to see the Pyrenees from Guildford High Street, though. Not impossible; just difficult.'

'I think I might have a look in the Jo Malone when we've finished. Do you mind?'

'Of course not. The bags will look nice and touristy at the airport.'

'That's a pretty decent excuse for overspending.'

A waitress places our order on the rickety table. '*Gràcies, senyoreta,*' says Polly, giving her a charming smile.

'Oh, you speak Catalan now.'

'A bit. You can never know enough stuff.'

'True.'

We eat, drink, sit and watch people walk by for a few minutes. There's a big bronze statue of Dali's *Nobility of Time* about twenty feet away. Two girls sit down on the low railing in front of it to smoke, drink coffee and talk. Their skin is glowing with the heat. They're both wearing smart black uniforms with small green ID tags and have a lot of professional-looking makeup on their faces. My guess is that they work at a cosmetics counter in one of the nearby department stores.

One of them has a fabulous, pneumatic figure that her uniform can't disguise, and a very short, silver-dyed pixie cut. What is it about women with that sort of figure and really short hair? I wonder if there's a book about it.

Polly finishes the last of her coffee. 'That was a pretty close call last night. I hate Dobermans.'

'Not as much as they hate me.'

'Quite.'

'It was bad luck, really,' I say. 'Nothing to do with us. Our reputation is not besmirched!'

She drums her fingers on the table, looks shifty and takes a deep breath. 'I know this isn't very professional, but...I don't have any family. I have no one, in fact. You know that. I don't feel comfortable about asking the other two, but I think I can ask you.'

I turn to look at her. 'Ask away.'

'Last night made me think. If something happens to me, I wouldn't be...I wouldn't want...'

'You wouldn't want it to be for nothing. I understand. You wouldn't want the perpetrators to get off scot-free. You wouldn't want some smirking scumbag to be walking the streets as if nothing had happened. We've always said this, Polly. We've talked about it before.'

'Sometimes I need reassurance.'

'I know.'

She looks down and nods her head. 'I'd do the same for you.'

'I know you would, Pol. Don't worry about it, OK?'

'Thanks.'

'You want to go to the Hard Rock Café tonight?'

'They have one here?'

'Are you kidding me? If we'd kept on down this road, we'd have walked past it.'

'I want a Double Decker Double Cheeseburger.'

'Come on. Let's go and look in Jo Malone's.'

I leave some money on the table with enough for a big tip. Polly sees, smiles at me and we get up and leave.

THE END

Books by Dominic Piper

Kiss Me When I'm Dead

Death is the New Black

Femme Fatale

Bitter Almonds & Jasmine

Printed in Great Britain
by Amazon